The Sins of the Fathers

Also published by Quartet Books
The Body and the Dream
translated and introduced by Jennifer Birkett

THE SINS OF THE FATHERS
Decadence in France 1870–1914

Jennifer Birkett

Quartet Books
London   New York

First published in Great Britain by Quartet Books Limited 1986
A member of the Namara Group
27/29 Goodge Street
London W1P 1FD

British Library Cataloguing in Publication Data
Birkett, Jennifer
   The sins of the fathers: decadence in
   France, 1870–1914.
   1. Huysmans, J.-K., *et al* —— Criticism and
   interpretation
   I. Title
   843′.8   PQ2309.H4Z/

ISBN 0-7043-2503-9

Phototypeset by AKM Associates (UK) Ltd
Ajmal House, Hayes Road, Southall, London
Printed and bound in Great Britain by
Nene Litho and Woolnough Bookbinding
both of Wellingborough, Northants

For Elsie and Gillian,
and in memory of Alice, Jane and Nick

Contents

Acknowledgements

I should like to thank those libraries whose resources have been used in the preparation of this book: the Bibliothèque Nationale; the University Library, Cambridge; the Bodleian Library and the Taylor Institute, Oxford; the National Library of Scotland; the University Libraries of Dundee and St Andrews and especially the British Library. I am grateful to Nigella Lawson for her initial invitation to write it, and to Jennie Bradshaw, Graham Bradshaw, Ian Johnston, James Kearns and Rex Last for their kind help and encouragement. Anne Shivers' expertise, patience and good-humour were of invaluable assistance in getting the manuscript together; and during the research and the writing, Valerie Smith and Hazel and Harvey Marshall gave much-appreciated moral support. Support, encouragement and advice have been unstintingly provided by Stan Smith, and to him as always go my love and thanks.

Author's Note

Translations are my own unless a translation is cited in the bibliography and page references are to first editions unless another edition is given in the bibliography.

The Sins of the Fathers

PART I

The Historical Perspective

1
The Energy of Byzantium:
The Enemy Within

Decadence in the late nineteenth century flowered – or festered – throughout Western Europe, but by common consent its centre was France, where it reached its apogee in the eighties and nineties. The starting and finishing points of the influences that fed it and the forms it spawned are not easily determined, but the period of history that gives the French variations a roughly coherent identity stretches between the end of the Paris Commune and the beginning of the First World War. Decadence in France is a style evolved by elites under threat for addressing the tensions and contradictions of that particular period.

Decadence is an attempt – and a very successful and entertaining one – to substitute fiction for history. It is the telling, for both pleasure and profit, of a story in which the tellers have invested their last remaining capital, and which represents their only hope of future returns. They no longer have very much by way of substance; for the buyer, all the appeal must go into the packaging, designed to the formula summed up by Edgar Allan Poe: '. . . much of Madness, and more of Sin, And Horror the soul of the plot'. It is ultimately a form of demagoguery, in which an elite competes for the mass market it despises. The market metaphor is a matter of historical fact. As Ellen Moers explained, rejecting Yeats' description of his 'tragic generation' and Holbrook Jackson's 'age of experiment':

> . . . the dominant note of the decade appears to be its commercialism: the *tragic* spectacle of literature and personality thrown upon the market

place, the great *experiment* of selling talent by advertising, publicity and showmanship (*The Dandy*, 1960, p. 292).

Moers quotes Arthur Waugh's own comment in *The Yellow Book*: 'It may be, indeed, that we ourselves are beginning to appreciate that the new era of letters is not so much decadent as vulgar.'

Commercial success is linked with selling particular political attitudes. Decadence, more than any other art form, involves the creation of imaginary solutions to real problems. Decadent artists sell their own desires to the populace as the image of a common dream, building on a thin foundation of historical fact the edifice of outrageous but seductive lies which is their own private fantasy. The proof of their success is in the ease with which, even today, we accept the decadents' versions of themselves. The dandy should not believe in his own poses, but his victims always must.

The self-images mirrored in the looking-glass world of decadent art are those of distinct, solitary egos: male and female locked in heroic conflict. Woman is usually the dominant figure, the key to all vital energies. Occasionally she is Ophelia, and, like man, the helpless victim of history. But more often she is Salome, Medusa or Mona Lisa, at best cold and enigmatic, at worst cruel and murderous. She is the Great Goddess, vampire and queen, a last representative of vanished rulers, seducing men to share her glamorous dispossession.

Her counterpart is the Artist (always male), who casts himself in the double role of Pygmalion, victim and creator of her beauty. She is the image of his desire, that inevitably destroys him; because his desire is to bend the whole world to his will, though he knows he has lost the power to do so. This gap between ambition and ability spawns neurosis, in all its forms.

Style totters on the edge of surrealism, dramatic, detailed, coloured with passionate intensity, to the point of hallucination. Vertigo is a form of escape, sought in dream, in the fumes of ether and alcohol, in opium, death, crime and the ecstasies of sexual pleasure and pain. Intensity comes from the crowding and confusing of effects: time and space are collapsed, categories – human, mineral, plant – thrown into an ultimate chaos. This is Byzantium, where all desires meet: private obsessions, fetishes, morbid fears and guilt are the substance of the decadent world.

This is desire of such urgency that all its contradictions are hidden. Intense self-consciousness is coupled with an insistence that the self is a mystery, and motives irrational and unknowable. Everyone is guilty, but no one is responsible. Reason is said to be the true ideal, but passion is the

Gustave Moreau, 'Les Prétendants' 1852 (Musée Gustave
Moreau), cf.p.5ff.

Gustave Moreau, 'Galatée' 1880 (Collection Robert Lebel, Paris), cf.p.68.

Jean Delville, 'Les Trésors de Satan' 1895 (Musées Royaux des Beaux-Arts, Brussels).

Sir Edward Burne-Jones, 'Perseus Slaying the Serpent' c.1885
(City Art Gallery, Southampton).

idol, and reason cannot control it. The greatest contradiction is that between the cult of individual desire and the neurotic craving for order. Rules and ritual are invoked to clamp down on the anarchy of decadent dream. The decadent imagination is simultaneously defiant and submissive, invoking energies which are immediately frozen, framed and trapped, surrendered to become images of ruin and waste. This is focused in a series of images which runs throughout the period. Mario Praz opened the first chapter of *The Romantic Agony* (1930) with the figure of Shelley's Medusa, face framed in her curling 'serpent-locks', in death still turning her 'brazen glare' on the living world, until both her beauty and horror intimidate it into stillness: 'humanize and harmonize the strain'. The spell of the Mona Lisa lies in the mystery of her curving, trembling smile which plays on the stillness of her oval face, both framed by her smooth, heavy black hair. Woman's vitality, in Pre-Raphaelite painting, or in Gustave Moreau's art, is trapped in ceremonial robes. The threatening power of the Sphinx's riddle reverberates under the weight of its implacable stone form. In that most delicate of decadent images, the Androgyne, all the potential of sexual conflict is fixed in a single, harmonious form.

In Gustave Moreau's epic canvas 'Les Prétendants' (1852), tellingly chosen by Jean Lorrain in *Monsieur de Phocas. Astarté* (1901) as one of the keys to the period, contradictions are at their most intense, and the political implications of decadence are clearest. A group of aspirants eager for power are the object of an unknown threat. They are defenceless, and they die. The painting is an expression of insecurity, but first and foremost a glamorization of submission. The dazzling figure of Athene, cool Greek goddess of Reason, hovering in an aura of light and coiling serpents, presides over the death-throes of Penelope's suitors, falling before the arrows of a near-invisible Ulysses. The violence is contained between her aura and the heavy stone walls of the ancestral hall to which the wandering King has returned. The painting, as J.P. Crespelle fretfully commented (*Les Maîtres de la Belle Epoque*, 1966) is so crowded with symbols as to be almost incomprehensible. The crowding is deliberate; profusion breeds confusion, and the dazzling light, dark shadows, and fumes of drunken orgy absolve the suitors of all need to struggle. Surrender is the only option, freeing each one to devote himself to his own heroic confrontation with death.

Least clear of all is who is responsible for the carnage. In the perspectives of the painting, it is the goddess who directs it – cold, implacable and vengeful. But the arrows have another source, to which all backs in the picture are turned, and which the spectator too can hardly make out. For the spectator, familiarity with the legend indicates that the source is Ulysses. The aspirants, suitors and usurpers are informed by their guilt. Whether the destroyer is the rightful owner of the property or merely another rival usurper, they know their right to be in the hall is hard to defend. Better to stay and accept what is offered, even death, than struggle out of their intoxication to escape a punishment which they know would be deserved.

Ambition for power and possession has collapsed into violence and chaos. Failure to take the queen, the symbol of the right to power, leaves only the ambition for death. This is the romanticized version of fear and failure that decadent art sells the public, eroticizing the urge for power and the failure to seize it – the source of that archetypal decadent identification of Love and Death, desire voluntarily locked in paralysis.

The suitors in the painting are the decadent generation, trapped in their own ambition and insecurity. Contemporary struggles for power are the true historical text underlying the symbols and fictions juggled by the writers whose work will be discussed in detail in the second part of this book. First we need to know who, in this generation, corresponds to the painting's rival suitors and who are the Fathers capable of their destruction, figures to whom they feel they owe allegiance, and against whom they can only fantasize rebellion.

Degeneration or Regeneration?

The most vivid sense of an historical period's fundamental conflicts comes from the most committed participants. From two opposite but equally partial perspectives on to those years of transition when the form of the new Republic was defined, the patterns of culture and politics are clearer, as are the alternative positions offered to the decadent generation. From the same evidence, the German author and philosopher Max Nordau lamented the decay of the world as he knew it, while the radical psychologist and 'sexologist' Henry Havelock Ellis charted with delight the signs of energy and regeneration.

Nordau's *Entartung* was published in 1892. The French translation, *Dégénerescence*, appeared in 1894, and the English version, *Degeneration*, in 1895. The book unashamedly declared itself the voice of middle-class philistinism. Greeted by waves of ridicule from his victims, the writer clung to his convictions and watched his sales soar. Nordau welcomed science, technological change, and material progress, but resented the pressures for cultural and political change to which these had contributed. In the heterogeneous progressive movements of the time, he imagined a single opponent. Socialism was one with feminism, naturalism, the decadents, symbolists, occultists and mystics, and:

> Mysticism is, as we know, always accompanied by eroticism, especially in the degenerate, whose emotionalism has its chief source in morbidly excited states of the sexual centres (English edition, p. 188).

His aim was to preserve threatened classical order in politics and culture:

> [*Fin-de-siècle*] means a practical emancipation from traditional discipline, which theoretically is still in force . . . it means the end of an established order, which for thousands of years has satisfied logic, fettered depravity, and in every art matured something of beauty (p. 5).

He referred with approval to Paul Bourget's definition of decadence in his *Essais de psychologie contemporaine* (1883): '[M. Bourget] recognizes that "decadent" is synonymous with inaptitude for regular functions and subordination to social aims, and that the consequence of decadence is anarchy and the ruin of the community' (p. 302). He saw no substance in the claim that the world needed new forms for its new ideas. There were no new ideas. At most, he thought, art might give a new gloss to traditional truths:

> The art of the twentieth century will connect itself at every point with the past, but it will have a new task to accomplish – that of introducing a stimulating variety into the uniformity of civilized life . . . (p. 550).

He was particularly concerned by the power of artistic interventions to determine the fate of new developments, restraining or giving comfort to the 'usurpers':

> Views that have hitherto governed minds are dead or driven hence like disenthroned kings, and for their inheritance they that hold the titles and they that would usurp are locked in struggle. Meanwhile interregnum in all its terrors prevails; there is confusion among the powers that be; the million, robbed of its leaders, knows not where to turn . . . Men . . . have hope that in the chaos of thought, art may yield revelations of the order that is to follow on this tangled web. The poet, the musician, is to announce, or divine, or at least suggest in what forms civilization will further be evolved (p. 6).

He thought that the decadents were in a minority, restricted mainly to France, and even there, 'only the upper ten thousand . . . I assert only the decay of the rich inhabitants of great cities and the leading classes' (p. 2n.). The backbone of Europe was still sound:

> The great majority of the middle and lower classes is naturally not *fin-de-siècle*. It is true that the spirit of the times is stirring the nations down to their lowest depths, and awaking even in the most inchoate and rudimentary human beings a wondrous feeling of stir and upheaval . . . [But] the Philistine or the Proletarian still finds undiluted satisfaction in the old and oldest forms of art and poetry . . . (p. 7).

But the influence of the decadent minority is still to be feared. The 'inchoate and rudimentary' spirit of the people might well fall prey to these 'fanatics'. It is the demagogic threat that alarms Nordau, and the possibility that artistic liberation could have a political corollary. He would like to see in Germany the kind of psychologist who had brought 'normal' standards to other European countries:

> A Maudsley in England, a Charcot, a Magnan in France, a Lombroso, a Tonnini in Italy, have brought to vast circles of the people an understanding of the obscure phenomena in the life of the mind, and disseminated knowledge which would make it impossible in those countries for pronounced lunatics with the mania for persecution to gain an influence over hundreds of thousands of electoral citizens, even if it could not prevent the coming into fashion of the degenerate art (p. 559).

His translator explains this as a reference to the political influence of the anti-Semite Passchen in some areas of Germany. But Nordau's concern is more general, and extends itself to any movement that disturbs the uniformity of consensus and makes a centralized State less governable. If decadence is lined up with socialism and feminism, it is because for Nordau there is too much of the incalculable, the unknown and the uncontrollable in decadent dream.

Henry Havelock Ellis, on the other hand, was excited by *The New Spirit* (1890) of political and cultural change inspired by science. Darwin had shown the importance of coming to terms with natural and historical fact in the construction of societies, acknowledging the need to 'build the lofty structure of human society on the sure and simple foundations of man's organism' (p. 9). Feminism was a new historical development, whose appearance was to be welcomed: 'The development of women means a reinvigoration as complete as any brought by barbarians to an effete and degenerating civilization' (p. 9). Science, feminism and democracy were the trio of new forces that must inevitably transform the age. Democracy had to be developed. Knowledge and education must be extended, and a new instinct for social organization should be encouraged, of which trade unions were a vital part. Democracy was not 'State interference'; it meant 'the community approach[ing] the point where the individual himself becomes the State' (p. 17).

He conceded that there was evidence of decline in some parts of Europe, especially France and England. But against this he set the rise of Russia. From a perspective that rose above petty nationalisms, it seemed to him that a whole new future lay open, in which Art had a major cultural and moral role to play. Though he noted that religious sentiment still lingered on, paralysing the energies of life, Art was increasingly a substitute, offering the same refreshment in more wholesome humanist form: 'the world remoulded nearer to the heart's desire' (p. 29). It was Havelock Ellis who in his essay on J.-K. Huysmans, in *Affirmations* (1898), spoke of the energies of decadence, arguing that individual development was a gain, not a loss, to the community. Sophisticated civilization delighted in pluralism and variety, and Huysmans had given a vision of the beauty in base things which had never before been seen: 'Therein the decadent has his justification' (p. 205).

The objects of these commentaries, the decadents themselves, were confused and hesitant in their politics. As will be seen, when pressed, most fell to the right. But all were aware of the ambivalence of their position, and there were some, like Havelock Ellis, who saw their work as a force for renewal, and one that could be social as well as artistic. Nordau's suspicions were not entirely groundless.

Anatole Baju, one of the movement's best-known if least-respected publicists, began his new review *Le Décadent* on 10 April 1886 with the declaration that modern civilization was 'deliquescent', modern man blasé and neurotic, and modern politics contemptible and of no interest to artists. Two years later, however, in the second series of the journal, Baju's 'Les Parasites du Décadisme' disowned art that abandoned content for abstruse and exotic form (1–15 January 1888). In the next issue, Ernest Raynaud's 'Chronique littéraire' pointed out the varied commitments of writers labelled 'decadent' by the public. What they had in common was a determined originality that 'attacked the public in its prejudices'. Baju was by then sufficiently interested in politics to cheer the younger generation for rejecting Boulanger ('Boulanger hué par la jeunesse', 1–15 May 1888), describing the demagogue as 'a rubber Emperor', come to power 'with the help of pimps, cheapjacks and bookmakers'. He felt that Boulanger in power would signal the triumph of mediocrity and the end of all that was vital and intelligent in France. His revanchist patriotism, far from being an admirable quality, was all that stopped the Prussian Empire from falling apart. In 'L'Art social' (15–30 September), Louis Villatte, reviewing Jean Lombard's socialist poem *Adel ou La Révolte future*, took contemporaries to task for writing too much of mediaeval legend and not enough of socialism. Finally, Baju himself defined an elitist form of socialism as the 'Caractéristique des Décadents' (1–15 October). The world, he thought, was certainly in decay, and about to fall to the Barbarians:

And we are the Barbarians of the Mind, only a few days in advance of the Barbarians of Action. We are representatives of the society of the future, strayed into your world; we despise your social Darwinism, your Laws, your Morality and your false Aesthetics.

Decadents were now enemies of art for art's sake. For them, the artist was the proper successor to the priest, preaching a simple message: 'Everything must work to the same end: the perfection of society'. In Baju's 'Orientation' (15–31 March 1889), the decadents were said to be working for:

. . . the complete education of man and the improvement of the life of society. They have tried to make literature serve these aims, which are Nature's own; they have tried to turn the book from an instrument of corruption and mental enervation into a handmaid of the Revolution, a work of intellectual liberation.

The editors called to 'young socialists' for their support, and urged writers to stop despising politics. As a token of good faith, they printed Eugène Pottier's socialist poem on a pair of leaky shoes, 'Les Souliers qui prennent l'eau'. Sadly, their appeal was as premature as the poem was bad. From 15 April the review became *La France littéraire*, and at the subscribers' request the political section was quietly dropped.

Recession and Repression

It was a very particular combination of internal and external pressures that turned France into the centre of the decadent movement, and provided material to justify the comments of Nordau and Ellis alike.

Nordau blamed the pace of modern life, 'the rank growth of large towns', and cheap, bad food. Even people's hair and teeth, he noted, were falling out faster than before. France, drained of vitality by the Revolution of 1789 and the Napoleonic Wars, 'nervously strained and predestined to morbid derangement', was more susceptible than other nations, and had had in addition to deal with the humiliating defeat by Prussia after which 'Thousands lost their reason' (p. 42).

The Franco-Prussian War was certainly a massive blow to national pride. But it did no more than confirm the fact that France was no longer the major European power. Roger Magraw's account of the period (*France 1815–1914: The Bourgeois Century*, 1983), gives the evidence. Demographic decline in the 1860s was compounded by economic decline which by 1869 had provoked substantial labour unrest. Diplomatic errors in the same decade alienated numerous foreign governments. All this was in galling contrast to the vigour of the emerging nationalist powers of Germany and Italy.

In the seventies, the economy was certainly weakened by indemnity payments arising from the war and by the loss of industrially advanced Alsace-Lorraine. But the European depression of the eighties was made more severe in France by *laissez-faire* prejudice. Profits and prices fell, and unemployment rose to over 10 per cent. This remained unchanged until the next economic boom in 1896.

Economic and diplomatic weakness, however, was perceived as far less of a threat than internal unrest, which was political as well as economic in its origins. Socialist and feminist movements producing 'disorder' within the nation – the 'mob'* and Medusa – are the major source of terror or, occasionally, excitement within the decadent text. The Commune that reigned in Paris from March to May 1871, after Thiers' capitulation, and was fiercely repressed by the Versailles government, scarred the imagination of the Right. Paul Lidsky's *Les Ecrivains devant la Commune* (1982), describes how the major writers of the period rallied behind Thiers to denounce the Communard 'rioters'. As he points out, those who in the past had been most eager to proclaim their loathing for the 'bourgeoisie' were now loudest in their condemnation of the attempt to overthrow its rule.

---

* With a few exceptions I have found the politically charged 'mob' the most appropriate term to convey the loading given by most decadent writers to the open French term '*la foule*', for which the English 'crowd' is often too innocent. There is room for an extended study of the place of the crowd in French literary contexts and its shifting semantics, along the lines of George Rudé's historical work.

He quotes Edmond de Goncourt, delighted to see the revolution 'bled white' by the use of 'pure force', putting off further popular rebellion for a generation: 'If the authorities seize the chance to go as far as they can at this moment, then established society can look forward to twenty years' peace' (*Journal*, 31 May 1871). Flaubert (like de Goncourt, a major influence on the decadent generation) thought the 'mad dogs' had been treated too leniently: 'The whole Commune should have been sent to the galleys and the bloody fools should have been made to clear the ruins of Paris with chains round their necks, like the criminals they are' (*Correspondance*, letter to George Sand, before 18 October 1871). No new political or economic idea, said Feydeau, would now be taken on its own merits: 'Behind it must always stand the spectre of popular power, horrible, repellent, drunk on wine and blood, stolen gold flashing from between its dirty fingers' (*Consolation*, 1872, p. 112). Catulle Mendès, who became one of the best-selling writers of decadent fiction, soon abandoned his initial sympathy for the Communards. For him, it was the Commune, not defeat by Prussia, that marked the collapse of France: 'It was Rome under Tiberius, Rome after the Barbarians!' (*Les 73 Journées de la Commune*, 1871, p. 327).

Amnesties to enable the Communards to return from exile were slow in coming. Partial amnesty in spring 1879 was followed by full amnesty in June 1880. It was a relief for the new Republic to have off the agenda an argument that had been divisive for the left wing, and the poor weak creatures who came back were clearly no threat. Nevertheless, the Right remained nervous. Henry James' novel, *The Princess Casamassima* (1886), shows a comically idealistic Communard in exile in London, a charming little man, who is also a key figure in a revolutionary cell whose doctrines catch the imagination of thoughtful working-class men and foolishly romantic aristocratic women. The Commune was a dangerous and a fascinating disease, whose capacity to spread disorder had no limits.

Fears of Communard spectres were reinforced by the hard evidence of working-class organization, beginning in 1876 with the first workers' congress. Trade unions were legalized in 1884, and in 1892 the workers' movement, moving towards anarcho-syndicalism, deliberately rejected party politics and decided to make its weapon the general strike.

The socialist threat was compounded by the feminist challenge which surfaced in the sixties and seventies. The impetus of the Société pour la Revendication des Droits de la Femme, founded in 1866, and whose members included Paule Mink, Louise Michel and Elie Reclus, was halted only briefly by the repression of the Commune. In 1879, Hubertine Auclert, founder of the group Suffrage des Femmes and the journal *La*

Citoyenne (1881–91), asked the Marseilles workers' congress to endorse political rights for women in return for feminist support. The alliance was, on the socialist side, mostly verbal, but it caught public attention. Auclert made the eighties a period of suffragist activism.

At the beginning of the decade, republican reorganization of the education system produced the first network of free secondary schools for women. In 1884, divorce was legalized. By the mid-nineties, demands had grown militant. The women's rights congress of 1896, the first to discuss women's suffrage, received substantial press coverage; and in 1900, three congresses met, one Catholic, one moderate and one militant.

The movement in France was backward compared to that in other countries. To some, however, it constituted a threat quite out of proportion to its numbers. When Joséphin Péladan (see below, Part II, Chapter 3) confronts what he calls the lesbian vogue of the 1890s, his outrage acknowledges that this was much more than a mode.

The future shape of such volatile developments was impossible to guess. The useful books (Gustave Le Bon's *Psychologie des foules*, 1895) of necessity came after the event. A measure of establishment unease was the hysteria that greeted the charismatic General Boulanger's successful mini-plebiscite in 1888. When the demagogue, with his winning blend of patriotism and social protest, gained his great victory in 1889 in a Paris by-election, his party, the Ligue des Patriotes, was prosecuted and he himself forced to flee the country.

The mostly middle-class elites who held the levers of power in the early seventies – the 'forces of order' – held on to them with increasing difficulty. Between 1871 and 1898, the conservative Republic was never totally secure, threatened by the Radicals in opposition and to the left of them the socialists, with the monarchists a constant irritant until 1877. In the 1880s, the Opportunists held on to power through a series of ephemeral coalition governments, representing the interests of the grande bourgeoisie under the rhetoric of a democratic programme. Distractions and diversions were the politicians' means of survival.

The colonies, expanded in the eighties and nineties, were not sources of profit, but 'a *psychological* necessity to dispel post-1870 despair, at a time when direct confrontation with Bismarck was not feasible' (Magraw, p. 236). The Algerian colony was extended into Tunisia and France took more of Indo-China, fighting China in 1883 for the coal and mineral resources of Tonkin. Madagascar was annexed, Morocco penetrated in the 1900s, and the Congo seized soon afterwards. To some extent the enterprise backfired, as the colonies became one more meeting ground for imperialist rivalries in which France seldom did well. France and Britain had been fighting in West Africa in the seventies, before Britain took Egypt. The Fashoda incident of 1890 was provoked by British resistance to French expansion in the Upper Nile. In the 1900s, France had to compete with Germany for Morocco.

The one indisputable advantage of the colonies, as Octave Mirbeau pointed out (see below, Part II, Chapter 6) was that they provided inferior races to confirm the superiority of the native-born French. These were a welcome addition to the traditional Jewish scapegoat. Anti-Semitism, never long dormant, revived in the eighties to unite a new coalition of the Right. Edouard Drumont's *La France juive* (1886), went into 200 editions in fifteen years. Mirbeau's *Journal d'une femme de chambre* (1900) shows how effectively the servant class could be persuaded to ally itself with its masters in contempt for a common enemy. The conviction of the Jewish captain Alfred Dreyfus in 1894 on charges of treason trumped up by the Army was initially a propaganda victory for the Right, which backfired as Zola rallied the Left with his pamphlet 'J'accuse . . .' (*L'Aurore*, January 1898). The year 1898–9 was one of anti-Semitic riots: the uneasy consensus had been split.

Between a bourgeois, capitalist and conservative Republican establishment and the new waves of socialism and feminism, the decadent generation was caught. It did not like the businessmen, the politicians, the military and the professions who made up an establishment that might be rather loosely tacked together but still held society in a firm grip. Conformism was the Republic's watchword: citizens were for use, not ornament, and sexual and intellectual freedom promoted inefficiency. For young rebels, there was more at stake here than literary fidelity to the Baudelairean pose – the dandy, flaunting his aristocratic disdain of the marketplace. Nobody in this generation, as Remy de Gourmont said, had any intention of dying for Alsace-Lorraine ('Le Joujou patriotisme', *Mercure de France*, April 1891).

On the other hand, the bourgeoisie had all the money. The new art could bypass the official Salons and the establishment journals, mount its own exhibitions, launch its own little presses. But it still had to sell itself. As the means of reproducing and distributing works of art improved, and the mass markets opened up, it was harder to resist the temptation of the big publishing houses. Some people had jobs in the despised establishment. Huysmans kept his head down and stayed at his Ministry desk, a useful regular income. De Gourmont lost his job at the Bibliothèque Nationale for his outspokenness. Aristocrats who still had money were more likely to hand it to middle-class bankers and stockbrokers than promising artists; Péladan's calls for (preferably female) patronage mostly fell on deaf ears.

Socialists and feminists could not fund art.

Economically and politically, this was a generation conscious of its dependence, and it is this dependence that fills its work with those morbid, vengeful images of frustrated adolescent eroticism. Decadents, Symbolists, Rosicrucians, Occultists shuffle the same motifs, with the same motives. Part of the desire for change, they are also part of a tenacious establishment, whose traditions they ransack for forms to contain their vitality. The second part of this book considers in detail the range of their exploitations. Joris-Karl Huysmans and Joséphin Péladan turned to Catholicism and the occult. Remy de Gourmont mixed indiscriminately pagan, Cabbalist and Christian myth. Rachilde (Marguerite Eymery) played eighteenth-century marquise or Messalina. Jean Lorrain blended folktale and mediaeval legend with the criminal drama of modern Paris and the Riviera, while Pierre Louÿs retreated into the temples and forests of Ancient Greece – or pornographic fantasy, which is a tradition of its own. Pagan revivals, mediaeval revivals, aristocratic revivals, Occultism, Catholicism are so many dead bodies to which these writers give new life. The vampires and ghouls in their texts are a dead culture feeding on its own children.

Women may be the villains in the foreground of their pieces, but their part is mediatory and instrumental. The real confrontation is with the apparently immovable order of a capitalist society in decline, which simultaneously nurtures and destroys. Decadence is not just Herod and Salome. It is the ageing Emperor Hadrian and his favourite, Antinoüs, voluntarily surrendering himself to all the Emperor's loves, hates and resentments, paying for security with submission, but still, in the end, facing his own solitary death, by drowning.

The modern decadents' vision of the last days of Empire, Rome or Byzantium, is not only, as Praz described it, a world in decay, 'an impression of a delicious death-agony', a 'monotonous background' scattered with occasional figures who are 'static personifications of the female lust for power' or 'a body full of bruises and decay enveloped in the symmetrical folds of a mantle of heavy gold' (pp. 396–7). The best decadent fictions draw Byzantium and Rome with all the ambivalence of their own period.

The most impressive evocation of the potential new life in the turmoil of falling Empire comes from Jean Lombard, in his two historical novels, *L'Agonie* (1888) and *Byzance* (1890). Both draw the confusion of a time when established order is threatened by enemies without and within, and usurpers and rightful inheritors of power are hard to tell apart. While elites struggle for political power, religions, philosophies and moral values are thrown into the melting-pot. Eros and violence reign; the animal is liberated in individual and mob.

In what Paul Margueritte described as 'nightmare', 'obsessive' novels (preface to the 1901 edition of *Byzance*), Lombard's originality lies in his focus on the crowds that are the real source of the ferment. Other writers, fearful of the crowd, push it to the margins; Lombard foregrounds it. He has no delusions: the crowd, as Boulanger showed, was a volatile thing, easily led, and more easily turned to destruction than to building. But it is the power of the crowd that is liberated when empire falls.

Lombard writes as the self-educated socialist, with anarchist sympathies, whose premature death in 1891 at the age of thirty-seven (on which Alfred Vallette wrote a sympathetic obituary in the August number of the *Mercure de France*) put an end to twenty years' engagement in political action and literary polemic. He attended the first workers' congress in Marseilles, was a regular campaigner and speaker at public meetings, a well-known journalist who at his death was editor-in-chief of *La France Moderne*, and a novelist whose popularity was spreading from the avant-garde to a wider public.

His novels restate Baudelaire's much-overlooked insight: that decadence is not only an aesthetic and moral but also a social and political question. He provides a context that gives political and polemic direction to what in Baudelaire's work had been a simple statement of fact. For Lombard, the other face of the violence and eroticism which the text offers for the reader's pleasure is the need for radical political change.

L'Agonie is a heady blend of violence, sexuality and squalor. In his obituary for Lorrain in *L'Echo de Paris* (republished as preface to the 1891 edition of the novel), Octave Mirbeau called it a 'historical hallucination', with 'a powerful smell of blood and wild beasts', displaying 'the universal, frenzied rutting of a delirious nation'. It was thrilling too in its decadent tumult of styles (visionary, epic, realistic and erotic) and the chaos of its language, where scholarly and technical terms jostled with plain, simple phrases.

The novel describes Rome in the third century, polluted by barbaric and voluptuous Asiatic cults and split by conflicts between those cults and Christianity. The Christians in their turn are split between the ascetic Western tradition and the gnostic, orgiastic Eastern. The heirs of the Christian Emperors are struggling for supremacy with the fifteen-year-old adolescent Emperor Heliogabalus. Heliogabalus, mitred, bejewelled, long-haired, painted and effeminate, wants to impose on Christian Rome the worship of the phallic Black Stone, symbol of his tyrannical power.

He processes round Rome at the head of a motley crew of naked women, eunuchs, priests, captives, subservient Senators, wild beasts in cages – a permanent erotic display which maintains a high level of confusion, whereby Heliogabalus keeps power. He leads the orgies, copulating publicly with both sexes. His intention is to reinforce the cult of the Black Stone with the cult of the androgyne, which in the Christians' eyes is the final abomination. The harsh reality of authoritarian power, an alien regime imposed by armed forces, will be coupled with a more seductive and correspondingly more potent symbol of opposites reconciled, joined in a new and harmonious whole. Lombard's androgyne is a repressive, corrupting myth, not a figure of perfection but a pretext for capitulation.

In another improper compromise, the cults of the Phallus and the Lamb come together in the scene of the Eastern Christian Mass, where young men and women, painting each other's breasts with the blood of the slaughtered victim, couple in bisexual orgies. The socialist puritan mistrusts the gnostic attempt to recuperate sensuality, and sees sexual excess as a threat to life itself.

This society which ostensibly celebrates individual desire is in fact devoted to death. Lions and leopards roar in the darkness behind Heliogabalus' tent. The foreign envoys who narrowly escape being thrown to the beasts for the Emperor's amusement are, instead, locked in a room and suffocated in flowers. In the glaring spotlight of the circus, the animals massacre the victims in the arena and then turn on the gloating spectators. They have their human counterpart in the brutal soldiers who maintain the Emperor's power, or sell their services to his opponents.

Most important, they have their echo in the Christian mob that rises in mindless and vain revolt against Heliogabalus' tyranny. The erotic play of his processions is shattered by the hordes rampaging through the city. The violent instincts of the crowd are the reality of which erotic power is a mere image. Lombard shows the danger of attempts to conceal political intentions with sexual tricks. Aroused by selfish desire, the crowd is the destructive element that swallows enemies and friends alike, returning hard-won humanity to chaos. Heliogabalus' mother and sister, escaping from their besieged palace into the anonymity of the surrounding mob, merge into the crowd 'as into the ecstasy of the void . . . They floated there, devoid of all awareness, seeing visions of vague faces, unknown eyes . . .' The two Christian lovers trying to escape from the vileness into a new order are murdered by their own people and their bodies thrown into the levelling filth of the *cloaca maxima*, the great sewer of Rome. In this last massacre, the only survivor left to inherit History is a greedy pig-merchant.

In *Byzance*, similar schisms reappear, as the Emperor Constantine V struggles to hold power against the icon-worshippers. This time the erotic gives way to pure violence. Sepeôs, the head of the conspirators, is ritually mutilated of a hand, a foot and an eye, and thrown alive into a dungeon. The populace is decimated by bloody massacres. At the end, the great church which is the heart of the city collapses on the rebels.

The pleasure of both novels may appear to lie solely in their sadistic display of suffering and pain. But contemporary readers would have encountered them in the context of Lombard's socialist reputation and, particularly, his prose-poem *Adel: La Révolte future*, published in 1888. Here, the chaos of 'Decadence and its debilities' is resolved, and the mob released from self-destruction. These debilities are those of the city in its death-throes, suburbs destroyed by Industry and Capital, howling crowds living under a pall of smoke and over the stench of sewers. An age devoted to money and material satisfactions is captured in the image of the female idol that presides over this vision of decay ('the flesh holds sway'), her breasts rotten inside, laughing through a toothless mouth, her belly a gaping hole, a mass of purulence under her fine brocades. It seems that the source of life itself is corrupt. Renewal is prophesied through Adel, the worker, who will throw the city into its own sewers, with the help of a Nature whose primitive vigour is only temporarily overlaid by the city's rot, and whose strength resurfaces in the city crowd. In a final Utopian vision, purifying violence in all its terrible beauty brings the promise of new life to a sick world.

This is the vision that will be renewed in the work of the anarchist Octave Mirbeau, with which the present book concludes. *Le Jardin des supplices* (1899), evoking the fascinating, sickening realities beneath all the play thrills and fears of Byzantium, is an indictment of generations of corruption, a demand for purification by fire and blood.

2
The National Tradition: de Sade and his Heirs

The art of French Decadence refuses to be limited by its national context, and the chapter after this one will consider some of France's exchanges with other European countries of influences and forms which are variations on a common crisis of values. In that wider perspective, a new threat emerges to the European elites and their dependants, in the double overshadowing of American capital and American democracy. Seldom given due recognition, its existence is nevertheless acknowledged in decadent demonology, where the Yankee businessman joins the Jewish banker, Medusa and the mob.

But the substantial origins of the language and philosophy of the decadence must first be looked for in France's own cultural history, where they appear predominantly and self-consciously rooted in the Sadean tradition.

After almost a hundred years' undercover existence, the case of the Marquis de Sade returned to the public domain in the eighties. In 1880, Alcide Bonneau published a study in *La Curiosité littéraire et bibliographique* of the first edition of *Justine*, and followed it in 1882 with one of *Juliette*. In 1884, he published with Isidore Lisieux a limited edition (150 copies) of the 1791 edition of *Justine*. An anonymous article in *La Revue indépendante* (January 1885), attacked the 'hypocrisy' and inaccuracy of de Sade's earlier publicists (Jules Janin, 'Le Marquis de Sade', *Revue de Paris*, November 1834, and the Bibliophile Jacob), and declared that nowadays: 'We are all more or less sadists.' Moderns, it said, appreciated the 'sickness' of de Sade, that exaggeration of normal responses which leads to the special association, often self-defensive, of cruelty and pleasure: 'Excess of pleasure takes the clear form of pain.' Sadism had surfaced at every decadent moment in history: '. . . all periods whose nervous systems are worn-out and overwrought: Rome under the Caesars, the Middle Ages of Sabbats and wizards, Rome under the Borgias, and the modern era'. It claimed that de Sade had gone to prison for fantasies, not real crimes, and pointed admiringly to his active sympathy for the Revolution.

De Sade was a natural focal point for the decadents – the aristocrat doubly dispossessed, out of place under both monarchy and revolution. He depended on the hierarchy of monarchy for his own privileges, but was tempted too by revolutionary ideologies of individual freedom, which seemed to give new scope to private desire. He attacked authority, in the form of the repressive Mother, the Family and the Church. In one of the decadents' favourite episodes, Eugénie, the eager pupil of the libertines, whipped, lectured, raped and sodomized, concludes her liberation and her education by sewing up her mother's vagina with a thick red waxed thread (*La Philosophie dans le boudoir*, 1795). But he reasserted authority in masculine form, in the shape of the libertines and bandits who direct the phallic orgy.

Like the decadents, he is torn between desire for chaos and desire for order. On the one hand, as Dolmancé explains in *La Philosophie dans le boudoir*, his model is the destructive ferment of Nature:

> Since destruction is one of the first laws of Nature, nothing that destroys can be a crime . . . murder isn't an act of destruction; a man who commits murder is only changing the forms of things; he is restoring to Nature elements which her skilful hand immediately uses to recompense other creatures . . . (pp. 421–2).

On the other, he turns to aesthetic rite and ritual for the means to control Nature, presenting the artist in the erotic as the new maker of order.

Two things, however, divide de Sade from his heirs. Where he places power in male monsters, they conjure up female ogres, disguising their own rebellion. And where his is an active rage against the limits of a world that seeks to enclose and restrain him, their violence, with a few exceptions, is febrile and inward-turned. When it entered the 1880s, the Sadean tradition found itself much debased.

After de Sade's death, access to his works was difficult throughout the nineteenth century. His legend was nevertheless current coin for men of the middle class and upwards. The Goncourts saw in *Justine* 'a sickness worth studying' (*Journal*, 4 June 1856), and noted that private collect-ions of de Sade's work figured in the most respectable men's libraries (10 November 1856) and 'aesthetic' and 'philosophical' discussions of it were current in men's clubs (October 1857; 28 February 1858). Though 'sickened' by him, they were intrigued to find that on a fact-finding visit to a women's hospital, the sight of 'the pale women we glimpsed on the pillows, bluish almost, transfigured by suffering and stillness' was 'an image that stirs our soul and draws us like some frightening veiled mystery', and filled them with sexual desire (18 December 1860). They visited the English sadist Henkey, son of a rich London banker, lodging in the Paris home of Lord Hertford, with his rich collection of erotic books and trinkets, waiting impatiently for a new binding of tanned female skin. In a nightmare, they imagined themselves taking part in the activities of Henkey's world (7 and 8 April 1862). All the same, Edmond was horrified when his own novels *La Fille Elisa* and *La Faustin* (with that archetypal English sadist, George Selwyn) were called 'sadistic' (27 March 1877, 7 February 1882), and not until 14 September 1884 did he admit to reading *Justine*, an 'abominable' book.

Sade's influence on the decadence was mostly exercised indirectly, through the authors who were the models of the movement: in particular, Baudelaire and Flaubert.

The poet of *Les Fleurs du mal* (1857) saw in de Sade a mirror-image of his own values and obsessions. First and foremost, they share the cult of self-conscious evil. For Baudelaire, in his notes on Laclos' *Les Liaisons dangereuses*: 'Evil which was conscious and self-aware was less terrible and nearer cure than evil ignorant of itself. G. Sand worse than de Sade' (*Oeuvres complètes*, éds. de la Pléïade, 1966, p. 640). 'To do Evil in full awareness' ('L'Irrémédiable') was the saving grace of the criminal, as of the dandy. The ironic knowledge that adds an extra frisson to his crime also absolves him, because it acknowledges the authority of the taboos he infringes. (Using the same argument, the Catholic avant-garde capitalized on the sadistic vogue of the eighties to claim both de Sade and Baudelaire for the Catholic tradition – an enterprise which shows the vulnerability of decadent revolt to conservative recuperations.)

Sometimes Baudelaire's version of de Sade is more projection than reflection. When he admires in him an example of 'natural man', drawn irresistibly by evil (*ibid.*, p. 521), he introduces values from his own residual Catholicism which do less than justice to de Sade's eighteenth-century amoral atheism. It is Baudelaire, not de Sade, who places the origins of evil in Nature rather than man, and, most of all, in the women who for him are Nature's chief representatives. Juliette is an exception in the Sadean world, while Baudelaire's poetry is dominated by the *femme fatale* and her innocent victims: '. . . every day a new heart in your manger/. . . dumb, blind machine, fertile in cruelties/. . . drinking the world's blood' ('Tu mettrais l'univers entier dans ta ruelle . . .'), 'Strong as a horde/Of demons . . .' ('Le Vampire'), 'Beloved tiger, monster with an indolent air' ('Le Léthé').

In his fantasy each exercises absolute power. The libertines who stage-manage Sadean orgies are masters of their world, their dreams turned to reality by bloodshed and force. Baudelaire claims only the magic power of poetry, but his rule is as absolute: 'I am the wound and the knife/. . . the victim and the executioner' ('L'Héautantimorouménos'). Power apparently conceded to women – vampires or goddesses – is no more than a snare. The heavy robe of his tears and desires that he weaves for his mistress-Madonna holds her locked fast while he plants his seven sharp knives in her 'panting . . . sobbing . . . streaming Heart!' ('A une Madone'). A mistress whose happiness mocks his own misery will have her just punishment: '. . . one night, I shall/. . . crawl silently/. . . to punish your happy flesh,/bruise your redeemed breast/Make in your side, amazed/A wide, deep wound,/And, dizzy sweetness!/Through those new lips/Brighter and more beautiful,/Filter my poison, sweet sister!' ('A celle qui est trop gaie'). After Joseph de Maistre, he links the vocation of poet with that of the priest and the soldier, equating: 'Knowing, killing, creating' (*Mon coeur mis à nu*, p. 1279). A few pages later, he plans a chapter on 'indestructible, eternal, universal and ingenious human ferocity. On the love of blood. On the intoxication of blood. On the intoxication of crowds. On the intoxication of the tortured (Damiens)' (p. 1287).

As this last note indicates, Baudelaire, like de Sade, is not only drawn to the pleasure of exercising power, but also of abdicating it, giving direct expression to that deep conviction of impotence from which the violence of both fantasy worlds springs. The reader to whom *Les Fleurs du mal* is dedicated, the *alter ego* of the poet, 'dreams of scaffolds as he puffs his hookah', conjuring sadistic fantasies out of willed passivity. In 'La Cloche fêlée', cobweb-wrapped lethargy alternates with outbursts of gratuitous violence – the characteristic mood, later, of Huysmans' des Esseintes, or Jean Lorrain's Count Noronsoff. Baudelaire dreams of physical dissolution, like the regicide martyr Damiens, or of moral surrender to the seductive promiscuity of the crowd. In the prose-poem 'Les Foules', he describes the pleasure of:

> . . . this universal communion. He who has the facility to wed the crowd knows feverish delights forever denied to the egoist, shut tight as a box, and the idle man, inward-looking, like a mollusc . . . What men call love is very little, weak and limited compared to that unspeakable orgy, that sacred prostitution of the soul that gives itself wholly, poetry and charity, to the unforeseen that suddenly appears, to the unknown that passes by.

Yet elsewhere, Baudelaire despises the surrender of self. In *Fusées*, the act of love is seen as an act of torture, a surgical operation in which the victim, out of control, is ugly and contorted, like someone suffering from electric shock, fever, opium or drink, his face marked with a 'crazed ferocity' that relaxes into a death-mask (p. 1249). This is not ecstasy but 'decomposition'.

To reproduce and fix, in art, the process of decomposition, reconciling the desire for chaos and the desire for order, is the purpose of both Baudelaire and de Sade. The wild orgies of tangled bodies in de Sade are careful theatrical productions, organized and harmonized by their libertine directors. They have their analogy in Baudelaire's poetry, where decayed and rotting flesh and disintegrating mind and spirit are gradually refined and fixed into the abstractions of art. In 'Une charogne', a decomposing dog's corpse, the future image of his mistress in her grave ('Legs in the air, like a lecherous woman/Burning, sweating poisons,/It spread out carelessly, cynically/Its belly, with its foul stench') becomes pure line and sound ('All rising and falling like a wave,/. . . A world of strange music,/Like running water and wind,/The forms vanished, and were no more than a dream . . .'). There is the same process in 'Les Métamorphoses du vampire', where the mistress biting his flesh becomes first '. . . a gourd with sticky sides, crammed full of pus!' and finally '. . . bits of a skeleton,/Rubbing together like a screeching weathercock/Or a sign in an iron frame/Blown by the wind on winter nights'.

This desire to force fresh order out of chaos through the despotic authority of art is a key motif in the decadence. It appears in Gustave Moreau's paintings, where hard metals and jewels fuse with pliant vegetation or soft flesh; in Odilon Redon's engravings, embedding human features into plants and objects; or the work of the jeweller Lalique, fixing coiling plant life into mineral forms.

For de Sade, Baudelaire and their decadent heirs, the desire is to enjoy the anarchy of Nature, the chaotic energy of matter, without letting that anarchy run its natural course. Art traps an image of freedom, to stand substitute for the reality.

Flaubert, according to the Goncourts, was interested in sadism long before he read de Sade (*Journal*, 10 April 1860), seeing in it the 'last word of Catholicism . . . the spirit of the mediaeval Church, horror of Nature . . . hatred of the body' (9 April 1861). In his *Salammbô* (1862), they saw a blend of de Sade and Chateaubriand (21 April 1861). As Flaubert pointed out in his letter of December 1862 to Sainte-Beuve, who had made similar comments in articles in the December *Le Constitutionnel*, such comparisons were dangerous for a writer whose *Madame Bovary* had already brought him before the courts on a charge of offending public morals. He felt that the violence and cruelty in his novel were justified by the historical situation, for he was describing the conditions of the aftermath of revolution, which France itself had known all too intimately: 'Need I remind you of Madame de Lamballe, the Mobiles in '48, and what's happening even now in the United States?'

It is Flaubert, with his vivid, visual imagination, who provides the decadent generation with the most striking images for the Sadean identification of Love and Death. The most famous of these appears in *La Tentation de Saint Antoine* (1874), the drama which reviews all the fatal human errors engendered by the mediaeval Church's 'hatred of the body'. At the climax of his self-imposed exile in the desert, the hermit Anthony is visited by the Devil in his double aspect: 'the spirit of fornication and the spirit of destruction'. Death and Life join forces ('You destroy, that I may renew'/'You give life for me to practise destruction!') and merge into a single monster: 'A death's head with a crown of roses. The head dominates a pearly-white female torso. Below, a shroud starred with golden stitches forms a kind of tail – and the whole body ripples like a giant worm standing erect.' This is the monster that inspired Odilon Redon, who produced two series of lithographs drawing on Flaubert's *Tentation*, in 1888 and 1896, as well as an album of 1889, *A Gustave Flaubert*.

The same corruption of pleasure is embodied in figures such as Salome and Salammbô. Salammbô, the priestess of the moon-goddess Tanith, dancing naked with the sacred black python, is both the vulnerable child-victim of the Sadean tradition, her fragility menaced by the python's strength, and the vehicle of a power greater than herself, that in its turn makes men 'her' victims. Her dance prefigures Anthony's grotesque vision of the pearly-white worm, but in a very different mode:

Her eyes half-closed, she leaned backwards under the rays of the moon.

The white light seemed to wrap her in a silver mist, the moist prints of her feet shone on the flagstones, stars throbbed in the deep water; the python tightened about her his black rings striped with gold. Under the great, heavy weight, Salammbô panted, yielded, swooned and died; he softly beat her thigh with the tip of his tail; then the music fell silent, and he dropped to the ground (p. 878).

Yielding to the python's cruel embrace, she gains even greater beauty, whose power is embodied in the heavy make-up, the elaborate priestess's robes, and the jewels she puts on to confront the Barbarian Mâtho. Her mirror reflects the dazzling power of sexuality focused by artifice:

[Her hair] was covered in powdered gold, curled back and front, and hung down her back in long ringlets fastened with pearls. The bright lights of the candles made more vivid the colour on her cheeks, the gold of her robes, the whiteness of her skin; about her waist, on her arms, hands, toes shone such a quantity of jewels that the mirror, like a sun, reflected her rays . . . (p. 880).

Through Salammbô as through Salome, the goddess shows her power by the shedding of blood. Battles, massacres, ritual sacrifices to Moloch build to the climax which is the ceremonial murder of Mâtho, the Barbarian who dared to challenge an oligarchy whose power seems unshakeable, rooted in its skilful exploitation of the darkest desires of the people. The rulers of Carthage debate his fate with relish:

. . . flay him alive, pour lead into his intestines, starve him to death . . . fasten him to a tree with a monkey behind him, to hit him on the head with a stone . . . ride him through the city on a camel, with linen wicks soaked in oil placed in various parts of his body; they liked the idea of the tall animal ranging the streets with this man writhing under the flames like a candelabra blown by the wind (p. 988).

In the end, he is given to the crowd to be torn to pieces. On that day, the 'female principle' dominates: 'a mystic lustfulness filled the heavy air; the torches were already alight in the depths of the sacred woods; there must have been an orgy of prostitution that night' (p. 987). He appears before Salammbô in inhuman tatters:

. . . a long shape, red from head to foot; his torn bonds hung along his thighs, indistinguishable from the tendons of his stripped wrists; his mouth hung wide open; from his eye-sockets flashed two flames that seemed to spurt up to his hair; and the wretch was still walking! (p. 993)

It is the women who are held responsible for the violence unleashed through sexuality. Yet at the end, Salammbô herself falls victim to the power of which she is the unconscious channel. At the moment of her betrothal to one of the victors, she suddenly collapses, 'pale, stiff, with open mouth, her loose hair hanging to the ground. Thus died Hamilcar's daughter, for having touched the cloak of Tanith' (p.994).

Continuing the Sadean tradition, Flaubert too is obsessed with the ambivalence of bloodshed. In his short story 'Hérodias', the severed head of the Baptist marks not an end but a beginning. The dripping trails of blood are replaced by the rays of the martyr's halo, inaugurating the new era of Christianity that will reinvigorate an old world. This tale, which closes the *Trois Contes* (1877), is in stark contrast to the bloodless banality of 'Un coeur simple', the account of contemporary French life which opens them. In between, the mediaeval 'Légende de Saint Julien l'Hospitalier' shows the second turning point in European civilization, where the spirit begins to deform the flesh. The natural cruelty of the child, imitating his father's pagan pleasure in the hunt, is turned into neurotic obsession by the repressive Christianity urged on him by his mother. Confronted with the choice between instinct and repression, unable to invent a middle way, Julien finally opts for his own death. In the language of the legend, he embraces Christ in leper's guise, preferring the vilest self-abnegation to the risk of living with instincts he fears he cannot control. Where Salammbô embraces the object of her fear in order to draw from it fresh sources of power, he fixes it to himself as a corrupting burden of guilt.

The same choice is set out in *La Tentation de Saint Antoine*. Facing the dilemma set by the mediaeval Church – that false polarization of carnal evil and spiritual good, which generates perversions – Anthony discovers the way out, which is to yield to instinct. His final temptation is that of the Spirit, the Ideal, presented in the celebrated dialogue of the Chimera and the Sphinx. The tempting presumption is that men can possess Truth by reason, either by intuitive leaps of the imagination (Chimera) or long thoughtful meditation (Sphinx). Neither is the answer. The Chimera runs round in circles, and the Sphinx sinks into the sand. Instead, Anthony is caught in a vision of material, chaotic reality. Forest and seas yield up all their rich variety, animal, plant and vegetable kingdoms merge and metamorphose, and he rides the primal chaos – 'and he's no longer afraid!' In his turn, he lets himself be engulfed by the vitality of Nature, craving to 'develop like plants, flow like water, vibrate like sound, shine like light, be absorbed into all forms, penetrate every atom, descend to the depths of matter – become matter!' (p. 164)

This is the instinctive freedom craved by de Sade, and denied him by religion and society. Anthony too is frustrated by the same forbidding powers. His ecstasy is shattered by the rise of the Sun, its face marked with the Face of Christ, figuring the humanist inheritance of abstract reason and the ascetic tradition of Christianity, which together make the laws of Western Europe. The morbid, denying power of the Spirit pushes him back to his visions of cruel domination, and his prayers, torments and self-lacerations.

Between Flaubert's Anthony and the decadent generation there is a considerable gap. When Huysmans' des Esseintes employs his dwarf ventriloquist mistress to mimic the dialogue of Chimera and Sphinx, a genuine source of metaphysical anguish has become a trick for sexual stimulation. Of Julien, Salammbô and Anthony, it is the first whom the decadents most closely resemble, stripped of the power to struggle, consciously embracing a morbid image of Love to acknowledge their guilt and their impotence.

A simpler version of sadism, both cruder and more perverse, is carried forward in the fiction of Barbey d'Aurevilly (1808–89), who uses it as a means of recruiting converts to his own idiosyncratic wing of the post-1871 Catholic Revival. As in Lombard's Byzantium, or Flaubert's Carthage, the erotic drive is harnessed to a political purpose.

Converted to Catholicism in 1846–7, well-known as a Romantic novelist, journalist and critic, Barbey linked to religion the prestige of the reprobate artistic circles to which he belonged. He was a friend of Baudelaire, whose style, sensibility and dandy image (the latter, by the 1880s, requiring assistance from wig, make-up and stays) he embodied for his younger friends, Huysmans, Péladan, Lorrain and Léon Bloy. Bloy saw in the sadism of Barbey's short stories, *Les Diaboliques*, a denunciation of the hell of the flesh into which modern society had sunk, a vigorous image of the hollowness of a world that refused to be regenerated by the Catholic Ideal: 'Is sadism, as we understand it, anything else but the starved craving for the Absolute, transferred to the order of the passions, and seeking in the practices of cruelty spice for the practices of debauch?' (*Un brelan d'excommuniés*, 1889). Sadism for Bloy became legitimate where it could be interpreted as a cry for help to Authority.

When published in 1874, *Les Diaboliques* had been pursued by the police and withdrawn from circulation. They received little notice when re-edited in 1882, but Félicien Rops' nine plates, published in 1886, produced a *succès de scandale*. The book was reissued in 1891, profiting from the vogue for the occult, and again in 1905 and 1912.

The tales evoke the passions that rage below the polite surface of society, with all its civilized games and rules. Society is always aristocratic, and sadism the last heroic gesture left in a world levelled by democracy. Barbey's cruelty has no ambivalent masochistic notes. His heroes – and more so, his heroines, who carry the final burden of guilt – are avengers, not expiators, who feel no corroding guilt. Only occasionally do they acknowledge authority other than their own, in the form of a Catholicism which, however, knows its subordinate place and decorative function: 'I know – all Paris knows – a certain Madame Henri III who wears at her belt rosaries of tiny skulls, carved in gold, over gowns of blue velvet, and indulges in self-flagellation, mingling, with the spice of her penitences, the spice of Henri III's other pleasures' ('La Vengeance d'une femme').

'Le Dessous de cartes d'une partie de whist' reveals intricate webs of suspected passions and poisonings. The Comtesse de Stasseville, pale and thin, with light red hair, thin lips ('narrow and murderous'), a tongue that flashes venomous epigrams like the diamond on her finger flashes poisoned fire, a cold sword glancing from her emerald-green eyes, with a reputation of irreproachable virtue, is the mistress of Marmor de Karkoël, a Scottish diplomat and connoisseur of exotic poisons. Her pale, white daughter Hermine is also in love with de Karkoël. Daughter and mother die in quick succession, and suspicion falls on the Scotsman. His viciousness remains, however, far inferior to that of the Countess, an unnatural mother who consumes her own children. The box of sickly-scented mignonette that always stood in her bedroom, whose flowers she carried everywhere, nibbling the blossoms throughout her whist games, is emptied out, and the corpse of a baby found at the bottom.

When cavalry officers swap stories in 'A un dîner d'athées', Captain Mesnilgrand tops them all with the adventure of Rosalba, a 'virgin Messalina' of immense sexual appetite, nicknamed 'la Pudica' for her habit of blushing pink before the slightest sexual initiative. Her husband finds irrefutable evidence of her infidelities. Watched by Mesnilgrand, hiding in the wardrobe, the couple exchange insults and blows, beating one another with the heart of their dead baby, kept in an urn on the mantelpiece, which Rosalba declares was never her husband's. In his fury, he tries to seal up her vagina with the pummel of his sword and the hot wax she's just been dripping on a letter to yet another lover; and Mesnilgrand must stab him to save her.

'La Vengeance d'une femme' celebrates the Duchess of Sierra-Leone, prostituting herself on the streets in her magnificent gold dress to punish an old husband whose Spanish pride would not allow her the innocent admiration of a younger man. Bursting with his servants into her chamber, he tossed her lover's head into her lap, and his heart to his hunting dogs. She now lavishes her magnificent and perverse passions on passers-by, dragging her husband's name through the mud. Her vengeance lives beyond the grave. When she dies in La Salpetrière, riddled with syphilis, she asks for her full title and the designation 'whore' to be carved on her tombstone. Concluding with the priest's naïve admiration of her humble 'repentance', this tale, like the others, simultaneously damns and enjoys the cruelty of its heroine, successfully obscuring the origins of her perversity with its protestations of outrage.

A more refined adaptation appears in the work of Villiers de l'Isle-Adam (1840–89), the last representative of an aristocratic ideal of which Barbey, at best, gave only a parody. Villiers first became known in 1862, with the publication of his esoteric novel *Isis*. Throughout the sixties, he headed the campaign to spread Wagner's influence in France. But his greatest fame was in the period 1885–95, after Huysmans' eulogy in *A rebours*. Three major works were published in 1886: 'L'Amour suprême', *L'Eve future* and the exotic *Akëdysséril*.

Villiers' heroes and heroines perform like figures out of de Sade, with, however, one vital difference. As Arthur Symons saw, they lack independent will: 'They are on the borders of a wisdom too great for their capacity . . . haunted by dark powers, instincts of ambiguous passions; . . . they have not quite systematically transposed their dreams into action' ('Villiers de l'Isle-Adam', *Studies in Two Literatures*, 1897).

In his heroines especially, Villiers incarnates his own dream of heroic despair. These exquisite creatures are mere carriers of power, lived by forces greater than themselves. They have, in Symons' words, 'the solemnity of dead people, and a hieratic speech . . . They have the immortal weariness of beauty, they are enigmas to themselves, they desire, and know not why they refrain, they do good and evil with the lifting of an eyelid, and are innocent and guilty of all the sins of the earth.'

Tullia Fabriana (*Isis*), whose family dates back to the twelfth century, is the archetypal *femme fatale*, all-powerful and self-sufficient. Through her esoteric knowledge and her skill with poisons, she has become a hidden political force who rules all Europe. She inhabits a closely-guarded palace, quickly sealed at the slightest threat of attack, festooned with bloody traps for intruders. But when she gives herself to the fair-haired young nobleman whom she at last decides is worthy of her, the pain he feels in her embrace comes not from her own strength but the glimpse of an ideal beyond them both: 'he had the impression of two arms joined – so painfully! – round his neck . . . and then the whole swarm of pale, infinite pleasures, the quiver of divine dream, torment . . .' She is only the gateway to knowledge of the overwhelming power of the instincts, the double forces of Love and Death of which she too is a victim. Villiers presents in their union a magnificent double vision of Nirvana and sensual plenitude: against the darkness of night and the heavens that envelop the hero like a shroud as he enters the crumbling tomb of sensual oblivion, he sets the pure marble whiteness of their naked bodies, the air filled with the scent of lilacs and white roses, and the silky touch of swans, greyhounds and kids.

In contrast, Mademoiselle d'Aubelleyne, the heroine of 'L'Amour suprême', is the classic victim. Appearing at a ball in strange half-mourning – pale oval face, white lilac in her black hair, a wreath of white lilac over a corsage of black silk embroidered with jet – she is a Beatrice figure, charming her would-be suitor with the mystery of her 'transparent soul'. She is spending her last night at the ball before taking the veil, to savour the delights she must surrender. He watches her next day as she is received into the order of discalced Carmelites, wrapped in a shroud, stepping into her coffin; the look in her eyes as her hair is cut will haunt him for ever. The anguish of Villiers' generation, denied its own life, is turned to pleasure with the cruel vision of female sensuality dedicated to death.

In *L'Eve future*, sadistic power is wielded by the scientist, who robs two living women, one of her beauty, and one of her intellect and her life, to make his android, Hadaly. A 'captive ideal', with all the charms of Hoffmann's Antonia, Poe's Ligeia and Wagner's Venus, Hadaly is the satirical, mechanical mirror of man's desire to worship a mystified image of his own power. A dark mourning-veil shrouds her face, caught with a band of pearls at the brow. Her body is encased in delicate armour of brilliant silver scales, moulding her virginal form. Her loins are hidden by a black linen scarf studded with diamonds. Her right hand holds the pommel of a sword, and her left a golden flower; her fingers are covered with rings. None of these attributes of mystery and power is her own. Einstein, the physicist, tears her beauty apart and reassembles it at will, to demonstrate his mastery of the ideal. In an ironic conclusion, a fire at sea destroys the android, crossing the Channel to enter real life with her lover on his English estates. The power men exert over women is only a shadow of the power Fate exerts over men, denying every effort to realize the ideal.

In *Akëdysséril*, it is again woman who seems to possess the power of destruction. The heroine is the warrior-queen of Benares, who at the death of her husband snatched power from his younger brother, and now leads her country to imperial triumphs at the head of an army mesmerized by her beauty. She stands among her legions as battle rages, waving her scimitar, 'on the jewel-laden howdah of her battle-elephant, beflowered with drops of blood'. She returns to Benares in triumphal procession, emblem of the cruel mystery which is men's desire to die for love. Tall, pale-browed, a diadem on her blue-black hair, dreamy and starry blue-black eyes, cruel nostrils, mouth with a bloody glint, teeth like a panther, the 'oppressive charm' of her features inspires 'unease' in her warriors. Despairing of possessing her, they die for her instead, 'thirst[ing] to feel the wounds received from her eyes'.

But the most compelling emblem of the identity of Love and Death is not the Queen herself, but the young couple, her rivals to the throne, whose death is arranged in her absence by the High Priest of Siva. Instead of following her orders, so that they die of passion fulfilled, in the 'nuptial ecstasy' of their first embrace, he engineers their death by suicide, about to exchange a first kiss so greatly desired that its reality could never equal the dream. The two bodies, twined together chastely like a marble statue, incarnate 'the dream of a pleasure accessible only to immortal hearts', fixing the death of sensuality as the image of perfect Love.

More than any other, this tale has an explicit political message. The stability of the country, according to the Queen, required the death of the lovers, as its greatness required the death of her adoring warriors. Order demands sacrifice – the death of the young, and the death of Love. Villiers' two symbols, the Lady and the dead lovers, give seductive force to an ugly statement of the sadistic and repressive nature of power.

The complexity of the Sadean tradition is much reduced by the decadents, in search of vivid images of the pleasure of pain, suffering and self-denial. Sacher-Masoch, at least as much as de Sade, is the representative figure of decadent sensibility.

In the eighties, Sacher-Masoch was a much-respected figure. As Gilles Deleuze has pointed out (*Sacher-Masoch: An Interpretation*, 1971), de Sade's rampant obscenity is in Masoch displaced, through fetishism, into a sickly decency. His politics and his language seemed entirely unexceptionable. When he visited Paris in 1886 he was fêted by the establishment. His *Femmes slaves* were published in *La Revue des deux mondes* in five instalments, between 15 June 1889 and 15 December 1890, and 'Le Cosaque' appeared in the same review on 1 February 1892.

Born in Galicia in 1835, Léopold von Sacher-Masoch found his work deeply influenced by the problems of nationalities, minority groups and revolutionary movements in the Russian Empire, and especially by the struggle of the peasants against the landowners. He was involved in the Panslavic movement. He was a respected Professor of History at Graz, and the respected author of best-selling historical novels where 'in the language of [his] folklore, history, politics, mysticism, eroticism, nationalism and perversion are closely intermingled, forming a nebula around the scenes of flagellation' (Deleuze, p. 10). His writing takes popular feelings of frustration and impotence and provides them with a rationale. *The Heritage of Cain* (a six-volume historical cycle of which he completed two parts, the first being the famous *Venus in Furs*, 1870) is a burden of suffering, entirely justified by Cain's crime. It is in the 'natural' order of things that Cain should shoulder his suffering, and die in free atonement for his unquestioned guilt. The success of Masoch's work in France is clearly connected with post-1870 efforts by the Right to urge ideologies of submission, rather than revolt. The Catholic cult of suffering, whose effects will be seen in later chapters, particularly in the writings of Huysmans and Péladan, belongs to the same movement.

For Sacher-Masoch himself, the origins of his sensibility lie in personal, not political experience. As Deleuze comments: 'He has a particular way of "desexualizing" love and at the same time sexualizing the entire history of humanity' (pp. 11–12). The writer describes his first whipping from an aunt, who regularly dealt out the same treatment to her husband:

> I both hated and loved the creature who seemed destined, by virtue of her strength and diabolical beauty, to place her foot insolently on the neck of humanity . . . Much later I isolated the problem that inspired the novel *Venus in Furs*. I became aware first of the mysterious affinity between cruelty and lust, and then of the natural hatred and enmity between the sexes which is temporarily overcome by love, only to reappear subsequently with elemental force, turning one of the partners into a hammer and the other into an anvil (*La Revue bleue*, 1888, cit. Deleuze, Appendix 1).

But personal relationships are elsewhere expressed in particular political contexts. The women in *Femmes slaves* rebel against the oppression of their male partners and become bandit figures looking for revenge. At the same time, they retain traces of their old nurturing role. 'Theodora', ill-treated by her first husband, is attracted by Baron A . . ., but has no intention of slipping back into another submissive relationship. In the course of a peasant revolt, she saves him by taking him captive, punishing him to appease the peasants and also to satisfy her own complex feelings towards him. Put to the plough, ridiculed and humiliated by watching women and children, he finally dies, accepting and enjoying the justice of his death.

Masochistic relationships, as Octave Mirbeau perceived in *Le Jardin des supplices*, are the key to the morality, aesthetics and politics of late nineteenth-century decadence, for they sustain and make palatable the inequality which is otherwise a source of revolt. Deleuze has shown how Sacher-Masoch's style displaces real anguish with fetishes and employs techniques to freeze and aestheticize violence, turning pain into art and torture into tableau. Rebellion is enclosed in the safety of a frame, which may be the cool image of the mirror, the reflection of a work of art, or the cold logic of contract. 'Disavowal, suspense, waiting, fetishism and phantasy together make up the specific constellation of masochism' (p. 63); and all these are characteristic features of decadent art.

Similarly, the cold, lovely female who protects and punishes is the point of reference for the moral values of Masoch and the decadent writers alike. For Deleuze, the masochist's dream of Woman is Nature as she appears in the prologue to Masoch's *Galician Tales*, with her 'threefold face: cold, maternal, severe' (p. 48). She is not evil, only the representative and the instrument of Death, the masochist's ideal. Masoch presents three female types: Aphrodite, who is warm chaotic sensuality; the Oedipal Mother, a sadist in league with male authority; and the preferred type, who combines both, 'the oral mother . . . who nurtures and brings death' (p. 49).

The oral mother is to be found throughout the decadent tradition. In, for example, Catulle Mendès' novel, *La Première Maîtresse* (1887), Honorine, 'vampire' and 'ghoul', a widow who preys on inexperienced, virgin youths, is both mistress and mother. Her irresistible charm lies in the cold, authoritative reserve she demonstrates in the depths of debauch. Honorine picks up Evelin Gerbier, convalescent from a serious illness, takes him home and rapes him. Evelin is a baby in her hands:

> . . . thrust back under the weight of a body slipping quickly down his own, the tearful Evelin, transfixed with terror, his legs waving in the air and his frail haunches held fast by two long, fine, brutal hands, suffered the greedy, frenzied, silent, consuming rape of his delicate, virginal puberty by a long foul kiss (pp. 74–5).

She initiates him into 'new pleasures, new humiliations: like a vile plucker of flowers fresh from the garden of Hell, she scattered in his bed all the accursed roses in her basket, black, red, bloody, stinking roses' (p. 116). And: 'In Honorine's arms, under her mouth, teeth, nails, Evelin trembled like a weak, bleeding, frightened victim, longing to escape, always overwhelmed. While he gasped in agony, she lay quietly laughing' (p. 117). Throughout Mendès' story, the victim is both innocent and guilty. He consents to his own ruin, but the real villain is the mother-mistress who leads him astray. Mendès' Introduction to the novel stresses the corrupting nature of woman. The Egyptian King Psamétik made every effort to preserve his body from decay. But all the embalmers' skills are useless at one spot, on his neck, 'a wound seething with maggots, spurting a tiny flame of putrescence', where a Greek courtesan once kissed him. It is woman who is 'the most active source of weakened will, deviant thoughts, surrender of conscience, duty unaccomplished, goals unreached, and finally, dissatisfaction with oneself, the worst of all sufferings'.

Such collapse of will, evasion of responsibility and determined search for scapegoats is the spirit of the decadence, and is not sadism but masochism. Though writers set themselves within the Sadean tradition, most of them are incapable of exerting that regenerative sadistic violence that expresses itself in negations, denials and anarchic revolt. What Sacher-Masoch makes plain is how much, unknown to itself, the national sensibility has changed between 1789 and 1870.

3
European Exchanges

Channel Crossings

The vigour that resurfaces in French writing in the late eighties owes much to the force of internal politics – the rise of anarchism – but much, too, to influences from across the Channel. Ideas which in the first place had come from France were now returned in new, invigorating form.

What mattered most was the personal influence of individual writers. As early as March 1873, the young Irishman George Moore had deserted the country he detested for Paris. His experience is recounted in his *Confessions of a Young Man*, first published in England and France in 1888 (in France, in serial form in the moderately socialist *La Revue indépendante*, March–August 1888, and in book form by Savine, 1889). In Paris, he discovered the pagan world of Théophile Gautier, whose *Mademoiselle de Maupin* taught him 'plain scorn of a world as exemplified in lacerated saints and a crucified Redeemer' (p. 74), and showed that 'a deification of the flesh and of fleshly desire was possible' (p. 81). He read the 'mad and morbid' literature of Baudelaire; he met Villiers and Mendès in the Montmartre cafés; he devoured Swinburne, Rossetti, Petrus Borel and Balzac. Through *Séraphîta*, Balzac's mystical study of the Androgyne, he acquired the love of the spirit, 'the white Northern women, with their pure, spiritual eyes' (p. 123). Moving on to Zola, he found himself in 1877 a convinced Naturalist. This concentrated course in modern French culture was the perfect preparation for his reading of *A rebours*, described in his *Confessions* as 'a dose of opium, a glass of some exquisite and powerful liqueur . . .' (p. 298). He added: 'Huysmans goes to my soul like a gold

ornament of Byzantine workmanship: there is in his style the yearning
charm of arches, a sense of ritual, the passion of the mural, of the window'
(pp. 299–300).

For Moore, however, the window of decadent style does not enclose the
observer in the seductive colours of an inner world; it holds up a prism that
casts afresh an intense light from the world outside. Mike Fletcher, the
hero of Moore's novel of the same name, published in 1889, is very
different from the des Esseintes of *A rebours*, with whom he has often been
compared. Like des Esseintes, he is the failed artist, struggling to realize
the forms of his own imagination, and transform Nature, by artifice, into a
more acceptable style. He, too, spices his pleasures with the low-life of the
city slums, and is constantly tempted to slip from modern civilization into
the refuge of mediaeval mysticism. But he is more robust than des
Esseintes, and though tormented by the same contradiction between
carnal and spiritual desire, can still for most of the novel take pagan
pleasure in his own sensuality and inspire the same pleasure in others, both
men and women.

In his projected poem on Schopenhauer, he gives his own version of the
dilemma. The flesh's blind, instinctive will to live is a 'stupid' but positive
force, sustaining a luxuriant, energetic universe. It is Reason that destroys,
restraining, repressing and corrupting the passions. Man's tragedy is that
he is now trapped in structures created by his own Reason, which Fletcher
defines as Christianity and Comtean socialism. He is forced to destroy his
carnal, vital self: 'As time goes on reason becomes more and more
complete, until at last it turns upon the will and denies it, like the
scorpion, which, if surrounded by a ring of fire, will turn and sting itself to
death' (p. 52).

Fletcher's poem evokes the last, apocalyptic days of the world, when the
Northern hemisphere has been devastated by man's desire for the ascetic
stillness of Reason. In the South, civilization has crumbled, but Nature
still flowers and flourishes. There the last man, seeking oblivion, like
Christ in Gethsemane ('Christ, that most perfect symbol of the denial of
the will to live'), meets the last woman, who urges him to regenerate the
human race. Her strong, healthy beauty has nothing in common with the
pale evil of the decadent *femme fatale*:

Her dark olive skin changes about the neck like a fruit near to ripen, and
the large arms, curving deeply, fall from the shoulder in superb
indolences of movement, and the hair, varying from burnt-up black to
blue, curls like a fleece adown the shoulders. She is large and strong, a
fitting mother of man, supple in the joints as the young panther that has

just bounded into the thickets . . . (p. 49).

But to the ascetic's distorted vision, she represents 'life's shame . . . listening to the fierce tune of the nightingales in the dusky daylight there, temptation hisses like a serpent' and 'to save the generations he dashes her on the rocks' (pp. 50–1). What is left is not neurotic anguish, but his still-deluded conviction of his own rightness. From the margins of life to which he has relegated himself, he contemplates the natural powers that are no longer his: 'Standing against the last tinge of purple, he gazes for the last time upon the magnificence of a virgin world, seeing the tawny forms of lions in the shadows, watching them drink at the stream' (p. 51).

Despite his love of carnal pleasure, Fletcher too is infected by his world's morbid desire to disown life and destroy beauty in the name of an ideal. He suffers from a growing boredom and malaise which neither love, travelling, politics, gambling nor philanthropy can cure. Fletcher, 'that type and epitome of Western grossness and love of life', finally ends, like his friend, the bored Lady Helen, in suicide.

The novel makes it clear that Fletcher's failure of will and nerve is a product of history, and especially of class. It is the aristocracy and the middle classes who are in decline. Unlike many of his French counterparts, Moore is reconciled to his own analysis. Fletcher, whose father was an Irish peasant and mother a French maid, bequeaths the wealth Lady Helen left him to the people: his own illegitimate child by an actress-mistress, and the child of a friend who married a pauper. He dies to allow a fresh generation to come to power. The energies of the future are in the streets and hovels of the city, to which the novel constantly returns, often in comic, but always in sympathetic vein.

In this respect, Moore's writing reinforces the anarcho-socialist strand represented by Jean Lombard. Later, his own views sharpen. In the 1904 edition of his *Confessions of a Young Man*, a dialogue between the pessimist 'I' and his nineteenth-century conscience rejoices again in the energies of the flesh disowned by Western culture: 'If you had read Schopenhauer you would know that the flesh is not ephemeral, but the eternal objectification of the will to live. Siva is represented, not only with the necklace of skulls, but with the lingam' (pp. 272–3). Still torn between love of living and dislike of the world that has to be lived in, he rallies the violence of his confusion for an attack on religion and the rich. 'I' foresees the inevitable, purifying and avenging revolt of the life instinct in the form of death:

Men are today as thick as flies in a confectioner's shop; in fifty years there will be less to eat, but certainly some millions more mouths. I laugh, I rub my hands! I shall be dead before the red time comes . . . The French Revolution will compare with the revolution that is to come, that must come, that is inevitable, as a puddle on the roadside compares with the sea. Men will hang like flies on every lamp-post, in every great quarter of London, there will be an electric guillotine that will decapitate the rich like hogs in Chicago. Christ . . . shall go out in a cataclysm of blood. The neck of mankind shall be opened, and blood shall cover the face of the earth.

As A. Norman Jeffares has pointed out (*Anglo-Irish Literature*, 1982, pp. 204–11), Moore's awareness is the product of his experience of the struggles of Irish nationalism, from the 1870s onwards. A novel like *A Drama in Muslin* (1886), confronting the evidence of exploitation in Ireland in society at large and in the home, and linking – as the nineties will do in France – the justification for socialist and feminist revolt, leads naturally to the awareness in *Parnell and his Island* that his own landowning class is finished, however exquisite its cultural mask. Increasingly, Moore's art is placed at the service of change: a voice from a dying elite who intends his passing to generate renewal.

George Moore's importance in these cross-Channel cultural exchanges was eclipsed a decade later by that of another Irishman. Oscar Wilde's first direct contacts with the major figures of Parisian culture took place on his first visit in February 1883, shortly after the publication of his *Poems*. He made the acquaintance of writers as varied as Hugo, Zola, Mallarmé, de Goncourt, Lorrain, Rollinat and Mendès, and visited Gustave Moreau's studio. In May 1883, this 'individual of dubious gender' scored a tremendous success with Edmond de Goncourt with his tall tales from America; just as in April he had entertained him with his revelations about Swinburne, whose pederasty and bestiality, according to Wilde, were only a pose to attract notoriety (Edmond de Goncourt, *Journal*, 21 April 1883).

Wilde ceased to be entertaining for de Goncourt's generation when circumstances required him and them to take these sexual 'poses' seriously. As in England, Wilde in France polarized public opinion by his determination to express his unconventional values in life as well as art.

In 1895, in *La Revue blanche*, Paul Adam was to inveigh against the illogicality of a society that attacked homosexuality while condoning adultery. Illogical or not, the lines were firmly drawn. Though scientific studies of homosexuality were on the increase, even these considered it as a form of disease (J. Chevalier, for example, *De l'inversion*, 1885, and

L'Inversion sexuelle, 1892; E. Laurent, *L'Amour morbide*, 1891). Marc-André Raffalovich's study of *Uranisme et unisexualité* (1896) challenged Krafft-Ebing's thesis that homosexuals were degenerates (*Jahrbücher für Psychiatrie und Neurologie*, 1894) with a list of major men of letters and politicians who had been homosexual, ranging from William Rufus to Michelangelo and Walt Whitman. But even this appeared in the series 'Bibliothèque de criminologie', and established its credentials with a censorious attack on the 'criminal' Oscar Wilde.

A few writers were straightforward in their advocacy of 'Greek virtue and Greek vice', especially in England. Under the editorship of Charles Kains Johnson, the review *The Artist and Journal of Home Culture* was a major source of Uranian propaganda. In France the subject was approached with a fascination hedged with ready condemnation and instant disavowals. As Raffalovich pointed out, it was not his neurosis that drove Huysmans' des Esseintes to embark on his highly satisfying liaison with the young man he met in the street, but it was certainly neurotic fear of censure that impelled him to break it off. The Gilles de Rais who sodomized his choirboys (*Là-bas*, 1891) required all the miraculous apparatus of the mediaeval Church to absolve him. Even Jean Lorrain, who turned his own homosexuality into parade, carefully censored his characters' desires. The blue-green gaze of the young farm labourer that tempted *Monsieur de Phocas* (1901), like the Primavera smile of the sailor that fascinated Claudius ('Ophélius'), are both equated with woman's invitation to destruction; both the farmer and the sailor are killed, leaving their victims to the sufferings of unattainable desire. For Rachilde, the homosexual passions that the red-haired painter Jacques inspired in a would-be virile aristocracy (*Monsieur Vénus*, 1884) were delightful proof of the weakness of her male contemporaries.

Lesbianism was a more acceptable vice, especially as practised by Pierre Louÿs' fragile creatures for the delectation of a male audience. When it was presented, like Wilde's homosexuality, as part of a deliberate challenge to sexual hierarchy, as well as a private indulgence, it was a threat to be condemned. The prototype is Balzac's heroine in *La Fille aux yeux d'or* (1834), the rake Henri de Marsay's twin sister who unwittingly finds herself competing with her brother for the same pretty mistress, and in her bloodthirsty jealousy tears her victim to pieces. Joséphin Péladan's crusade against the Amazons claims to be conducted more in sorrow than in anger; but Lorrain's article 'Autour de ces dames', which earned him a 3,000 franc fine from the censor (letter to Oscar Méténier, February 1892) is a vicious account of how Mizy, now Catulle Mendès' mistress, a drug addict and a degenerate, allowed one of her lesbian lovers to leave her new-born baby boy to die of exposure. Lorrain's *Une Femme par jour: Femmes d'été* (1896) includes a Baudelairean description of 'the legion of the great Damned', sadists, morphine addicts, 'their pleasure-seeking mouths stuffed with the ash of reality' (p. 172).

Many writers are in no doubt that lesbianism is a response to some cruelty inflicted by lover, family or society at large. Catulle Mendès' *La Maison de la vieille* (1894) describes the misfortunes of Stella, a survivor of the Commune, brought up on dreams and fairytales, brutally awakened by a husband who raped her, disgusted by the orgies which are modern society's substitute for love. She almost succumbs to the seductions of Anaïs. But Anaïs too is evil, a vengeful, mercenary sadist who torments little children. Confronted with the alternatives of modern Byzantium – lesbianism or rape – Stella takes what Mendès thinks the wisest course, and commits suicide by jumping out of her bedroom window.

Goncourt's *Journal* shows increasing venom in the face of Wilde's open homosexuality. Léon Daudet was one of his best sources, having been in England when the Marquess of Queensberry was hounding the Irishman. On 28 May 1895, Goncourt is told that Wilde is being pursued round all the London hotels by Queensberry's slanders, and is glad to record that all his family, including his mother, are either mad, alcoholics, or both.

At the time of Wilde's trial, the younger generation of writers in *La Plume* and *La Revue blanche*, including some of Goncourt's acolytes, spoke up vigorously in his defence. Goncourt kept his distance. On 1 December 1895, he noted Henri Bauer's angry denunciation of timorous French writers who would not sign Stuart Merrill's petition in *La Plume* for the commutation of Wilde's condemnation to hard labour. He commented smugly that no one now *could* sign the petition, for fear of seeming intimidated by Bauer.

Wilde had become a focus for the new energies of the nineties. His *Salome* (written during the year he spent in Paris from December 1891) was not only an important reinforcement of the lush language, sensuous imagery, and morbid motifs that were already part of decadent stock-in-trade; it also brought together Decadents and Aesthetes in active co-operation. The plan for a London production with Sarah Bernhardt having been thwarted by the Lord Chamberlain, the play was first staged by Lugné-Poë at the Théâtre de l'Oeuvre in February 1896, where Stuart Merrill was manager, and while Wilde was in Reading Gaol. Pierre Louÿs, Adolphe Retté and Merrill read and corrected the French of the manuscript, and Louÿs later took care of the proofs for the 1893 French edition of the book.

The Picture of Dorian Gray, first published in June 1890 in *Lippincott's*

Monthly Magazine, and in book form in July 1891 (and by A. Savine in French in 1895), gave as a major source of Dorian's corruption the 'yellow book' presented to him by that arch-corruptor Lord Henry, 'partly' suggested by Huysmans' *A rebours* (letter to E.W. Pratt, 15 April 1892). More than Huysmans is involved here; Wilde's novel is a fantastic compendium of every cliché of French Decadence. In the yellow book, the sins of the world passed before Dorian in exquisite guise, with 'metaphors as monstrous as orchids, and as subtle in colour' (p. 101), and in 'curious jewelled style'; and all modes of escapism, 'means of forgetfulness, modes by which he could escape, for a season, from the fear that seemed to him at times to be almost too great to be borne' (p. 111). What he seeks to elude, like every decadent hero, is his tainted aristocratic inheritance ('the monstrous maladies of the dead') and his dread of the decay to come – the passing of time, which, Lord Henry had warned him, would steal his youth and beauty. He reads with pleasure of a hero like himself, in love with artifice, creating a whole range of moods to be savoured with equal, amoral pleasure, tasting impartially of vice and virtue, enjoying equally flesh and spirit, rejoicing in the confusion of conventions: 'one hardly knew at times whether one was reading the spiritual ecstasies of some mediaeval saint or the morbid confessions of a modern sinner' (p. 101).

Wilde's text explains: 'Dorian Gray had been poisoned by a book. There were moments when he looked on evil simply as a mode through which he could realize his conception of the beautiful' (p. 115). Wilde's version of decadence is subversive in such precisions; he makes it quite plain what potential challenges to order it contains. His novel is a survey of the implications of the new Egoism, or Individualism, which has far more cutting edge than its French models. Dorian Gray's hedonism is a radical challenge to conservative order, being of a new kind whose aim 'was to re-create life . . . Its aim . . . was to be experience itself, and not the fruits of experience, sweet or bitter as they might be . . . it was to teach man to concentrate himself upon the moments of a life that is itself but a moment' (p. 104).

The Preface stresses that art does not dictate values to the spectator, but that he discovers through it the values which are his own: 'It is the spectator, and not life, that art really mirrors.' To demand such freedom for individual desire has socially disruptive implications, as Lord Henry calmly spells out. Aristocratic logic upholds the right to rebel. Crime is only the lower classes' version of the freedom the elite demand in art: 'Crime belongs exclusively to the lower orders. I don't blame them in the smallest degree. I should fancy that crime was to them what art is to us, simply a method of procuring extraordinary sensations' (p. 160).

In other work, Wilde's resistances produce explicit political challenges. The ill-fated anarchist drama *Vera, or The Nihilists*, which ran for a week in New York in August 1883, and which Wilde was revising during his 1883 visit to Paris, sets rabid decadent cliché at the service of revolution. The mysterious, fascinating woman who heads the revolutionary cell stabs herself with the poisoned dagger meant for the Czar. The Czar has become a convert, who will use his power to give power and freedom to what at present is an ignorant and self-destructive mob, incapable of setting itself free. The same impulse appears in *The Soul of Man under Socialism* (*The Fortnightly Review*, February 1891), which argues that the finest flowering of Individualism will be in an (anarchist) socialist society. Private property and the competitiveness it engenders are charged with crushing individuality out of possessors and dispossessed alike. Revolt is the only moral response:

> A poor man who is ungrateful, unthrifty, discontented and rebellious, is probably a real personality, and has much in him. He is at any rate a healthy protest. As for the virtuous poor, one can pity them, of course, but one cannot possibly admire them. They have made private terms with the enemy, and sold their birthright for very bad pottage. They must also be extraordinarily stupid.

The enemy is 'brutal popular control', in the shape of the uneducated masses and the State institutions which manipulate them, with the help of canting journalists. Art is the weapon which will put an end to State-organized stupidity:

> Art is Individualism, and Individualism is a disturbing and disintegrating force. Therein lies its immense value. For what it seeks to disturb is monotony of type, slavery of custom, tyranny of habit and the reduction of man to the level of a machine.

If Art fails, mass violence is a legitimate answer:

> It is often said that force is no argument. That, however, entirely depends on what one wants to prove . . . The very violence of a revolution may make the public grand and splendid for a moment.

Wilde's vigorous call for freedoms of all kinds was a message that certain sections of the French avant-garde were eager to hear. What was never, unfortunately, clarified, was the disabling effect of the elitist centre of his call for revolt. The problem should have been plain from *The Picture of Dorian Gray*. In Dorian's particular case, the hedonist enterprise is doomed to failure because it is never simply the product of his own exercise of freedom. Lord Henry speaks of 'project[ing his] own soul' on to the youth:

> . . . to hear one's own intellectual views echoed back to one with all the added music of passion and youth . . . there was a real joy in that – perhaps the most satisfying joy left to us in an age so limited and vulgar as our own, an age so grossly carnal in its pleasures, and grossly common in its aims . . . He would make that wonderful spirit his own (p. 41).

For Basil Hallward, the painter of his portrait, 'What . . . the face of Antinoüs was to late Greek sculpture, . . . the face of Dorian Gray will someday be to me' (p. 24). Dorian will provide 'a new personality' for art, a fresh combination of passion and idealism that will mirror Hallward's own vision of the ideal.

The conclusion of the novel links the fate of the individual in this 'free' world to his position in an unshakeable hierarchy of power. Dorian Gray dies by his own hand, always the creature dependent on the past, whether in the form of his family, his cultural inheritance, or these two older men, eager to live out their dreams through another generation. He blames, and murders, Hallward, who in fact is another victim: Art is only a shadow of the real power it portrays. That power lies in the hands of Lord Henry, who goes scot-free, denying all responsibility for the outcome of a situation he has machinated, blaming instead Fate, the world and the victims themselves, telling Dorian:

> You and I are what we are, and will be what we will be. As for being poisoned by a book, there is no such thing as that. Art has no influence upon action . . . The books that the world calls immoral are books that show the world its own shame (p. 161).

Secure in his established world, the English Lord – the archetypal Father of decadent nightmare – has the power to make others see themselves in the mirror of his choosing, and play-act their freedom on any stage he dictates.

The little Paris magazines of the eighties and nineties kept their readers up to date with changing London fashion in art, morality and revolutionary poses.

The Pre-Raphaelites, who had exhibited at the International Exhibition in Paris in 1855, were to remain influential throughout the second half of the nineteenth century. As late as 1894, *La Revue blanche* was recommending to its readers the re-edition of Tennyson's poems in the 1857 version, with Pre-Raphaelite illustrations.

Gabriel Sarrazin's articles in *La Revue indépendante*, November and December 1884, on 'L'Ecole esthétique en Angleterre', were the first major account of the movement, formed in 1848, and the Aesthetic school which had developed from it. The poetry of Swinburne and Dante Gabriel Rossetti, he thought, was now recognized. The painting of Rossetti and Burne-Jones ('the greatest contemporary English painter') would shortly be given its due place. The Pre-Raphaelite movement, as defined in the *Germ*, had rid Art of sermonizing and Romantic reverie, and replaced them with strict observation of nature and sincere, strong emotion, after the Primitives. Similarly, the Aesthetic school divorced art from moralizing, and sought to harmonize and spiritualize passion through form, after the manner of Gautier, Poe and Baudelaire. Determined to shun banality, the Pre-Raphaelites were open to the most archaic and the most modern of influences: Queen Anne architecture, Botticelli's painting, the music of Liszt and Wagner. Their emblems were the sunflower, the lily and the peacock's feather; they drew Constance, Purity and Beauty; their women wore floating garments; they supported the new decorative arts.

The encyclopaedic introduction is informative, but of most relevance to the immediate needs of French culture are Sarrazin's studies of Swinburne and Rossetti. Swinburne, still too scandalous a subject for lengthy discussion, is briefly congratulated for a lyricism unrivalled in Europe, which presents the modern conflict of flesh and spirit in the opposition of plastic beauty and moral beauty, and combines extreme pessimism with fanatic devotion to Love, Revolution and Humanity. But in Dante Gabriel Rossetti, who had died two years before, Sarrazin has an artist on whom to hang a justification of the new place given to sensuality in modern art. He emphasizes the contrast between the ascetic mysticism of his poetry and the sensuality of his painting, in which, he believes, Rossetti focuses the basic contradiction of the new sensibility. In his painting, the 'pomp of life' overwhelms Dantean dream. He has created a new female type in his 'Venus Verticordi', Lady Lilith, and the Blessed Damozel, eyes filled with a mysticism that is also 'the languor of sublime passion', an 'angelic siren' proud of her physical beauty, aristocratically elegant, with her 'broad pearl-white neck', her gauzy silk drapes and a sea of red-gold hair. Sarrazin chastely reserves most of his attention for the Blessed Damozel, Rossetti's sensuous version of Beatrice, who draws men to salvation with her erotic charm. He discreetly omits Rossetti's other bequests to the decadence: the *femme fatale* (not only Lilith, but also Helen of Troy, Circe and Pandora), the fallen woman and the innocent victim, Ophelia. Through Sarrazin, Rossetti's sensuality comes enveloped in an aura of respectability, in striking contrast to the storm he had provoked in England, little more than ten years earlier:

> . . . shameless nakedness . . . flooded with sensualism from the first line to the last . . . a veritably stupendous preponderance of sensuality and sickly animalism . . . abnormal types of diseased lust and lustful disease . . . (Robert Buchanan, 'The Fleshly School of Poetry – Mr D.G. Rossetti', *Contemporary Review*, October 1871, cit. David Sonstroem, *Rossetti and the Fair Lady*, 1970, pp. 166–7).

La Revue indépendante returned to the defence of sensuality in subsequent months, with its article on de Sade (January 1885), another on 'La Liberté de la chair' (February), defending Rabelais, Diderot and Danton, 'those colossal geniuses, [who] taught us to mistrust the chaste!' and in March, Jean Moréas' review of Th. Ribot's seminal work on *La Philosophie de Schopenhauer*, which discussed the philosopher's view of love as the overwhelming instinct that drives men to accept 'individual unhappiness for the good of the species'. In May 1888, François Viélé-Griffin published his translation of Swinburne's 'Laus Veneris'. But not until June 1889 – the year in which the Pre-Raphaelites scored a major success at the Exposition Universelle – was it possible for Gabriel Mourey to risk an extended article on Swinburne.

Mourey began by stating that Swinburne was still unknown in France. This was not entirely true; the late sixties and early seventies saw substantial artistic interest in his work (Eileen Souffrin, 'Swinburne et sa légende en France', *Revue de littérature comparée*, 1951, XXV, p. 311). The eighties sees rather a revival, encouraged, as Mario Praz points out, by the sensational revelations of sadism and child prostitution in London (*Les Scandales de Londres dévoilés par la Pall Mall Gazette*, 1885) with which Swinburne's name was immediately associated. Villiers de l'Isle-Adam's article on 'Le Sadisme anglais' (*Le Succès*, 18 September 1885) imagined a conversation between two Englishmen in which Swinburne qualified for the title of 'our truly national poet', for the success with which his poetry evoked 'the sensibility of most Englishmen':

These thousands of children and young girls kidnapped, purchased and exported in our island all serve, I swear, to procure us the kind of pleasures of which our national poet speaks; we exhaust on their bodies whole sequences of painful refinements, and ever more subtle tortures. And if they die, we know how to dispose of their unknown remains (cit. Praz, p. 444).

Mourey began with Swinburne's double call for erotic and political freedom. His apocalyptic style, lurching between the Ideal and the 'Gehenna of the flesh', full of 'rut', 'spasm', 'sweat' and 'blood', was 'the great cry of revolt of an independent mind and a free heart'. With his attacks on religion and the old idols, he was 'forcing the gates of the new era'. The lyrical and visionary *Poems and Ballads* (first series published in 1866), from which Mourey gave lengthy translations, responded to the needs of: 'our overheated brains, our insatiable imaginations, our souls gnawed by vague desires'.

This collection, dedicated to Burne-Jones, should, thought Mourey, be prefaced by the painter's 'Sybilla Delphica': 'She has the cruel smile, the complex flesh tints of the Swinburnian muse, and her flanks enfold whole worlds of lust'. Felicia's eyes, cat-circles, signalling perversities, are the 'glorification of abnormal pleasures and forbidden spasms of lust'. It is the inspiration of 'Dolores', Our Lady of Pain, that makes the poet an apostle of Revolution, and he returns to her constantly for refreshment. Mourey quotes too from the 'sadistic lyricism' of 'Anactoria', Sappho's address to her lover, where 'blood seems to flow from the page'; and he gives the whole of 'calm', 'melancholy' 'Fragoletta', Swinburne's poem on bisexuality. This was, for Mourey, analysis and dream forced to extremes, where the reader experienced the 'cold terror of that hell of sensuality where human creatures writhe' and the bliss of 'a Hindu inhaling the ecstasy of his bloody wounds before a mysterious divinity'.

Sacrilege and sadism had become the fashion. Rémy de Gourmont's play *Théodat*, on the subject of the bishop seduced from his vows of chastity, was printed immediately after Mourey's piece. De Gourmont's own account of Swinburne appeared in May 1891 in the *Mercure de France*, as a review of the *Poems and Ballads* (published in Mourey's translation, with Maupassant's 'Notes on Swinburne' as a preface). For de Gourmont, Swinburne is less revolutionary than mystic, who, unlike Rossetti or Tennyson, approaches sensuality as a means to reach beyond reality to: '. . . a beyond where the carnal banquet continues unsated, for ever unfinished. Bodies of woman, androgyne, ephebe, every form or whim of beauty seen or imaginable, is evoked by the poet to slake desires that reach vampiric extremes.'

Maupassant's 'Notes', in contrast, emphasized the carnality of Swinburne's writing. They began with personal anecdote that satisfied the public craving to believe that Swinburne practised all he preached. As a young man, Maupassant had helped rescue the drowning poet from the sea at Etretat, and had been rewarded by two invitations to lunch at the chalet baptized in honour of de Sade ('Château Dolmancé') which Swinburne shared with his friend Mr Powell. They were 'two visionaries', whose conversation cast a disturbing and macabre light; they talked of literature and politics, strange Irish legends which Powell translated, perverse and magic poetry. Dried bones and a parricide's hand cluttered the tables, and the party dined on roast monkey.

Maupassant defended the *Poems and Ballads*, which, he said, hypocritical English critics condemned and artists acclaimed. He dismissed charges of sadism as irrelevant. The poems certainly belonged to 'the most sensual, idealistically depraved, highly-wrought, enthused with impurity, of all literary schools'. They were disordered and difficult. But they conveyed 'the irresistible, tormenting appeals of pleasure beyond reach, and the unspeakable desire, with no precise form, for an impossible reality, that haunts the truly sensual soul'. From feverish carnality, Swinburne conjured visions of inaccessible desire: '. . . the tender aspirations of the flesh, the hunger and thirst of mouth and heart, tormented passion haunted by visions that spread fever in our eyes and our blood . . .' Maupassant gave long excerpts from 'Laus Veneris', including the much-censored love-bite sequence, and from 'Dolores', 'a kind of despairing hymn to Ideal Lust, which produces that dreadful, convulsive, dreamless spasm of the flesh'. He recommended 'Fragoletta', 'that jewel', and finally noted that Swinburne had abandoned love for political poetry, in the defence of republican causes.

What is striking at this late date is the failure of the French to pick up the transformation of Swinburne's politics. 'A Song in Time of Revolution' had supported the cause of Italian freedom, and presented revolution as the universal remedy for the ills of Europe, and *Songs Before Sunrise* (1871), dedicated to Swinburne's mentor Mazzini, put martial trumpets and Baudelairean imagery to serve the same causes. But when Sadick Bey undertook the bloody suppression of the Bulgarian rebellion of 1876, Swinburne had been more entertained by the Turk's cruelties than distressed by the fate of the revolutionaries. As Donald Thomas points out, the erotic is a powerful political force, but an ambivalent one. For Swinburne, 'to see Italy set free was sublime, though not as sublime as the ecstasies of Sadick Bey' (*Swinburne: The Poet in his World*, 1979, p. 155). Flaubert's *Salammbô* and Jean Lombard's novels had made precisely this point. Most aware, however, of the repressive forces that touched them most closely at home, the decadents' attitude was a simple one: all freedoms were one, and freedom was what every decadent individual required.

The *Mercure de France*, which in the nineties was the major channel of English culture into France, attributed to itself a revolutionary role, which it defined as the defence of individual freedom.

Founded in 1890 by Alfred Vallette and Remy de Gourmont, the magazine polemically declared its regret that the term 'decadent' had been so misused by the contemporary press. In his first editorial (January 1890), Vallette found the 'decadent' label not inappropriate, in so far as decadent writers were defined as young men opposed to artistic and moral cliché. The editors proposed to make room for trends which might now seem subversive, but in ten years' time would be common currency. Their magazine was helping demolish a crumbling house, with a view to hastening the moment of reconstruction.

In the next (February) issue, Vallette argued that 'decline' was the older generation's description of a world slipping from them, of which the young were glad to see an end ('L'Evolution égoiste'). 'Egoism' and 'Individualism' challenged the basic errors of that old world; the young saw neither Nature nor themselves as evil, and were not convinced of their powerlessness to make changes. Vallette's thesis found concrete illustration in Remy de Gourmont's major anti-revanchist article, 'Le joujou patriotisme' (April 1891).

The *Mercure* set out to create a newer, freer culture, in which the rebellious had pride of place. There was a place for the occult, beginning with reviews of Villiers' *Axël* (March 1890), Stanislas de Guaita's *Au seuil du mystère* (June) and Joséphin Péladan's *Coeur en peine* (December). Vallette himself reviewed Lombard's *Byzance* in September. In February of the following year, de Gourmont wrote of the new fashion for 'La Littérature "Maldoror" ', Lautréamont's sadistic prose poems, in which liberating stylistic flourish, proliferating metaphor, and magnificently obscene violence opened the door to mystery. De Gourmont's review of Swinburne's *Poems and Ballads*, in May, is in appropriate company.

The magazine drew on English culture to support two very different trends: the dreamy, mystical evasions represented by *Axël* and the grotesque, energetic flamboyance of Lautréamont. In March 1892, the editors published 'Un manifeste littéraire anglais' of English poems with parallel French translations, taken from the *Book of the Rhymers' Club* (founded 1890–1), and including the work of Yeats and Arthur Symons,

Richard Le Gallienne's 'Beauty Accursed' and Ernest Dowson's 'Nuns of the Perpetual Adoration'. (The latter, with its discreet sadism that sets the veiled heads and 'coarse attire' of the nuns, 'Calm, sad, secure; with faces worn and mild' against the 'wild and passionate' world, its fading roses and 'Man's weary laughter and his sick despair', is precisely in the style of Villiers' 'L'Amour suprême'.) October 1892 saw Charles-Henry Hirsch's article on Thomas Lovell Beddoes, the minor Romantic precursor of Swinburne and Wilde. The contrast is glaring between the Rhymers' subtlety and Beddoes' grotesque supernatural, all demon lovers and spectres dancing by moonlight. Hirsch puffed Beddoes' 'The Bride's Tragedy' and 'Death's Jest Book' and gave long translations from his macabre poems, 'The Ghost's Moonshine', 'The Boding Dreams'.

In February 1894, Arthur Symons' 'La Littérature anglaise en 1893' reported that the new generation was firmly established. The realism of George Moore, the English Huysmans, was still popular, and there was a new frankness, while *The Celtic Twilight*, by a promising new poet, W.B. Yeats, marked a growing fashion for mystery and imagination.

Unhappily, the new frankness was not to last long. The trial of Oscar Wilde lay just over the horizon, and shortly beyond it those political events that were to provide the stimulus for collapse of consensus and a new crack-down: in France, the Dreyfus Affair, and in England, the Boer War. Interestingly, Arthur Symons, although originally one of the main mediators of the new ideas between England and France, a channel of subversion, played, like Huysmans, a major part in the later earthing of much of the movement's energy into conventional forms. Already in November 1893, his presentation of decadence in *Harper's New Monthly Magazine* was less a defence than a guilty apology: '. . . this representative literature of today, interesting, beautiful, novel as it is, is really a new and beautiful and interesting disease' (cit. Holbrook Jackson, *The Eighteen-Nineties*, rpt. 1976, p. 50). And in 1908, in *The Symbolist Movement in Literature* (originally, the 'Decadent' movement), he wrote a priggish dismissal:

It pleased some young men in various countries to call themselves Decadents, with all the thrill of unsatisfied virtue masquerading as uncomprehended vice . . . No doubt perversity of form and perversity of matter are often found together, and, among the lesser men especially, experiment was carried far, not only in the direction of style. But a movement which in this sense might be called Decadent could but have been a straying aside from the main road of literature. Nothing, not even conventional virtue, is so provincial as conventional vice; and the desire to 'bewilder the middle classes' is itself middle-class.

Symons is sneering, but he is partly right; for the interest of decadence lies precisely in grasping its 'middle-class' nature. It is the volatility of the class from which it springs that explains the volatility of the movement – one that could produce not only a Jean Lorrain, an Oscar Wilde and an Octave Mirbeau, but also a Huysmans and an Arthur Symons. In the eighties and nineties and, indeed, in 1908, the 'main road' was still under construction. Whether moral and political anarchy, or the old order, would point the direction of the highway, was yet to be established.

The Cult of Wagner

That same volatility is in evidence in the history of the Wagnerian cult in France, after 1870. With its complex blend of radical and conservative elements, giving voice simultaneously to nationalist and internationalist aspirations, Wagner's music spoke directly to the restlessness, insecurities and idealism of the decadent generation. Nietzsche's assessment is accurate, though in a fuller, and less scathing, sense than he intended:

> All of Wagner's heroines, without exception, as soon as they are stripped of their heroic skin, become almost indistinguishable from Madame Bovary! . . . Indeed, transposed into hugeness, Wagner does not seem to have been interested in any problems except those which now preoccupy the little decadents of Paris. Always five steps from the hospital. All of them entirely modern, entirely *metropolitan* problems (*The Case of Wagner*, 1888).

For the decadents, ransacking his work for the building materials of their own fantasies, Wagner spoke of their inner confusion, figured in the Christian division of flesh and spirit, in which carnal desire and pleasure is never separated from guilt, nor spiritual ambition from fear of failure. He had images for the chaotic forces threatening to overwhelm the divided individual from 'outside': the insurgent crowds created by the great city, or the threat from other nations. He had a language that could express vital chaos, with all its terrors and its fascination, and could also appear to control it, diverting its discordant energies into familiar, reassuring artistic and religious evasions. What was wanted by many of his French admirers was a fresh version of the Christian myth which in the past had successfully blended the dream of transcendence with the reality of submission to established order. (Wagner himself, in *Religion and Art*, 1881, had spoken of the duty of art to rescue religion which was no longer meaningful to the people [see R. Furness, *Wagner and Literature*, 1983, p. 88].) Wagner presented rich pickings for ideologues who sought to recuperate the right-wing failures of the past, while seeming to reject them, and found artistic harmony sufficient substitute for social harmony based on genuine democratic change.

This particular tendency appears most clearly in the work of Joséphin Péladan, whose fiction makes ample use of Wagnerian references and motifs, whose Salons de le Rose ✠ Croix were an important centre for Wagnerian painting in France, and who published in 1895 a collection of annotated librettos, *Le Théâtre complet de Wagner*. It is summarized in Edmond Barthélemy's articles in the *Mercure de France*, November 1893–February 1894 ('Etudes d'art religieux. II: Des cycles germaniques et scandinaves dans la Tétralogie de Richard Wagner'), which are an act of faith in the ability of the Wagnerian synthesis to reconcile all the contradictory aspirations of the moment. Barthélemy reconstructs the Ring cycle as an allegory of Fall and Redemption. Wotan, the Father who is the 'focal point of Wagner's creation', is doing his best to save all, not just his own children, but those who have released the forces of chaos. Siegfried (the predestined Redeemer), Brünnhilde, Siegmund and Sieglinde, are not replacements for a failed God, but his 'reflections' and 'echoes', 'incarnations' of his desire for a new world, his dream of freedom and his ideal, figured in Valhalla. Gods and humanity are struggling together in a project filled with ruptures and new beginnings, but beginnings which always recall the past of which they are built. Continuity is the theme, and all that is, is the 'prolonged vibration of the original Soul'. Seen in this perspective, Wagner's music is transformed into an act of faith that the Catholic ideal will return, in the teeth of its failure. Barthélemy lists the swings of history, concluding as 'Barbarian disorder gives way to the pious constitutions of the Middle Ages'. His message is clear: a call for return to traditional values, to religion, hierarchy and authority.

The context of such uses of Wagner's work is too far removed from that of the 1930s to see here more than prefigurations of later deformations, but Furness' comment on d'Annunzio's use of Wagner is not inapposite:

> The temple of art and the cult of the hero, aestheticism and victory, death-intoxication and triumph: a disturbing synthesis seems here to prepare the way for that 'aestheticizing of politics' which Walter Benjamin would later associate with fascism (p. 52).

D'Annunzio's substantial debt to Péladan's work should not go unremarked.

Wagner made his first impact on Paris in the 1860s. Concert performances of his work held in January and February at the Salle du Théâtre Italien (extracts from *Der Fliegende Holländer*, *Tannhäuser*, *Lohengrin* and *Tristan und Isolde*) were very badly received. The first defence of his music was written by Théophile Gautier, whose daughter Judith was later to become one of Wagner's main disciples and publicists in France. But it was Baudelaire whose responses came closest to the enthusiasm of the decadent generation, after the successes of the 1881 Paris season.

In his letter to Wagner of 17 February 1860, Baudelaire described himself as 'swept away and dominated' by the sensuous power of this grandiose, proud music, into new revelations and a heightened sense of understanding. He experienced 'a feeling of being penetrated, invaded, a truly sensual delight, like that of rising into the air or rolling on the sea . . . these profound harmonies seemed to me like those stimulants that accelerate the pulse of the imagination'. In 'Richard Wagner et "Tannhäuser" à Paris' (*Revue européenne*, 1 April 1861), he spoke of Wagner's profound appeal to the imagination, articulating individual aspirations and bestowing the same sense of effortless potency as the opium dream.

This 'tyrannical' music, Baudelaire saw, was aimed primarily at mass audiences, to arouse and channel collective emotion:

> Wagner seems especially drawn to those feudal pomps and Homeric assemblies where lies an accumulation of vital force, enthusiastic crowds, a reservoir of human electricity, from which the heroic style leaps forth with natural impetuosity.

Using the techniques of the religious public theatre of Greece, with their emphasis on a total artistic experience, Wagner, Baudelaire explained, turned to myth to give the crowd a self-image that included both their own time, nationhood and place, and an understanding of their essential, universal humanity. In Baudelaire's interpretation, humanity is Christian in its essence: all the fables of all races speak of sin and redemption ('There's nothing more cosmopolitan than the eternal'), and the motive forces that eternally renew human history are man's double attraction to body and spirit, and the struggle within him between passion and reason. These, for Baudelaire, are the root of the harmonies that speak so powerfully to the crowd.

Baudelaire saw Wagner as double, 'man of order and man of passion', who delighted his audience with a hellish, yet totally modern vision of the flesh:

> The true, terrible, universal Venus . . . Languors, delights mingled with fever and cut through with anguish, incessant returns to a lust that promises to quench thirst, yet never does; frenzied palpitations of the heart and senses, the imperious commands of the flesh . . .

In its Baudelairean paraphrase, Wagnerian love careers down to the devil, 'among the screams of victims and the sadistic shouts of victors', as if by some fatal necessity: 'as if the barbarous must always have its place in the drama of love, and carnal pleasure lead by inevitable Satanic logic to the delights of crime'. At these extremes of vicious ecstasy, the mood of his music suddenly turns to religious themes, in a refreshing contrast that opens the mind to higher inspiration and restores harmony and order.

What attracts Baudelaire, as it will attract the decadents, is his sense that Wagner has resolved two contradictions – the desire for chaotic vitality and the desire for order. Baudelaire describes his music as cathartic, leaving the listener with the impression of healthy, masculine, dynamic vigour that in real life follows on the satisfactory resolution of a great moral or physical crisis. In the context of Wagner's music, the violence of emotion and instinct finds safe release.

Villiers had also heard Wagner in the early sixties, and became an ardent admirer, campaigning in *La Revue des lettres et des arts*, the first Wagnerian review in France. He emphasized Wagner's demand that the flesh be renounced in the service of a spiritual ideal, and his vision of the renewal of the world by Art.

Unlike Baudelaire or, indeed, Wagner himself, Villiers spoke to a very small elite of fellow-artists. Teodor de Wyzewa (*La Revue wagnérienne*, 8 June 1886) named Villiers and de Quincey the major representatives of the Wagnerian tradition in prose fiction, for their musical and emotional prose. Yeats' 'Rosa Alchemica' was written under the spell of Villiers' Rosicrucian fantasy *Axël*, the work most influenced by Wagner. But when *Axël* was staged posthumously at the Théâtre de la Gaîté in 1894, it folded immediately – exquisite poetry, but near-inaccessible. Axël, the young count in search of his lost family treasure, and Sara, a renegade nun, confront one another in a castle in the depths of the Black Forest. Before them is the choice between sensuous and spiritual life – love, gold, power and wisdom, or the Infinite. Sara, the temptress, offers Axël all the painful, fatal pleasures of the senses:

> All the favours of all the women in the world are as nothing, compared
> with my cruelties! I am the Dark Virgin. Dimly I remember the day I
> caused angels to fall. Flowers and babes, alas, have died in my shadow
> . . . I can lull you with deathly caresses . . . Bury yourself in my whiteness,
> abandon your soul in me like a flower lost under the snow! Wrap
> yourself in my hair and breathe the spirit of dead roses . . . Yield. I shall
> turn you pale with bitter joys; I shall have mercy when your soul is in
> torment . . .

But she is tamed by Axël, and together the two choose the Infinite,
which is Death. Only slaves, they say, struggle to live. This is the 'ultimate
consummation' of *Tristan und Isolde*, in all its negative force, described by
Furness, 'a sexual climax accompanied by physical death. At the moment
of highest ecstasy, and at the point of death itself, the Romantic
imagination had glimpsed the infinite' (Furness, p. 41).

The Wagner welcomed by the eighties is filtered through both Villiers and
Baudelaire, providing the pleasures of both refined mysticism and violent
emotion:

> The vague, mist-laden mysticism, the taste of genesis, the ethnic
> horizons, the brusque, excessive, quasi-mystical emotions that charac-
> terize Wagner's dramas seemed to the weary youth of France a promise
> of liberation. We studied his most fanciful characters with intense
> ardour, as if Wotan held the riddle of the world, as if Hans Sachs would
> reveal free, natural, spontaneous art. I smile at it all today, and feel
> foolish when I confess it, but what we particularly admired was his
> librettos (Léon Daudet, cit. André Coeuroy, *Wagner et l'esprit
> romantique*, 1965, p. 274).

The librettos, initially, were almost all there was. Paris had to make do
with concert performances between 1880, when Charles Lamoureux
defied the ban on Wagner's music which had been in force since the defeat
of 1870, and May 1887, when *Lohengrin* was first staged at the Eden-
Theatre. The latter was a short-lived affair, nipped in the bud by
revanchist demonstrations organized by the Boulangists. Police reports
absolved left-wing revolutionaries from all part in the demonstrations:
'They're internationalists, and they leave this kind of demonstration to the
boulevard loiterers and the Ligue des Patriotes . . . No one in the Socialist

Party would go to the expense of a seat at the Eden; they're generally much more positive, and see Art as nothing but ornament' (cit. M. Kahane and N. Wild, *Wagner et la France*, 1983, p. 67). *Tristan* first appeared in full production in 1899, and *Rheingold* not until 1909. Pilgrimages to Bayreuth were in vogue, but not within everyone's reach. *La Revue wagnérienne* (1885–8) performed a public service by publishing summaries of the librettos, together with its own writers' expositions of the mysteries behind them. For the French, the symbolic meaning of the female figures was especially important – an emphasis reinforced in the painting of Gustave Moreau, Odilon Redon and Fantin-Latour filling the Salons (see Teodor de Wyzewa, 'Peinture Wagnérienne. Le Salon', *La Revue wagnérienne*, 8 June 1885).

Catulle Mendès gave his account of the Ring cycle, closer to the original than Péladan's or Barthélemy's versions – 'guilty God saved by innocent Man' (14 March 1885). Brünnhilde was the Goddess announcing with her own death the transfer of power, the end of the old Gods and the coming glory of Man who would ascend in an ecstasy of Love. Odilon Redon's lithograph of the Valkyrie in triumph appeared on 8 August.

In the 8 November issue, the occultist Edouard Schuré expounded the lurid mixture of lyricism and exacerbated sensuality which is *Parsifal*, paying special attention to a different female image, Kundry, accomplice of the wizard Klingsor, sworn enemy of the Knights of the Grail. Kundry symbolizes the fatal double attraction identified by Baudelaire. 'Ghoul, enchantress, lustful vampire', conjured up by the wizard from the black gulf, she oscillates between two moods: demonic lust that ensnares men and self-abasing remorse that craves their forgiveness. With the coming of Parsifal, she is transformed into a Magdalene by the sign of the Cross and finally released, like Sara, into death. Schuré points to her acolytes, the thirty flower maidens who surround Parsifal, 'man besieged by a heady, entrapping vegetation'. Like Kundry, the image of Nature's ambivalence, they represent both heady fascination and fearsome threat. (They will be seized on with delight by the Wagnerian painters: 'Les Filles-fleurs', of Fantin-Latour's celebrated lithograph, and Georges Rochegrosse's 'Le Chevalier en fleurs'.)

In his book, *Richard Wagner* (1886), Catulle Mendès devotes considerable space to Kundry, the model for his own dangerously seductive heroines, guilty and yet strangely innocent:

Woman both hellish and divine in her lack of self-awareness, all instinct, servant of good, slave of evil ... She it is who opens her arms to trap the sacred heroes and drags them ecstatic to their damnation. Ragged, wild, dishevelled when she dwells with the Knights of the Grail, like a well-disposed hyena; in Klingsor's enchanted gardens, dressed in magnificent cloths from which gleams her even more magnificent flesh, flowers and jewels mingled in her caressing, coiling locks, twining like lianas, she lives the double life she lived in all her former existences; she was the Herodias who summoned before her on a golden dish the head of the Precursor, and seeing it lie there dead, as she had required, embraced it on the mouth – brimful of bloody remorse! (pp. 255–6).

What is missing from his account is any reckoning of Kundry's dependence on the men who, in theory, are her 'victims'. For the French decadence this is the ultimate charm of Wagner. His female figures, running the entire range of decadent typology, have one thing in common. Mothers and sisters, protecting and nurturing, or seductive temptresses, deceiving and destroying, they may appear to be men's equals ('Sisters', Péladan calls them), or even, at times, prime movers and transformers of history. In fact, they are instruments of men's power, and scapegoats for men's failures. It is their fathers, brothers and husbands, gods, kings and wizards, who in the end make history through them.

In the decadents' version of Wagner, it is Death, dressed in flowers and jewels, or dressed in rags, that is the end of all his art. The thrill of strong emotion, manufactured out of the contemplation of private and public collapse, gives a perverse illusion of vitality. The terrors of collapse are held at bay by another, reassuring, illusion of a protective, over-arching order, produced partly by the total satisfaction of a spectacle that addresses itself simultaneously to all the senses, and partly by the limited motifs and strict patterns – the ritual – of Wagner's art.

One novel that echoes this pattern very simply is Elémir Bourges' *Le Crépuscule des dieux*, written between 1877–82 and published in 1884. A hymn to the decay of Latin culture, the novel traces against a background of Wagnerian music and through Wagnerian motifs the fall of the ancient house of d'Este (riddled with inherited neuroses, weakened by perversions, divided by illegitimacy) which is displaced by the stronger power of imperially ambitious Prussia. Degeneracy in private life and political failure are linked. The novel opens in June 1866, with Wagner himself summoned to entertain the Duc d'Este, conducting fragments of the *Ring* and the overture to *Tannhäuser* that flatter the Duke's family pride, and the Siegmund–Sieglinde duet that hints at the incest and corruption hovering about his household. The concert is interrupted by news of the Prussians' attack on the Duchy, and audience and musicians all take flight. The story closes ten years later in Bayreuth, with the Duke, a revolting, decayed tyrant, despised and snubbed by his peers, in attendance at the première of *Götterdämmerung*. The Duke has fallen; Wagner is the last bastion of order in Europe.

Between these two performances, the whole family has taken refuge in Paris, where the Duke squanders his fortune on gardens and palaces. Wealth buys the show that is one substitute for political power, and it buys too the erotic indulgence that now holds the centre of the stage. The whole family is locked in struggle for possession of the treasure-chamber, at the heart of the palace. Giulia Belcredi, a former opera singer, manoeuvres to become the Duke's mistress and disinherit his children. She tempts the twin brother and sister to incest and suicide, seduces Otto, the Duke's favourite, into further crime and perversity, and finally leads him into attempted patricide. The Duke survives, but goes mad, as does his son; Giulia takes poison.

With the collapse of the family complete, the novel pulls out of its erotic displacements and back into the current of history. Giulia, scapegoat for the family's fall, is no more than the vehicle of historical forces. While these individuals were obsessed with private greeds and passions, the whole world changed. At Bayreuth in 1876, facing Wagner's music again, Charles d'Este is forced to acknowledge a series of unpalatable truths. Whatever the length of his pedigree, he is now outranked by his rival, the Emperor Wilhelm of Prussia. While the Norns sing on stage, he begins to realize the ludicrous figure he cuts in the eyes of others, a rag of an old man, tottering round the hotels of Europe. It is no longer the aristocracy who crowd the boxes of this theatre. Wagner has assembled a new audience, of industrialists, businessmen, magistrates and men of letters: 'all confused, levelled, confounded, all become people, great and small, known and unknown, all dressed in the same clothes. No more rules, no more hierarchy!' He turns in desperation to Wilhelm, to offer him allegiance; Wilhelm is the one single leader strong enough to hold the line against the new spirit. To his horror, he finds Wilhelm's strength comes from compromise with the new order. The Emperor doesn't see Charles. He is bowing to two Jewish bankers, the 'hooknosed usurers' who share with the Yankees the privilege of holding society to ransom. Individual power and wealth count for nothing against those who can manipulate collective power and wealth. Charles' elite has been displaced by a new elite, the demagogues. His vindictive, resentful vision of the rise of the mob ('an immense gulf, ready to swell with furious waves') and of a universe ready for transformation into 'a foul trough where the herd of men would eat its fill' is absorbed into Wagner's music.

Other writers – Villiers, Péladan, even Lorrain, mourn the passing of the aristocratic tradition. Bourges gives Charles no quarter. The Duke dies in apoplexy, perched on his commode. The elaborate, costly ritual he has commanded for his funeral is ruined by the clumsiness of careless servants: his entrails, badly embalmed, burst out of the urn, to the horror of the congregation. This aristocratic twilight is grotesque, cruel and final. It leaves nothing behind but the stench of decay and the delusion of grandeur: a stage, and an artist, turning the death of a world into his own music.

PART II

Transformations of
Decadence

1
Consuming Passions:
J.-K. Huysmans 1848–1907

In the words of Mario Praz, *A rebours* is 'the pivot upon which the whole psychology of the Decadent Movement turns', containing in embryo 'not only [Huysmans'] own novels, but all the prose works of the decadence, from Lorrain to Gourmont, Wilde and D'Annunzio' (*The Romantic Agony*, pp. 322–3). Arthur Symons, in the *Fortnightly Review*, March 1892, is more succinct and more accurate: *A rebours* is 'the quintessence of decadence', or, in *The Symbolist Movement in Literature* (1908), 'the breviary of the decadence'.

Huysmans' novel of 1884 is less a source of new beginnings than a catalogue of mature achievements, crystallizing all those themes and forms in which other, often more gifted, artists had already begun to express the unease of the age. But it does indeed represent the spirit of decadence: a self-contained work of art, written to hold life at a pleasurable distance, to be delicately savoured, snared and immobilized in the safety of aesthetic form. In his *Journal*, 16 May 1884, de Goncourt claimed it for his own school, 'our kind of literature'. This was literature as opiate: 'a book that brings a slight fever to the brain'.

The book is important not only in itself but as a stage in Huysmans' development from Naturalism to Catholicism, which in its turn casts light on the underlying continuity of late nineteenth-century middle-class culture and its ability to transform revolt into order. On the one hand there is the fascination of the real world, in all its physical and sensuous detail. The celebration in 1884 of Diderot's centenary recognized the grip which his version of rationalism – empirical, sensuous and materialist – had taken of the French mind and eye, training both to demand clarity and truth. This is the source of Naturalism, with its emphasis on scientific observation. On the other hand, there is the unwelcome fact that modern reality – the effects of industrialization and democratization – is not necessarily pleasurable, and for some its mutations are unacceptable.

The art of decadence is to confine that vividly perceived reality, with all its natural tendency to change, in forms that halt its movement. Decadence fixes the real with repressive and regressive ritual, religious, erotic, aesthetic, piling form on to form to stifle truth; but still, out of some residual, guilty recognition of fact, allowing glimpses of historical reality to persist. The Pre-Raphaelites, drawing what they called the essential truth within the real, were engaged in precisely the same rewriting of evidence.

Huysmans' transition from Naturalism to Symbolism and Catholicism is a logical one. His critics have noted that the power of his work lies in that tension between his Naturalist vision and his rejection of what he sees. For Remy de Gourmont, in his 'Notes sur Huysmans' (*Mercure de France*, June 1891), *A rebours* was 'the consecration of a new kind of literature . . . draw[ing from crude reality] themes for dream and inner transcendence'. Havelock Ellis (*Affirmations*, 1898) claimed 'his very idealism has been nourished by the contemplation of a world which he has seen too vividly ever to ignore'.

It was the intensity left over from his Naturalist origins that led Havelock Ellis to see Huysmans as incarnating the recuperable side of the decadence. In his essay in *Affirmations*, he described Huysmans' work as a reversal of the dynamic tensions of the Latin decadence. Tertullian and Augustine wrote powerfully because they incarnated 'a fantastic mingling of youth and age, of decayed Latinity, of tumultuously youthful Christianity'. Huysmans also 'incarnates the old and the new, but with a curious, a very vital difference'. Nowadays, Christianity is the dying power and the new pagan moment the source of vigour. What Huysmans presents is the image of massive force misdirected, a decaying ideology struggling to control the upthrust of the new, and giving only a vision of painful futility. This is the sum of decadence: the vain attempt to freeze the new energies:

> Huysmans had wandered from ancestral haunts of mediaeval peace into the forefront of the struggles of our day, bringing the clear, refined perceptions of old culture to the intensest vision of the modern world yet attained, but never at rest, never once grasping except on the purely

aesthetic side the magnificence of the new age, always haunted by the memory of the past and perpetually feeling his way back to what seems to him the home of his soul!

Preliminaries to Nightmare

Huysmans' restless explorations from Naturalism to Catholicism are all part of a single struggle, testing, modifying but never moving beyond the decadent pose. In that trajectory the energies Havelock Ellis saw are not recuperable. At every stage in his work, the same patterns and structures are repeated. A neurotic, fragmented imagination constructs the world outside in its own image, obsessed with the menacing fascination of a decay it is determined to perpetuate.

Though he first became known as a writer of Naturalist fiction (*Marthe, histoire d'une fille*, 1876; *Les Soeurs Vatard*, 1879; 'Sac au dos', in *Les Soirées de Médan*, 1880; *En ménage*, 1881), Huysmans' first work was an experiment in forms outside the Naturalist aesthetic. *Le Drageoir à épices* (1874), is an act of homage to an alter ego, François Villon, whose poetry likewise blended nostalgia for a lost, lovely past with a craving for life and a morbid love for the realities of his impoverished, plague- and war-ridden world. Huysmans' tone in these prose-poems is robust, with no trace of decadent languor. But his themes are those that will reappear in later decadent pieces. The introductory sonnet sets the tone. This is the debris of a culture, made over into art: 'A choice of bric-à-brac, old carved medallions,/Enamels, pale pastels, an engraving, an etching, the colour of rust,/Huge-eyed idols, with treacherous charms'. 'Rococo japonais' is a Japanese beauty, a she-wolf with indolent smile, fantastic eyes and red mouth. 'Camaïeu rouge' features a red-haired 'goddess' downing port, head haloed by the sun, like a virgin out of Fra Angelico or Cimabue. There is a 'Déclaration d'amour' for debauched Ninon, and for 'La Reine Margot', the salacious Marguerite de Navarre, debauching her servants, fishing the head of her lover, the Chevalier de la Môle, out of the charnel-house. Death, the cruel and lovely mistress, haunts the volume. Phthisis is the 'implacable ghoul' delivering deadly kisses, with her ambivalent smile, long, streaming hair, purple-flecked skin, pale deathrays glancing from her eyes ('Ballade chlorotique'). A 'Ballade en l'honneur de ma tant douce tourmente' is for the sweet tormentor with eyes sparkling like diamonds, rubies, emeralds and topaz, glowing like stormy seas, spilling opium and oblivion, and blood-red lips with teeth that bite cruelly at the heart.

Croquis parisiens (1880), illustrated with engravings by Forain and Raffaelli, is a clear prelude to *A rebours*. The model is Baudelaire, transforming the sordid landscape of the modern city with fleeting glimpses of perverse beauty. Grotesque details plucked from the whole, intensified to dreamlike disproportions, turn ugliness into a source of pleasure. In *A rebours*, the imaginative powers of the neurotic 'artist' des Esseintes are permanently flawed; but here, as in Baudelaire, dream and art are both effective means of escape.

Artifice transforms city landscape into exquisite still life, that gives off the scent of repressed pain. In 'La Bièvre', a Parisian suburb with a choked-up stream prefigures the dead moonwashed fields of *A rebours*: 'a desolate corner of a big city, a scorched mound, a trickle of water weeping between two frail trees'. The tears are pleasure for the observer: 'Nature is only interesting when she's broken down and broken-hearted.'

Paris's charm lies in its gamey contrasts. The rough, natural energy of the crowds at the Folies Bergère and the Bal de la Brasserie Européenne is set against a close-up of the streetwalker ('L'Ambulante') who caters for more jaded palates. Her appetizing aura of decay is enhanced by her garish make-up and showy dresses. The Baudelairean contrast between her dying body and the living colour of her paint generates a 'mysterious, sinister beauty':

For her as for the others, vice has performed its usual task, refining, making desirable the shameless ugliness of her face. Losing none of the charm of her suburban origins, in her striking costumes and charms boldly emphasized by paint and paste, the whore has become a tempting, tasty morsel for jaded appetites, sluggish senses only stirred by the violence of cosmetics and the tumult of grand evening gowns.

Sexuality, already perverted by the artifice of the whore, dressing up the natural woman into a commodity for market, is twisted further by the writer's art. 'Le Gousset' substitutes for woman the fetish of her smell, taking the body's crudity, through exaggeration, into the refinement of art. The smell 'unleashes the animal in man', with its range of different notes for the discriminating nose, heady acrid scents blended to make a female essence, at once more stimulating and more relaxing than the scent of one woman. Des Esseintes' later experiments on his keyboard of liqueurs are a displacement of this original erotic experience:

. . . the range runs through the whole keyboard of smells, bordering on the obsessive perfumes of seringa and elder, reminiscent sometimes of the sweet smell from rubbing together fingers that have held and smoked a cigarette. Bold, sometimes exhausting in brunettes and black-haired women, fierce and sharp in redheads, in blondes the scent is vague and heady like certain sweet wines . . .

But already less important than these paraphrases of modern life are the paraphrases of the latest Paris has to offer in modern art, the subject of Huysmans' closing sketches. Already the three major motifs of decadence are present: the artist's struggle to snare reality in the magic of form, the morbid threat of the real, and the vision of the threat in sexual terms.

'Nightmare' passes in sequence before the lithographs of Odilon Redon (from his album *Dans le rêve*, 1879, dedicated to Goya). At this stage, Redon was still relatively unknown. Huysmans' accounts of his work, here, in *A rebours*, and in later articles such as the review of the album *A Edgar Poe*, 1882, in 'Le Salon des Indépendants de 1881', or that of *Hommage à Goya* published in *La Revue indépendante* (February 1885), helped make Redon's reputation as a key figure of decadent art.

Seen through Huysmans' eyes, this is a world of pain frozen into hieratic images. An Assyrian head, sheets of stagnant water, a flower with a pallid, anguished human face, the sun's eye, a wide-eyed juggler, a desolate steppe, all reflect the fixed stare of the onlooker, who sees the intensity of his suffering in their sharp, closely confined articulation of Redon's own anguish. Beyond the calm resignation of Redon's still images, Huysmans' panic gaze metamorphoses one figure into another, creating a dramatic, near-uncontrollable narrative, an intense, nightmarish re-enactment of his own repressed terrors. The ironic smile of the final flower is charged with personal threat both for Huysmans, looking at the painting, and his reader, seeing its echo in his text. At this stage, the threat is also a pleasurable thrill, generated by an artistic game in which the spectator dictates the play.

The same interplay between the desire to surrender and the desire to dominate is evoked in a re-creation of Wagner's Overture to *Tannhäuser*. Here Art is said to stage a demonstration of 'essential' philosophical truths, in a drama played out in 'a landscape Nature could never create'. In abstract, man can believe in his own potency. The song of the pilgrims, rising against a clear but colourless backdrop, is sure of its own phallic power ('worshipping yet proud, male and upright').

That confidence rests on its submission to the authoritarian certainties of religious faith. Against a different backdrop, the twilight shades and confusion of the real world, the same song becomes tentative, no more than wistful desire. Real life is 'fluid and fantastic', full of colours, shades and shadows, but 'dead', 'dying', amorphous and menacingly uncertain. The music evokes cloud-formations, and flower images that display its morbid but fascinating beauty: 'dead violets, dying roses, sickly white of anemones', all 'exhaling unknown perfumes, the Biblical reek of myrrh mingling with the complex, voluptuous scents of modern essences'.

The sudden appearance of Tannhäuser is a 'heraldic' evocation of the anguished struggle of spirit with flesh, which is the legacy of Christianity. Tannhäuser strides confidently through an apparently submissive landscape suddenly transformed into a shifting, overwhelming, erotic threat of revolt:

> Tannhäuser advances; – and the darkness is shot through with light; the cloud spirals take on the arched lines of haunches and stretch and swell like breasts; the blue avalanches in the heavens throng with nude forms; cries of desire, lubricious summonses, impulses of yearning for a carnal Beyond, leap from the orchestra, and above the undulating espalier of fainting, swooning nymphs, Venus rises . . .

For Huysmans, Wagner's modern Venus incarnates the problematic nature of the modern world, made more deadly and more lovely by the transgressions of modern man: 'a white Belluaria, soaked with perfumes, crushing her victims with blows of heady flowers'. Tannhäuser succumbs to the 'polluting' clouds, sinking into a triumphant sunset orgy of regal crimson and gold, to the swelling blast of trumpets. Miraculously, he survives: in natural harmony, the evening colours of his fall must be followed by the redemptive rays of dawn, and Wagner's music fuses the two motifs of Lust and Purity, presenting Art as the God who redeems all confusion. Huysmans' text is a vicarious enjoyment of the pleasures of sin, within the absolution of Art.

'Les Similitudes' is a collection of feminine essences, a Baudelairean blend of colours and scents, sensual refinement and animal vigour. In this swift summary of female types, women are without menace because without identity, reduced to simple sensuality for rapid, easy consumption. There are ash-blondes, draped in the nostalgic charm of the past, whose symbol is autumn melancholy and the scent of verbena and mignonette; a bouquet plucked from Fragonard of 'snow-powdered hair, playful, caressing eyes, huge flounces of azure and peach'; 'banal beauties', whose artifice has gone sour, 'with black greasy hair, cheeks lacquered with rouge, plastered with talcum powder'. There are nightmarish women out of Poe, Baudelaire, or Delacroix, 'distraught, gloomy beauties' in 'tormented poses', with 'cruel, bleeding lips, eyes blackened by burning nostalgia, widened by joys beyond the human . . . nameless perfumes streaming from their sumptuous skirts'. Last of all, there are whores in triumph with 'voracious lips, eyes like furnaces, exhaling raging, terrifying breaths of patchouli and amber, musk and opopanax, a hothouse heaviness . . .' A single kiss unites all the colours and scents, in a syntax that re-creates their living, blending movement, reconciling reality and dream. The dream vanishes, but the dreamer wakes to see the cat perched calmly on the foot of his bed, Baudelaire's symbol of sensuality refined and tamed: 'At the foot of my bed, there was my cat Icarus, who'd lifted her right leg and was licking her gown of ginger hairs with her pink tongue.'

The proses of *Croquis parisiens* present a subject that is secure in its possession of the world and confident in its ability to mould the rest of that world into its own image. Huysmans' Naturalist novels of the same period present the opposite: the human subject possessed by the world, the mere product of heredity and environment, of physiological, economic and historical determinations. From the contradiction of dream and reality rises the decadent neurosis for which Gustave Moreau's art provided the first solution. This was painting that incorporated all the terrors of the real world and made them safe, creating a territory that simultaneously was and was not history, populated by figures who seemed vividly real but were totally controlled by their maker's imagination.

In Huysmans' account of 'Le Salon Officiel de 1880' (collected in *L'Art moderne*, 1883), the painter is a mystic who rejects the whole of modern life for art, plundering the cultural tradition for a new synthesis that evokes the 'opium-eater's dreams'. He borrows from Mantegna and Leonardo da Vinci, Hindu art and the feverish colours of Delacroix, engraving, mosaic and illumination. In literature, he echoes the Goncourts, Flaubert in his Romantic mode, and Baudelaire, whose 'Rêve parisien' stirs precisely the same sensations. (In this poem, Baudelaire evokes a Paris remade in the image of his own desire, sheer art and fantasy, devoid of people and organic life, all 'metal, marble, water', with naiads dwelling in the pools and the mystical waters of the Ganges streaming from the heavens into 'diamond gulfs'. Moreau's art has this, and more besides. Whereas Baudelaire's exotic visions are deliberately undercut by reversions to the sleazy urban context that generates them, Moreau's work completely represses its terrors.)

The two canvases Moreau submitted in 1880, like his earlier 'Salomé', were both visionary images of woman. Between them, they evoke the two contradictory faces the decadent attributes to Eve, which displace into themselves the fear that fills his landscape. In 'Hélène sur les remparts de Troie', the pale blonde in her jewelled gown, standing against a bloody, phosphorescent sky, dominating the Trojan carnage, is the fatal beauty who is the source of all evil: 'like a maleficent deity, poisoning, all unconscious, all that draws near, all she sees or touches'. 'Galatée' is beauty as victim, caught off-guard and vulnerable, confirming man's strength. The nymph asleep in her cave walled with jewels, wrapped only in her long, fair hair, is pinned by the covetous eye of the giant Polyphemus. Under that monstrous gaze, both nymph and landscape are frozen into harmless gems:

> Coral branches, silver twigs, starfish, pale and filigree, spring up simultaneously with green stalks bearing real flowers and dream blossoms, in this cavern lit like a tabernacle with precious stones, enclosing an inimitable, radiant jewel, the white body and pink-tipped breasts and lips of Galatea asleep, wrapped in her long, pale hair!

A Rebours: Devouring Dream

Between Moreau's dreams, Redon's nightmares and his own Naturalist vision, Huysmans created the ironic celebration of decadence which is *A rebours*. In 1882, Folantin, the anti-hero of the short novel *A vau-l'eau*, was the Naturalist bourgeois cornered. Like des Esseintes, he tries to retreat into a Thebaid of his own creation, a domestic interior answering simple ambitions – clean, warm rooms and decent food. None of these ambitions is realized; a none-too-well paid bureaucrat, like Huysmans, in one of the ministries, Folantin hasn't the money to keep the world's spite and shoddiness at bay. In 1884, des Esseintes lavishly realizes all Folantin's wishes. With social position, an enormous private income, and all the resources of Paris at his disposal, he can try to dream his way out of the corner. Though he still fails, his is a heroic and colourful collapse. As much a comic grotesque as Folantin, he can at least enjoy his neuroses in style; and when his doctor, speaking with the hateful voice of both science and nature, orders him back to the ruck of the city, he can at least pay servants to carry him there.

Des Esseintes' project is a conservative one: to maintain a personality and a tradition in decay. He gathers under his roof all he knows of instinct and intellect, mind and senses. None of it gives the pleasure it should. Experience turns to poison as it filters through a memory that retains only degradation and pain, and an imagination geared to vice, crime and ugliness. The present is marred by his own neuroses. Mind and body jaded from having known too much, and unable to control or enjoy the world that in theory he possesses, he is left with the morbid, vengeful contemplation of his own frustrations. At the edge of the text are the masses and the rising generations who will inherit his world. At the centre is des Esseintes' frenzied lament for his own fading powers, insistently expressed in sexual terms.

This systematic eroticization represents one of the decadence's most potent political effects. The thrill of sexual pleasure holds the reader's attention focused on the wounded would-be hero. Decadent sexuality displaces politics; performing for his audience, like Salome dancing before Herod, the decadent usurps power with erotic promises that can never be cashed. The real truth – the political and cultural failure of the tradition he represents – is seen in glimpses, like the vulnerable flesh of Salome under her veils. But as long as the variety, the movement, and the glitter of the dance remain, the spectators will buy his illusions.

A rebours is a hymn to consumption, by which des Esseintes establishes his hold on his world. Whether he deals with food itself, with Nature, or with Art, he reviews, in all its variations, the pleasure, and the glamour, of devouring. The pleasure is also pain: maintaining the position of major consumer is not an easy task, and results, all too often, in the consumption of his own substance.

Eating is not the hero's greatest passion. In this – by design – he distinguishes himself from the Folantins of this world. But since he is tied, like lesser mortals, to the degrading need to eat in order to live, he experiments with ways of distinguishing his own modes of consumption.

In the past, his eating was an imperial triumph. He held a wake for his lost virility, an all-black dinner where art and spice took precedence over nourishment. Naked negresses served turtle soup, black olives, caviar, rye bread, game with licorice-coloured sauces, chocolate creams and dark heavy wines. Sadly, such 'self-consuming' (VII, 20) extravagance is unrepeatable. Gestures of magnificent indifference must be unique, or they wear thin. In the present, demonstrating his distinction is increasingly difficult, and he is driven to increasingly strained devices.

He follows a routine of light, regular meals but eats by night instead of by day. He takes his drinks in bizarre combinations, with the help of a 'mouth-organ' of exotic liqueurs that turns liquids into notes, imitating different musical modes, or pretending that each liqueur is a different musical instrument. His interest is not in taste, but in what taste can become through art. His greatest success is in the recuperation of a masochistic memory with a glass of real Irish whiskey. In minute detail, he recalls the pain of a visit to the dentist, and his panic terror as the huge figure mercilessly rammed its index finger into his mouth, pulled and tore at his head, shoved its hand into the depths of his gullet, and finally brandished its trophy, a decayed blue tooth dripping with blood. The end of the pain is a moment of orgasmic relief. What des Esseintes lingers over is his pleasure as he left the surgery, dimming the memory of the pain, so that what remains is 'the horrible charm of the vision' (p. 77).

In the English tavern in the rue d'Amsterdam, an illusion of change of place creates an illusion of appetite. As at the dentist's, domination is the spice. Des Esseintes' jaded appetite is stimulated by the sight of boy-faced, large-toothed, arrogant Englishwomen devouring their solitary dinners. Back home, he is tempted by a different kind of crudity, in the form of the 'foul dish' in the hands of an urchin in his garden, with 'seaweed hair full of sand, two green bubbles under his nose, and his mouth disgustingly smeared with white filth from a sandwich of cream cheese sprinkled with chopped green chives' (p. 253). He sends a servant to buy it, but at the last minute, his stomach revolts. Instead, he finds a different kind of pleasure in sending it back for the boy and his friend to fight over.

Over-indulgence in spicy pleasures finally unfits him for normal consumption. The independent aristocrat regresses to childish states. At first a beef bouillon provides healthy nourishment, descending, in language implying the child's erotic pleasure in its own faeces, 'like warm marrow, like a velvety caress' (p. 268). In the last stages, des Esseintes' stomach refuses even this. The doctor prescribes peptone enemas, administered three times a day by a manservant. This is the 'supreme fulfilment' (p. 318) of his craving for artifice and his unspoken longing for a passive, dependent role, and he dreams in his excitement a whole set of enema menus. But his release is short-lived. Doctors are cruel parents, who require their children to be responsible for their own lives, and des Esseintes is instructed to return to normal consumption, or risk madness. Protesting, the rebel submits to order.

Nature ingested in *A rebours* in the form of food is also made over as landscape. While the common run of humanity is at the mercy of the environment, the aristocrat claims the ability to transform and transcend it by force of imagination, memory, will and cash. These too are failing powers, and, as they decline, reality returns to take revenge.

Again, the past was more satisfying than the present. In the pre-lapsarian landscape of his childhood, he reigned undisputed and self-sufficient. His father was dead, his mother uncaring and ill, and the servants too old to pay him attention. In his idyllic solitude, he would read and dream and look down on the little villages in the valley of the Seine. All his present negotiations with landscape are attempts to recover the womblike security of this substitute mother Nature, that unfitted him for the struggle for power in a harsh world. But when he tries to re-create his dream, all he can reproduce is the cold, decaying sterility of his real mother. His attempts are only parodies of life.

His preferred natural landscapes are those which seem most crudely artificial. In the night landscape around Fontenay, Nature is a badly made-up, raddled old whore. The moonlight plain is 'dusted with starch-powder and covered in white cold-cream', with 'faded grass distilling a scent of cheap, spicy perfumes, trees chalk-rubbed by the moon . . . their shadows lying in heavy black streams across the plaster soil' (p. 38). There is a marked contrast here with Oscar Wilde's Nature, who has the sophistication to imitate the best, not the worst, in art. Her model is not the fading whore but the young Impressionists who embellish corruption by painting only its surface and declining to probe the ugliness beneath. 'The Decay of Lying' praises those 'wonderful brown fogs . . . lovely silver mists . . . that white quivering sunlight one sees now in France, with its strange blotches of mauve, and its restless violet shadows' (*Intentions*, 1891). Des Esseintes' sole attempt to beautify Nature murders its object. On the shell of his pet tortoise, he has a Japanese bouquet marked in jewels, so that the flowers will flicker with the illusion of life as the creature moves over a rich Indian carpet. But the jewel crust stifles the tortoise, leaving the bouquet an inert mass in a corner, grotesquely emphasizing the dead flesh beneath.

Nature is the female, inviting defilement and degradation. Under Huysmans' jaundiced gaze, even the flower is corrupted by its associations. Des Esseintes still enjoys the suffering of the common kinds ('low-class flowers, wilting in the sewer- and lead-laden air of the poor districts' [p. 132]). But the aristocrat prefers hothouse flowers, 'princesses of the vegetable kingdom' (p. 132), whose perverse forms, imitating man's art, acknowledge its superiority. He collects flowers with a look of cloth, metal, or raw meat; flowers made of artificial flesh and skin, raked with diseases, ulcers, scars of leprosy and syphilis. He has carnivorous plants, luminous plants, plants that defy conventional categorization, unholy mergers of animal, vegetable and mineral, all symbols of rot and decay: 'Everything is syphilis' (p. 141). In Nature's loveliest forms, he finds the pervasive corruption of feminine sexuality.

In the intense heat of his conservatory, des Esseintes dreams his own nightmare of life's impossible alternatives. He dreams that he is walking through a forest with a straggle-haired gipsy woman with a bulldog-face, when the two of them are confronted and pursued by the monstrous mounted figure of the Pox. The unknown and unwanted woman becomes a scapegoat. She hinders his escape, and for his own protection he must strangle her. A tiny door offers the only way out. On the other side is a moonlit clearing full of giant white Pierrots that would crush him with their weight. Sterile fantasy is the only alternative to a reality figured in its most repulsive form by the deadly, degrading female. Des Esseintes closes his eyes and stands frozen on the threshold, fixed between the glare of the pox and the self-confessed impotence of his fantasies.

He opens them on an erotic image of the obscene power of that world outside him – woman and Nature – he had sought to devour, and that now returns to consume him. At the centre of a sterile mineral landscape, a naked woman in green silk stockings materializes. She mutates into the grotesque forms of his hothouse flowers, figuring all the terrors of the trap of the Eternal Female, Venus Flycatcher and *amorphophallus*, that confronts him with his own complicity in the obscenities of sex. Suddenly her eyes turn chill blue, and the images of phallic power turn into the trap of the *vagina dentata*. All that saves him is the chance awakening manufactured by Huysmans' text. On the brink of destruction, all the pleasure of temptation and the thrill of danger are safely enclosed, by art, in the form of dream:

> . . . he moved slowly forward, trying to dig his heels into the ground to stop himself walking, falling, getting up despite himself to come closer and closer; he was almost touching her when black *amorphophalli* sprang up all around, leaping towards the belly that rose and fell like the sea. He pulled them away, pushed them aside, swept by unspeakable disgust at the warm, firm stalks squirming between his fingers; and all of a sudden the hateful plants vanished and two arms were trying to embrace him; and his heart hammered with fearful anguish, because the woman's eyes, her horrible eyes, had turned a clear, cold, terrible blue. He made a super-human effort to pull from her embrace, but with an irresistible movement she held on, grasped him tight, and he watched haggard as the dreadful Nidularium bloomed between her waving thighs, bloody and gaping between two sword-blades.
>
> His body was caressing the plant's hideous wound; he knew he was dead; and he jerked awake, breathless, cold and mad with fear, sighing, 'Thank God, it was only a dream' (pp. 148–9).

Dreams are not always so easy to wake up from, and des Esseintes knows the dangers of relying on his own imagination to control Nature's seductive terrors. Nature is best enjoyed in the form of texts. In Zola and Mallarmé, those two opposite extremes, he finally finds his childhood idyll re-created. Zola's Eden, Le Paradou (from *La Faute de l'abbé Mouret*, 1875) is a Hindu poem to the flesh, in all the robust, hyperbolic colour of its 'fantastic heavenly copulations and long earthy ecstasies' (p. 277). In Mallarmé, it is the 'Après-midi d'un faune' (1876) that rewrites fear into delicate eroticism. Despite his best efforts, the virgin faun never catches the nymphs. But he fails from inexperience, not exhaustion; the phallic image, untested, remains strong, 'tall, white and rigid' (p. 299), and the marks of the nymphs' passing make the forest more lovely. The frustrations of the androgyne faun are real, but passing. The mood of the poem is perfectly balanced. All that can spoil it are the morbid preoccupations des Esseintes deliberately imposes, fastening over the snow-white cover two silk strands, one pink and one black, to introduce a perverse note into the innocence of the text: 'a discreet intimation of the regret, and a vague threat of the sadness that succeed the extinguishing of passion's flame and the satisfaction of the senses' clamour' (p. 300).

Abandoning Nature, des Esseintes retreats totally into the world of art. In Fontenay, the final refuge, his walls are covered with bookshelves and paintings. He picks over the cultural tradition for fragments to make a mirror in which to view himself. In the end, what he is is what he has bought.

His own renunciation of originality is disguised by his choice of models. He seeks out the novel, the strange and the bizarre. In painting, it is the icon-like work of Gustave Moreau, Jan Luyken, Odilon Redon and Rodolphe Bresdin, Redon's tutor, that hangs on his walls. All are fantasies built on precise, intense portrayals of reality. Moreau's vivid colours and sharp outlines, Jan Luyken's scientifically precise re-creations of ancient architecture, and Redon's studies from prehistory all build on and away from the sharp perceptions of positivist science. At the root of its fantasy, the century likes the semblance of hard fact. Thematically, too, there are resemblances. All four produce a theatre of strong sensations, in a strict frame, enclosing the same obsessions with sexuality, death and the threat of the mob. Des Esseintes buys works of art as drugs, to savour a fantasy image of his own terrors.

In his study, between his rows of books, hang the two watercolours Moreau exhibited at the Salon of 1876. 'Salomé dansant devant Hérode' is pure surface, movement and flashing light, Baudelaire's ideal mistress, the real woman transformed into an idol. Fixed in place by the gaze of Herod, Herodias and des Esseintes, she can never retaliate by turning that gaze back. She is held prisoner by the weight of a whole culture, figured first in the eclectic architecture of Moreau's setting, those pluralities of time and space which produce the no-time, no-space realm of pornographic fantasy. Des Esseintes himself burdens her sensuality with a weight of literary references. The child Salome of the Gospels, the Old Testament's Whore of Babylon, Flaubert's vigorous Salammbô are all subsumed in her hieratic figure, which becomes a device for contemplating in safety the intimidating vision of sexuality. Unlike Flaubert's Salammbô, or, indeed, his Salome, or even Wilde's lyrical creation, this creature has no identity of her own. The evil influence she radiates is attributed by her audience.

The images des Esseintes selects from the canvas systematically evacuate her of life. The lotus flower in her hand, the image of fertile female sexuality, is twisted to an image of impurity and death, reattributed to Egyptian burial rites.

Des Esseintes dwells here on the symbols of male impotence, Herod and the eunuch. In 'L'Apparition', in contrast, male power is recuperated in a perverted form. Herod leans forward 'panting with emotion' (p. 88), and the severed head of the Baptist, poised above the charger, fixes the dancer with its glassy eyes, light streaming from its halo. The sole purpose of this recuperation is to terrorize the female victim. Des Esseintes adds his own cruel assessment of the goddess-dancer's 'real' nature. She is nothing but a harlot and an actress. Her mask of divine self-possession is torn away, like the veils torn from her body in the dance, leaving her struggling under the eyes of her male accusers, speechless in her own defence. Des Esseintes enjoys the vulnerability of her naked flesh, clawed, squeezed and burned by the imposed images of divinity. Into Moreau's hieratic original, Huysmans introduces a violent frenzy:

> Salome, with a gesture of terror, is pushing away the frightening vision that nails her motionless on the tips of her toes; her eyes are dilated, her hand convulsively clutches her throat.
>
> She is almost naked . . . dressed only in jewelled cloths and shining minerals; a gorgerin clasps her waist like a corselet . . .
>
> In the burning rays emanating from the Precursor's head, all the facets of the jewels catch fire; the stones come to life, outlining the woman's body in glowing streaks; points of fire pricking at her neck, legs and arms, red as coals, purple as jets of gas, blue as burning alcohol, white as starlight (p. 87).

And yet, in obvious contradiction, des Esseintes claims it is Salome who is the sadist, man her victim:

> Here, she was truly a whore; obedient to her hot, cruel female nature; she was alive, more sophisticated and yet more primitive, more hateful and more exquisite; she stirred more vigorously a man's lethargic senses,

bewitched and enslaved his will more surely . . . (pp. 88–9).

The sadistic fantasy generates an energy of its own. To his abuse of Salome, des Esseintes adds a second abuse, of Moreau, whose picture he exploits and whose personality he puts at his own service – almost, a double rape. His placing of Moreau, enumerating his antecedents in his own art, connecting him to the modern literary context, transforms the painter into one more projection of his buyer's own image: tradition's heir, in despair from knowing too much, 'in eternal anguish, obsessed by symbols of love and perversity beyond the human, divine debauch, consummated with no abandon and no hope' (p. 90). His conclusion complacently lingers on the artist's captivity. These canvases only live at the pleasure of des Esseintes' gaze, 'hanging on the walls of his study on special panels between the rows of books' (p. 90).

If the place of the erotic is in his study, then the bedroom is the place for religion. Des Esseintes hangs in his dressing-room the series of 'Persécutions religieuses' by the seventeenth-century Dutch engraver Jan Luyken, a catalogue of 'the spectacle of human suffering', all the tortures ever invented by religious folly (p. 92). The anguish is intensified by the swarming crowds of victims (a discreet act of revenge on the mob) and at the same time held at a distance by a historical setting, lovingly reconstructed: Nero's Rome, the Spanish Inquisition, the French Wars of Religion. Des Esseintes intensifies the effect with an extra frame, considering the engraver himself, an austere Calvinist, whose sadistic hallucinations are generated by asceticism.

In the next room are Robert Bresdin's engravings ('La Comédie de la Mort', 'Le Bon Samaritain'), fantastic, chaotic landscapes inhabited by death and demons. In both, the dream of an unlikely redemption at a distant future (a Christ-figure vanishing in a sky full of fleecy clouds, a fairy city on the horizon, on the far side of a river) is constructed on the pain of one individual in the present. The couple of the Samaritan and the wounded victim is paralleled in the first engraving in the couple of a praying hermit and a starving pauper ('a wretch dying, exhausted by deprivation, worn out by hunger, flat on his back with his feet on the edge of a swamp' [p. 95]). Pain is intrinsic to this world's economy.

Finally, Odilon Redon matches Moreau's dramatic tableaux with a new kind of visionary fantasy. Des Esseintes' catalogues of the contents of Redon's frames detail the bizarre combinations that throw conventional categories into confusion ('A horrifying spider with a human face stuck in the middle of its body', 'an enormous dice blinking a sad eye' [p. 96]). There are too the structures from pre-history, the Darwinian ancestors of plants, animals, man, that disturb him by their distance from the evolved type. He sees in Redon's work the grotesque inventions of the heat of sickness, disease, fever, recalling the Gothic horrors of Goya or Edgar Allen Poe. He thrills to the terror and the 'unease' he feels at these intimations of the fragility of the human form, reminding him of the vulnerability he felt as a child, in the grip of typhoid fever, suddenly confronted with the fluid and formless nature of the universe, and the tentative nature of his own identity. Confronted with Moreau's images, he played at intensifying their terror. Faced with Redon's style, he flees.

Huysmans' reading of Redon in *A rebours*, which made the artist famous, is in fact a misrepresentation, transforming scientific delight in Nature's chaos into Huysmans' own Gothic fears. From the botanist Armand Clavaud, Redon had learned about microscopic entities, the new discoveries of evolutionary science, and most of all, comparative anatomy. He knew of the order under apparent chaos, no less authentic for being only newly seen. He was impressed by the evidence of a common structure to all living things, that made nonsense of conventional hierarchies and categories, and by what he learned of the expansive force of evolution, which is what his art tries to evoke. In Redon's own version, his monsters came not, as Huysmans claimed, from microscopic observations, but from his own artistic experiments with the expansive potential of forms (*A soi-même: Journal 1867–1915*, pp. 22, 27–8). His blends of skeletons and flower-faces were attempts to explore the limits to which natural lines could be extrapolated and like structures combined without betraying Nature, 'putting the logic of the visible at the service of the invisible' (p. 28). Redon is a humanist, concerned with beginnings, not dead-ends.

Even Redon's huge eyes, his most powerful symbols, are distorted in des Esseintes' account. For Redon, they represent the evolutionary doctrine that intellect and spirit gradually transform the animality of Nature (Sven Sandstroem, *Le Monde imaginaire d'Odilon Redon*, 1955). All des Esseintes sees is deformity, the incompatibility of desire and the world, faces 'devoured' by 'huge, mad eyes' which are the image of his own frustration and despair.

When des Esseintes turns to literature, it is to piece together from tradition a canon not unlike his strange dietary arrangements. His consumption of literature follows the same patterns as his consumption of food, ranging from gamey off-meats to ordinary, healthy nourishment, from rich extracts to colourful junk. The Latin Decadence offers the highly spiced hors d'oeuvre of Petronius' *Satyricon*, satirizing 'the vices of a decrepit civilization, a cracking empire' (p. 48), exposing the squalid ruts of the bestial mob and the luxurious debauch of the wealthy, beds crawling with lice, parents who sell their children for cash. Apuleius' neo-Latin *Metamorphoses* have in contrast a robust, comic salacity. Still more piquant is the contrast between the sober asceticism of Tertullian's writing and the vicious rule of his emperor, Heliogabalus, whose perversities are after des Esseintes' own heart – 'walking in a cloud of silver powder and gold dust, a tiara on his brow, his clothes spiked with jewels . . . titling himself Empress, changing his Emperor nightly and choosing him for preference among barbers, scullions and charioteers' (p. 50).

Literature is diverted to sexual purposes. Perversely, and with the help of a few aphrodisiac pills, Dickens' chaste lovers launch him on a nostalgic digression into the masochistic experiences of his own past. He recalls the acrobat whose brutal, masculine features aroused and disappointed his hopes of taking a passive female role, the tiny ventriloquist who threw him out, tired of playing out his fears of exposure and humiliation, and the pale-faced, long-haired homosexual youth with small mouth and big lips who picked him up in the street. Their relationship lasted several months. He 'had never known such dangers, nor felt such full, painful satisfaction' (p. 166).

Baudelaire offers a language for des Esseintes' own morbid dissatis-factions, the diseases of a decaying soul facing the failure of all ambition and the emptiness of the future, calming pain and boredom with sex, drugs and drink. Of his sadism he says nothing. Here his idol is Barbey d'Aurevilly, whose *Le Prêtre marié* and *Les Diaboliques* blend sadism and mysticism. Sadism is not merely the infliction of pain but also the transgression of Christian taboos; the naughty child enjoys 'playing with forbidden things, simply because his parents have said he must not' (p. 241). In Barbey and de Sade, what des Esseintes clearly appreciates is the depiction of Satanism as an assertion of the father's authority and a challenge to the mother's. He alludes to the episode in 'Le Dîner d'un athée' that Barbey borrows from *La Philosophie dans le boudoir* (the sealing up of the mother's vagina); and in his reading of the Black Mass, culled from Jacob Sprenger's *Malleus maleficarum*, the degradation of the female is central. The mass is celebrated 'on the back of a woman, crouched on all fours, with her naked rump, repeatedly fouled, serving as the altar' (p. 243).

Flaubert, the Goncourts and Zola, echo his own longing for another time and place, each providing a different frame for the same neurotic self-image. But these writers are too robust for him now. He prefers the spotted, uneven work of minor artists – Verlaine, Corbière, Hannon, Villiers and Poe. Poe's studies of 'the Demon of perversity' are incisive analyses of the failure of will under the pressure of fear, and the effects of morbid anxiety. His neurotic, androgyne heroines, des Esseintes' sisters, learned in German mystical philosophy and the Cabbala, are terrifying instances of the female threat, commanding not only natural instinct, but also the masculine citadels of reason. 'Gloomy white spectres engendered by black opium's relentless nightmare!' (p. 293) – these women are far more frightening than Baudelaire's cruel sensualists. There are days when des Esseintes can't endure them, any more than he can swallow food, or Redon's nightmares.

Villiers de l'Isle-Adam provides an antidote, in tales that exalt the masculine power of will and imagination. But only 'Véra', Villiers' less threatening version of Poe's 'Ligeia', ruling her lover from beyond the grave, really interests des Esseintes. His other tales are Romantic toys, of no interest to a generation convinced that its powers are faded, and its place in history gone.

Dreams of Debauch: Woman and the Devil

A rebours charts the spiral of frustration that characterizes decadence. Powers constantly and consciously turned in on themselves are self-destructive; and the individual, turning for support to an over-heavy tradition, collapses under its weight. The decadent hero tries to eroticize his failure, deliberately pressing sensuous pleasure beyond the limits of natural endurance, and provoking from Nature an expected retaliation. Desire takes the form of masochistic anticipation of failure, or sadistic fury. In the works that follow *A rebours*, the intensity of his desire increases, running through new scenarios of frustration in which woman increasingly takes the centre of the stage. In *A rebours*, she was a mere memory, or an image in picture or text. Now she is an active agent of evil, or object of punishment, the perfect scapegoat for man's failure. At the same time, the evasions of *A rebours* take on increasingly fantastic form.

In *En rade* (1887), Jacques Marles is an impoverished version of des Esseintes. He is bankrupt, through no fault of his own, and is not an aristocrat. But he was once wealthy, middle-class and a Parisian – a distinguished figure, then, in the rural backwater where poverty has driven him. He is also intelligent, cultured and neurotic. Both metaphorically and literally, he inhabits a crumbling house, the old château de Lourps, with its wild garden of seeding vegetables and rampant weeds.

Like des Esseintes, he feels around him the imminent collapse of familiar order, figured most potently in the local peasantry who exploit him, and threaten his tenure of the castle – which is, in fact, theirs. He is their relative, but must pay rent. In the ominous silence of the overgrown garden, he sees figured the disorder that Nature, it seems, prefers:

> ... this Jacquerie of peasant species and weeds, rising at last to rule over soil made rich by the slaughter of feudal essences and princely flowers ... A fine thing, vegetable mobs and nations! (IX, 51).

Like des Esseintes, he is the victim of 'irrational' fears which in fact are totally rational fears of displacement.

With unexpected honesty, the text admits that Jacques' terrors are engendered by the old house itself, and that the ghosts he fears to meet in it are only his own inherited phantasms and prejudices. But they are also engendered by his fear of being infected by his wife's nervous illness, and his guilt at having caused it by the clumsiness of his first attempts at intercourse with her. The sexual frustration it imposes creates more unease.

Increasingly, he defines his wife's 'refusal' of sexual satisfaction as the real cause of his suffering. In his resentment, he dreams her and her femininity into scenarios in which sexuality becomes sadistic and grotesque.

His dreams are figurations of fears which leave him, wakening, drenched in sweat; but they are perversely enjoyable, richer, fuller, more dramatic than the waking experience of the same fears. Decadence may have no answers, but it gives flattering projections of an egoist's anguish.

The first of Jacques' three dreams is a pleasurable experience of desire fulfilled. As he drifts off to sleep, the walls of his bedroom liquefy and spread open into an arch, over a road down which a fairy palace soars to meet him. He finds himself in a spacious room opening on to many corridors, with womb-like domes in the ceiling, coiled over with jewelled vines. As in a Moreau picture, the vegetation is reassuringly inorganic, but gives an illusion of life. Fiery fruits sparkle on the vine; on the 'cradles' of branches hang 'symbolic' pomegranates, whose 'gaps reddened with bronze' caress the tips of phallic columns that rise from the ground. Among these exquisite images of petrified sexuality, the king appears, dominating the whole scene, gloriously bejewelled, but his face unmoving, lava-grey, hollow-eyed, drained of all emotion. An old man presents to him a young woman, fair-haired, blue-eyed and perfumed with myrrh and cedarwood, the symbols of death and eternal life. Three vivid, still frames follow. The old man tears off her dress, leaving her naked on her knees before the king, 'annihilated' by the anticipated violation of her virginity. She sees reflected in the black marble of the floor her breasts and belly, and the golden speck between her parted legs. The king's eyes bore into her childish nakedness; he holds out his sceptre for her to kiss; the palace floods with mist, and when it clears, the white figure of the woman is lying across his crimson knee, probed by his crimson arm.

The highly coloured detail exalts the power of the male and takes a lingering pleasure in humiliating the female victim, reduced beyond woman to child and supplicant. At the same time, the king's own potency is delicately questioned. These are negotiations between old men, with phallic substitutes for true power, and the climax is not penetration but masturbation.

In the second dream, a sterile lunar landscape is a sadistic representation of Jacques' wife's illness and their lost love. Towns made of medical probes, needles, saws and scalpels are spread out over a white sheet, with one dead Gothic city carved in a silver mountain, covered in rocks, lava salt, boils and blisters, and ending in a petrified sea. His wife's material presence beside him allays the terrors of such desolation, but still he feels as empty and hollow as the scene before him. When the rising sun flames the landscape into light, she ruins the effect with a banal comment that transforms all his guilt to resentment.

The last dream is a nightmare chaos of long pursuits through staircases, tunnels and wells that brings together all Jacques' fears of intellectual, social and physical impotence, in a hotch-potch of allusions to his dilettante studies, his terror of other people, his sexual desires and frustrations, and most of all his loathing of women. The dream revolves around a familiar decadent motif: self and world are a rag-bag of experiences, tackily stuck together in a desperate attempt at order, poised between shock and surprise, terror and thrill. An intolerable flight, from fears that can find no one satisfying form, is finally resolved in a single, vengeful image of woman who is the source of all pleasure and, most significantly, of all pain. A wall that bars his escape becomes a sheet of glass, and behind it foams a turbulent mass of water. In the water, a woman's head slowly rises, followed by a firm, attractive body. The jaws of a trap are clenched on her haunches, spotting the water with blood, adding an 'atrocious pleasure' to the smile on her lovely, tragic face. Jacques' desire to rescue her is frustrated by horror as her blue eyes fall out, leaving red sockets, where the eyes grow again; the 'nameless horror' of this alternation of heavenly beauty and bloody ugliness leaves him powerless. The woman rises from the water, right to the top of one of the towers of Saint Sulpice, where she perches, laughing, transformed into a pox-ridden, toothless old hag, with flabby breasts and vast thighs.

This is Truth, Jacques tells himself: man's desire for the ideal constantly aroused and cruelly cheated. In his dream, the local driver corrects him: not Truth, but old Mother Eustache's daughter. Jacques wakes up as this 'patriarch', swearing and blaspheming, without provocation, turns in fury to thrash him. Fear of the female, fear of the father, and most of all, fear of the unknown threat of the people, join in a climax which turns them all into a thrilling self-abandon to destruction.

In the art criticism of *Certains* (1889), Huysmans continues to juxtapose hieratic representations of frustrated desire to frenzied and distorted images whose aim is to defile and degrade their female subject. His desire is still to escape from the ugliness of the modern city, the cult of money, the democratization of politics and the relegation of art to the marketplace, into 'the gulfs of bygone ages, into the tumultuous space of nightmare and dream'. But his dreams are more hostile, and his nightmares more cruel. Alongside Moreau and Redon he now invokes Félicien Rops, whose Satanic satire strikes a cruder note.

Huysmans is still entranced by the myths of Moreau, whose heroines are aristocratic incarnations of the disorder lurking below the surface of things. They have the frozen beauty of virgins whose chaste flesh is devoted to 'spiritual onanism', locked, exhausted, in their private secrets, brooding inwardly on 'sacrilege and debauchery, torture and murder'. Huysmans describes the watercolours in the Goupil gallery in the rue Chaptal in 1886, Moreau's series illustrating the *Fables* of La Fontaine:

Against these noisy, shrieking backgrounds pass silent women, naked, or decked in cloth studded with brilliants, like the bindings of ancient Scriptures, women with flossy, silken, hair, hard, staring pale blue eyes, icy milk-white flesh; Salomes holding motionless in a chalice the head of the Precursor, soaked in phosphorus, streaming light, under quincunxes of dark, near-black green; goddesses riding hippogriphs, streaking the dying agony of clouds with the lapis lazuli of their wings; female idols, crowned with tiaras, standing on thrones whose steps are drowned in astonishing flowers, or sitting, stiffly posed, on elephants whose brows are mantled in green . . .

Whistler's silver-blue 'Nocturnes', opium-dreams of colour, are invitations to the mind to lose itself in a limbo of pleasure. But Huysmans lingers over his more recent work, the portraits of Miss Alexander (1884) and Lady Archibald Campbell (1885), disclosing the deadly enigma of the female:

. . . ghost portraits, in retreat, pressing back into the wall, with their enigmatic eyes and their icy-red ghouls' mouths . . . From her otterskin coat and dark dress, supremely elegant, rises Lady Campbell, her tightly laced body quivering, her mysterious face bent forward, invitation in her haughty, commanding eyes, and repulsion in her dull red mouth. Once again the artist has drawn from the flesh an indefinable spiritual expression, transforming his model into a disturbing Sphinx.

A new version of Redon ('Le Monstre') gives an erotic slant to the old nightmares of confusion, focusing on the guilty anguish of the female. From Redon's first series of illustrations (1888) for Flaubert's *La Tentation de Saint Antoine*, Huysmans takes the vision of Lust and Death. A rose-crowned death's head joined to a white female torso – in Redon's version, a mummified body – trails off into streaks of stars; the whole body undulates like a gigantic worm poised on the tip of its tail. In another album, a long thin larva coils round the column of a temple, with a pathetic female head resting on top, longing for death to free it from some unnamed crime: '. . . the pale, emaciated face, eyes heart-breakingly closed, mouth pensive and suffering, hopes vainly, like a victim on the block, for the liberating fall of some invisible axe'.

Crime and punishment are the themes of an extended account of modern erotic art ('Félicien Rops') in which Huysmans' tone acquires a new violence. He takes up a moralist's stance, commenting that cold, respectable works of art are repressions by the artist which intensify his real-life desire for obscenity. The English are the best example. The prudery of their art hides and breeds cruel, perverse sexuality:

The hypocrisy which so consciously cloaks the depravities of old England, prey to the infantile passion for rape, easily explains the way the English people behave, in their private lives and in their works . . . only the chaste are truly obscene. Everyone knows that continence engenders fearful libertine ideas . . .

Though he concedes, from his own experience, that even the satisfied sensualist has lascivious dreams. Or rather, the unsatisfied sensualist; though Huysmans boasts ample sexual experience, he is 'sated', feels 'sincere disgust for sensual pleasure'.

In the concluding article of the volume, on the fifteenth-century painter Francesco Bianchi's 'Virgin and Child with Saint Quentin', he flirts discreetly with the temptation of the androgyne youth. The saint provokes 'disturbing reveries':

That tomboy figure, with its slightly swelling haunches, girlish neck with flesh white as stripped elder, mouth with ravishing lips, slender waist ... This androgyne bears all the vertiginous signs of Sodom, and yet his insidious, anguished beauty is already purified and transfigured by the slow approach of a God.

The dream drifts into a gloating account of the saint's martyrdom, flagellation and transfixion, suddenly cut short, as Huysmans confesses there are no signs of pain in the tranquil picture before him, only in his own dreaming response.

There are no traces of guilty homosexuality in the piece on Rops. Instead, the focus is entirely on woman and the evil principle she represents. Those exacerbated desires that for des Esseintes were the simple mark of aristocratic distinction become the Satanic temptations denounced by the Church. In this new form, the erotic can simultaneously be enjoyed and rejected, and the burden of sexual guilt, through the vehicle of religious tradition, be transferred wholesale to woman.

Japanese erotic art in Huysmans' view rehabilitates lust by showing the intense suffering that accompanies it. In his Japanese album, sketches of physical passion show the paradoxical identity of pain and pleasure at the limits of sensual experience. He sees nothing to distinguish the symptoms of sexual orgasm from those of death, transposing the sketches into the language of torture. Men and women, this time, suffer alike:

Their women, with their indolent, white, emphysematic flesh, lie dying, bodies thrown back, eyes closed, teeth biting on bloody lips; their bellies, with their fearful slits, gape wide under a kind of powder puff, like lanced boils; their men lie gasping, prostrate, sporting incredible phalluses with parasol tops and tubes bulging and streaked with veins. All lie tangled together, in impossible poses, like corpses, bones broken by a rain of powerful, thrashing blows.

But, predictably, in Huysmans' favourite engraving woman is the sole victim of her own sexuality, which monstrously drains her of life:

The finest engraving of this kind that I know is horrific. A Japanese woman lies covered by an octopus. The terrible beast pumps her nipples and ransacks her mouth with its tentacles, while the head sucks at her lower parts. The almost superhuman expression of pain and anguish that contorts the long face of this hooknosed clown and the hysterical joy at the same time streaming from her brow, the closed eyes of the corpse-like creature are admirably portrayed!

Japanese art is too 'anecdotal' to satisfy Huysmans' larger desire for a context that will certify the foulness of sexuality and woman's responsibility for it. He finds this in Félicien Rops' Biblical version, as he terms it, of Lust, where Woman is 'the great Whore of Saint John's vision', and Salome the figure of the erotic force that drives humanity, rivalled only by Money. In the Christian contradiction of Purity and Lust, Huysmans sees a new source of vitality for art.

Some of Rops' best early work was done for Poulet-Malassis, the publisher of erotica (1864–9, including the 1868 frontispiece for Baudelaire's *Les Epaves*). In these female figures, drawn by Rops with some affection, Huysmans sees woman's essential frivolity. They are 'dwarf nymphomaniacs', 'cats in heat', frenzied devotees of the phallus, which, unlike them, has a personality of its own. At best, women are nothing but insatiable desire for the male. At worst, desiring each other, they lose all trace of humanity. Rops has captured the viciousness of a new type:

. . . the absinthe drinker, brutalized, starving, all the more threatening and voracious, with her empty, icy face, cheap and hard, her limpid eyes, with their cruel staring lesbian gaze, her over-large mouth, a straight slit, her short, straight nose.

This unnatural void invites the Devil. In the framework of Catholic symbolism, woman acquires a new grandeur. Rops draws demons, temptresses, succubi of Satan – Huysmans reels off a catalogue of invective. From Rops' *Sataniques* he reconstructs in his own prose the tableaux of the Black Mass, writhing, naked women, possessed by carnal frenzy.

He draws the witches' ride through the air, drunk on strange philtres made of 'menstrual fluids, sperm, cats' brains, donkeys' brains, hyena's belly, wolves' genitals, and hippomane, which flows from the genitals of mares in heat'. He recounts their descent into the clearing, the kiss on the Devil's backside, and the drinking of blood and devouring of children's flesh which is the Black Mass itself, reaching its climax in incestuous orgies. Huysmans dreams of extremes of pleasure and pain that only mystics can know. The naked woman in 'Le Sacrifice', nailed to the altar by the double-headed phallus of a demon made of a horse's skull is 'shrieking, crazed with horror and delight!' The demon is Death, immobile and pitiless, head locked in its own dreams, phallus drenched in blood: this is 'the bitter symbolism of Lust foundering in Death,

Possession desperately desired and, like all dreams that are realized, straightway paid for'. In 'L'Idole', the woman who leaps to meet the Devil's monstrous phallus knows her wickedness and the disillusionment and destruction that await her. Huysmans watches, mesmerized, as she embraces and shares this phallic power, a 'devilish Theresa, saint turned Satanist'. In 'Le Calvaire', the Devil with rampant phallus who has displaced Christ from the Cross is using his feet to strangle a naked, ecstatic Magdalene in her own hair. This Devil, who has finally ousted Christ, is more than the flesh. His power is also that of the forces of democracy and capitalism, the peasant and the Yankee, who have a power to attract and to satisfy that Huysmans can never rival: 'The Accursed One, with the sniggering, smirking expression of the vicious peasant, the Yank, and most of all, the Satyr; a bestial Satan, foul and wine-sodden, with jaws like a cashbox and walrus teeth'.

Woman herself is Love and Death in Rops' illustration for Barbey d'Aurevilly's *Diaboliques* (1883). In the frontispiece, 'Le Sphynx', a naked woman tempts the monster to reveal new secrets of the flesh. Rops introduces a modern variation into the traditional image. The Satan who watches her, as he has always watched humanity, waiting for its fall, is a Devil ill-at-ease, conscious that his reign is near its end and his own powers fading. Flesh and money will rule the future; and only woman, it seems, can unlock their secrets. The old Devil is pushed to the margins, forced – like the men of Huysmans' generation – to admit his day is done:

> This is the true tamed Satan of our closing century, a gentleman, dumb, proper, longsuffering, stubborn; he's imperfect, worn-out and old . . . he no longer has the colossal attraction of his maturity. He has to listen from outside, no longer hears what's going on within; in his hunt for souls, all he uses now, perhaps, are the limited faculties of man.

Huysmans, his bourgeois contemporaries and the modern Devil ('a gentleman in a black coat, a peasant, John Smith, in all his foul respectability'), move into an unexpected alliance as their power falls into the hands of women. With relief, Huysmans finds the means of containing the female threat in the Catholic tradition from which Rops draws his satirical forms. Rops' women are not the dangerous figures of the real, historical present, but fantasies for whose taming Catholicism has tried and tested formulae: 'essential Woman and, outside Time, the poisonous naked Beast, the mercenary of Darkness, the total slave of the Devil'. A hierarchy in which woman is subject to the Devil and the Devil to God reasserts men's authority and competence to control.

The price of re-establishing this authority is that the 'aristocrat' align himself with the despised forces that originally displaced him – John Smith, peasants, Yanks – and share their ideology, if not their material privileges. It appears to be a price Huysmans is willing to pay. However much in later work he rails against the philistine mediocrity of the Catholic bourgeoisie, here he faces the truth: in the face of the common female enemy, all differences disappear.

In its later stages, Huysmans' involvement with decadence is increasingly an attempt to glamorize essentially middle-class and conventional values. In the novel *Là-bas* (1891), his entry into Catholicism 'à rebours', a hero who has clearly reverted to the Folantin type yearns for the distinction conferred by sadism and Satanism. The pious bellringer of Saint Sulpice, Carhaix, and his wife, with their homely dinners and suppers, provide the context for most of the information Durtal gleans about Satanism, interrupting scabrous details of spell-casting with offers of extra carrots. Carhaix' wife is the prototype of the female figures who will appear in Huysmans' Catholic novels, reliable, motherly housekeepers, devoted to the Virgin Mother Mary. Returning to the ranks of the respectable, this new hero reaches for baroque forms as a last gesture to express so much that has been repressed. *Là-bas* places decadent motifs in their proper context, by the bourgeois fireside.

Satanism is also made respectable by an appeal to science. Charcot's accounts of the behaviour of hysterical women are uncannily like traditional accounts of demonic possession. The newly discovered world of microbes hints at the possible existence of an equally unfamiliar world of spirits. Brown-Séquard's work on drugs, which has provided a miraculous cure for impotence, could be said to vindicate the old spells. Durtal plays the sceptic, but he dreams his wishes very close to fulfilment.

He chooses sides at the novel's outset. His model for the history he plans to write is Michelet, whose way of reaching the truth of history (like des Esseintes' approach to art) is to write himself into its characters. For Durtal, history is essentially unknowable. Significantly, the 1789 Revolution and the 1871 Commune are the episodes he uses to illustrate his contention – periods where truth, for him, is at its most unpalatable.

In *Là-bas*, he turns to the Middle Ages, to invent drama and mystery. The figure he takes for his point of perspective is the enigmatic Gilles de Rais, the 'Bluebeard' of tradition, 'inexplicably' transformed from sinner to saint. Behind de Rais stands the faceless mediaeval populace, the passive material of aristocratic perversions. Even when the people revolt, it is only in the name of the higher authority of Church and State, whose

Félicien Rops, 'L'Idole', cf.p.85.

Fernand Khnopff, 'L'Art', 'Les Caresses' or 'Le Sphynx' 1896
(Musées Royaux des Beaux-Arts, Brussels).

'Le banquet de Satan et de ses fidèles'. Illustration for
Le Satanisme et la Magie by Jules Bois, 1895, cf.p.92.

dignity de Rais has flouted. Their submissiveness contrasts with the insurgency of the modern rabble, the 'loathsome populace', heir to the Commune, who cheer the newly-elected Boulanger in the closing pages of the book. Socialism has not improved the masses, sneers Durtal, and never will; the future is in the hands of swarming, soulless generations, devoted solely to the pleasures of food and drink. The text here does a double-take, for the hedonistic instincts he condemns in the crowd are also his own. The crowd is an object of contempt and fear, but also a mirror of his own vices, and the repression he practises on them is a displacement of his self-repression.

If Durtal, in consequence, presents a banal, uniform surface, Gilles de Rais is all he has repressed, the projection of the crowd's animal instincts and a creature of huge, varied and discordant appetite. The historian pins him securely to the page with all the instruments of scientific method, and then proceeds to savour his monstrous, irresponsible criminality. Whether psychopath or possessed by the Devil, he enjoys a freedom Durtal envies.

His crimes were the product of scientific curiosity, devices to draw the Devil. Women never attracted him. He began by sodomizing his own choirboys and then moved on to murder, dismembering children in heroic quantities for his Black Masses. The victims were kept in caverns, and brought up for necrophiliac orgies with the baron and his accomplices, senses aroused by drink and spiced foods. Huysmans adds precise and sickening detail. The most outrageous exploit of this 'virtuoso of murder and pain' was to half-hang a child, cut it down with the pretence of rescuing it, and then, when the child was reassured, slowly cut off its head.

With such refined cruelties, de Rais reached the limits of evil. His frustration at having no more taboos to transgress drove him to madness, and then to remorse. Caught in this contradiction, he tore himself and his victims apart. The climax of Durtal's Bluebeard fantasy is de Rais' hallucination in the forest depths around his castle. His very presence depraves the landscape, summoning up a vision of the primitive obscenity of matter that the language of the text subtly transforms. The erotic evil de Rais imagines in Nature 'really' is there; he is simultaneously found guilty of corruption and absolved, victim of Nature's 'innate' corruption. For the observer – Durtal, Huysmans and the reader – his drama is a heady mixture of erotic pleasure, guilt and fear:

> He wanders through the forests around Tiffauges, thick, black, deep forests like those still hidden at Carnoet, in the heart of Brittany.
> He sobs as he goes, distraught, pushing away the clutching ghosts, then stares, and all of a sudden sees the obscenity of the ancient trees.

Nature seems perverted before his gaze; his very presence seems to deprave her; for the first time, he sees the unchanging salaciousness of the woods, the priapic orgies of the forest.

Here a tree is a living creature, standing erect, then plunging head downwards, buried in its mane of roots, lifting its legs in the air, parting them, splitting into fresh sets of thighs that open in their turn, smaller and smaller as they move away from the trunk. Or else another branch thrusts between the legs, fornication without movement repeated on smaller and smaller scale from branch to branch, right to the top of the tree. Or the treetop is a phallus, lifting and falling under a leafy skirt, or rising from a green fleece to plunge into the velvety belly of the earth . . .

On all sides, obscene forms rise from the ground, erupting chaotically in a firmament fallen prey to Satan. The clouds swell into nipples, split into fat rumps, round into fertile gourds, scatter in spilt trails of milk, in harmony with the dark, swelling forests, replete with images of dwarf and giant thighs, feminine triangles, great V-shapes, mouths of Sodom, splayed scars, oozing moist fluids! (XII[b], 18–20).

Like des Esseintes' fantastic plants, these eroticized images of Nature erupt into ulcers and polyps, while a syphilitic red holly drenches de Rais in a rain of blood. He answers Nature's violence with a counter-attack on the dryad dwelling in the tree: his desire, to rape the divinity, degrade and despoil the corrupting Mother. He takes refuge in his castle bedroom, pursued by incubi, succubi and the ghosts of his dead.

At the height of battle, he suddenly surrenders. Lapped in a rising tide of blood, he appeals to the crucified Christ, hearing at last in his own tearful voice the tears of his victims, and the way is clear for his redemption and reintegration into the world of order. A long account of his penitential humiliation, on trial before the representatives of God, King and populace, concludes Durtal's narrative on a glamorous symbol which confirms both order and self-indulgence.

The contradictions of decadent sensibility, oscillating, since Baudelaire, between frenzy and torpor, cruelty and remorse, rebellion and submission, find a home in the dramatic doctrines of reparation and redemption on which the romantic Catholicism of the late nineteenth century is founded. What the doctor was to des Esseintes, so God is to de Rais.

Compared with his imagined version of Gilles' career, Durtal's own excursions into sin in the company of Madame Chantelouve are 'pretty shabby', mere 'bourgeois sin'. Only the feelings of guilt are as strong. In her, as in Gilles de Rais, he sees a fragmented personality, both *allumeuse* and creature of mystery. He pieces together the signs that she's a Satanist:

her nervous laugh and pointed teeth, her claim that she sleeps with Byron and Baudelaire, the strange contrast of her cold body and burning lips, her talk of free love, her boast that her first husband committed suicide for jealousy, her craving to have priests for lovers. When she admits that the black magician, Canon Docre, once her confessor and lover, taught her how to summon incubi, she becomes for him the occult incarnate. When Durtal speaks of inventing a new sin, Pygmalionism, making love to the creation of one's own imagination, Madame Chantelouve is his Galatea.

'Pygmalionism' is not a new sin. It is the decadent cliché which asserts that women are only the image of men's dreams, and that dream turned to reality will always disappoint. Durtal's efforts to penetrate the mystery he imagines in her eyes lead to the squalid world of the Black Mass. Satanism, as des Hermies warns him, is not what it used to be. Modern 'Satanists' are neurotics whose lust drives them to obscenity. Woman is no longer the centre of the rite, which has turned into a sodomite orgy.

At the door of Docre's chapel, Durtal and his mistress are greeted by an obvious 'sodomite' with 'a corrupt face, sticky, liquid eyes, cheeks plastered with powder and painted lips' (XII[b], 156), who reappears as one of the grotesque 'choirboys' serving the Mass. Docre officiates at an altar dominated by a blasphemous crucifix that displays a naked Christ with erect phallus. Docre too is naked except for a pair of gartered black stockings under a chasuble the colour of dried red blood, marked with a horned black goat. While Docre hurls streams of abuse at the God who failed to save the world, incense pours out, bells ring, women in grotesque convulsions tear off their clothes. At the moment of consecration Docre turns and exposes himself to the congregation, and fouls the host. While he continues to defile the wafers, the choirboys couple with the men in the congregation, and the women masturbate with the chalice and the crucifix. Durtal's reactions are mixed. He stands up to see better; then, 'disgusted', 'half-choked', demands to leave, taking Madame Chantelouve with him.

Her real sin is to insist he continue the orgy with her in the back room of a wineshop, forcing him to realize his perverse fantasies. She becomes an Eve, making him sin, while he pleads innocence and remorse:

> She took hold of him and revealed to him slavish desires, foul practices he had never suspected of her; she spiced them with ghoulish frenzies, and when he finally escaped, he suddenly fell to trembling, because in the bed he saw the fragments of a wafer (p. 171).

As de Rais' character is unexpectedly healed by conversion, a descent of grace at his trial that provokes a frenzy of repentance and forgiveness, so this feverish account of modern Satanism has a luminous codicil. The abbé Gevingey describes a White Mass, the 'Sacrifice de gloire de Melchissédech', which invokes the reign of the Holy Spirit, descending to purge souls and bodies and enable men to produce children free of original sin. The Vintrasian Doctor Johannes, a Lyonnais mystic, had performed it to lift from Gevingey a spell Docre had cast with poison and menstrual blood.

Absolute evil, in which Huysmans includes every kind of instinct, is circumscribed in a frame of absolute good. Within the frame is a chaos that cannot be understood, only contemplated and perversely enjoyed. This frame is the pledge that one day some higher authority will conjure a change. In the meantime, as the bellringer says, down here, everything's 'dead' and 'decomposing', while 'up there', the Paraclete waits to descend. True sin is the spawning masses, contemptuous of the Ideal, 'stuffing their bellies and flushing their souls out through their guts! (pp. 265–6).

Huysmans himself, as Robert Baldick describes in *The Life of J.-K. Huysmans* (1955), was as fascinated as his fictional heroes by Satanism and the occult. It was Villiers de l'Isle-Adam who first took him to Edmond Bailly's bookshop, rue de la Chaussée d'Antin, where he met the poet Edouard Dubus, 'addicted to magic and morphine', Stanislas de Guaita, Paul Adam and Papus (Gérard Encausse). On 31 October 1887, he wrote to Emile Zola of his plan for a new book on 'the fringes of the clerical world', with whom he'd been mixing, Naundorffists, hagiographers and alchemists, 'a collection of nuts' (F. Zayed, *Huysmans, peintre de son époque*, 1973, p. 433). Edouard Dubus told how, in that year, 'He used to tell strange tales of witchcraft, esoteric cults, werewolves and – even then – of Satanism; and after a long pause, he'd generally finish with: "All very odd . . . very odd . . ." ' (*Le Figaro*, 14 May 1927).

At Villiers' death in 1889, Huysmans and Mallarmé were left to supervise the publication of *Axël*. The Rosicrucian drama seems to have had little influence on Huysmans' concept of the occult. Whereas Villiers speaks of aspirations to the divine through beauty, art and knowledge, Huysmans dwells on the crudest and most unsophisticated aspects of the supernatural – spells, sacrilege and perverted ritual. When he attacks the Rosicrucians in *Là-bas*, lumping them together with the Satanists, it is clearly of the disreputable magus Joséphin Péladan that he is thinking. There is no attempt in the novel to redress the balance by considering other faces of a movement that for many artists was a fresh source of lyrical energy. Yeats, for example, who in March 1890 joined the Rosicrucian Hermetic Students of the Golden Dawn, and who in his *Autobiographies*

(1926) acknowledged a considerable debt to Villiers (pp. 394–5), describes in his *Rosa Alchemica* the ritual Dance before the Rose, which is certainly, for his narrator, a diabolical challenge to Christianity. At the same time, its pattern and his partners have a seductive, stimulating loveliness. The Dark Lady whose eyes destroy the soul is also the initiator into the sensual life.

In 1889, Huysmans also met Rémy de Gourmont's mistress Berthe Courrière, 'a cabbalist and occultist, learned in the history of Asiatic religions and philosophies, fascinated by the veil of Isis, initiated by dangerous personal experiences into the most redoubtable mysteries of the Black Art' (Rémy de Gourmont, *Portraits du prochain siècle*, cit. Baldick, p. 138). A year earlier, he had met Péladan's mistress, Henriette Maillat, whose letters he used for Madame Chantelouve's correspondence with Durtal. Most important, 1889 was the year in which, through Berthe Courrière, he first came across Joseph-Antoine Boullan, the unfrocked priest who became one of his major sources of information on occult practices and who was instrumental in his conversion to Catholicism. Boullan's activities as an exorcist in connection with his Société pour la réparation des âmes, encouraging unwary clients into intercourse with Christ and the saints, had led to his being thrown out of the Church in 1875. Immediately he made contact with Pierre-Eugène-Michel Vintras, 'a devout labourer, with an excitable but weak brain' (Eliphas Lévi, *The History of Magic*, tr. A.E. Waite, 4th ed., 1948, p. 332), who in 1839 had been drawn by an angelic vision to the cause of the Bourbon Pretender, Louis XVII and, along with the restoration of the monarchy, preached the imminence of the Third Reign of the Holy Spirit. On Vintras' death in December, Boullan took over as high priest of the Vintrasian sect, supervising such rituals as the 'Sacrifice de la gloire de Melchissédech', described by Huysmans in *Là-bas*, or, with a few selected disciples, the 'Unions de Vie' in which celestial beings, or, failing such, higher initiates, had intercourse with lesser adepts to help them up the ladder of salvation. Lévi gives an account of similar practices from an anti-Vintrasian pamphlet of 1851:

> . . . the devotees of Tilly-sur Seules . . . celebrated in their private chapel, which they termed the upper chamber, sacrilegious masses, at which the elect assisted in a state of complete nudity . . . It was like the orgies of the old Gnostics, but without even taking the precaution to extinguish the lights. Alexandre Geoffroi testifies that Vintras initiated him into a kind of prayer which consisted in the monstrous act of Onan, committed at the foot of the altar, but here the accuser is too odious to be believed on

his own word (p. 335).

Stanislas de Guaita denounced Boullan's ritual unions in his *Le Temple de Satan* (1891) as doctrines leading 'firstly, to unlimited promiscuity and indecency; secondly, to adultery, incest and bestiality; thirdly, to incubism and onanism . . . all exalted to mysterious and sacramental acts of worship' (cit. Baldick, p. 157). In 1890, Oswald Wirth and Edouard Dubus had already tried to warn Huysmans, who refused to take any notice; he had in Boullan the material for a good novel. Wirth reported: 'He listened to us with a smile on his lips, and then remarked that if the old man had found a mystical dodge for obtaining a little carnal satisfaction, that surely wasn't so stupid of him . . .' (cit. Baldick, p. 162). He also took some of Boullan's lunacies seriously. De Goncourt's entry in his *Journal* for 15 March 1891 notes that Huysmans was ill, and carried everywhere with him a bloodstained scapulary sent by the abbé Boullan, to ward off attacks from succubi.

Adding other documentary sources to Boullan, Courrière, Dubus and the Bibliophile Jacob, Huysmans found himself, with the publication of *Là-bas*, the accepted expert in the subject, and, as with *A rebours*, well-placed to exploit a lucrative new fashion. Occultism, as Jules Bois said, offered an 'active mysticism, a noble Tolstoyism' more satisfying than that of its rival, Buddhist nihilism, and a forceful creed (Jules Huret, *Enquête sur la littérature contemporaine*, 1891, p. 50). A gullible public was eager to believe in dreams – and nightmares – turned to reality. In his preface to Jules Bois' 'well-documented' account of Satanism past and present, *Le Satanisme et la Magie* (1895), which drew its most substantial evidence from *Là-bas*, Huysmans stressed the practical usefulness of the book, claiming to have known many people who had been destroyed by Satanism. Scientists, magistrates and the clergy conspired to deny its existence, but there was evidence that the most ordinary-looking people walking the streets were adepts. The most banal bourgeois could mask the blackest mystery. Decadence, he implied, was within the reach of the man in the street. He cited recent examples: the theft by an old woman of fifty consecrated hosts from Notre-Dame in Easter Week, and two examples of child murder linked with Black Masses. His 'Canon Docre' was the centre of a cenacle of Belgian Satanists, and had corrupted his flock with aphrodisiacs and orgies.

Huysmans' introduction raised hopes amply fulfilled by Bois' text, with its graphic descriptions of Satanic rites (of which Sabbat and Black Mass are both taken straight from *Là-bas*). Bois gravely sketches the politics of Satanism, linking Vintrasianism and the Bonapartist cause. The disastrous war with Prussia in 1870 was the result of misinterpreted advice from spirits summoned by Napoleon III and his Empress. He explains the nature of incubi, succubi, vampires, all projections of human dreams and desires that spring from menstrual fantasies and unsatisified lust. Charms and spells are effects of magnetic forces, harnessed by particular rituals.

But of all his explanations, the most important is that of the new role of women in contemporary cults. In occultism, woman was no longer the destroyer Hecate, or Circe, which men's antagonism had made her, but priestess and mediator. Bois' preamble argues that though Jewish and Christian misogynists may have tried to reserve power for men and refused to admit priestesses to the Church, the future reign of the Paraclete will be mediated by the Mother: 'the Paraclete is not only the Spirit, it is also the universal Mother forever repressed by the Church, the Mother suppressed by the Virgin, true woman, with no false shame for her nature and her gifts'. Huysmans' preface had already referred to Diana Vaughan and her Luciferan review *Le Palladium*. Bois adds to the roll of honour Katie King and Madame Blavatsky, and points to the role of women in the current revival of Catholicism. There was the Blessed Margaret- Mary Alacoque, who revived the cult of the Sacred Heart, and the Virgin Mary, the weeping Mother of Lourdes. Eugène Vintras had campaigned for the recognition of the cult of the Immaculate Conception.

When feminism later became fashionable, Bois turned his dream of women prophets and martyrs into more practical politics. For the misogynist Huysmans, however, the new vision of woman as priestess and mediator led only to the further mystifications of Catholicism.

Paying for the Dream: Redeeming Eve

In Huysmans' post-conversion fictions, women atone for the evil of Eve. Sadistic impulses are transposed into contemporary Christian doctrine. Woman still suffers, and causes men to suffer, but the message of the Immaculate Conception of Lourdes, the Dolorous Virgin of La Salette, and the Sacred Heart of Mary, is that all suffering is a participation in the Crucifixion and the Redemption. This is a new inflection of the cruel Mother, the priestess with distant, pain-filled eyes. With the image of her own grief, the new Woman invites compassion, rather than forces submission. In the language of the doctrine, her 'victims' are voluntary, joyful participants in a creative act of renewal.

Such language, however, is belied by the facts. The image of the Dolorous Virgin still has the function of fixing the contradictions and tensions of the present, rather than provoking reactions and resolution.

Woman still exists to make pain a pleasure. The cults of the Sacred Heart and the Immaculate Conception, both invoked after the Franco-Prussian War to encourage the nation to return to authoritarian, monarchist and Catholic tradition, only offer renewal by way of greater repression.

This is the call Huysmans responds to in his conversion, retreating into an inner world clearly and authoritatively shaped by Christian doctrine. The centre of that world is his soul, focus of a cosmic struggle between God and the Devil, into which all energies are concentrated and locked. The struggle drains the life out of all that is merely human. Sexual desire is repressed, a major obstacle to stillness of mind and soul.

In Huysmans' first Catholic novel, *En route* (1895), there is still some vigour in Durtal's struggle with the 'ghoulish' whore, Florence. But already his attention is moving to the 'dirty' female saints who engage in reparatory suffering, and who are ready to take on disease and death for his sake. To give him calm of mind, the outside world must consent to its own degradation and destruction.

Durtal turns to the fourteenth-century Saint Lydwina of Schiedam (to whom Huysmans, in 1901, devoted a whole book), who offered her physical sufferings in atonement for the sins of others. The decay of her body is charted in sadistic detail, riddled with gangrene, eaten by worms, attacked by plague. The Blessed Angela di Foligno to whom Durtal turns after a night plagued by succubi was, like him, a guilt-ridden former libertine. She spent her life in masochistic atonement, using burning coals to cauterize 'the very wound of her senses', humiliating herself in the service of the poor and sick, drinking the water where she had washed a leper's sores, to punish herself for her revulsion. *La Cathédrale* (1898) introduces a little-known figure from the thirteenth century, Saint Christine de Stumbèle, who was pursued by the Devil. He filled her bed with lice, whipped her till she bled, turned the food in her mouth to toads, snakes and spiders, and drenched her with warm faeces.

Almost all the female figures of *La Cathédrale* undergo the same degradation. The type is as in the carving of the woman on the porch of Dijon Cathedral, who slips the clutches of the devils in hell to implore the sinner to repent:

> Her eyes haggard and dilated, her hands joined, she pleads with you in her terror, points to the holy place and cries you to enter . . . Charitable and severe, she threatens and implores; and this image of woman excommunicated for eternity, driven out of the temple, banished for ever to its threshold, haunts you like a remembered pain, a nightmare of terror (XIV [b], 257).

The Queen of Sheba, who in Moreau's paintings would have been a potent and disturbing source of mystery, a 'lustful virgin, coquette and casuist', with her 'spicy flesh' and 'innocent sphinx-like smile' is described as too complex for the innocence of mediaeval art (p. 92). On cathedral walls, she generates for Durtal neither mystery nor unease, while the image of Solomon still stirs him to rich dreams of exotic palaces filled with music, incense, flowers, monkeys, peacocks and a harem of naked women. The magician king is magnificent even in his decline, writing Ecclesiastes, and after his death a continuing enigma – apostate pessimist, saved or damned? – Durtal wonders, in self-regarding sympathy. But Sheba is no longer an object of desire. When Durtal dreams of her now, her place on the pedestal is taken by his ugly middle-aged housekeeper. Too late, he 'inveighs against the canons, vainly begging them to take away his housekeeper and bring back the queen' (p. 106).

His image of female beauty is now the Virgin, given a form that refuses all links with her fallen sisters. Botticelli's pagan brush made the Virgin and Venus identical, with their 'slightly turned-up nose, mouth like a folded cloverleaf . . . pink eyelids, golden hair . . . and the same expression . . .' (p. 139). Durtal prefers the Flemish Primitives. Roger Van der Weyden's Virgin is both simple woman and spiritual beauty, with her long red hair, high brow, straight nose and melancholy, innocent gaze.

This figure of unearthly purity holds only a 'minute' baby Jesus (p. 142). Huysmans' feelings are unspoken, but obvious: still the Mother of God, she is free of the degrading aura of fertility.

All beauty in *La Cathédrale* is locked away in the purity of art. There may be carnal terrors on the threshold, but inside all is safely dead. Beauty is frozen into the statues, the stained glass, the fixed categories of mediaeval symbolism. Durtal and his guide, the aptly named abbé Plomb, list the symbolic meanings of colours, flowers and jewels. Huysmans is transformed from poet to pedant, indulging a neurotic obsession with 'fact' from which all pleasure is absent. Des Esseintes at least drained the meaning from living objects. Durtal sucks the dry bones of a tradition picked over by past generations, left dusty and arid.

A would-be robust appeal to 'treat souls like men' (p. 58) by a return to the frank carnality of the Middle Ages, turns into one more denunciation of the sinfulness of the flesh. Desire must be 'purged' and 'pilloried' into submission. The life of the Church Huysmans enters is negative, all its vigour channelled into the destructive forms of denunciation, vituperation, castigation. Huysmans' aim, as in *A rebours*, is still to return to the tranquil security of the womb, and the price is still negation, disgust and pain.

Durtal's last vision of the Virgin of Chartres presents her in forms reminiscent of one of Moreau's priestesses. Her power – so the Church guarantees – will be used with mercy, as long as Durtal submits to her rule.

This last evocation of the Virgin draws every decadent image of woman's beauty and power into the safe confines of the Church. In the process, it makes plain the structures of power which both decadence and Catholicism underwrite. Durtal, claiming to submit to an authority not his own, abdicating both power and responsibility, is in fact reclaiming power without responsibility. For the source of the Virgin's power is the masculine authority of the Church. The exquisite image in which that power is focused is the product of men's labour and men's imaginations. The Virgin of Huysmans' text, consoler and destroyer, is forever fixed in the theology, the poetry, the anthems, stone and glass of the cathedral:

> . . . I seem to see her in the contours, in the very expression of the cathedral; her features are slightly blurred in the pale splendour of the great rose window that flames like a halo behind her head. She smiles, and her luminous eyes have the incomparable splendour of those bright sapphires that light the entrance to the nave. Her fluid body flows into a dazzling, fluted gown of flame . . . Her face has a pearly whiteness and her hair, woven on the spinning-wheel of the sun, is a flight of golden threads. She is the spouse of the Canticle: *Pulchra ut luna, electa ut sol* . . . the vaulted roof joined above her like a dais tells of her charity, the stones and glass echo her anthems; and all things, from the warlike fashion of the detail in the sanctuary, to the accent of chivalry that recalls the Crusades (the shields and sword-blades of rose and lantern windows, the helmeted ribs, the old tower in its coats of mail, the iron trellis of certain windows), all things . . . translate that *terribilis ut castrorum acies ordinata*, tell of her privilege to appear, when she wishes, like 'a terrible army drawn up for battle'.
>
> But here, I think, she seldom wishes that; this cathedral is most of all the reflection of her inexhaustible gentleness, the echo of her indivisible glory! (pp. 294–5).

The stratagem is hardly worthwhile. The authorities Durtal would reinstate have had their day, as the novel itself admits, setting out the gap between Durtal's fantasy and the reality. He will never possess the Virgin of his dreams, only Madame Bavoil, his simple, waddling housekeeper, and her maternal assurances of his impotence. It is Madame Bavoil who answers his effusion to the Virgin ('Ah, much shall be forgiven you, because you've loved Her so much'), and who has the last word of the novel, calling on the Virgin to seduce him to his salvation: 'It depends on you, aid him in his poverty, remember he can do nothing without your help, kindly Temptress, Our Lady of the Pillar, Virgin of the Crypt!'

2
Satyrs and Amazons:
Remy de Gourmont 1858–1915

At this distance, it is hard to picture Huysmans and Remy de Gourmont as friends, even though that friendship lasted only two or three brief years from their first meeting at the end of 1889. What they had in common was elitism, idealism, scorn for conventional values, and the desire for something different. De Gourmont's 'Souvenirs sur Huysmans' sketch a personality 'full of unease, eager for the rare, the unknown and the impossible' (*Promenades littéraires*, Vol. III). But the search for the rare and unknown leads the two men down very different paths. Despite declarations of independence, both are ultimately men of tradition eager to be part of an orthodoxy, yet de Gourmont was disappointed by the ease with which his friend succumbed to a limiting religious ideology. His own approach is more critical and more creative: art, not religion, provides the tools with which to shape and reshape the image of his desire.

What he wants, however, is not fundamental change but superficial variation, just as Huysmans did. From the cultural tradition, he is eager to preserve the concept of the individual as the centre of both public and private worlds. 'The true cement of any community is egoism; when a man grows taller and stronger, that very fact ensures a powerful and healthy Republic' ('La Morale de l'amour', July 1900, coll. in *La Culture des idées*, 1900). At another level, he knows that this idea of the subject is seldom supported by the facts. What he sees as the repressive institutions of the modern State, the bourgeois Republic, and the levelling banality of public opinion they create and thrive on, are constant threats to the would-be

Egoist. The answer is to slip out of public being, into the personal life, to deal with areas that seem the intimate and indisputable property of the private individual: language and sexuality. De Gourmont's fiction undertakes to rewrite human relationships and ways of communicating.

Ironically, as he discovers, what seems most private is in fact shaped by collective forces beyond individual control, and language and sexuality are themselves sources of limitation and frustration. The craving for impossible transformations is the theme of all his fiction, which, unlike Huysmans', is doubtful, ambivalent and sceptical. His description of Stéphane Mallarmé's work could be applied to his own. This is the poetry of hesitation:

> ... the most wonderful pretext for reverie yet offered to men wearied by so many heavy, futile affirmations: poetry full of doubts, changing nuances, ambiguous perfumes, the only kind, perhaps, we can still enjoy. If 'decadence' did indeed stand for all these autumn, twilight charms, we could most certainly welcome it and make it one of the modes of our music ('Stéphane Mallarmé et l'idée de décadence', 1898, rpt. in *La Culture des idées*).

De Gourmont's aim is to preserve the egoistic heart of the bourgeois tradition by reforming the surface. This is clear in his essay of 1899, 'La Dissociation des idées' (rpt. *La Culture des idées*), which confronts the prejudices which are the base of modern society: 'The brain of civilized man is a museum of contradictory truths.' Of these, the most important are those concerned with the nature of sexuality and art. Sexual repressiveness is a historical accident for which Christianity is to blame, associating sexual pleasure with reproduction, and disassociating pleasure from love. These links have nothing to do with reason, and everything to do with the vested interests of individuals and societies. By another historical accident, art has been contaminated with sex, associated with the ideal of female beauty, to which the observer's response is erotic, when traditionally, de Gourmont argues, it should be a question of pure, aesthetic harmonies. For the modern, the beauty of art provokes both an aesthetic and an erotic response. 'Art is love's accomplice,' he declared in 1901 ('Success and the idea of Beauty', rpt. *Le Chemin de velours: Nouvelles Dissociations d'idées*, 1902). This, he believes, is not legitimate, and gives art a social role to which it is not entitled, using strong emotions to focus the popular imagination. He failed to add that this double response is the source of the seductive power of decadent images and ideology; and its effects are conspicuous in his own writing.

Sexuality is in every sense the matter of de Gourmont's writing. There is no mistaking the erotic quality of his language, authoritative in its use of abstracts, precise in its analyses and definitions, but incarnating abstracts and analyses in vivid concrete images, with sharp physical detail that brings them to compelling life, consciously recalling the mystical sensuality of the troubadours. His subject is the inherited repressions which have deformed the individual. 'La Morale de l'amour' (July 1900) argued that the State should allow free rein to sexual instincts, which are a private matter. It challenged the imposition of ascetic Christian morality, which generated the vices it professed to attack. Sodomy and sapphism, he claims, come from convents: 'Every attack against freedom of love encourages vice. When you dam a river, it overflows; when you repress a passion, it goes off the rails.' Worst of all, constraint on the body is constraint on the mind's development: 'Everything is connected, and intellectual freedom is certainly linked to the freedom of the senses.'

The subject of his fictions is also desire itself, figured in the enigmatic image of Woman and the even greater enigma of man's relationship to her. De Gourmont's fictions collect up contemporary images of the female, and delicately interrogate them – reserving the right to ignore his own answers. In decadent fantasy, women are stereotyped into supporting roles, their function being to affirm that men are the heroes – tragic heroes – of the drama. In his study of algolagnia (finding sexual pleasure in pain, or more specifically, 'reinterpret[ing] relationships of dominance, subordination and brutality as sexual'), Jerry Palmer has explained that the images of the persecuted virgin and fatal beauty, the two opposite masks in which the decadence envisages the female, have nothing to do with what women really are, or even what men think they really are:

> . . . the Fatal Beauty is that which saps the male ego, with scant attention paid to the effects the situation has on the lady; and the Justine-figure is similarly restricted by her function as reinforcement of the male. Both figures are male gender-role fantasies ('Fierce Midnights: Algolagniac Fantasy and the Literature of the Decadence' in *Decadence and the 1890s*, ed. I. Fletcher, 1979, pp. 97–8).

De Gourmont's orginality is that he admits that the ego-reinforcement supplied by these female fictions is not enough. When he sadistically torments his fantasy to compel her to produce a better image of his desire, he 'knows' she never will, because she is nothing but that desire, the projection of his own dream. He thinks he might like her to be something different, which could give independent confirmation of his superiority.

But faith in his own potency depends on his belief that the only creative mind in his world is his.

De Gourmont's fictions declare that his world is unsatisfactory; that it will never change unless the balance of power within sexual relationships is redistributed; but that he is afraid of change, and will not have it. He creates cruel, frightening heroines in revolt against the images imposed on them, and evokes the bloody threat of a reality that could at any moment rise in anger against false, distorting definitions. There is as much fear and misogyny in his writing as in Huysmans', but it is linked with a guilty awareness which almost – but not quite – opens the door to the new. Unlike most of his contemporaries, he writes of *and against* the female myths.

From the beginning, de Gourmont intended to create heroines who would fulfil his own dreams. In his diary for 31 December 1874, at the age of sixteen, he wrote: 'I should like to create characters, stamp them with the seal of my own mind, move them according to my own will; I should like heroines all of my own, owing me everything, from their birth to those qualities which make one love a woman as one would love an angel.'

What he actually invented were not angels but demons. In his first novel, *Merlette* (1886), his hero Hilaire, who, like all his later heroes, combines indecisiveness with blind egoism, is a dreamer who lacks the force to turn dreams into reality. Merlette, the miller's daughter who is in love with him, 'natural' woman ('the very poetry of nature in all its grace and fulness'), is totally dependent on his will. By his unthinking indifference, Hilaire turns this angel into a devil. The 'poetry of nature', brushed aside, turns from pastoral to melodrama. The love that Hilaire rejects, having no means to express itself, becomes formless hatred which is intensified by its sense of its own powerlessness. De Gourmont's writing gives that hatred body, but like Hilaire he changes its shape, twisting it to his own cruel sophistications.

Merlette's own language is a weak echo of Nature's threatening power, figured in the shapeless violence of the riverwaters caught in the millrace: 'As if in a trance, Merlette murmured her accompaniment to the song from the abyss, three sustained notes rising insistently from the depths, intermittently dominating the dull lapping of the waves and the noise of the waters' (p. 236). She is the only victim of her violent resentments, falling accidentally in the millrace to drown, unnoticed in death as in life. But de Gourmont gives this powerless victim his own incisive and sadistic language, transforming her into a conscious source of evil. She dreams her rival drowning in cruel, caressing images that are embodiments of man's desire:

> The wicked thought came to her that with a flick of her finger she should
> have thrown [Bette] on to the sharp cutting stones of the dried-up river
> bed. The blood dripping from her wounds would have plastered down
> on her brow that provocative fleece of curly hair that fell over her eyes.
> The cutting stones would have lashed through the ribbons of the bodice
> where the fine, slender waist dwindled to a spindle-point. The sharp
> stones would have put out the impertinent eyes where Merlette had read
> contempt and fear . . . (p. 233).

And after her death, Hilaire makes her the scapegoat for the sense of
failure and frustration that fills his marriage and his life.

In later novels, de Gourmont's versions of his heroes' self-delusions are
more sympathetic.

Sixtine (1890), dedicated to Villiers de l'Isle-Adam, is a celebration of
the decadent's hero's incapacity in any world except that of his own
dream. Like *A rebours*, it claims to mock its own hero for his failure to
secure the object of his desire. Hubert des Entragues is the victim of his
own grotesque misunderstandings, and of his determination to preserve
the textbook shadow between dream and its realization. His capacity for
cliché is pathetic, as Sixtine herself tells him when at the end of the novel
she slips off the worktable to assert her own identity by a vicious attack on
his incapacities.

But what the novel argues is that willed incapacity coupled with
imagination is more satisfying than anything the real world can offer.
Unlike des Esseintes, who foolishly thought he could improve on reality,
des Entragues knows that the function of the creative imagination is to
find devices to delay the disappointing moment of possession. The
function of woman is to be the vehicle of the ever-changing images and
ambitions which incarnate man's dream. As long as she remains silent and
mysterious, the game goes on. Regrettably, the moment always comes
when reality resists, and spoils the story. Few women are as co-operative
as Berthe Courrière, de Gourmont's mistress from 1886, the inspiration of
this and later novels, duly grateful to the poets who grant women:

> . . . those wonderful, immortal lives, living for ever, whole, imperishable,
> in the memory of man. She might have been no more than a tyrannical
> queen, a rough warrior, or some commonplace virtue. The hearts of
> poets have decked these faces in splendid gems and diadems, made of
> them magnificent idols, raised to heights where oblivion cannot touch

them ('Le Fantôme', *Mercure de France*, May 1893).

Des Entragues is a tragic hero, the Wounded Knight scarred by his own
civilization. Too much thinking is his downfall. He was brought up on the
Cartesian *cogito*, reinforced by Schopenhauerian idealism: 'The world is
the Idea I have of it.' In fact, he has nothing. He is an aristocrat, without
the status and wealth that should go with his name. He complains: 'I don't
know how to live. My existence is perpetual cerebration, the complete
negation of ordinary life and its ordinary loves' (p. 34).

He makes a virtue of necessity. If dream is all he has, then dream is all
that matters: 'What use would reality be to me, when I've got dream, and
the ability to play Proteus, to possess in turn all the forms of life, all the
diverse and passing states of the human soul?' (p. 27). Impotence is his own
choice. When Sixtine, at the end of the story, abandons him for a less
dilatory Russian suitor, his anger is brief, and he returns with relief to the
peace of his library and his favourite author, the voluntary castrate
Origen.

Reality is best used as a frame for art. He is writing a contorted Gothic
romance, 'L'Adorant', whose chapters are strung out along the thread of
the still-born affair between himself and Sixtine – fantasy embedded
within fantasy. In 'L'Adorant', no one challenges the dreamer-hero.
Guido Della Preda, Count of Santa-Maria, is a redoubtable aristocrat,
locked unjustly in solitary confinement in a high tower. Prison leaves him
free to dream. He desires the Madonna Novella, a new image of the Virgin
with the two contradictory qualities men most desire in woman. She is still
the Mother, consoler and refuge, but a Mother who might almost be
Mistress. The game his imagination plays is to image in words all the joys
of the flesh, without requiring their realization, which would mean
admitting their absence. The dream Madonna appears in a drifting cloud
of peacock's feathers, pure, white and mysteriously wonderful. She strips
off her crown of stars for him. The buckle of her girdle and the clasp of her
cloak fascinate him, with their promise of surrender. The traditional
symbols of Mary fill his room with dizzy, sensuous perfumes and textures,
counterpointed by the mystic and moral values each represents. Image
moves to abstraction, in an incantatory ritual, simultaneously arousing
and curbing erotic desire:

> She blossomed into a mystic Rose exhaling an exquisite scent.
> And Guido's heart was filled with sweetness.
> Then she became a pure Mirror reflecting a burning sword.
> And Guido's heart was filled with justice . . .

Then a Vase appeared, first of bronze, then of silver, then of gold; there swirled up smoke of incense, cinnamon and myrrh.

And Guido's heart was filled with worship.

Then there rose up a Tower of Ivory, and other visions, and last of all a dazzling Gate that Guido saw was the Gate of Heaven, and he began to wonder if this adventure wasn't about to end as speciously as his encounter with Pavona (p. 279).

A fiction can hold passion on the brink of realization, so that the dark, carnal side of woman remains hidden under the fair Virgin Mother of tradition. All the poet has to fear is release from prison and return to the conditions of real life. When that comes, he throws himself from the top of the tower. His death, he claims, is what the Virgin craves. She wants the worship not of his body but his words, prayers and litanies. He dies with the greeting, '*Ave Rosa speciosa*', with its lingering, ironic pun: the Virgin dazzlingly lovely, and pure deceit.

The greatest pleasure the text provides its author is the poet's undisputed control over his images. The Virgin on her pedestal is subject to his fantasy, all her identity in the attributes he imagines. He may call her Queen, but she is as much his slave as Pavona, the Ethiopian he possesses in dream, who has no eyes until her lover opens them. The eyes that then gaze at him from his bed are 'frightening. They were like the eyes on peacocks' feathers, white peacocks' feathers' (p. 144). They are the eyes of the Virgin, watching, reproaching and punishing from his supposed betrayal of chastity, and the focus of a masochistic fantasy that turns enforced chastity into fresh pleasure: 'Forgive me, most reverend Madonna, and punish me in your wisdom' (p. 145).

He rewrites and remodels Sixtine, as he does the Virgin, into his dream of the ideal. The dream again includes masochistic fantasy: the 'fact' that she's cold and evil, and intent on humiliating and abandoning him. He projects on to her the monstrous depths of criminality he fancies exist in himself. In her mouth, he 'observes' an ambiguous violence. When he wakes in the 'portrait room', the image of her that forms in the empty mirror is a Medusa. As Sixtine explains in her farewell letter, what the magic mirror reflects is the image of the watcher's own desire. From the memory of the dead viper he had watched her pick up, he fashions a complex symbol of evil – green water, green willows, moon and snake:

Above the mantelpiece, the mirror slowly changed colour: its moon-green, green of transparent water under willows, was shot through with golden life. At the centre of the light, as if on the face of the moon,

shadows seemed to fall into a semblance of human features, and around
this vague face coiled waves of light like loose, floating blonde hair. In
the blink of an eye, before I could analyse the rest of the sudden
transformation, I saw it complete. Bright, alive, the portrait looked
back at me; line for line, the young woman with the snake (p. 39).

Sixtine, flattered by the image, would, she admits, have surrendered to
his vision, had he not chosen instead to write a novel. To her, his choice
makes no sense:

So why did you desire me? If nothing exists outside your fantasies, what
phantom did you pursue? Perhaps we should try to understand each
other, and find out the kind of lies we have before us. What an
awakening there'll be in the shadowy harem, of all the forms you've
slain, Bluebeard of the Ideal! Have you counted them all? And I am
the seventh, no doubt about it, the one who opens the cupboard of
secrets . . . 'And they pierced his body with their swords.' And so Life
kills Dream. Goodbye (p. 305).

But Sixtine, for all her bullying, has killed nothing. Fairytale Bluebeards
are indestructible. In choosing to deny her desire, des Entragues has kept
for himself the aura of mystery that usually glamorizes woman. Sixtine's
charges of sadism acknowledge power which might have been disproved if
put to the test. The price she set on her surrender was too high:

I'm the dough, waiting for the kneader's hands; I can't make myself
alone . . . Tell me what it is I want . . . conjure up for me what I want, let
me see it with my eyes, touch it with my hands, you can do that, you
must be able to, because you're a man! . . . (pp. 175–8).

Paralysis is the safest mode of existence. The chapter with Sixtine's
farewell letter, 'The Key to the Casket', has an epigraph from Goethe's
Wilhelm Meister that gives the image of des Entragues' real desire, a
longing for nothing: 'We'll put the locked box between us, then we'll open
it and we'll see . . . I want to find nothing in it . . . nothing at all . . .' Des
Entragues envies the passivity permitted to women, longing to hand over
responsibility to some stronger force. Like many of his contemporaries, he
plays with the language of homosexuality as a figure for a different kind of
desire. But this represents no real change; sadism and exploitation are still
its foundation. The only alternatives des Entragues can envisage are
suffering or self-destruction. For the Egoist, the second is unthinkable:

If desire . . . leaves me, even in thought, with freedom of choice, what's the good of loving . . . Perhaps what I need, like a woman, is to be possessed, to be rid of my doubts . . . Where am I? I tried to penetrate to the essence of all things; I saw that there was nothing but movement and at once the world vanished, reduced to invisible forces. I thought I could double my sensations by duplication, and I've destroyed them. Nothing is worth lifting a fingertip for. It's all only thought, vague movements in the atoms of the brain, a small inner murmur (p. 160).

Christian images in *Sixtine* open up a rich vein of language for de Gourmont to explore in the early 1890s. The major dogmas – Incarnation, Atonement and Redemption – are appropriate figures for de Gourmont's contradictory impulses to hedonism and abstension, and for the masochism with which those contradictions are resolved. The rituals, litanies and literature of the Church provide fresh decor and new motifs and rhythms to express the lyrical seductions of cruelty.

At the same time, a return to early Christian or Jewish tradition can challenge modern Christian antagonism to sensual pleasure. De Gourmont reserves the right to play with such images and philosophies as he pleases.

Le Latin mystique (1892) is a collection of the major neo-Latin poetry of the early Christian Church. Huysmans' Preface to it does the book a disservice, in its emphasis on the churchmen's hostility to the flesh. De Gourmont is certainly fascinated by their vindictiveness. But his introductions to individual poets suggest a certain ambiguity:

With the battering-ram of their homilies, they vainly assail the ramparts of the eternal flesh, and the stones from their holy slings glide over breasts and bellies to caress, perhaps, rather than to wound.

His authors, he believes, dwell with his own morbid sensuality on:

. . . the amazing sadism of the torturers, who, with their female victims, turn their painful attention to the specifically female organs, torturing the breasts with their dreadful tools, grasping with the iron claws of some monstrous beast at the hidden virginity of brave virgins!

The sequences of the eleventh-century monk Goddeschalk rehabilitate female carnality. His hymn for Mary Magdalene dwells on Christ's forgiveness for the prostitute, while 'In Communi Virginum', to the Brides of Christ, is full of lurking images of sensual pleasure. In the Mary Magdalene sequence, de Gourmont finds his own thesis that woman is the simple mirror of man's desire: ' "You [Christ] love her that she may be lovely, – *Amas ut pulchram facias*", – what a noble brain so far advanced in Idealism!' Similarly, in Claudius Marius Victor, he discovers that: 'Women are like excellent mirrors, giving a faithful reflection of the objects held up to them: women take on the likeness of their men.'

The mirror-relationship of man and woman and the problem of sensuality are at issue again in *Lilith*, also from 1892. In this dramatic narrative, de Gourmont rewrites the myth of the Fall in the light of the Cabbala. This is in every sense a blasphemous drama, using the backdrop of the Garden of Eden to set out the entire gamut of sexual perversions, and in the process challenging the authority of the Father-Creator, for whom Creation is only a 'short-lived toy', a mirror for his vanity, and whose chief concern is to keep it subjugated.

Adam and Eve enjoy the uniform, untroubled, sensual and sexual bliss of ignorance. Satan and Lilith, incarnations of the animal instincts of sexuality and power which Jehovah most fears, experiment with all the variations and varieties of carnal knowledge, culminating in sodomy and bestiality. Satan is the initiator, but Lilith rapidly outstrips him, the 'archangel of debauch' (p. 96).

With this new knowledge, Satan tempts Adam and Eve. Jehovah punishes them by making his authority plain in all the boundaries, limits, rules and divisions – including the great division of life and death – he now imposes on the freedom of their garden. But that freedom, the text suggests, was illusory, so long as they remained mere mirrors of their Creator. Death and carnality produce pain, but they also produce human knowledge and a limitless unknown. Adam and Lilith copulate, and Lilith gives birth to all the vices of Lust, who celebrate their own perverse beauty:

> We have wide, dark, luminous, savage eyes, and cruel mouths more blood-red than the sucking vampire. Our breasts are as hard as the chests of youths hammered by wrestlers' fists, our legs supple as ash wands – and our androgyne souls will be double, like our loins, and hold sway in the hell of our loins! (p. 97).

Satan and Eve produce Cain, that even greater paradox, the murderer who opens the way to Crucifixion and Redemption. Unknown to Jehovah, an angel restores to the garden a sprig of the Tree of Life, which will become the Wood of the Cross.

Cruelty, crime, perversion, sensual knowledge and sensual excess are the material of new worlds, all in the gift of women, and to be used against the Father's will.

In the prose-poem 'Litanies de la Rose' (1892), modern woman blends all the attributes of Lilith and Eve. Through traditional mediaeval art forms (the litany and the blason), de Gourmont re-creates the traditional female symbol of the rose, as a *summum* of all the variations of female nature. His originality is to evoke also the sensuous reality of both woman and rose, creating an illusion of life so erotically compelling that the reader is seduced into accepting de Gourmont's version of femininity as natural truth.

This 'lyrical satire', as Ezra Pound called it, accuses woman of hypocrisy, venality and cruelty at the same time as it invokes these vices as part of her mystery, with the refrain: 'Flower of hypocrisy. Flower of silence.' Like the sadism of the pagan executioner, the satire attempts to torture meaning out of the enigma. The poem is both imprecation and invocation: 'Wreathe us in the perfume of your lies.' De Gourmont demands an end to the separation of flesh and ideal. The Mystic Rose of the Virgin's litany, in its dazzling purity, 'terrifies'. The black rose perhaps has 'nothingness' at its heart, but it is in the carnal mystery of the black rose that the supplicant longs to put his faith. Where *Sixtine* preached abstension, this poem longs for satisfaction. Both are simply word-games; it is the poet who is duplicitous and projects his duplicity into his Rose.

The Rose of this poet's dream is a treacherous, irresistible invitation to the unknown. She is dominant, powerful and strong: 'Blonde rose, with the light chrome mantle over your frail shoulders, blonde rose, female stronger than the male.' She is rapacious: 'Orange rose . . . patrician, the tiger's maw sleeps under the pampas of your leaves.' She consumes: 'devourer of flesh, rose with bloody lips, if you want our blood, what need have we of it? Drink it all.' Yet she longs to be hurt: 'red vase where teeth bite when the mouth comes to drink . . . you smile at our bites and weep at our kisses'. She dreams of being dominated: 'Corn-coloured rose, you want to be moulded, you want to be kneaded.' She longs to be opened: 'Crimson rose, you lie down and offer yourself, imperial sacrifice, to the covetous desires of beardless youths.' Tyrant and victim, promiscuously offering herself, she becomes a centre of communion. Her lovers are legion, not 'I' but 'we', the shepherd, the goat and the wind, noblemen, youths, brothers.

Despite its anger and bitterness at desire frustrated, this is a litany in praise of desire. In the final verse, Woman is both saint and sinner, source of life and death, Christ's representative on earth and also his murderer:

Rose, papal rose, watered by the hands that bless the world, papal rose, your golden heart is only copper, and the tears that bead your vain corolla are the tears of Christ, hypocritical flower, flower of silence.

Le Fantôme, written towards the end of 1891 and published in 1893, uses other images drawn from Church ritual and mystic theology to evoke the impossibility of reconciling dream and reality. Woman is again both inspiration and disappointment.

Hyacinthe solicits the hero's attention from a room crowded with faceless women. Her appearance – like a ghostly figure stepping out from a fresco or tapestry – should be a warning that this can be no more than a repetition of the eternal drama of disappointment. But he believes her when she points to the doubleness of her name, and its promise that contradictions can be reconciled – jewel and flower, order and stability and organic change: 'I am stone and flower, hard and full of perfume, transparency and flesh, harsh and soft, double and yet one. Hyacinthe: is that stone, or flower?' (p. 16).

She claims she wants to be more than a shadow, and to live her own dream. She has, though, no dream of her own, and must depend on Damase to invent one for her, begging: 'Don't do violence to my will' (p. 20). But her will is to be violated and dominated, to have others' dreams forced on her. When later he accuses her: 'You're just like the others – just a sheath!' her answer is a plea for the impossible: 'Can't I be that and something else besides?' (p. 48).

The ironic chapter 'Duplicity' sets out the logic. Woman wants to be worshipped. An idol who is worshipped is one who is used. Its function is to feed its worshippers with a glorified image of themselves, to 'rejoice in the pain of being crushed in the press and drunk, pure wine, dispensing intoxicating splendours'. Hyacinthe can realize her dream, but the reality will horrify her.

Man has the same dream of passivity, but will never realize it. Woman has no image to impose on him. Damase tells her: 'I'd like to be imbued with your spirituality, and I can't be. You flee before the sharp edge of my intelligence like tangled seaweed before the blade of a scythe' (p. 58). Like the seaweed, woman has no shape or direction but that given by the moving waves of man's world. Damase is impressed by Schopenhauer, for whom the World-Spirit is female, with no essence or form of its own, shaped by the collective and private imagination of men:

Schopenhauer . . . understood that intelligence and automatic functioning can co-exist. His World-Spirit is Woman raised to the power of infinity – a kind of highly dangerous God, whose reign is attended with all kinds of cataclysm, a God unknowable for humanity and for itself (p. 58).

Hyacinthe doesn't understand what he's saying. 'Hyacinthe seemed distracted by the [surrounding] images' – of martyred saints, Scholastica, Ida, Catherine, Christine, penetrated by the cruel knowledge of divine love. This, she asserts, demanding intercourse, is the way she can be known. Hyacinthe is content to live through others' symbols and rituals. Damase is not content, but will play this game as well as any other.

Losing her virginity gives Hyacinthe an illusion of enlightenment, and considerable pleasure. Her first orgasm is 'a second that lasts almost an eternity' (p. 30), though waking up is disappointing. 'It's not much better than eating a peach' (p. 31).

Together they explore the whole range of sexual 'sins': 'We know sensation gives nothing; but let's enjoy that nothing. When it returns in imagination, it can seem everything. Let's admit our contradictions, so we can smile at ourselves when tragedy befalls' (p. 38).

To intensify sensation, he turns to sadism. He humiliates Hyacinthe with insults for her dullness, and takes her when she's racked by terror and tears. In the rhythms of de Gourmont's sentences, orgasm is a carefully calculated counterpoint of pleasure and pain:

> In a series of abrupt reversals she passed from suffering to pleasure. But even when lost in the music of sexual arousal, she could not forget the discord of those painful impressions; she was torn between the irrefutable violence of her immediate sensations and the fear that when ecstasy was past the monstrous vice of hate would squeeze her tight in its arms for ever.
>
> I bravely prolonged the experiment, measuring out carefully rests and movements, varying the rhythm to frustrate her expectations, and Hyacinthe, terrified by the contradictions torturing her fortunate flesh, suffered in delight, ready to die of love in a hellish paradise. At last her tears burst forth: and I drank them like pearls of precious blood (p. 68).

This is the point of no return from which they move into 'the mystical forest', or at least into 'mysticism as we understood it', subordinating the Christian mystique of sacrifice to the demands of their own desire. The Christian cult of purity is hardly appropriate here. In the chapter 'Les Licornes', Christ the unicorn flees from Hyacinthe in contempt which her lover clearly shares. But she is not only contemptible but gullible. Damase easily convinces her that repentance for lost virginity, like the Magdalene's, is even more laudable than virginity preserved.

In the next chapter, 'Les Figures', carnal love replaces divine love on the altar, and the Mass is reconstructed as a sensual communion. The whole apparatus, bells, trumpets, incense, and the entire hierarchy, clergy and laity, are invoked to reproduce the orgasmic moment. Ascetic ritual is reversed. The priest is young, blonde and handsome; the virgin nuns are released from the grilled choir; there are no more penitents; angels are young, fertile flesh. Only the Poor Man is retained, to stand eternally excluded on the threshold. Without the weeping scapegoat, the elect have no way of perceiving their good fortune. The egoist's mirror is the suffering of others.

Prayers to the Spirit rise in a Baudelairean blend of incense and roses. Gospel and Epistle declare that love between man and woman is the Kingdom of God, and that pleasure, not reproduction, is its purpose. The prayer of Oblation stresses that Incarnation, in blood, is the beginning of Redemption: 'The belly of Woman is a sacrificial altar and the first station of Calvary, the first dwelling chosen by the Host; an obscure oblation, the bloody prelude of Transfixion' (p. 85). The Antiphone declares that the union of the couple is the apotheosis of humanity. The darkness of earthly exile is transformed by rolling waves of light, colour, scent, summoned to calm the erotic blue-green terror of the sea. Abstract and concrete images merge in a passionate climax:

> The human waves swell up to the heavens, and hearts flutter in transfigured bodies like roses in the dawn wind, and eyes are turned into pure amethyst: bellies shivering with love slip away on shining white clouds and all things are raised up in an apotheosis of white (p. 87).

The counterpart of this dream of sensual transcendence is the pain of the Lamb crucified on earth. Imitating the divine scapegoat, the lovers introduce a ritual language of suffering into their caresses:

> She learnt that the caresses of the left hand are the first acts of suffering, proof that the sacrifice is accepted; and the caresses of the right cover the whole bloody manual of love: the kiss of thorns, the touch of lead-tipped thongs, the lovesome bite of nails, the carnal penetration of the lance, the spasms of death, the joys of putrefaction (p. 101).

This aestheticization of sexuality might have continued for ever, but

Hyacinthe demands too much reality. One evening, she arrives naked, demanding to be whipped with knotted cords. Damase is offended by the coarseness of total nudity, and has no wish to see her body spoiled by scars. He complies, until terrified by her avidity and her cruelty, far beyond anything, he says, that he might have dreamed:

> Under [her] half-hidden irises flickered gleams of madness, flames and flashes of a cruelty that her executioner did not share.
> She had been on her feet. Suddenly her arms fell about my neck and she dropped down, dragging me with her into an unforgettable gulf of voluptuous excess – and we stayed at the bottom for ever (p. 104).

In fact, what repels Damase is seeing his own dreams so precisely translated into reality. At last, Hyacinthe, recognizing for herself that she is nothing but his reflection, reflects back his repugnance. Once she stops offering her own sexual and spiritual desire to feed his dreams, she is of no more use. But the text absolves him of selfishness, as it did of cruelty. It is Woman who volunteers and then withdraws her favours. Hyacinthe herself asks to go back into the tapestry of his memories: '. . . back to the crowds of faceless women from which my love had drawn her – back to become the ghost that all women are' (p. 113).

De Gourmont's later work makes far less use of Christian imagery, especially the more esoteric forms of Christian symbolism to which Huysmans, for example, increasingly turns. Other older, or more popular, versions of the supernatural are more vivid. He moves away too from the paralysis of pure Schopenhauerian idealism. In his essay 'Dernière conséquence de l'idéalisme' (*Mercure de France*, March 1894), the ego is still the centre of its own world, but there is a new twist to its relationship with others which comes from the acknowledgement that Narcissus cannot know himself except in the mirror of others' self-knowledge. The difficulty is that those mirrors threaten Narcissus with unwanted images of their own.

There are three choices: to give up and die, to enslave others to one's will (as Nietzsche suggested, the 'slave-owner of Idealism'), or to negotiate. The individual should have confidence in his own powers of resistance:

> Thought by others, the ego acquires a new, stronger awareness of itself, multiplied according to its essential identity. Multiplying a rose gives a garden full of roses; multiplying a thistle gives a field full of thistles.

Where Huysmans makes a religious act of faith, de Gourmont makes a humanist one:

Mirrors can be good or bad – and mirrors only take in and reflect a way of being, not the being in itself. Being in itself is inviolable, but it has to undergo attempts at violation to know that it is so.

For all the brave words, the experiment of negotiating the world is full of terrors. The *Histoires magiques* (1894) are tales of mirrors mistaken. In these frightening little fantasies, individuals are caught in false images of desire, sometimes their own, sometimes those of others. In each one, sexuality is the main motive force. Indulged to excess, or repressed, it produces neurosis, madness and death.

The tales are magnifying mirrors, vivid dramas whose imaginative distortions evoke the precise configuration of each sexual trap. Like all good fantasy, they objectify unspeakable desires in a way that declares the fascination of the horrible and the perverted, at the same time as it suggests there should be something different. They cannot say what a liberating magic is. They can however reveal the identity of the black magician: all those institutions and individuals that are mediators of repressive, patriarchal authority – Church, mothers, husbands and lovers.

'Péhor' and 'Le Secret de Don Juan' are the two poles between which the tales move. These are the two distortions of what de Gourmont considers essential female and male character, by 'nature' respectively passive and active. In the first, female nature is deformed by repression and ignorance. In the second, sophisticated man is destroyed by Nietzschean egoism.

In 'Péhor', Douceline's mother leaves her to cope unwarned and uninformed with the onset of puberty; menstruation is an unexpected, terrifying trauma. The mystery of sexuality is mediated through the Bleeding Heart of Christ, the morbid form of displaced sensuality preached in the country church. Her first experience of intercourse is as rape. With no other outlet for her desire, she turns to obsessive masturbation. In her unenlightened, guilt-ridden imagination this is possession by the demon. Trapped in a circle of carnal fantasies and self-abuse she could – and would – never communicate, she becomes mentally and physically ill, and finally dies in anguish, vomiting blood.

In the name of liberation, de Gourmont takes sadistic revenge on the 'pure'. A salacious description of masturbation climaxes in a revoltingly anal death: 'A kiss stinking of excrement was precisely planted on her lips and the soul of Douceline left this world, swallowed by the entrails of the demon Péhor.' (For Douceline, the peasant's daughter, he at least has sympathy. A later essay, 'La jeune fille d'aujourd'hui' [1901; rpt. *Le Chemin de velours*], attacks the daughters of the middle classes whose venality makes them accomplices of parental repression, and whose hypocritical sensibilities are made the pretext for authoritarian censorship.)

Don Juan, on the other hand, is Narcissus. He sees in the women he meets only images of his own power, and attributes he can steal to enhance it. Given entirely to carnality and the pleasure of exploiting others, he has no soul, only the semblance of one, borrowed from one of his victims. Forced at last to look into the mirror of death, he sees his borrowed plumes fall away, leaving nothing at all: 'an empty ghost, a rich man with no money, a thief with no arms, a dismal human larva reduced to the truth, spelling out his secret!'

In contrast to much of de Gourmont's other fiction, women in these tales are more often victims of men than their destroyers. The sadist of 'Stratagèmes' locks his mistress into a virginity she does not want. He prefers the chase to consummation; he wants her to play Daphne to his Apollo and Galatea to his Pygmalion. He sets her on a pedestal and pretends to worship her. In fact, she is a slave. When she demands intercourse, he simply pours her tea.

In 'Les Fugitives' another sadist, devoted to an impossible longing to possess all the beautiful women in the world, gives form to his 'Neronian' dream by reciting to his terrorized mistress the litany of the women he desires: from the passers-by in the street (a huntress, a pale blonde, a green-eyed succubus, fur-clad creatures, women in light summer dresses) to Helen, Salome, Mary Magdalene, Ophelia. She can mirror them all, he says, because she is Nothing – vacuous, plain, stupid. He is a vampire: 'a magnificent drinker of souls!'

A dying wife ('L'Autre'), reduced to an empty, worm-eaten box, an abandoned shell, by a husband who has treated her solely as a sexual toy, dreams what she's become:

> . . . the obsessive, grotesque vision of a woman with her face veiled by a kerchief while a brutal hand lifted her dress. All night, the shame of it writhed behind her eyelids, and the sight filled her with an overwhelming disgust and an impotent anger that exhausted her, destroyed her fragile vitality.

In her dying moments, he brings to her bedside her sister, already his mistress, her own cruelly indicting mirror-image.

The perverted forms that modern society imposes on female desire can surprise, horrify or even kill the woman who tries to see herself reflected in the ideological mirror of passion. The heroine of 'Le Faune', shaped by a loveless husband and puritanical parents, puts together the fragments of the dream of sensuality they gave her. Tiny burning cherubic kisses fall in sparks down the chimney, as the creaturely warmth of her fur wrap domesticates her fear of the animal force of the erotic, and a first glimpse of the faun's shadow reassures her with its immaturity. The obscene truth of sexuality shatters her sentimental delusions. Instead of 'the agreeable and obedient reflections of a mirror identical to her dream', what she sees is a monstrous satyr, 'not shaped by desire but deformed by the most strict reality. He was so ugly, with his cruel goat's face – so ugly, bestial, drunk with such precise, base desire – that she sat up, furious.' The alternative to accepting the truth of the satyr is nothing. The tale avenges itself for her rejection of man's sexuality by abandoning her: 'She saw herself naked in the tall looking-glass at the back of the room, completely naked and completely alone in her gloomy bedroom.'

'Danaëtte', locked by her lover into the empty round of adultery, is entranced by the mirror-image of her own chill sterility – the falling snow that insidiously drifts into her room and into her body through a window she herself never opened. Hers is Madame Bovary's dream of being carried away to an ideal unknown, an abdication of selfhood which is both intense pleasure and death:

> The snow fell on and on, penetrating so deeply into her swooning body that she felt only the one, single sensation of dying buried under the wondrous snow kisses, embalmed in snow – of being carried off and away, in one final gust, to the land of eternal snow, the endless, fabulous mountains where sweet little adultresses, loved for ever and ever, swoon endlessly to the commanding caresses of perverse angels.

A juxtaposed pair of tales – 'Les Yeux d'eau' and 'Le Suaire' – both contain the same image of those aquamarine eyes beloved of the decadence, derived from Baudelaire's cat's eyes, where what the cat-lover sees is the image of himself. The tales use the image to present two different ways of exchanging reflections, which imply two very different modes of male and female relationships. In both, the same cluster of motifs – eyes, water, death and crime – is essentially ambiguous. Symbols are not there to be passively endured, but to be unlocked by individual choices.

In the first story, the hero, rowing down a river, is snared by a mysterious pair of eyes full of ruined elegance and beauty: 'half-green, half-purple, aquamarine melting to pale amethyst, cold, tempting eyes where countless lovers must have drowned, thinking they were falling into heaven!' Their owner rejects his advances. Her eyes are her only weapon against men's desire, and if she yields to emotion, she knows she will lose them. For her own safety, she defines her eyes as 'two fountains of hatred . . . the way to Hell'. The innkeeper tells the rejected suitor that she's mad, and has been ever since she was fished out, drowning, from the river. This woman, by a freak of chance, has survived the passion that initiated her into an identity, which is an identification with the egoism of the male. What she practises now is a distancing, Nietzschean cruelty. What she is now is not certain. Neither male nor female, she is a servant at the inn, but with the language and bearing of a lady. Her crazed egoism infects others with her madness and her hatred.

'Le Suaire' plays with the tantalizing possibility of a different kind of relationship, in which men and women might accept the risk of passion and transform the familiar images of antagonism and death into new life. This time, man and woman meet as equals, walking along the same beach. Hubert is attracted by Sarah's pale anemone eyes, her liquid tones, her mother-of-pearl teeth. But the water-imagery that this time attracts him is not that of the river, raging between the limits of its banks, but the sea. With all its contradictions and surprises, an emblem of power, freedom and fertility, the sea becomes a new dream of the eternal feminine, a far more complex mirror.

Hubert is torn by contradictory longings, for the maternal 'warm solitudes' of the lonely sands, and for the chilly risks of the open sea. Sarah offers both. He throws into the sea her warm swansdown cloak, the maternal illusion, and turns to Sarah as the new woman, with all her terrifying 'criminal' mystery. Both will accept the risk of passion; safety lies not in huddling in paralysis for warmth, but in accepting the challenge to action. Negative images are transformed into positives, symbols of death to symbols of life. The receding sea throws back Sarah's wet, salty cloak, and she picks it up. She can still be a mother, but of a different kind; she's 'reborn' to the 'death-rattle of the ebbtide'. From 'frail serpent with anemone eyes', treacherous and poisonous, she becomes a 'travelling swan', promising fidelity but also new horizons. Plucking her cloak from the waves, she flourishes it as a banner for the future.

But even in this most optimistic of de Gourmont's dreams, the conclusion is full of terrors. The ego that opens itself to the outside world, venturing to engage with the mystery of new forces, risks being over-whelmed. The power to choose and act no longer lies with men, but with women:

With an air of triumph, shaking her flaming hair in the wind, she threw herself at the wrecked, floating garment, wrung from it the streams of water, and threw it over her arm, saying innocently: 'It will be a shroud for whichever of us survives.'

Sarah's dress whipped in the wind.

The new woman of 'Le Suaire' appears again in the novel *Les Chevaux de Diomède* (1897), as a promise of change which – by man's fault – never comes to fruition. In the myth, which also inspired Gustave Moreau's painting, Diomedes was the king who fed his horses on the flesh of his enemies. He was overthrown by Hercules, and his body tossed to his own beasts. Tyranny is inevitably consumed by its dependants; all that the master can expect back from his slaves is the image he gives them to feed on.

The Diomède of the novel is not a simple tyrant. He is dissatisfied by the world he has inherited, with its paralysing division between flesh and spirit. His vision of a new life attracts Néobelle, who is his ideal on the brink of realization: 'a strong young woman, full of sap and intellectual vigour . . . she isn't stupid flesh, ready to enjoy animal pleasures and then withdraw, return to her pasture; there's intelligence and grace in her animal majesty; she has the gift of laughter' (pp. 35–6).

Diomède has grasped that to liberate instinct means to change the balance of power in society:

A new morality means a new world. The most moral creature is not he who humbly obeys the law, but he who makes his own law, according to his own nature and his own mind, and realizes himself according to that law, as far as his own strength and society's obstacles will allow him . . . Such a morality is loathed by States, who punish it, and historians, who are there to censure. Both are right. It destroys authority, because it is hard to understand what physical authority one soul can have over another (p. 60).

Diomède remains paralysed, and Néobelle with him, because he retreats into games and dilettante fantasy, afraid of the challenge Néobelle might represent. Like his friends, he is ruled by fear of what change in conventional roles might bring:

I'm afraid of this woman who's moved me, the woman I desire, the woman I love. I'm afraid of finding the only one, the real one . . . I want to play with life, go by in a dream; I don't want to believe; I don't want to love; I don't want to suffer; I don't want to be happy; I don't want to be taken in. I just watch, observe, judge, smile.

What about Pascase and Cyran? Why are they afraid? Pascase is afraid of the unknown, Cyran of the known. I'm afraid of having to kneel (pp. 34–5).

His fears are well-founded. Néobelle writes to him, deferentially, asking advice on how to realize a dream as vivid as his own, of a new intimacy between the sexes that would satisfy both mind and body:

I'd be a fat, velvety bumblebee, vanishing down into the depths of a foxglove bell, then pushing open the door and leaving powdered with gold . . . and afterwards I would be more beautiful, dazzling with the golden dust that adorns the palaces of the mind.

I dreamed this dream and let it go, and then took it into my head that it would be more seemly to take a lover. That's in line with the usual, decent conventions.

. . . perhaps the two roads are not altogether irreconcilably hostile. Perhaps they intersect here and there, in among the trees of the forest, like in the labyrinths drawn on the frontispieces of old books (pp. 67–8).

Like Diomède, she is reluctant to commit herself. He encourages this, answering her challenge with ironic evasions. He knows irony breeds illusion, but at least this is the illusion of his freedom, which Néobelle threatens:

Irony is the faceted eye of the dragonfly, transforming a bramble blossom into a lordly garden. Néobelle is a horizon. She stands there like a mountain; real, demanding calm, direct contemplation (p. 71).

Retreating into dilettante play, Diomède destroys both their dreams of change. Divorced from an ideal, the body is an object of contempt, and carnal love no longer the gold-dusted image of infinity, but ugly perversion:

Ah, Néo, contempt is a major part of love. Without contempt, most carnal encounters would be inexplicable. Man takes enormous pleasure in playing the animal, rolling in the litter of instinct, enclosing his ideal in the narrow limits of the sexual garden, turning it into a prison. He lifts his head to look his partner in the face only to read there the satisfaction of a fall . . . (p. 125).

Néobelle, driven back by Diomède's advice and evasions to the conventional alternatives of female passivity or male dominance, chooses a masculine role. She decides to lose her virginity to find out who she really is: 'I want to follow my own desires and not the order established by others' egos' (p. 178). All virginal mystery gone, she is left with nothing, and 'discovers' in herself the essential coldness which she has been taught is the prerequisite of power: 'Néo is the marble statue I thought she was, and I'm glad of it . . . Now I know myself, I can easily rule the passions aroused by my futile beauty' (p. 183).

Diomède acknowledges himself defeated by the sadistic monster of his own creation. In the wake of her emancipation, all his other mistresses vanish, dying, or leaving him for other lovers: 'Diomède's horse, I pray your bites aren't poisoned! The old team is dissolved. One horse has broken the leading rein' (p. 187).

Les Chevaux de Diomède was chosen for translation and serialization by Ezra Pound and Richard Aldington in the *New Freewoman*, in twelve episodes, between 1 September 1913 and 2 March 1914. The defeat of Néobelle by the Artist is a narrative with striking analogies to the neat marginalization by Pound and Aldington of the women running the English magazine, whose title was changed to the *Egoist* part-way through the run of de Gourmont's text, since: 'The present title of the paper causes it to be confounded with organs devoted solely to the advocacy of an unimportant reform in an obsolete political institution' (15 December 1913). Like Néobelle, the women dug their own graves by their uncritical adoption of the ideas of authoritative, radical-sounding men. Under both its titles, the magazine was sub-titled *An Individualist Review*. Its authors insisted that they were Individuals, Egoists, Aristocrats, devoted to a sense of Selfhood, rather than any part of something collective, be it men, women, or any political category. They were not, they said in their second issue, political, but they knew that at any public meeting they could expect the Tory to speak most clearly and straightforwardly, and they saw socialism and democracy as threats to enslave the Individual. They noted with horror the developing connection between the Woman Movement and the Labour leader George Lansbury, well-intentioned, but a victim of 'cultural brain-rot' (15 July 1913).

Like Néobelle, they too had thought confusedly that there must be new options. Hoping to stay 'flexible', to appear with 'a different air in each issue' (No. 11, 15 November 1913), they reviewed a wide-ranging set of alternative female images. The first issue attacked Mrs Pankhurst and the Woman Movement, at the same time as it presented the mysticism of Mrs Blavatsky and Mrs Eddy as a promising way forward. An anthropologist offered evidence that Woman's true role was that of Mother, while another contributor enthusiastically advocated free love. Later, there was lengthy debate and correspondence on the Individual's right to choose to prostitute herself. These were at least attempts to be something different. When the magazine's title changed, woman was pushed back into being a figment of male fantasy. In the fifth issue of the *Egoist* (2 March 1914) appeared drawings from André Rouveyre's *Le Gynécée*, for which de Gourmont had written the text, 'morbid' caricatures of the animal nature in woman, almost all showing woman in her erotic moods and, as the female reviewer gloomily pointed out, slave to her own passions when not dominated by those of men. The sixth issue included a review by Aldington of de Gourmont's *Le Latin mystique*, a reassertion of the most traditional values.

In 1898, de Gourmont published *D'un pays lointain*, a collection of fantastic tales bloodier and blacker than the *Histoires magiques*. The distant lands in question are those of the origins of European civilization: pagan, early Christian, mediaeval and Renaissance. In their myths, legends and folktale, de Gourmont obsessively re-creates his vision of an essential law 'by which all that changes changes in form, not in essence'. Diana of Ephesus becomes Mary, Christian churches rise on the ruins of pagan temples, but the cult of the unattainable remains the same ('La Métamorphose de Diane'). In 'La Ville des Sphinx', the hero who rides the riddling Sphinx all around the world, pursuing the delusive image of desire on the horizon, can only return to the high-walled town he started from.

Out of pity, the Sphinx destroys him. The mood of these stories is deeply pessimistic. If life is only the pursuit of changing metaphors, it is not worth living. As the prologue seems to say, the ideal must be found in sensuous experience, but of a new kind.

The distant settings generate images more vivid that those of modern life. Humanity is heroic and aristocratic, in the robes of kings and queens of a lost past. At the same time, before the centuries of rationalism, these dream figures have more primitive and more animal colours and contrasts. Watching the melodramatic conflicts of body and spirit which they re-enact, the temptation is to believe that these dead systems might have some value; the old lies were deadly, but they had a certain vigour. 'Régelinde', the Barbarian princess, put out her own eyes to resist the seductions of nature and the flesh, believing that 'salvation comes from acting in negation of natural laws'. Those Barbarian Christians, de Gourmont points out, who destroyed the simple pagan beliefs of Rome, regenerated Europe with their errors.

But to divide body and spirit has its dangers. Women placed on pedestals as virgin goddesses and queens turn in vicious resentment on the men who ask them to step down into ordinary, human carnality, imposing a simple alternative: princess or prostitute. 'La Révolte du plèbe' describes the futile efforts of the humane nobleman, Sansovino, who forbids the annual ritual slaughter of virgins, only to find both populace and victims rise in revolt. The queen at her loom is weaving a silken serpent that suddenly turns from the frame to bite the melancholy king ('Mains de reine'). Phénice ('Visages de femmes') complains of the men whose crude carnality has reduced her to their image: 'I'm "Woman"; obviously, because I'm "a woman"; I have that "certain mystery", and that's why so many suitors hang on my lips. And know this: what I despise in myself is the animality of men which has made me what I am – an animal.' 'La Dame pensive' drowns herself with her fisherman lover, who has 'stolen' her identity by raping her as she lay entranced in her virginal dreams.

It is this vision of just retribution that turns man's dream of woman into nightmare, from which only art can save him. Claude and Anna (*Le Songe d'une femme*, 1899) are only seen dimly, in the mirror of an enigmatic and allusive correspondence that gives occasional glimpses of depths never recognized by their lovers. They depend on men for their realization in the world. Paul chooses the conventional symbol by which each is to be known. He paints Claude as Leda, ravished by an ideal of purity, and sees Anna as the Giaconda, the mystery of sensuality: 'woman with no soul, or a cluster of tiny fleshly souls; every pore of her skin, every downy hair, has its own sensual life' (p. 144). Both names are only half-truths. Claude longs for sexual experience, while Anna is an ambitious, thoughtful writer.

By his own confession, Paul is the decadent type, greedy and grasping, eager to remake the whole world in his image, and committed to what he admits is a destructive, if convenient, separation of spirit and flesh. Torn between the desire to possess all women and the pursuit of the One Ideal, he resolves the conflict without difficulty. He is his own Ideal, and women are to serve him:

The One, in fact, is me; my property is to attract all flesh to mine, and to live happily among the cries of love that rise in chorus from all those anxious hearts devoted to my satisfaction . . . I'm afraid, Bazan, that what I'm telling you are things I've read in decadent literature. I'm awfully much a man of my time . . . I'm not taken in by female beauty, nor the traps of the unconscious. Women are beautiful because we desire them. There's no more Absolute in the female than in the male (pp. 179–80).

Paul's dream of Woman produces the unconscious terror, violence and guilt beneath his confident assertion. The female, whom he has reduced to a lump of flesh to be broken and remoulded at will, returns to mock and humiliate him as a monstrous, vengeful, jumble of bits and pieces. In a sequence of metamorphoses reminiscent of Redon and Huysmans, swelling, maternal forms and colours are transformed into bloody, raw meat or sterile, prickly plants. The slave is a cruel responsibility. Deprived by man's decree of intellect and spirit, woman must find them in him. If man decides he is her God, she necessarily becomes octopus, leech and sucker, draining his life and strength:

I'm still thinking of [Anna] long after I've locked the door and hidden the hellish key in my case. So I fall asleep in a harem, for each of her charms lives and blooms in my troubled dreams.

A plump, saffron-coloured Indian girl, dressed only below the navel, leads me solemnly into a great conservatory filled with blue-green light, saying: 'Don't go to sleep, the flowers are about to open.' I go in, and there's the miracle. In front of me, huge, throbbing white mushrooms. The top of their caps is the shape of a pink shell, like a nostril, swelling and sinking, and the whole mushroom, along with it, starts beating like a wing. The whole thing moves, spins, turns into a ballerina's skirt, and from the skirt springs a woman in a pink tunic, then the tunic tears and falls away like the skin of a ripe fig, and the woman stands naked and motionless, an offering. Her two tiny breasts stiffen and quiver; turn into balloons; smother the naked, proffered woman; settle on to their short stalk; two huge white mushrooms topped with a pink shell, like Chinese parasols.

Everything starts again, proliferates, but I'm watching other trans-formations . . . Another plant looks like an orchid. It's hideous, the colour of raw meat. It opens up like a casket; gapes like a red apple ravaged by finches; then suddenly twists and tears, and its lips hang like pink ears; the ears drape round a female form and there again, rising up on her sweet, insolent stem, is a woman, waiting, dreaming, remem-bering. I turn away so as not to see the pretty, chaste, delicate woman turn back into the flower the colour of raw meat, gaping with shameless stupidity.

Further on is a host of cactuses, stalks that are legs cut off at the knee or below the belly like truncated columns; crawling bellies covered with tufts of hair, tree-trunks, where I sense traces of quivering human life; shaven heads, with no organs, completely round, half pink, half white, like sucking-pigs. There is something devilish here. I'm not afraid now,

I'm ashamed, and I aim a kick at one crawling belly that looks like a sack of flour. The belly jumps up on to the truncated columns. Arms and a bust spring suddenly on to its damp flesh. The arms select a head, eyes, mouth, pluck one of the meat-coloured flowers, and the monster minces towards me to deliver an address.

'Don't you recognize me, my love? We're all those separate parts you so love, that you've just been worshipping. Put together somewhat hastily, I confess, we're the beauty you enjoyed last night; every part of her, every one of the chapels where you knelt with such fervour. Does the order of our design matter so much? Would you like legs instead of arms, arms in place of legs? There you are – look . . . Do you want my head down to my belly, my belly in place of my head? There you are – look. See, I express myself very well, even though I've no teeth. Am I any less lovely? . . . You love me, don't you? Give me your lips, my love. Give me your soul. Drink in my life and my thought from the mouth I yield to you. Come, take me, hold me in your arms. Oh, how I love you! Only the most beautiful women know how to love. I'm most beautiful, and I love you. Where's the little mirror? Thank you. Oh, I think I've found my final form. Come, all of you, to life!'

And without letting go of my limbs, where she twined like an octopus, the monster waved for resurrection, and the creatures rose up, their suckers pressing forward, to take my life . . . I screamed and woke up. Bazan, do you think the dream means something? Anyhow, the only thing it's affected is my nerves. I've slept badly, but I haven't repented (pp. 145–50).

Paul copes with the nightmare by clinging to his familiar symbols ('I'm getting used to the Giaconda'), by aestheticizing and eroticizing the threat of rebellion, and by crude, egoistic violence. 'I'm getting used to the Giaconda, until the day I finally get sick of her. On that day, I'll be completely heartless, because I'm very selfish.' And selfishly he drops his mistress, Anna, for a better, richer match.

Like Villiers and Huysmans, de Gourmont finds that science, as well as art, can be used to turn dream into reality. His treatise *Physique de l'amour. Essai sur l'instinct sexuel* (1903), with its long would-be scientific incursions into the sexual habits of butterflies and toads, might seem at first sight the antithesis of his creative fiction, in both argument and style. According to Ezra Pound, it spoke out for the essential animality of human love, in contrast with *Le Latin mystique*, which presented the traditional Christian attack on carnality. Between these two poles, he thought, de Gourmont's philosophy of love oscillated. In fact, though the language of the two works is different, their content is the same. Subordination to man's desire is the law of the universe. There is pleasure to be found in disorder, as long as it is contained. Cruelty, violence and murder are Nature's way of pointing to the limits; but man is the artist who finally draws the lines.

In one sense, this text is liberating, in its claim that sexuality is amoral and that the private life should be freed from the censor. It was tremendously successful in France and Europe for these reasons – and for the same reasons, took some time to reach English translation. Arthur Ransome bitterly remarked in the *Fortnightly Review*, June 1912, that: 'This book is in its eighth edition in France, and has been published in all European languages except our own.' In another sense, it is both conventional and oppressive. The defence of the animal and therefore free nature of desire goes with the assertion that sexual practices based on domination and subordination are Nature's norm, and it is woman who takes the subordinate place. The text confronts directly the contemporary challenge for women's equality. Science supports the lyrical prejudices of the fictions, and the whole is held together with a stiff dose of threat.

De Gourmont rejects Darwin's evolutionary hierarchy. All that distinguishes man from the other members of the animal and insect kingdoms is the rich variety of ways in which he satisfies the sexual drive. In the first chapter, man is 'an animal of extreme complexity' and 'Love is deeply animal; therein lies its beauty.' The animal function of maintaining life is primary, and everything that furthers this is legitimate.

He reverts to this theme in Chapter 9, 'Le Mécanisme de l'amour', reviewing Nature's varied methods of intercourse to argue for the indulgence of so-called 'perverse' sexual desires. The manners of the praying mantis put de Sade into the shade. Nature in her courses gives support to Baudelaire, who ridiculed the notion that 'decency' and love could ever be bedfellows. Sodomy and onanism are common habits, as the casuists' as well as the naturalists' studies show: 'Practices common to an entire ethnic group cannot be called anything but normal and it is of little importance whether they have been stigmatized by the apologists of sound morality. What is good is what is and what is includes what will be.' De Gourmont is not willing to go to the stake for sadism, and would rather seem confused than criminal. So he also says that cruelty is as much an aberration as chastity, and an equal threat to the proper development of the intelligence, 'depriving the sensibility of one of its healthiest and most stimulating sources of nourishment'. But he is impressed by the blend of pleasure and pain (not really, he says, pain at all) in the sexual act: 'The pain that accompanies the sexual act must be carefully distinguished from passive suffering. It is very possible (as women could testify) that the sighs or even cries uttered at such moments are the expression of a mixed sensation where pleasure has almost as much part as pain.'

What cannot be mixed are the traditional gender roles. Nature provides evidence of fundamental and unchangeable differences between male and female. Women are usually smaller, weaker and fatter than men. Their skin is more delicate and their hair longer, their brains smaller and their intelligence more practical and less spontaneous. In compensation, they are more beautiful. Their lines are more harmonious, because their genitals are not visible.

In his chapter 'Le Dimorphisme sexuel', de Gourmont concedes that civilization has accentuated morphological and psychological differences, but argues that they must be presumed to have been there in Nature. Changes of activity can produce physical change, he thinks, but not intellectual changes. On this dubious basis, he presents the sexual division of labour in present society. Man protects and woman breeds. The couple is the keystone of biological and social order. Equality of education, reducing differences, makes it unstable: 'and from that', he warns darkly, 'come adultery, divorces and rampant prostitution' (p. 38). Exchanging the roles of breeder and protector is neither useful nor possible. His science moves into mysticism, as he argues that each creature has a duty to retain its own form.

In a chapter which brings together 'Le Dimorphisme sexuel et le féminisme', de Gourmont returns to a statement made earlier in his text, that the primary human form was female, and the penis a supplementary development. 'The male is an accident; the female would have been enough.' In modern society, the male has centred upon himself the non-sexual activities, 'disinterested works'. As far as civilized development goes, these are the most important; but in terms of mere survival of the species, the unwelcome evidence from Nature is that the species could manage quite well with the female alone. In excited tones, blending irony and threat, de Gourmont suggests to the feminist enemy that parthenogenesis and its concomitant, the absolute reign of the female and the end of the male, would be more natural and more logical than any equality of rights ('social promiscuity'):

> The idea of feminism leads to these chimeras. But if what women want is to destroy the couple, not reform it; if what they want is to establish a vast social promiscuity, and if feminism can be summed up in one formula: free women and free love – then feminism is a greater chimera

than all the others, which at least have an analogue somewhere in the diversity of animal behaviour. Yes, human parthenogenesis is less absurd. It represents an order, whereas promiscuity is a disorder. But social promiscuity is also impossible for this simple reason, that woman is weaker and would be crushed. She can only struggle against man thanks to the privileges man concedes her when he's disturbed by sexual intoxication, lulled into ecstasy by the vapours of desire. The factitious equality she claims would restore her former slavery the day that too many, or all, women took the notion to enjoy it . . .

From the viewpoint of natural logic, it is very difficult to sympathize with moderate feminism. It would be preferable to accept feminism to excess. Because where there are numerous examples of feminism in Nature, there are very few of sexual equality.

Frenzy is always very close to the surface of this text. The devices which in fiction divert attention from the weight of the chains to their exquisite workmanship, or modulate shrill resentments into the plaint of the child betrayed do not exist in the scientific mode. Personal prejudice sticks out in all its ugliness, distorting the harmonious lines of the argument. The threat to crush women is paralleled by the desire to make subordinates of the whole black race, suddenly introduced in an unexpected aside to a discussion on the behaviour of ants, in the chapter 'L'Amour chez les animaux sociaux'. De Gourmont justifies slavery in Nietzschean terms. The white race in giving up this 'advantage' was perpetrating an act of irresponsible sentimentality, 'betraying its destiny, renouncing, under Christian inspiration, the complete and logical development of its civilization'. Octave Mirbeau's analysis of decadent egoism, by which the politics of murder is made to seem the natural way of life, could have been modelled on de Gourmont alone.

Alan Durant, a recent commentator on Ezra Pound (*Ezra Pound: Identity in Crisis*, 1981), has pointed out that most Poundian critics pass over in silence his translation of and comments on this text, while happily charting his debt to de Gourmont's work for his theory of the image, internationalism, individualism, and the importance of originality and the cultural tradition. Pound was particularly interested by the Frenchman's linking of sexual and intellectual development, adding a lengthy postscript to de Gourmont's hypothesis of 'a certain correlation between total, deep copulation and cerebral development' (Pound trans., p. 169).

For Durant, the underlying pattern in Pound's poetry and politics is concern to defend his own ego, asserting his own authority by ordering and dominating what he sees as the chaos around him. As with de

Gourmont, this appears most forcefully in the imagery of the male–female relationship. Man is the inventor, the thinker, his brain 'a sort of great clot of genital fluid held in suspense or reserve' (ibid., p. 169), and his sperm is 'the form-creator'. The female reflects and supports him: 'Woman, the conservator, the inheritor of past gestures, clever, practical, as Gourmont says, not inventive, always the best disciple of any inventor' (ibid., p. 179). (In the essay 'Les Femmes et le langage' in *Le Chemin de Velours*, de Gourmont described women as transmitters of male language, culture and 'the whole of society's strategies', but never creative users.) The artist is 'the phallus or spermatozoid charging, head-on, the female chaos' (Pound trans., p. 170). Durant's analysis of the *Cantos* shows its recurring imagery: the emissions of the penis invest the female, the earth and the reader with knowledge, law and light, while the female constantly figures chaos, not an intellectual but a biological process, permanently subordinate.

The only difference between the processes of the *Cantos* and those of de Gourmont's writer-heroes, from des Entragues to Paul, is one of confidence. The order that Pound took for granted, locked in the madness of ideology, is one that de Gourmont saw as problematic, requiring violence to maintain it. The nineties' decadent is aware of the resistances offered by others to his dreams of domination. His more extreme inheritors firmly close their eyes to everything but their dream.

The frank attack on feminism in *Physique de l'amour* seems to dispose of de Gourmont's hostility. The women whose images embellish the rest of his fictions, from *Une nuit au Luxembourg* (1906) onwards, are no longer vengeful rebels but consoling angels – the gentle fantasies of an ageing poet. In his preface to his translation, *A Night in the Luxembourg* (1912), Arthur Ransome, praising the novel's 'crystalline Epicureanism', described it as the new *Mademoiselle de Maupin*. This is rather unfair to Gautier's clear-edged account of sexual ambiguity and sexual desire. De Gourmont's tale is mere self-indulgence, a mystical hotch-potch of sensual metaphysics and dying gods.

James-Sandy Rose is found dead in his rooms in Paris. On the floor is the dress of a mysterious woman, who was seen entering his rooms but not leaving. The answer to the puzzle is found in his diary, which tells of a miraculous confrontation in the Luxembourg gardens with a 'Christ', accompanied by three women, who is also 'Apollo', son of God, but not immortal, former tutor of Epicurus and friend of Spinoza – the one a hedonist, the other an ascetic, but both materialists, philosophers and truly happy men. Epicurus shared his wife with the god, and Spinoza his glass of milk: 'We drank milk while discovering the identity of reality and perfection' (p. 166).

The god explains the mistake mortals have made with women – teaching them a sense of sin, and teaching them to think – and the mistake made with life, desiring happiness rather than reaching out to seize it in the momentary pleasures of the senses.

The gods know 'the uselessness of all that is not pure sensation, and our chief business is the cultivation of our senses . . . We give ourselves over with divine ingenuity to all possible pleasures' (pp. 127–8). All that stops Rose from enjoying the same delights is his Christian education. When he listens to the voice of conscience, to qualms of guilt and sin, the magic spring light that has filled the gardens is veiled by winter night again, and the women changed into whores. Christ explains the creative power of the imagination:

Women are part of metaphysics . . . creatures of sensibility, intelligence and faith; all depends on the moment and the man. Between the goddess and the wench in the public harem, the difference lies in the idea of sin. Sinner, you see courtesans where I, a god, see goddesses. The world is what you make it; you create without knowing (p. 179).

With Elise in the lilac grove, James-Sandy experiences the perfect fulfilment that evaded des Entragues, Damase, Diomède:

Her gown, a mere tunic, slipped slowly down, disclosing one by one the charms of my goddess, who to me seemed Beauty itself. She was so beautiful that for a moment my admiration was stronger than my desire. But the sight of her pure belly, mother-of-pearl conch, flowered with gold, cast me to my knees in a sacred frenzy, and mad kisses parted the chalice of the flower that was soon in full bloom and soon deep breathed in. We were both happy at the same moment. My ecstasy carried me to the top of such a high mountain that I was dizzy and my head spun. When I came to myself, dying in the arms of my dying love, I felt as though I had put on a new dignity and that the resurrection that had snatched me from a delightful death was raising me into a more precious life.

My love, dressed in her gown, her flowery hat on her freshly fastened hair, was picking branches of lilac. I stood up to help her; her white arms were already full of an enormous sheath. She gave it to me, then picked a harvest of lilies and roses and we went back to my master (pp. 123–5).

All the images are of submission, to a 'master', a 'goddess', to the heady power of the senses. The submission is to a Beauty of James-Sandy's own choosing, though not of his own invention. From a synthesis of religious and philosophical dream and romantic cliché, the text puts together the image of a self desperate to be deceived by the tissue of old lies.

Elise left the magic garden with him for his room, where he was found dead three days later. The fantasy enters the real world, like so much of decadent experience, through the mediation of the doctor who diagnoses death by 'sexual, followed by cerebral, excess' (p. 202); as he says, a 'very natural' way of dying.

Where contemporaries like Huysmans or heirs such as Pound end in melodrama and madness, de Gourmont's creative genius finally fritters away into slight deceptions and quiet resignation to the dying of the light. The decadent mellows into a mildly salacious old man. In the *Lettres d'un satyre* (1913), the satyr-hero counts his blessings. The creature of instinct, hounded into hiding by Christianity, released by the Renaissance, saved from oblivion by sensuous young women or adventurous artists, is finally civilized by the prostitute Cydalise. Once she teaches him to write, love becomes language. He loses in spontaneity, but, he consoles himself, gains in self-perception. This is the decadent manner: to trade for the images of selfhood the proper sense of self.

The benefits of soft, civilized life must be paid for by the repression of raw instinct. He no longer chats to little girls in the park. He takes his loves light and easy, ridiculing the modern fashion for 'the pleasure of suffering and the delights of abjection' (p. 140). He is frivolous; but in return, he is free and happy.

Writing his *Lettres à l'Amazone* (1914), to Nathalie Barney, he returns to his idea that personality involves a free and equal exchange of vision between men and women: 'Perhaps renewal of oneself by the lover is the psychic basis of love . . . the interplay can't be disentangled; we are at one and the same time Pygmalion to a statue and statue to Pygmalion' (pp. 133–4). He admits his still lingering suspicion that 'in love, perhaps one only loves oneself', but generously transfers the enjoyment of selfhood to the daughter-figure, who is the new woman:

At least let that strengthen you in your wonderful Amazon egoism, which is the foundation of all goodness and sensitivity. To be good, you must first be very selfish; and you must be selfish to be sensitive (p. 139).

3
The Spell of the Androgyne:
Joséphin Péladan 1859–1916

Max Nordau, that expert on degeneracy, rather liked Joséphin Péladan. He was 'intellectually the most eminent' of the occultists, and 'to be taken in good faith' (*Degeneration*, p. 219). Though exactly why Nordau should think so is not clear from his book, which is a check-list of what in Péladan's life and work he found most offensive.

Nordau's chief target was the flamboyant theatricality of the self-styled 'Magus' and 'Sar', who had declared himself the heir of the Knights Templar, the Rosicrucians, the Magi, Zoroaster, Pythagoras and Orpheus:

He dresses himself archaically in a satin doublet of blue or black; he trims his extremely luxuriant blue-black hair and beard into the shape in use among the Assyrians . . . in the corner of his letter-paper is delineated, as a distinctive mark of his dignity, the Assyrian king's cap, with the three serpentine rolls opening in front. As a coat of arms he has the device of his order: on an escutcheon divided by sable and argent a golden chalice surmounted by a crimson rose with two outspread wings, and overlaid with a Latin cross in sable. The shield is surmounted by a coronet with three pentagrams as indents . . . He possesses a special costume as Grand-Master and Sar (in which his life-sized portrait has been painted by Alexandre Séon), and a composer, who belongs to that order, has composed for him a special fanfare, which on solemn occasions is to be played by trumpets at his entrance (pp. 219–20).

In the second place, he attacked the three basic themes of Péladan's work: Wagner's music, which Nordau particularly disliked, the cult of the androgyne and the renunciation of sexuality, and the possession and operation of occult powers. Every one of his unusual 'romances' seemed to Nordau to follow the same pattern:

> . . . a hero appears who unites in himself the distinctive marks of both sexes, and resists with horror the ordinary sexual instincts, who plays or enjoys the music of Wagner, enacts in his own life some scene from the Wagnerian drama, and conjures up spirits or has to repel their attacks (p. 222).

Finally, the German writer attacked Péladan's mysticism, a hotch-potch of ideas brought together, in his view, on the flimsiest of connections. He saw, not unreasonably, a link between the confusion of Péladan's thought and the dramatic conflicts between reason and instinct that were evoked in his writing with considerable frankness:

> He has the peculiar sexual emotionalism of the 'higher degenerates', and this endows him with a peculiar fabulous shape, which, at once chaste and lascivious, embodies, in curiously demonstrative manner, the secret conflicts which take place in his consciousness between unhealthily intensified instincts and the judgement which recognizes their dangerous character (p. 223).

The fact that Nordau contined to admire Péladan's work is a testimony to the repressive part played in it by the Magus' strictures on the 'dangerous character' of the instincts. In Péladan, the contradictory desire of the decadence for both power and powerlessness, to be both rebel and slave, takes its clearest form. Under the mystical mumbo-jumbo and Romantic posturing of his 'individualism' lies a fierce authoritarianism, founded on the longing to subject and, most of all, to be subjected. The French Magus and the German Philistine have much in common, and not least, the belief that the function of art is primarily a social one: that of reconciling individuals to a subordinate place in an established hierarchy. For both, individualism is an ideal that cloaks a rigorous and repressive self-censorship.

Sleight-of-hand, deception and ambiguity are the characteristics of Péladan's work. Music and magic – stylistic and intellectual trickery – are his tools, and his ideal is the androgyne, that double and duplicitous symbol in which opposites can be reconciled and weaknesses, personal and political, rewritten as strengths. His whole life and work are devoted to the elaboration of a conjuring trick to flatter himself and his followers with an illusion of power. A simple illustration of his technique is the celebrated confrontation between the artist-magician Nébo and his neophyte, princess Paule, in *A Coeur perdu* (1888), the third volume of Péladan's fourteen-volume epic cycle, *La Décadence latine*. Quoting the highly erotic sequence in *The Romantic Agony* (pp. 337 ff.), Mario Praz presents the androgyne Paule as the dominant partner, a strong-willed masculine figure, a second Mademoiselle de Maupin, who seduces Nébo against his will, and ironically mocks his failure to perform. The sequence is certainly constructed to demonstrate Nébo-Péladan's impotence, but the pleasure it evokes is not only that of being dominated but also of domination. Nébo and Paule are both figures of Péladan and his double desire to be both active and passive – the artist who sets up the ritual and the woman who ridicules, as well as the impotent male and the woman enslaved.

Paule is Nébo's puppet, and her power is circumscribed by her master's elaborate rituals (in this instance, 'Le Rituel d'Amour', which occupies the entire third part of the book). At his invitation, she enters a room with carefully placed lights and carefully chosen perfumes, its walls painted with phallic symbols, and puts on the exotic jewelled costume Nébo has selected for her. In Nébo's own good time she is drawn on to a throne to play the part of Istar-Aphrodite, under his direction. The priest worships only an idol of his own creation, which remains under his control. He makes her take up the hieratic pose of Moreau's Salome, in which he watches her enjoy the sensuous contrasts of her own smooth flesh and the jewels' hardness. Like Salome before Herod, she is fixed and fascinated by the image of her beauty that her observer dictates. When he throws her on to the bed of roses, lilies, daphne and myrtle which symbolizes the ambivalence of sexuality, his intention is not to penetrate her but to make her understand the power of the male symbolized by the sexual act. Making Paule wait demonstrates his ascetic self-control and her dependence. For Nébo, performing the sexual act matters far less than creating a context in which woman is disarmed by the delusion that she holds all the weapons. She has only those weapons his fantasy attributes to her.

In their first embrace, it is uncertain who yields. Paule takes the initiative; but the centre of the text is a scream without an author, in a chaotic darkness of undefined torments with no named torturer or victim. At the end, however, one clear statement emerges. The female is generically the possessed, and the male, even when choosing a submissive, feminized role, is always the phallic possessor:

> Her arms surrounded him, and with a kind of hysterical strength she lifted him off the ground and pulled him on top of her, embracing him as though she were the male, raping her victim . . . Was there a smothered scream? It was almost inaudible; the flames on the tripods had almost gone out. Ah, the ecstasy of opposites; in boudoirs and torture chambers there sizzles the same carnal emanation, floats the same scent of excited skin; the machinery and the emanations of lust are unbelievably akin to the machinery and exhalations of torture. Are we perhaps the dupes of traditional categories, conditioned by our predecessors to divide our sensations into pleasure and pain, as though the saint possessed by Antinoüs would not feel more anguish than if she were impaled by a reddened lance? (pp. 301–2).

The text shows all the traits that, according to Deleuze, typify masochistic fantasy. The relationship is based on a pact, not rape, and fetishistic displacement (lingering over jewels, flowers, Paule's breasts) is substituted for explicit and obscene accounts of the sexual act. The dynamic violence of sadism is replaced by the suspension of reality; the fantasy is frozen for passive and contemplative enjoyment. But here, as always in Péladan's novel cycle, the pleasures of masochistic surrender are doubled by the assertion of power, and the narrative argues that to kneel in worship is the way to possess.

The confrontation of Nébo and the princess throws into relief that triple constellation of sexuality, art and religion which is the particular characteristic of Péladan's work. On the one hand, he declares himself victim of his own urgent sexual desire (on which, he said, he built the whole of La Décadence latine). On the other, as Artist and Magus, he claims to know the techniques that can control that desire and give it any physical form he may choose. His work – and his life – reiterate the bankruptcy of the claim but continue to re-enact the obsession. In Péladan's prose, Baudelaire's evocation of the lover transfixed by the vision of naked, bejewelled female beauty is no longer presented as private fantasy but as the stuff of which real life is made. The perfect androgyne, Tammuz, whose mission is to rescue Paris from decadence, is assured by his mentor that ' "Les Bijoux" belong to normal sex' (La Gynandre, 1891, p. 40). The aim of Péladan's art is to recuperate the pleasures of masochism, turning the masochist into a new, heroic model.

What distinguishes Péladan from Baudelaire is the novelist's desire to have society's sanction for his dreams. More accurately: Péladan's intention was to rewrite the society of his time into the form of those dreams, making no distinction between his private fantasy and public reality. Of all the actors on the decadent stage, Péladan alone seems to have been taken in by his own theatre, confusing history and his own fictions. The initiates in his novels rub shoulders with historical personalities; or they step outside the narrative to inscribe their names alongside those of real-life contemporaries on the membership list of the Rosicrucian society of artists, with which Péladan planned to challenge the atheistic and democratic Barbarians of the Third Republic. The novel cycle itself was intended to function as a pattern for others aspiring to the status of Magus, who would form the nucleus of this warrior-guild. Bizarre as the enterprise may now appear, it won adherents: Péladan's private and political fantasies were shared by a not inconsiderable collection of artists, mystics and dreamers of the Right.

Péladan was born into a tradition of redeeming political failure with fantasy. He was an ardent disciple of his father Adrien, who for much of the century had devoted his talents as a journalist and polemicist to the cause of traditionalist Catholicism and militant monarchism, in their long retreat before anti-clericalism and democracy. Joséphin had considerable difficulty with the repressive morality of his father's Catholicism, but found its emphasis on authority and hierarchy entirely acceptable. One of the principal sources of his masochism is his relationship to the Catholic Church, another version of the decadent mother who nurtures, cradles and stifles, offering a sense of place and self in exchange for self-denial.

In the 1840s and 1850s, in Nîmes and Lyon, Adrien Péladan had been instrumental in drawing numbers of intellectuals and creative artists into the traditionalist and ultramontane camp. Like his son in the eighties he offered a more interesting alternative to the timid and narrow-minded Gallican Church that had frightened away the liveliest minds of his generation. He found a fresh audience in the early seventies, when the aftermath of the Franco-Prussian War produced, briefly, a monarchist majority in the Assembly and a revival of Catholic hopes of political power. The Basilica of the Sacré-Coeur was founded, as an act of atonement for the national apostasy (and the Commune) to which the Right attributed France's humiliation by Prussia. Pilgrimages of reparation were organized, penitential devotion to the Sacred Hearts of Jesus and Mary flourished, and a spate of prophecies promised the reign of the Holy Spirit on earth, if only the nation would repent its republicanism. Adrien was responsible for some of the best-selling pamphlets (approved by the Pope) on the supernatural apparitions and apocalyptic prophecies (*Le Dernier Mot des prophécies*, 1878–80; *Le Secret de La Salette*, 1889). The madness that swept France was short-lived; but even so, the popularity of Adrien's elucubrations makes it easier to understand the ease with which Joséphin assumed the national imagination could be captured.

In the tenth volume in his cycle, *Le Dernier Bourbon* (1895), the Sar describes the cession to himself of his father's prophetic mission. The novel is set in 1879, the year in which Jules Ferry banned unauthorized teaching orders (effectively, the Jesuits) from France, depriving the Church of its most effective means of disseminating its doctrine. Faced with this direct attack, the Catholic hierarchy crumbled. Péladan wrote his description of the débâcle in 1895, provoked by what he saw as a second and final betrayal – the Pope's appeal to Catholics to settle their differences with the Republic. He sets out with desperate clarity the political failure of the Catholic Right, which for him was at the origin of France's decadence, and which appeared to leave art and morality as the only remaining spheres of action.

Ilou, the Westerner turned Brahmin who, with the Chaldean Magus Mérodack, is the principal incarnation of his author's own magical powers, explains the purpose of the Rosicrucian crusade. If the image of God can be reinstated in the national imagination, then new leaders can be created in place of the bankrupt Fathers on earth: 'The duty of initiates is to foment individual personalities who are fitted for great actions, so that when the event arrives, the man will also be there' (p. 101).

Ilou proposes a union of the highest cultivated minds in Europe, who would be both traditionalists and internationalists, prepared to admire equally Italian painting, German music and French literature and to replace the flags of war with the flag of culture. This will be a state within a state, carrying 'the symbol of the Rosy ✠ Cross which is the search for God by free secular paths'. This is a Wagnerian dream of a 'freemasonry of high culture', but whose aim is to install not humanism but theocracy: 'Our fellow-citizens are men of culture who love the same masterpieces; the foreigner is the man with no taste; the enemy is the bourgeois, the democrat, the civil servant.'

Defining the science of the Magus for Jules Huret's *Enquête sur l'évolution littéraire* in 1891, Péladan emphasized that his blend of authoritarianism and heroic individualism was a marriage of the best of tradition and the modern world: 'the inheritance of high minds across time, place and race, preserved for eternity'. It was, indeed, a synthesis calculated to appeal to adepts of religion, philosophy and, most of all, modern art.

From his father's Catholicism, he borrowed the prophecy of the renewing Reign of the Holy Spirit. He took also the doctrine of the Communion of Saints, who can transform the world by the force of their prayers, and modelled on it the magic powers of his Rosicrucian initiates. The theory of history as cycles of defeat redeemed by triumph is in the traditionalist de Bonald, before Péladan discovers a variant form in Wagner's myths. The mystic philosophy of Fabre d'Olivet (*De l'état social de l'Homme ou Vues philosophiques sur l'histoire du genre humain*, 1822) reinforced his dream of an imminent reign of the Spirit – a return of theocracy – as well as supplying his bizarre doctrine of the androgyne, who plays a key role in inaugurating the new world. The androgyne heroes and heroines of his novels represent a unique fusion of eroticism, mysticism and politics. In the early eighties, he was much influenced by the occultist Saint-Yves d'Alveydre's vision of society as a 'synarchy' in which every class and group would slip obediently into its due place, ordained by Providence – basically, an ideology of hierarchical order (*Mission des ouvriers*, n.d.; *Mission des souverains*, 1882; *Mission des juifs*, 1884).

In art, he found models in the fiction of Balzac and Barbey d'Aurevilly, da Vinci's figurations of the androgyne and the music of Wagner. In Wagner's search in the national past for myths to create a new unity in the present, Péladan found a mirror of his own. In Wagner's librettos, he perceived an echo of his own obsessive struggle for self-realization in an apparently pre-ordained universe, and his guilt-ridden attempts to resolve the divisions between body and spirit. And last of all, the musician provided the model of a new style, incantatory, emotional, overpowering, that could sweep an audience into its own vision, beyond the critical reach of reason.

These mystico-literary credentials were Péladan's passport, in 1882, to the cafés and clubs of avant-garde Paris. In the painter Rodolphe Salis' Montmartre club, Le Chat Noir, headquarters of the review of the same name, the most baroque dreamers were the most welcome, as the decor declared:

Two walls painted with frescoes showed some lively pseudo-mediaeval inventiveness: a scholar burning the effigy of Aristotle, a witch cutting the hanged man's rope, noble ladies with unbelievably pointed caps, watching unlikely tournaments, drinking-scenes culled from Hals, Rabelais jumping out of his Divine Bottle and Villon, patron saint of likely lads, with his retinue of whores and sausage-makers. A whole museum of stuffed cats and stuffed owls hung from the ceiling; a crocodile did duty for a chandelier (*Curieuse!* pp. 63–4).

Péladan began his literary career by writing art criticism. He pinned his flag to the mast: 'I believe in Ideal, Tradition and Hierarchy' (*L'Art ochlocratique*, 1888, p. 45). He found these best expressed in the images of woman and the flesh presented by modern Catholic art. Puvis de Chavannes and Moreau were his idols, but his most sincere admiration was reserved for the satire of Félicien Rops, capturing the new face of the Devil, who is the nineteenth-century bourgeois ('. . . he has no horns, no tail, no claws, this devil, he wears a suit, sports a monocle; his feet may be forked but they're hidden in fine shiny shoes; all that's satanic is his smile and his eyes, and he's terrifying') and the diabolical grace of the Parisienne, the Devil's new instrument. 'La Dame au pantin' is a chilling celebration of modern woman and her triumph over her former masters:

Tall, slender, almost androgyne, she lifts up with her black-gloved arm a puppet in a suit, with an indescribable smile of contempt for this mannikin who represents you, or maybe me. Rops' smiles slip from the corners of Mona Lisa mouths, and irony, cold, silent irony, has found in him a fearsome interpreter (p. 50).

As always with Péladan, a personal problem is inflated into a universal dilemma. The spite vented here finds more violent expression in the pornographic *Femmes honnêtes* (1885), for which Rops provided a frontispiece, in which Péladan (under a pseudonym) denounced the 'exhibitionists', 'sadists', 'onanists' and 'lesbians' whose indifference to his charms had clearly disappointed the Magus' expectations: 'It was reserved for the Latin decadence to astonish psychologists with the spectacle of these continent Messalinas, incapable of lust!' (p. 105).

But it was as a novelist that Péladan became famous, attaining instant success in 1884 with the first volume of his epic cycle, *Le Vice suprême*. The Catholic camp was delighted with the book, for its denunciation of modern decadence and its advocacy of the 'true' ideal: 'aristocracy, Catholicism, originality' (Barbey d'Aurevilly, *Le Constitutionnel*, 16 September 1884). But the vogue for the occult which it popularized rapidly divided Péladan from his Catholic acquaintance, to the accompaniment of considerable ill-will. Personal quarrels, abuse, sexual slanders, challenges and duels filled the eager columns of the newspapers – all, of course, excellent publicity for the Magus. In the February 1892 issue of the *Mercure de France*, Edouard Dubus complained bitterly of his talent for grabbing the limelight – a mere buffoon who fascinated the 'gawpers' with his carnival costumes. Dubus claimed there was far more to real magic than Péladan told the public. In the future, there would be: Paul Adam and

Jules Bois were to move in the direction of socialism and feminism, and Péladan's own contribution to the encouragement of major symbolist artists would be an important one. For the present, the mystifications and the quarrels of the sects were a major part of occultism, and when Huysmans accused Péladan and his allies of murdering the abbé Boullan long-distance, by magic, public attention was riveted.

In May 1888, with the decadent mystical poet Stanislas de Guaita, Papus (Gérard Encausse) and the novelist Paul Adam, Péladan founded the Ordre de la Rose ✠ Croix. As Jean Pierrot points out (*The Decadent Imagination, 1880-1900*, 1981, pp. 102 ff.), they were a motley crew, with little in common. De Guaita was the thinker, author of the three-volume *Essais de science maudites* (*Au seuil du mystère*, 1886; *Le Temple de Satan*, 1891; *La Clef de la magie noire*, 1897), whose aim was to revive the Western tradition (Eliphas Lévi, Hoene Wronski, Fabre d'Olivet, Boehme, Swedenborg and Saint-Martin) at a time when the theosophists had brought the East into fashion and were threatening to move the centre of occultism from Paris to London. Papus, author of *L'Occultisme contemporain* (1887), was an organizer, founder in 1888 of the review *L'Initiation* and interested in connections between science and metaphysics and the practitioners of magnetism, spiritism and hypnotism.

The group began to split as early as 1890, when Péladan, objecting to the masonic connections of his fellow-Rosicrucians, concluded his novel *Coeur en peine* with a declaration of his own devout Catholicism. In 1891, he founded his own Rose ✠ Croix Esthétique, combining occultism, Catholicism and art. While the rest of the occult movement discussed magical doctrines and astral light, he stressed its social and political purpose. The founding notice of his society, printed at the end of *La Gynandre*, included an act of (qualified) submission to Papal authority and a declaration of an intention to turn dilettante artists into warriors of the Spirit:

The ideal must be made manifest once more before the slavo-mongol invasion. Latin civilization in its declining days must hand over to its successors a book, a temple and a sword. There must be an inventory of the treasures bequeathed by the past and of our modern conquests; above all, there must be action in a mode capable of civilizing the Barbarians who will come after us.

Where mysticism has failed, only Art can act on the collective soul. We all know men who believe in Phidias and Leonardo, but care nothing for Catholic truth.

To instil the theocratic essence in contemporary art and especially in aesthetic culture: this is our new way forward (p. 349).

Self-appointed Grand Master of the Order (which in his preface to
Typhonia (1892) he compared with the English Pre-Raphaelite renewal),
Péladan found the Salons de la Rose ✠ Croix catholique. The statutes of
the Salons were first published in a pamphlet of 1891 and reprinted in 1892
with *La Panthée*. An annual month-long exhibition (March–April) was to
promulgate the cult of the Ideal, through the cult of Beauty and Tradition.
Priority would be given to works based on legend, myth and allegory, on
subjects taken from Catholic dogma and oriental theogonies (though not
those of the 'yellow races'), or the 'idealized nude' as exemplified in the
work of Leonardo and Michelangelo. Patriotic, military and modern
themes were excluded, and work by women artists was banned. In the
evening, there would be performances of the music of Bach, César Franck
and Erik Satie, and of Péladan's own dramas (regularly rejected by the
established Parisian theatres).

The statutes concluded with an attack on the Catholic Congress of
Malines, which had just published a ban on Baudelaire, Verlaine, Barbey
and Péladan, the theatre, and all works whose subject matter might be
considered sinful. Against such repressive philistinism, Péladan's Salons
were to provide a rallying-point. The *Figaro*, scenting good copy, offered
publicity. Support had been promised by Puvis de Chavannes, Redon,
Fernand Khnopff, the sculptor Astruc, and Eric Satie, and Péladan
planned also to invite Burne-Jones, Lehnbardt and Boecklin. Neither
Chavannes nor Redon produced the promised work, and no more was
heard about the Germans and Burne-Jones. But Satie composed the
incidental music for the tremendously successful first exhibition, held at
the Durand-Ruel Gallery and preceded by processions and Mass on the
Champ de Mars.

The report in the *Mercure de France* (May 1892) gave all the credit to the
financial backer, the Comte de la Rochefoucauld, for what it described as
an original attempt to inscribe a mystical essence in sensuous reality. The
critic praised Filiger's religious miniatures, in the manner of the Primitives
and the Flemish mystics, Trachsel's watercolours of Chaldean palaces,
haunted by chimeras and larvae out of Redon, Khnopff's 'Sphinx'
(painted, apparently, on mirrorglass, so that female spectators found their
foreheads resting on its genitals – 'resting their intellect, by naïve instinct,
on its proper organ'). The mood overall was one of dreamy languor,
encapsulated in Charles Maurin's 'Dawn', showing 'all the ways in which
humanity wakes, tired in advance of the day to be lived, eager to escape,
yet falling back into the snares of humdrum tasks and humdrum

pleasures'. Jean Lorrain's countess, who only went to the opening out of loyalty to the La Rochefoucaulds and 'poor Antoine' was less impressed:

It's absolutely PUTRID . . . disembodied heads, like great waterlily flowers floating on stagnant water, women like maggots with their bodies trailing off into long worms, those awful earthworms you cut with a spade, huge horribly luminous eyes blinking over nocturnal landscapes . . . it's a nightmare (*La Petite Classe*, 1895, p. 65).

Interestingly, when the *Mercure*'s critic turned his attention to Jeanne Jacquemin's exhibition of pastels, excluded from the Rosicrucians' Salon because of the artist's sex, he found striking similarities in models, tone and themes. Jacquemin offered the same uneasy blend of mysticism and perversity, in the same ambivalent images: a drowned child, a severed head of Christ, a prodigal son, with 'eyes dead to all desire', an androgyne Séraphîta, clasping in her hand an 'unknown flower', and a man and woman dying in despair indistinguishable from ecstasy, yearning for an impossible ideal. In 1892, Péladan was on the crest of a wave; he had found exactly the right language to speak to contemporary unease and draw it back to traditional order.

The basic grammar of this language was erotic experiment and erotic discipline. Though women were banned from the Salons de la Rose ✿ Croix, they had a vital role to play in the formation of the Magus, the new man who would restore the old values (Preface to *La Science de l'amour*, 1911). In his two guides 'Comment on devient Mage' and 'Comment on devient Fée', published in 1892 and 1893, Péladan set out the male and female disciplines. As in the novel cycle, the Magus's struggle to perfection was seen essentially as a struggle with his sexuality, harnessing and dominating the power of the female at the risk of being possessed and destroyed by it. Péladan's magic is a morality, and one in tune with contemporary sexual fears and fantasies. Aphrodites, Isoldes, Kundrys, Ice Queens and androgynes crowd his pages, adoring the magnetic power of the Magus.

In the first volume, Péladan explains that magic is a science of will, desire and renunciation. The Magus is the man who has experienced and conquered desire and now in his detachment possesses all things, with the simple watchword: 'Neither fornicate nor vote' (p. 42). Destiny depends on the stars, which alone determine whether a man will be a leader or a follower.

Sexuality is both means and obstacle to power. Carnal pleasure is less important than desire, but it is the way to desire, introducing the neophyte to the virtues of longing, suffering and dream. The best part of sexual pleasure is not orgasm but the protracted 'calm caress' (p. 109) that stimulates the pleasures of the imagination. (Extended foreplay is the fate of most of Péladan's heroines, as of most of his aesthetic and political projects.) Péladan manoeuvres desperately against strict Catholic morality to make a case for pleasure. He condemns perversity but defends the 'ambivalence' of sexual experience, in which good and evil, 'the chimera and the monster', are hard to tell apart.

But for the Magus rather than the Catholic, it is not the sexual act itself that is the problem but the fear of being trapped, through sexuality, by feminine wiles. Woman, Péladan explains, is an overwhelming and overpowering force: 'Kundry, femininity personified, forever fluctuates between the Grail and Klingsor, equally excessive in good and evil' (p. 107). If not impressed into service, she imprisons.

The good fairy learns from her guide how to be inspiring, undemanding and unobtrusive. Péladan begins with Fabre d'Olivet's account of an alternative Hebrew version of Genesis which explains the androgyne origin of man and his fall. Adam's disobedience was not sin but part of the Providential order, for without it he would have had the capacity for self-knowledge and perfection. Since the Fall, the constant struggle of passion with reason extends the bounds of human understanding. The ultimate product of this conflict will be the reconstitution of Adam's original androgyne being, enriched by a new element of divine self-consciousness.

Since the Fall, woman represents passion, and man, intellect. Woman, with no will of her own, is 'attracted' to two opposing principles: instinct, the 'vertiginous force' of the Serpent, and intellect, which resides in man. What the serpent of instinct proposes is not necessarily evil. Woman mediates his good and bad suggestions indiscriminately to her partner: 'Woman, in her rashness, is equally an occasion of danger and a mirror of the ideal' (p. 42). Man's duty is to save her from the Serpent by passing judgement on her libidinous suggestions, distinguishing for her and himself between vice and virtue. Man, in short, assumes the responsibility and the credit of action, while woman takes the risks, prepares the initiatives, and bears the guilt.

Though she is said to lack the faculties of reason and discrimination, she is expected to perform a double role that requires both: Eve, who must 'move man by offering visions of the unknown, as you did at the time of the original sin', and Mary, who must 'present man with the senti-mentalization of his concepts', taming the beast she arouses (p. 47). The

Fairy is to teach young men desire while ensuring they stay virgins as long as possible; and when the inevitable fall comes, she will make sure their dreams remain intact. Péladan might usefully have referred his readers to the best of all fairies, Stella, who is the heroine of his novel *L'Androgyne* (1891), a 'priestess of sexuality, shameless, triumphant' (p. 231), who initiates the future androgyne Samas with a sequence of exhibitionist displays from her bedroom window. The moral intention is a pretext for near-pornographic cliché, as Stella bares her breasts:

> Opening the slits she's just cut in her robe, she reveals both her breasts at once, her hands drawing aside the cloth, leaving them naked . . . entranced by the spell she casts, she continues to hold back the parted cloth with her delicate fingers (pp. 205–6).

Art and literature are invoked to legitimize erotic response. Naked after her bath, Stella stands in a ray of sunlight like:

> . . . the princess of German legend who to ensure her knight's fidelity as he left for the Crusades showed herself to him without a veil, so the memory would preserve him from seduction.
>
> The slenderness of Theban paintings, but rounder, the same structure, but plumper, shone from Stella's breasts and mound, and the likeness of breast and rump was repeated between her arms and her round thighs. Her elbows echoed her knees, and her wrists her ankles, in smoothly swelling alliteration.
>
> Before this unexpected picture Samas trembled, his eyes burned, his heart beat in anguish, his hands clenched on the window-sill . . . he swayed. Overwhelmed by the splendid reality . . . (p. 223).

The Fairy is never permitted to be more than a mirror, reflecting men's passions and inhibitions. To explain why, Péladan refers to Fabre d'Olivet's hypothesis ('sufficiently probable to count as proven') that woman, who came into history as the priestess, transmitting messages from the divinity to male rulers, was cast out because she abused her power and invented human sacrifice. All women, the Magus asserts, are egoists and vampires at heart. This is why their roles must be carefully limited: 'Woman is only suited to the theatre, piano, drawing room, bed or convent – artist, singer, pianist, coquette, mistress or saint' (p. 49).

The Fairy, whether Melusine, Morgan le Fay, Vivian or Isis, knows she depends on men. She will respect the artists (Plato, Dante, Shakespeare, Wagner and Péladan) who set her on her pedestal, and in gratitude make herself the sexual initiator and the patron of youthful genius. This is her contribution to social order:

> Revolutions have only ever been the enterprise of exceptional individuals on whom society has tried to force the common yoke. Privilege, exemptions, favours, are seen by the statesman as safety-valves for order. Whatever force may be latent in a group, its explosion depends on the single entity that joins with it and makes it effective by giving it a physical form.
>
> A woman who mediates in this way between the law and the individual who is beyond it does not dishonour the nation but rather strengthens her society (p. 69).

A Fairy lives by ritual. She begins each day with a bath, removes all superfluous hair, applies a strong perfume (to her clothes, not her body) and says her prayers. She walks through her home in a floating housedress, diffusing a spirit of joy and peace. After a delicate lunch of fruit and vegetables, she goes driving in a tight dress that shows off her breasts but reveals nothing below the waist. She may not visit other women. Before dinner, she sits in a her low-necked evening dress in a quiet, statuesque pose, allowing the contemplation of the Ideal she mirrors. She copies the slow, melancholy gestures and smiles of the women drawn by Leonardo, Correggio and Prud'hon. At the day's end, before falling asleep, she reads a little poetry and glances towards her crucifix.

Though her domestic role, so described, may seem somewhat ornamental, in Péladan's scheme for historical renewal the Fairy plays a vital part. In the reign of God the Father, a woman knew her place: Esther, the victim who voluntarily offered herself to the tyrant to save her people. In the present Christian dispensation, the reign of the Son, women have too much power and misuse it. Péladan blames the spread of war and democracy on women's refusal to sacrifice themselves. If only they could submit, and place their sexuality at the disposal of the artist, then the Holy Spirit could reign, the androgyne Adam be created, and a new and better relationship of man and woman begin. Women are urged to revert to their traditional roles, recover power from the new women and the new democrats, and hand it back to the patriarchy: 'Our own times offer us the spectacle of a mob of intellectual eunuchs who let the crowd be feminized and have let women rejoin the crowd. That is why, dear sister, you must serve or perish' (p. 349).

A useful corrective to the intimidating female figures in the first few volumes of *La Décadence latine* is the novel *Mélusine*, whose poet-hero reconstructs his female ideal in his own crippled image, and who writes his prose-poem 'Aux Vénus mutilés' for all poets and women who know that the modern world has cheated them of glory and love (*Diathèse de décadence. Psychiatrie. Le Septénaire des Fées. Mélusine*, 1895). These poems to the corrupted Ideal, flawed as the Fairy Mélusine herself – 'half woman and heavenly, half serpent and devil' (p. 58) – draw Mary, the American heiress, to the poet with a Giorgione face and 'strength hidden under his feminine appearance' (p. 45). Mary's own vigorous beauty is marred by an ugly secret: she has a wooden foot, a repulsive stump, and a cupboard full of false feet that her lover glimpses while spying on her undressing. In exchange for her patronage, Péladan and his hero forgive and accept the defect of their own invention. The poet kisses the stump, marries the heiress, and fathers a child on her, while she pays for him to write and stage his major play on the death of Sardanapalus.

The message of this fiction within a fiction is a clear summons to the vigour of the new world to share in the holocaust of the old: at its climax, the dying king, swaying on his throne on a pyre of useless treasure, summons his whole harem to leap into the flames beside him. This is the pattern of devotion for the poet's household, women and servants alike. Mary's maid vows herself to eternal virginity to serve the master she secretly loves. All three spend long, chaste hours on one bed, the maid at her employers' feet, exchanging long, languid, 'decent' caresses, 'like gods'. In theatrical fiction or domestic fact, the dream attributed to the Fairy is the same: to surrender herself to death for the sake of someone else's passion.

In *The Romantic Agony*, Mario Praz suggested that all Péladan's women belonged to a single androgyne type. Péladan himself counted seven types in all in his Fairy guide, one for each of the seven planets, and these can be reduced to three: the ideal androgyne, Sister and Friend; the Mother-mistress, who is the Enemy; the Wife-mistress who supports and consoles. All appear in *La Décadence latine*, helping or hindering the fulfilment of the epic's many heroes, who are all, in their turn, so many projections of Péladan himself. The Magus persevers in his quest to reinvent the androgyne, forever betrayed by his recalcitrant Fairy but enjoying in compensation a rich and varied range of erotic fantasy.

The first volume of Péladan's cycle, *Le Vice suprême* (1884), investigates two androgyne images, the princess and the actress, each a soured version of the ideal – 'a living allegory of the Latin decadence' (p. 83). Pale, flat-chested and perverse, both are destroyers of men. But one is an authentic perversion and the other a cheap copy. The monstrous Léonora d'Este is devoted to an aristocratic dream of old heroic values, for the sake of which Péladan would willingly forgive all her sins. La Nine belongs to the modern, materialistic world, acting the androgyne because it pays, cash. In these two women, Péladan opposes aristocratic and democratic values – the one, for him redeemable, the other hopelessly corrupt.

Léonora's beauty, transformed into a symbol of the new moral and political world of the Magus's vision, is presented in a series of artistic frames. Surrounded by the velvet curtains and silk cushions of her boudoir, reclining on her sofa, a figure out of the Italian primitives, she represents the over-spiritualized and over-sophisticated Ideal of aristocracy, anticipating its imminent renewal by the barbaric vigour of the modern world. She stands for the reconciliation of warring opposites:

> . . . the 'Venus Anadyomene' of Primitives experimenting with renascent paganism with brushes still soaked in mysticism, a Botticelli where the saint, in nymph's undress, still preserves a gawky innocence in the perversity of the plastic form of her debauch; one of Dürer's mad virgins . . . (p. 22).

Framed naked before the mirror beside her friend Bianca, her superiority is obvious. The sensual, plump Bianca makes shameless lesbian advances to her friend, too impatient to wait for 'true' fulfilment with a male lover. Léonora's aristocratic self-restraint, waiting for her destined lover, is evident in her refined form:

> . . . the pallor of her slender arms flowed down her hands; the paleness of her slanting shoulders flowed into her long neck. Her thin frame was comfortably fleshed-out, with no protruding bones. Her small, precisely formed breasts stood out abruptly on her flat chest, straight and pointed, with no modulating transition. The line of her body swelled only slightly at her haunches, vanishing into a pair of excessively long legs, like an Eve from the brush of Lucas van Leyden. The long slender lines, the slimness of her joints, the narrowness of the extremities, the dominant verticals, rendered immaterial flesh whose hues were already unearthly: she might have seemed one of those saints stripped naked for martyrdom by the pen of Schongauer the engraver; but the ambiguous gaze of her green eyes, her wide mouth with its disturbing smile, the red-gold flash of her hair, her whole head belied the mystic aura of her body (p. 46).

The best and worst of Léonora comes from her Borgia inheritance: her pride, and her mystical idealization of chastity and courtly love. She strips and whips her guardian's mistress for having tried to usurp her place in the household, experiencing a piercing pleasure as the woman's flesh is bruised and streaked with long red and purple weals. Married to a libertine who rapes her on her wedding night, she responds again with violence. Too weak to whip men, she finds subtler forms of revenge, arousing desires she has no intention of satisfying, driving men to duels and suicide or the diseased embrace of prostitutes. The 'supreme vice' is her 'satanic' delight in the havoc she wreaks, seeking out all the perverse pleasures that the theologians condemn.

By the time she meets her saviour, the Magus Mérodack, her image of love is the drowned Antinoüs, the morbid perversion of the androgyne ideal, who rises to her from the depths of the sea: 'Open your arms, my limbs are soft from their bath of eighteen centuries, I am ready for your embrace' (p. 94). The ghoul is joined in her dreams by the incubi who (in Péladan's strictly materialist mysticism) are made of the physical substance of repressed sexuality, emissions of fluid turned into phantoms that hover about their source. Léonora's obsession with dead or imaginary heroes sweeps her into masturbatory visions of:

> ... the obscenity of all things. Goats, reeling with lubricity, break horns in furious embraces: a delirious phallic procession passes before her, the inner friezes unroll of a temple of Priapus ... A sudden clear space. Clinging to her pride with an effort that turns her pale, she reins in her flesh.
>
> Quivering, enervated, panting, her eyes clouded, her arms hang limp with depression and fatigue ... (p. 98).

Léonora is saved because she turns for rescue to living heroes, Mérodack and the Dominican Father Alta, who alone are capable of resisting her sexual challenges. As the cycle nears its end (*Finis Latinorum*, 1899), she hands to them her wealth and influence, and in return receives the redeeming kiss of Tammuz, the perfect androgyne lover.

La Nine is her demonic caricature, the modern Parisienne, straight out of Rops. She has no haunches or breasts; all maternal softness is replaced by a 'she-cat's charm and feline grace' (p. 185); she shaves her head and wears men's clothes: 'She was consciously the pale androgyne, the supreme vampire of ageing civilizations, the last monster before the fire from heaven.' The difference is that she is from the city populace, sold into prostitution by her mother. Like most of her class, in Péladan's ideology, she can only imitate, usurping with her counterfeits the place left empty by a defaulting aristocracy. The three-act operetta in which she stars as the androgyne in search of the chimera is a cabaret vulgarization of Wagnerian motifs. It generates in its audience a collective sexual excitement which Mérodack's derisive hunting call easily rallies, and which strikes fear into the forces of Republican order; but all it can inspire is riot, not revolution. Mérodack uses her charms to collect the clutch of social outcasts – failed artists, libertines, anarchists, monarchists, atheists and sceptics – from which he will attempt to forge his new elite. But this symbol of corruption turns out to be a two-edged weapon. La Nine's self-seeking intrigues destroy her lover, the Prince de Courtenay, who was to lead the aristocratic revival. He kills himself, leaving her pregnant with his child. This failed attempt to restore the androgyne ideal leaves the future hostage to corrupt women and corrupt democracy.

The next three volumes – *Curieuse!*, *L'Initiation sentimentale* and *A coeur perdu* – trace the pact made by the sculptor Nébo with the Russian princess Paule to re-create the Platonic androgyne. This is an attempt to treat women not as enemies but as equals, which similarly ends in disaster. Some souls, the sculptor explains, are born androgyne, with 'a woman's heart and a man's brain'. Of these, a few become men and women of heroism or genius by their own volition, while others can only achieve perfection as a couple. In exchange for the inspiration of Paule's beauty, he offers the power inherent in his own knowledge of the world and his ability to resist the temptations of money, politics and love: 'I shall be the great doctor who will abort all your base desires, depoeticize passion for you, save you from the defiling marks of instinct' (p. 18). She will end as Beatrice; but she begins as Séraphîta, Minna, and most of all, Mademoiselle de Maupin, as Nébo initiates her, disguised in men's clothing, into all the circles of the Parisian hell.

Paule wants active sexual experience, but it is precisely this that Nébo will not let her have. She learns as a spectator, sharing Nébo's own marginalized and voyeuristic perspective, to see sexuality and democracy as the enemy. She is shown women of all classes with nothing but their bodies to offer, eternal dependants and victims. The wives of drunken workers are starved, beaten, humiliated and driven into brothels. Upper-class women prostitute themselves to buy clothes and catch a husband. Female sexuality brings unique humiliations; Nébo shows her a hut outside the city walls, where three raddled old whores make love to a legless client, an 'animated trunk' perched on a trolley. To dissuade her from joining what he describes as the feminist campaign for a reversal of roles, Nébo takes her to the Sex Bureau, where a madam parading her stock exploits the new female clientele. Péladan's crude satire presents a fairground Hercules, in sheepskin and gold sandals, off-the-peg for Semiramis; for Cleopatra, a Mark Antony in crimson tunic and laurel wreath; a provincial Romantic dandy for Emma Bovary, and a vicious schoolboy. The Chatterton ordered for Paule proudly refuses her advances, and as a reward for his genius is set free from the brothel.

The disorders of passion are identified with those of democracy. Nébo teaches his princess to identify the threat of sensuality and the threat of the crowd:

> Caliban rules the whole island; his sons have produced sons, atrocious, godless beings – let them wallow in their filth. Hide your quivering wings my Ariel, they only cause sedition among the swine; as I hide my knowledge, Prospero who scorns to dispute an inch of the land with these moles, or pick up a crimson mantle where the slugs have trailed their slime! . . . together, my Ariel, we shall build a lovelier, greater world than theirs, an inaccessible world of ineffable mystery! (p. 315).

Unfortunately, in the middle of Nébo's exposition to Paule of the doctrine of the androgyne on which the new world will be built, the text breaks off. It resumes with Péladan's description of his arrest and imprisonment for ignoring his call-up notices, laced with violent invective against the militarism of the Republic that threatens individual freedom and reduces genius to 'a beet in Caliban's soup' (p. 355). Péladan calls an unholy alliance to his support, including not only women but also Zola and the working class, declaring that the Communards may have been bad but the bourgeois State is far worse.

His populist enthusiasm is short-lived. In the prologue to *L'Initiation sentimentale*, the old battlelines are drawn again: the Orphic elite of intellectuals against Nimrod, the masses, moved by instinct. Too proud, Nébo says, to struggle for political power, Orpheus has other devices. Paule, made over into the perfect androgyne, is to become an image of repression and abstension which will provide an erotic focus for the popular imagination and a model for national passivity. Essentially, she is to create a vacuum for theocracy to fill. The prologue closes with Nébo's invocation to his new statue of Eros, the god who rules the masses ('the poor flints of humanity, who only spark when struck by sex' [*A coeur perdu*, p. 66]) but serves the artists who give him form. Nébo's project, however, is thwarted by Paule's determination to seduce her mentor. Finally, the sculptor decapitates his own image of Eros in masochistic, frustrated rage.

The third volume is a desperate attempt to save the dream by compromising with the enemy – sexuality, if not democracy. Ultimately 'forced' to sin against chastity for the sake of higher political and religious good, Nébo experiences a brief illusion of fulfilment:

> In that naked embrace, their souls touched . . . he discovered . . . the ability of the sexual embrace to restore for one brief moment the primitive androgyne, in a dual sensation where, sisters in ecstasy, the intoxication of life and the intoxication of death followed one another (pp. 327–8).

But Paule again destroys his dream, this time with her Circean desire to make him into her creature. To preserve the ideal from her sensual corruptions, he must abandon her and destroy the androgyne couple.

Having established to his own satisfaction that it is woman, the people and the State who obstruct the old world's return to power, and not the incapacity of that old world to respond to modern needs, Péladan abandons the ruins of this particular scenario and begins the round again with fresh sets of actors.

In *Istar*, crammed full of androgynes and angels, genius finds its sister-soul. This time it is middle-class spite and mediocrity which prevent the androgyne couple from transforming the world. The novelist Nergal and Istar, the Jewish beauty who becomes a Catholic for his sake, are two aristocratic androgyne souls descended from the fallen angels (Oelohites) of Cabbalistic tradition, heirs of a Miltonic Satan who disobeyed God in their desire to know real life and love and now wander the earth, dispossessed and desiring. The couple have fallen into the hands of Nimrod, the jealous provincials of Lyon, where Istar has had the misfortune to mismarry. She herself is something even higher than an androgyne – an 'Ereckéenne', a creature of perfect desire, the vibrant image of redeemed sexuality, whom Nergal could legitimately enjoy but for the accident of her marriage. In Péladan's prose, the pleasures of repression reach new, grotesque heights. The lovers, lying together naked in innocent cerebral lechery, enjoying the 'refusal of desire' which is the highest form of love, generate between them a magnetic atmosphere whose force, denied its natural expression, is unnaturally diverted:

> Abruptly drawn from their contemplation by a crazed caterwauling, they saw the cat, drunk on their sexual emanations, mad with love, rolling on the carpet, victim of two nervous currents flowing over him in a burning stream (p. 339).

Péladan's narrative resolves the intensity with an equally futile and fatuous diversion into separation, followed by Istar's decline and death. Dead, at last she becomes physically available to Nergal, as, with her husband's approval, he tries to bring her back to life with a necrophiliac ritual.

Finding that the symbol of the androgyne provides, at best, only limited satisfaction for his attempts to deal with the contradictions of his own sensuality and his double terror of sexual and political failure, Péladan turns elsewhere for assistance. In an introductory note to *La Victoire du mari* (1889), he expresses his admiration for the music and, especially, the myths of Wagner. He sees in them the image of his own attempts to reintroduce idealism to the modern public by the stirring depiction of heroic passion.

Péladan's orphan heroine Izel is the ideal new woman, taught to acknowledge beauty, art and sexual desire as intrinsic parts of Catholic religion, and to consider it her religious duty to patronize genius. She has read Balzac, Barbey and Nergal and plays the music of Chopin and Wagner. She combines the loveliest features of both Latin and Germanic races: the familiar long neck, pale skin and slender figure of Botticelli's virgins, dark, romantic German eyes, Parisian grace and the Valkyrie's strength: 'She exuded a sensation of fabulous femininity . . . she seemed a woman of the harem – an ideal harem, containing the whole series of archetypes of modern desire, in all its diffuse complexity' (p. 35).

Her sensuality is still suspect; she casts herself in the role of the forbidden Isolde, waiting for her Tristan. Péladan acknowledges that the Ring cycle depicts 'the fatal antinomy of Beauty and Power' (p. 73), the opposition of body and spirit that his novels perennially lament. But in other operas he finds a fresh pattern whereby Power is achieved *through* Beauty and the spiritual ideal reached by means of the flesh:

Wagner first perceived man's salvation through the purity of woman, a naïve idea: a woman can never save man, and besides, pure love lacks fire; then he saw the hero, and finally the saint, and the work that begins as an artistic epic ends in mystery at Saint Peter's in Rome (p. 74).

This is the pattern he exploits in *La Victoire du mari*, where desire oscillates between satisfaction and repression and the hero enjoys in turn both anarchic self-indulgence in passion and the security of restrictions and rules. Romantic defiance coexists with a proper sense of guilt and the need for punishment (effectively diverted on to convenient scapegoats). The result is an illusion of heroic, vigorous and orderly life where all contradictions are apparently resolved in a new image of the ideal. This ideal is entirely enclosed in the world of art, structured on Wagnerian motifs, rhythms and repetitions and locked into a closed circle of ideological prejudice disguised by stylistic tricks.

Izel and her husband are presented as Siegmund and Sieglinde – brother and sister, both elect and equals. Together they confront the threat of sexual passion, listening for the first time to *Tristan* in the darkened auditorium at Bayreuth that so offended contemporary proprieties ('darkened', said Léon Bloy, 'for the convenience of the gropers and feelers who go off their heads when the violins start'). The music and the drama are a 'whiplash' to heart and senses, making the audience 'pant, writhe with lust'. In the overture, Izel recognizes 'the sounds I make when I swoon in ecstasy, my invocation to the tomb at the moment when my whole being rears and beats against the limits of feeble human nature' (p. 84). They return obsessively to the opera, twice a week, and afterwards make love in the fields by moonlight. Izel, passive femininity, sinks into a Nirvana of passion, a 'delightful decomposition', in which identity evaporates into a 'pearl-grey mist' (p. 101). Adar, on the contrary, experiences a sense of wholeness and expansiveness, a perfect unity of 'idea, feeling, sensation' in which 'orgasm, instead of ending pleasure, opens up ecstasy' (p. 99). But both are trapped. This is the limbo of extreme sensation, where spirit literally slips away from body and into the embrace of the mystical Fiery Serpent – to surrender to a single one of the world's mystical powers is a betrayal of the Magus's destiny, which is to dominate them all.

Adar slips from Izel's bed to hear *Parsifal*, and the overture frees him from her 'witch's' magic. At first he retreats in anger to devote himself to his neglected studies of mysticism and magic. Eventually he realizes that his wife, like Kundry, is an irresponsible creature who must be rescued from her own vulnerability. The couple fall victim to the trickery of a German Magus who takes possession of Izel in his astral body. Izel's description of her rape emphasizes how close their own passion had been to forbidden experience:

> We make love asleep . . . so I didn't wake up at the touch, which was very like what we felt in Bayreuth, what you called our 'Nirvana of love', that kind of completely nervous excitement . . . I was yielding when a more violent movement made me open my eyes: the lamp was lit, and yet I couldn't see you.
>
> I was dumbfounded, I felt possessed but there were scales on my eyes and I could only see emptiness . . . I lay there listening to what should be

you, though you were invisible to my sleepy, weary perceptions, and what should have been you melted in my hands, fluid yet resistant, like mercury, and then I leapt out of bed, snatched up my long hairpin and pursued the obsession with the ridiculous weapon, and then I was aware that the monster had fled before the pin (pp. 154–5).

The husband's guilt is purged by scapegoating his wife and her 'lover'. He kills the musician. At first, he rejects his defiled wife: 'A slug had crawled between them, and they felt they could never again touch each other's lips, hands or hearts!' (p. 158). Later, he repossesses the resisting Izel, first by violence, like the German, in the form of an incubus, and then with the help of Wagner's seductive music, calling her back with their original lyrical motif. After the redemptive catharsis, life can now alternate between Eros and Hermes, Sexuality and High Magic, echoing the tumult and peace of Wagner's own harmonies.

Wagner's music appears again in the triumphant finale of *La Gynandre* (1891), to mark the victory of the androgyne ideal. This novel is an elaborate revenge fantasy in which the androgyne Tammuz asserts man's ability to defeat the challenge of Lesbos. Having disarmed all the lesbians in Paris with his gentle virility, Tammuz marries them off in a solemn ritual to an equal number of replicas of himself, thereby avenging, he says, 'the death of Orpheus' (p. 317). To the music of *Lohengrin* and the 'Ride of the Valkyries', four female androgynes pour out aphrodisiacs and heavy perfumes, the lights darken, the couples link hands, a hymn strikes up and a central pillar is unveiled, revealing the Phallus, which all the women worship.

The excesses of this novel are a gauge of Péladan's distress at what he saw as the fashion for lesbianism, rife, he claimed, for ten years, invented by journalists short of licentious copy, and an evil imitation of true androgyny, to which women can only come under men's instruction. In the new movement, he saw an alliance of two usurping forces: 'The crowd reigns, and Woman seeks emancipation' (p. 5).

The novel is the account of a crusade by the writer Nergal, assisted by Tammuz. The Church offers them no guidance; theologians, casuists and confessors are full of dark warnings but no hard information on what lesbianism involves or how lesbians can be cured. There is more enlightenment to be found in literature: not in Sappho, who Nergal says was a heterosexual confused with a lesbian contemporary of the same name, but in Lucian, Brantôme, Ninon de Lenclos, Balzac, Diderot, Gautier and, most of all, Baudelaire, described as the only writer who both recognizes the perverse beauty of his subject matter and gives it its due religious condemnation. Sodomy destroyed Greece and Rome, so France must be saved from the Gynander. The term, Nergal claims, is his own coinage:

> The Androgyne is the virgin, still feminine, adolescent; so the Gynander will be the woman who lays claim to masculinity, the sexual usurper, femininity aping virility! . . . The first term is out of the Bible, and designates the original state of the human creature . . . I have borrowed the other from botany, and baptize with it not female sodomy but any woman with an inclination to imitate Man; and that means a Mademoiselle de Maupin as much as a bluestocking (p. 43).

Tammuz embarks on an exhaustive tour of the lesbian circles of Paris. The *Orchidées* are a harem of a dozen young women, lean as greyhounds, who smoke and drink liqueurs in the house of their patron, Aril, a successful architect, hard-working but untalented. She and Tammuz are instinctive enemies, but the others are no more than 'nervous animals', soon tamed by his Orphic piano-playing. They're only Wagnerian flower-maidens, he decides, fixed in adolescence. The 'Royal Maupin', devoted to fencing and athletics, are simply aping men, while the 'Pentapole', five women draped round a communal bath, smoking opium and cigarettes, is a bad joke. There are a few untalented lesbian women artists and writers whose 'art' is only a pretext to seduce other women. Tammuz' great discovery is two genuine androgynes, misnamed lesbians by a slanderous press. The Russian princess Simzerla, frigid, addicted to opium, and the Countess Limerick, an American heiress, captain of her own yacht, *Sappho*, and its all-male crew, both readily yield to his authority.

Lesbianism, Tammuz establishes, to his own satisfaction, is not so much a female attribute as a male invention. Women who find sex repellent have had brutal husbands or incompetent lovers. Husbands encourage their wives to take female lovers, a less threatening proposition than a male rival. Journalists need copy to satisfy their editors; sensation-seekers like to watch women make love. Tammuz finally declares in triumph: 'Lesbos, physical imposture, slander on the human soul, nightmare of decadent nights; Lesbos, you never existed!' (p. 269).

Only the very few women who have had lesbian intercourse are beyond rescue. Aschtoret, the actress (and the only non-aristocratic woman in the text) forces Tammuz to watch her strip and violate the pitiful Madame de Maudore, flaunting her power over the other woman and jeering at his impotence to intervene – too horrified, he claims, by the 'tragic' spectacle of her victim.

Between 1888, when he discovered Wagner, and 1895, when *Le Dernier Bourbon* was published, Péladan's sexual fantasies celebrated the success of magic and music in forcing the female will to a hero's wishes. But by the time *Finis Latinorum* appeared in 1899, the Magus's Rosicrucian salons (six in all between 1892 and 1897) had been laughed out of fashion; and politically too the tide had turned, with the Catholic Right on the defensive in the Dreyfus Affair.

La Vertu suprême (1900) makes a last forlorn attempt to urge the middle classes back to mediaeval values. A new ally, Maître Baucens, modelled on William Morris, has a project to restore the guild system and the pride of the individual artisan. But the market is already too powerful. It is publicity, not genius or craftsmanship, that sells a work of art.

Mérodack sets up his own crusading guild for European culture at the abbey of Montségur, his Monsalvat, where his Rosicrucians enthusiastically swear the oath of the Knights Templar. But he sinks the enterprise by demanding an oath of chastity he knows will be refused. His justification is expressed in terms of Christian logic: if 'supreme vice' is the perversion of the spirit by carnal desire, then 'supreme virtue' must be the surrender of the flesh to spirit, which is the folly of the Cross. His real motive is his conviction that hierarchical order depends on sexual repression. The Magus' doctrine that carnal love can be a route to mystic knowledge can only be applied to the elite and in their embattled situation the Rosicrucians cannot risk setting an example of sexual anarchy:

> The only value of the curse laid on sexual pleasure is that it is a means of order. Magic is only dangerous and forbidden for the common horde; and lust is a form of magic (p. 216).

While Mérodack laments what he sees as a necessary absolutism that has ruined the cause and exiles himself in penitence, the friends he leaves in disarray praise his heroic idealism as their last remaining ray of hope. The concluding symbolism speaks the same language as Edmond Barthélemy's Catholic version of Wagner. Mérodack-Wotan may appear defeated, but individual failures are compensated by the overriding Providential ordering of the universe which will eventually create the new world of the Ideal, whatever the logic of human history might be. In Mérodack, Romantic, occult and Christian figures of suffering artist, Wandering Jew and martyred Christ are combined into an image of complete destitution that in Péladan's occult logic *must* be followed by a redemptive reversal. This is the symbol which speaks the most effectively to the national imagination in the nineties, and for the religious revival of that period it is crucial in bringing decadents and aesthetes back to the Catholic fold.

In Péladan's final analysis, the blame for failure lies not with Mérodack but with women, too possessive or too promiscuous to form the androgyne ideal, capable only of the role of mistress or mother. Their resistance frustrates Tammuz' attempts to use the sexual services of a hand-picked force of attractive men and women in the Rosicrucian cause. Tammuz' most obedient agent, Bélit, saved an Eastern country from colonization by keeping an unsavoury politician in her bed during a crucial vote, but she refused to repeat the experiment. His mistress, Rose de Faventine, abandoned him in resentment at his recruitment efforts, which she termed infidelities. Rose is denounced as the type of self-seeking, over-ambitious woman; as a convent schoolgirl, she 'tricked' the almoner into teaching her the secrets of magic by studying hard to prove she deserved enlightenment, and she shows her true colours by reverting to the 'pose' of lesbianism as soon as she leaves Tammuz.

Nannah, on the other hand, is the over-compliant woman, equally destructive. Her submissiveness is to blame for the excesses of her sadistic English husband, which Péladan charts in a sequence of disproportionate length and unusual detail. Before their marriage, she modelled for him as a beggar-girl in rags and as a bloodstained martyr; as his wife, she walked the streets dressed as a gin-sodden whore so he could play-act her client; to earn a substantial divorce settlement, she let herself be locked in the cellars of a remote manor house, dressed in rags and chains, tied to a stake, starved, splashed with blood in an obscene witch-trial, and submitted to increasingly realistic games of torture until, tied to a table with all her hair shaved off, she was finally rescued by the Rosicrucians.

At the end of Péladan's epic, the ideal woman is no longer the androgyne or any of her variants but the passive, devoted mother-mistress, Bélit. She closes the last novel as Léonora opened the first, silent, waiting, motionless as a work of art. She is not one of Leonardo's delicately enigmatic figures but a strong Amazon, sculpted by Michel-angelo, sincere, supportive, suffering without complaint:

> The Ideal for every one of us, were we not decadents, would be a Bélit, quenching our sexual desire without argument or opposition, leaving the whole of our being to the chimeras who are the sole corsairs of Art (pp. 86–7).

The walls of her octagonal boudoir are patterned with Zacharie Astruc's paintings of gigantic flowers transformed into human creatures – Wagner's flower-maidens, but all now unambiguously devoted to the magic quest for purity and perfection:

> ... most holy lotus and royal lily, mystic rose and magic Solomon's seal, Masonic acacia, Druidic mistletoe, speaking mandragora and verbena, flower of enchantment (p. 2).

Bélit, like the paper flowers, is all surface. Unlike Léonora, she has no qualities, dreams or desires of her own. The silent, passive focus of men's dreams of knowledge and power, her only willed act is the surrender of her beauty to her chosen god. A less grotesque version of Huysmans' Madame Bavoil, she figures the same decline of the perverse vitality of the decadence into consoling conformism – the return to the enfolding, stifling embrace of the Mother.

At the end, Péladan himself, one-time heroic champion of the ideal, the scourge of the State, watched his theatrical career trickle away into a round of lecture tours, sporadic articles and unsuccessful applications for academic posts. The logic of submission that runs through his rebellious fictions, in his androgynes, his Magi, and most of all, his women, finally worked itself out until he could find much to approve of, he said, in the politics of Waldeck-Rousseau. Yet some of the charm lingered: Muriel Ciolkowska, in the *Egoist*, found room to write (1 December 1916) of his 'enthusiasms and convictions', his 'erudition', his 'vast intellectual capacity'. The short obituary she wrote for him on 1 August 1918 bears witness to the durability of both decadent magic and the decadent disease: 'He marked a period, exercised an influence, and his vogue will return some day.'

4
'La Marquise de Sade':
Rachilde (Marguerite Eymery) 1860–1953

Woman's place, for the writers and artists of the decadence, was inside the work of art, as an image to fix the male imagination. If Rachilde, almost alone of women writers of her period, was accepted into the Club des Hydropathes and Le Chat Noir, patronized by Victor Hugo and Barbey d'Aurevilly, approved by the misogynists Huysmans and Léon Bloy, and befriended by Verlaine, Jean Lorrain, Catulle Mendès, Laurent Tailhade and Camille Lemonnier, this had much to do with her willingness to play and play up to the decadent stereotypes. Squeezing every possible thrill from her autocratic, sadistic heroines, casually dismissing effeminate and inept anti-heroes to madness and death, she nevertheless respected the limits of the images allotted her – Salome and Scheherazade, but never Herodias. She is the real-life counterpart of Clara, heroine of Octave Mirbeau's bitter satire on decadence, *Le Jardin des supplices*, maker, vehicle and victim of other people's dreams, whose function is to reproduce the values of a world with no energy of its own. For admirers and reviewers, she embodied all the contradictions of Baudelaire's women: animal and goddess, ingenuous infant and perverse adult. Albert Samain wrote sonnets to 'her eyes iced with green', and 'the 'enigmatic cat locked in the woman's form', observing 'The marquise's fine teeth/Crunch endlessly on exquisite caramel', as she savoured 'The voluptuous pleasure of being no man's conquest'. Camille Lemonnier, in an article in the *Mercure de France* (February 1891), reprinted as preface to her novel, *La Sanglante Ironie*, savoured the blend of physical innocence and intellectual corruption which, he said, made her young heroines so much more vulnerable than Barbey's mature *Diaboliques*:

> Neurotic, their senses precociously aroused by the ferment of heredity, sick of an excess of reverie that delivers them to man already initiate and deflowered, they take on a kind of ingenuous perversity, and as long as they can they remain, in their subtle spiritual corruption, girls who have dabbled in sin but postpone its bodily embrace.

Like her male contemporaries, Rachilde found a market and packaged herself for it. Like them too, she paraded an ironic self-awareness that turned her concessions to the market into contempt, proclaiming her independence by caricaturing the parts she was forced to play. She boasts in her memoirs (*Quand j'étais jeune*, 1947) of going to the *bal des Quatz-z-Arts* in 1885 with Jean Lorrain, she in a short white spotted muslin dress, socks, baby shoes and a blue satin belt, he in a pink tunic and panther-skin cache-sexe he had got from a wrestler in Marseilles. The man's suit she wore to shock the Latin Quarter was a statement of intent, like the eighteenth-century marquise's costume for which she exchanged it to confuse and intrigue a staid suitor, her future husband and future editor of the *Mercure de France*, Alfred Vallette. But these carnival costumes, like the flamboyant gestures of her writing, have no alternative, more authentic, identity beneath them to justify the bravado. These masks, like Ensor's, are also the real face. In her pamphlet of 1928, explaining *Pourquoi je ne suis pas feministe*, Rachilde joined her claim to be an independent individual, an enemy of all groups, to an unrecognized and deeply rooted social conservatism: 'I have always acted as an individual, never dreaming of founding a new society or upsetting the one that existed.' She confesses to insecurities that are exactly those of her male contemporaries, the difference being that in her case the origins lie in gender. She knew, she wrote, that masculine privileges would have been useful in her struggle for financial survival and a career of her own, but she had no right to them: like all women, she said, she was neurotic and had no self-confidence. As the publisher's notice for her pamphlet observed, the celebrated artist spoke with the voice of 'the French middle class, faithful as ever to time-honoured experience and an entire tradition'.

In her pamphlet, Rachilde blamed her own contempt for women on her mother. All the family money came from her mother's side, from a radical anti-Bonapartist newspaper that Rachilde's grandfather had edited. The mother encouraged her daughter to despise her father, and at the same time did her best to frustrate her ambition to be a writer. In her autobiography, Rachilde describes, in contrast, her devotion to her father, commander of the cavalry regiment which covered Bazaine's retreat to Metz in 1870 and illegitimate son of an aristocratic family, with whom, Rachilde decided, her preferred allegiance lay.

From childhood, Rachilde was caught in multiple insecurities. She identified herself twice over with defeated causes: the aristocratic tradition, and a father whose authority was in dispute. She had no desire to be identified with her mother, the usurper, daughter of a radical, challenging every kind of established order. And yet, her mother's strong-minded example was always there, to point out the weaknesses and failure on her father's side, and life was further complicated by her father's undisguised regret that the daughter had not been a son.

It is out of these divided and confused loyalties that Rachilde puts her creative imagination at the service of male masochistic fantasies, acting out the temporary triumph of the vengeful female and the humiliating overthrow of the male – subject to the reinstatement of paternal power in the last act. Like Baudelaire, she plays all the roles in the fantasy, which becomes her own, both executioner and victim.

For all their anarchic pretensions, Rachilde's rebellions never took her far outside the family circle. She gave plays and patronage to Paul Fort's Symbolist Théâtre de l'Art, founded in 1890; her pleasure in shocking the sensibilities of respectable theatregoers was greater than her understanding of some of the plays. She wrote for the anarchist and later Dreyfusard *Revue blanche*, but took care to mark her distance from its editorial policy. Her defence there of Oscar Wilde in 1896 ('Questions brûlantes'), was chiefly a defence of Lord Alfred Douglas, in the chaste name of romantic love, echoing the self-justifications Douglas had just published in the *Mercure*. When the literary anarchist Laurent Tailhade was caught in the blast of a real bomb in the café Foyot, she and Vallette drove to the scene of the accident to find their friend, and defended him against the jubilant sneers of the right-wing press; but five years later, Tailhade took her to task in a letter for drifting to the side of reaction, concluding hopefully: 'basically, you're on our side; the Triumph of the Republic, just, true, fraternal, is the triumph of all independent people. You'll support it – despite yourself, out of your love of independence and beauty' (20 November 1899). Rachilde was *not* on his side, though her 'love of independence and beauty' like those of other decadent contemporaries were of considerable help to a Republic that was more conservative than Tailhade recognized, displacing as they did more fundamental political issues.

To some extent, Rachilde's own writing acknowledges and deprecates its conservatism. Among the many mediocre works she poured on to the market, certain texts indicate her awareness of the closed nature of decadent ideology, and of the destructive readings of social and personal relationships that its images reinforce. But this awareness leads to no search for alternatives. On the contrary, it locks her more firmly into the same symbolic patterns, and into a self-lacerating pessimism which finally turned to despair – particularly after the First World War, with its irrefutable evidence of the bankruptcy of the father-figures on whom she depended.

Rachilde's obsession with a fantasy of female power has led to considerable misinterpretation of her work by modern feminists, who repeat, in a different language, the appropriations to which she was subjected by the male reviewers and readers of her own day. The author of the introduction to the 1982 reprint of *La Jongleuse* (Editions des femmes) argues on the evidence of its domineering and sadistic heroine that Rachilde writes 'to proclaim that woman had the right to love in her own way and to remain mistress of her own fate', and that she is 'despite her reservations about feminism in 1900, an effective writer who by her verbal and imaginative powers must be inscribed in the ranks of those whose aim is to furnish other women with the means to their own freedom'. This is a novel in which woman indiscriminately hands on misery to woman, as well as man, and where no one is free. At best, Rachilde's writing stirs the reader to uneasy awareness of the ugly implications of contemporary fantasies. At worst, it reinforces the fantasies, making fear and guilt an integral part of their pleasure.

Marcel Schwob's preface to her collected short stories (*Le Démon de l'Absurde*, 1894) is still the most perceptive assessment of her work. Rachilde is not Scheherazade but Cassandra, enclosed in her own prophecies of doom, unconscious of their real meaning, but fixing accurately and intuitively on the tiny signs of inexpressible, imminent disaster:

This is the same obscure ability to make connections that sets death at the end of sexual desire, that invokes the obscenity of plump little hands, that brings a blurred edge of sadness to a spring landscape with its branches of flowering almond . . . With those delicate filaments that extend her intelligence, she sniffs the scent of death in love, obscenity in healthiness, terror in calm and silence. Like an alert cat, she pricks her ears and hears the little mouse of death gnawing away at walls, thoughts and flesh. And she stretches out a voluptuous paw to play with the little mortal creature.

Rachilde's first successful novel, *Monsieur Vénus*, subtitled 'a materialist novel' and dedicated 'To physical beauty', was greeted on publication in Brussels in 1884 with a fine of 2,000 francs and a two-year prison sentence. For the French edition of 1889, Rachilde begged a preface from Maurice Barrès. The preface assured the book's success, but defeated its purpose. Barrès turned the would-be female subject back into object, humiliating the humiliator, with his invitation to readers to be titillated by Rachilde's motives for creating a heroine who exploited men in the ways men usually exploit women. In these fantasies of a twenty-year-old virgin, the blend of innocence and vicious sophistication was 'one of the most mysterious riddles I know, mysterious as crime, genius, or infant madness, with elements of all three'. In Barrès' view, the novel had no ethical, psychological or artistic merit. Its author was a typical young woman, writing out of animal instinct, 'for her own sexual thrills'. To the perverse spectacle of Rachilde's own sexual naïveté was added the pleasure of seeing her heroine suffer, modern woman punished for her cold arrogance. Finally, Barrès reduced the distinctive female problem to one more manifestation of 'our' decadence:

> The sickness of our age, to which we must constantly revert, and which *Monsieur Vénus* shows us in woman taking one of its most interesting forms, is one of nervous fatigue taken to excess and a hitherto unknown arrogance. This book is the first to point out the strange forms it brings to the sensibility of passion.

The fashionable decor of Raoule de Vénérande's bedroom mirrors her adolescent sexuality, repressed and perverted by the bigoted aunt who brought her up. The walls, draped in red damask, are covered with weapons and licentious paintings; a bed of black ebony, loaded with cushions, reeks of heavy oriental perfume. Besieged by suitors of wealth and breeding equal to her own, she keeps an ironic distance. A marriageable – and marketable – virgin has power over men; a married woman does not. Unwilling to surrender to men of her own class, she turns instead to a man she plucks out of the city poor, with all the good looks and subservience that traditionally draw upper-class men to their female servants. Jacques Silvert is an untalented painter, earning a scanty living making artificial flowers. Raoule sizes him up like a prostitute: 'very dark red hair, almost tawny; a slightly stocky torso on jutting haunches, straight legs, slim ankles' (p. 5). He has damp, beseeching, doggy eyes; he is young; he smells of fried potatoes. His harpy of a sister is quick to become his pimp.

Raoule's pleasure in Jacques is in seeing how much humiliation he will accept. Apparently there are no limits. She sets him up in his own studio, where she wanders in and out as she likes; he rebels at the intrusion, and then gives in. She watches him take a bath; he suspects she's watching but daren't challenge her. She gives him hashish, watches him under the influence of the drug, and makes love to him while he lies powerless, 'arousing terrifying ecstasies, with such exquisite skill that pleasure constantly rekindled at the moment of exhaustion' (p.60). He becomes the mistress, referred to as 'she', and she visits him in men's clothing. She confides her experiment to de Raittolbe, one of her suitors, declaring modern women have no intention of reproducing an aristocracy whose time is done, and see no point in giving pleasure they don't share to men who don't know how to make love. De Raittolbe, who should have been shocked, is simply entertained.

Jacques is gradually reduced to a passivity which he learns to enjoy. Raoule beats him, demands increasingly effeminate behaviour, and imposes on him 'degrading habits'. De Raittolbe too thrashes him, irritated eventually by such flagrant betrayal of masculine authority. Raoule, rightly suspecting the beginnings of homosexual attraction, falls furiously on Jacques' bleeding body, tearing off his bandages:

. . . she bit his marbled flesh, squeezed it in handfuls, scratched it with her sharp nails. She ruthlessly deflowered all those wonderful charms that had once given her mystical, ecstatic happiness.

Jacques writhed and squirmed, his blood flowing out through the deep gashes that Raoule pulled wider, in a refinement of sadistic pleasure (p. 138).

She marries him, as much to keep her possession safe from her male rival as to flout convention.

The men at her wedding, like de Raittolbe, find themselves coveting the bridegroom. On the wedding night, Jacques' transformation and Raoule's discomfiture are complete; he bursts into tears because she isn't a man. One night shortly afterwards, he tries to seduce de Raittolbe, who resists, but the final result is a duel in which Jacques inevitably dies. Raittolbe, who genuinely loved him, mourns the boy, while Raoule is still more interested in possessing a property of her own. In the penultimate chapter, she works mysteriously over the corpse with a pair of gilt pincers, a velvet-covered hammer and solid silver scissors. In the last pages, her bedroom has become a shrine for a wax figure of Jacques. The hair, eyelashes, chest hair, teeth and nails are all natural, and a spring in the figure's mouth automatically presses open its thighs. The figure is an anatomical masterpiece, made by a German.

The images are ludicrous, and the text in one sense scarcely justifies more than one reading, since it relies for its effects on surprise and shock, which are not reusable commodities. What holds the reader is the sense of being introduced into a highly private but real world. Partly this comes from the intensely sensuous and idiosyncratic detail of Rachilde's observations and descriptions. But mostly it comes from the clarity with which she sets out the exploitative patterns in the relationship of men and women on which fantasy and reality are both structured, and the frustrating impossibility of breaking them. The *femme froide* is a social construct, the only part given to an independent woman to play. But even the *femme froide*, trying to play executioner, is forced back into the role of victim. Everything she invents for herself is recuperated for men's pleasure. And without their support – be it de Raittolbe's amused approval or the German craftsman's skill – she can neither rebel effectively, nor sustain her own fantasies.

For Rachilde, class is the insurmountable barrier which must always prevent change in women's condition. With Jacques, Raoule came closest to disrupting her world, first by taking a paid lover to challenge the sanctity of family order, and secondly in marrying him, to bring disorder inside the closed circle. This particular outsider was doubly dangerous, introducing sexual ambivalence into a hierarchy built on rigorous gender as well as class distinctions. The aristocratic de Raittolbe's response – to kill the destructive element – was a logical one. But Raoule, who shares Rachilde's own faith in hierarchy, was never more than half-hearted in her challenge to order. Her chosen instrument from the people, mindless and malleable as the wax doll he became, was no match for the men of her own world. Her retreat into her bedroom with her toy makes surrender an integral part of her fantasy of revolt – surrender made palatable by redoubling her sadistic cruelties against a totally powerless Jacques.

La Marquise de Sade (1887) performs precisely the same self-castrating movement against would-be castrating woman. The symbolism is as heavy as that of *Monsieur Vénus*, and the scenes of torture and sexual licence equally morbid and violent, but the fantasy moves in a more realistic setting, with a detailed analysis of the domestic, social and political circumstances that construct the female sadist. The opening scene at the abattoir, where Mary walks daily with her aunt, between the military parade ground and the cemetery, to fetch the pint of blood prescribed for her anaemic mother, actualizes the hostility and hatred in the child's environment, which adults conspire to conceal. Mary's formative trauma is the accidental sight of the slaughtered bull, dying in slow agony and splattering her with blood. She wakes from her collapse to see the anxious, fatherly face of the butcher bending over her. Growing up is the progression from this initial, shocking confrontation with the father who loves and kills, through states of indifference, masochism and passive resistance to vengeful violence. The counterpart of the butcher and the bull in Mary's adult life is her lover, her husband's illegitimate son, Paul, whose nose bleeds copiously over her dress at their first meeting, and later, with her encouragement, over her feet. She pricks him with hairpins, tattoos her name on his flesh, and longs to tear him to pieces, like a dove, or the kitten she had as a child, that grown-ups pulled to bits.

The moral and physical violence that Mary's family practises on her is returned by the child with interest to family, lovers and society at large. She is neglected by her dying mother, and brutalized by a beloved father. When her mother dies giving birth to a son, she competes unsuccessfully with her baby brother and her father's new mistress. Her first chance for revenge comes when a drunken nurse overlays the baby in bed; she watches without intervening, enjoying the power of irresponsibility. After her father's death in the Franco-Prussian War, she falls to the care of a misogynist uncle, who proposes to send her to a convent. At this point, the silent victim makes her first protest: 'I'm in the way, because I'm not a boy!' (p. 234). Intrigued by her resistance, her uncle takes an interest, and begins to educate her. Her initiation into anatomy becomes an initiation into debauch. She connives at his advances, which leave her technically a virgin, and him vulnerable to her blackmail; from this moment, the victim of sexuality begins to reverse her role.

Marriage with a rich, ageing libertine is an escape into a lesser domestic dependence. She threatens to poison her husband if he tries to force her to have children. She is a mistress, not a wife, prepared on occasion to indulge all his desires, at a price. She stages a humiliating confrontation between him and her lover, his bastard son. Maddened by her perversity, poisoned by the aphrodisiacs she feeds him, exhausted by the mistresses she sends him, her husband dies of what the doctor calls 'a strange case of satyriasis' (p. 370). Discovering she has poisoned his father, Paul leaves her in disgust, literally tearing himself away from her claws and teeth.

Mary is both victim and heroine, greater than her circumstances and the men around her, a daughter of the Roman decadence forced to live through 'their' pale imitation. She is an admirable monster, a robust carnivore, a salamander untouched by the flames of modern neurosis, a vampire:

. . . she lived on others' nerves, not her own, sucking the brains of everyone around her with the exquisite pleasure of a mind that can analyse to a degree the value of others' infamies and will frankly confess to regretting its cruelties, since so many of its chosen dishes are in such doubtful taste (p. 376).

The ethics Barrès complained were missing from *Monsieur Vénus* appear here, and they are his own, the 'cult of the ego' which he made the watchword of the Third Republic. If force is its own justification, then Mary has every qualification for preying on the weak – physical vigour, intellectual strength, and a powerful ego. She has no alternative occupation. Only politics attracts her, and politics, she knows, is closed to a woman who will not be satisfied with a supporting role. In her eyes, the world is too corrupt to be worth saving. She roams Paris at night in a restless quest for blood and strong emotions, in the company of her most recent suitor, chosen for 'the freshness of his complexion'. The vampire images decay into sadistic reveries: 'Sometimes a new wound would rise hideous from the city mists, and she would touch it with a raging finger, probing it with pleasure that erupted in shafts of irony' (p. 377).

She stays in cheap hotels in the hope of seeing a murder, but never does; she avidly leans over balconies to watch fights in squalid dancehalls, surrounded by the unspoken contempt of her gigolo escorts. Her fantasies finally settle on a band of male transvestites being propositioned by a group of young aristocrats, all useless to society. One of these would be an ideal victim:

Her nostrils dilated behind the velvet of her mask. She would take an ideal pleasure in the death agony of one of these men, incapable of defending himself against a woman. One spring night, she would toss her handkerchief into this heap of animals for sale, bring him home, cover him with her jewels, wind him round with her laces, intoxicate him with her best wines and then, asking nothing in exchange but his repulsive life, tie him with satin ribbons to her antique bed and kill him with pins glowing red from the fire.

A subtle plan . . . that she wouldn't, perhaps, carry out, but would brighten her thoughts on her many dark days (p. 384).

What restrains her from challenging man's indefensible claim to privilege is the risk of laying herself open to a jury that might misconstrue her act as a crime of passion. The 'true female from the era of the Earth's primitive fire' could never fall in love with 'one of these sexless creatures', 'fallen males' (p. 385). Mary locks herself into a dream of murder she will never realize. The story comes full circle, closing in a bar at La Villette by the slaughterhouses, where she mingles with the butchers' apprentices, pretending to have the same lung complaint as her mother, so that, like them, she can mix her wine with blood. She is a vampire and a beast of prey, but also a sick woman and a pathetic child:

> With her pallid face, wrapped in her marten furs, half little girl craving forbidden fruit, half lioness yielding to instinct, she slipped in among those people, held out her cup like them, drank with a delicate enjoyment concealed by a tubercular mask (p. 386).

Unlike her usual escorts, the apprentices respect and pity her. There is an unspoken parallel between her 'strange mystic desire' to murder the weak males of her own class, and the slaughter of the butchers' victims; it brings Mary on to the fringes of the fathers' potent world. She enjoys their warmth, company, bad language, and the smell of blood from the open slaughterhouse door. But she drives away hermetically sealed from their reality in her furs and her carriage. She has nothing in common with workers. Dreams of destruction are enough. The novel hints darkly at the forces that could be unleashed by a misused woman, combining her animal vitality with that of the working people, and loosing it on a corrupt ruling class. It also swears its author would never dream of lowering herself to such levels, and reassures the reader that she *will* be good.

With its own limits abjectly stated, Rachilde's hatred is displaced from men to women. Paul's contemptuous abandonment of Mary had been quite justified, anticipating a conclusion in which the heroine, with only her own resentment to add to her husband's money and status, accepted again the marginalization she had suffered as a child. In *Nono* (1885), the poor young secretary whose adoration is mercilessly exploited by the General's daughter Renée, mistress of a duke, turns out to have a dignity, purity and nobility that puts the woman to shame. He goes to the guillotine on her behalf; she dies in madness at the moment the guillotine falls; and her father stands by Nono's bier to renounce his daughter and adopt the dead boy's family in her place. In *Madame la Mort*, Rachilde's three-act symbolist drama staged at the Théâtre d'Art in March 1891, all the sympathy is for men, whose dreams can only be cast in empty or morbid female images. The wealthy hero, a morphine addict, tired of life, commits suicide by smoking a poisoned cigar. In the central dream sequence, Life and Death compete to win him. Life is Lucie, his treacherous mistress, who in the last act inherits his fortune. He prefers Death, the unknown woman who promises peace.

In the two other plays Rachilde wrote for Paul Fort, *Le Vendeur du soleil* and *La Voix du sang*, men are again the centre: the anarchist poet, whose lyrical tongue seduces the crowd and subverts the State, and the son stabbed in the street outside his home, while his screams go unrecognized and ignored by his parents, secure in their middle-class complacency.

In her preface to the collected edition of her three plays (1891), she noted the tremendous success of Shelley's *Cenci*, which had been Fort's second production, but makes no reference at all to his Beatrice, the heroine who incarnates almost all her own fantasies. And yet Camille de Sainte-Croix' review in *La Bataille*, included in her book's Appendix, spelled out the significance of this 'parricide for freedom', who murdered her incestuous father for revenge and for the public good, to expose the unholy alliance of dying powers – religion and aristocracy – by which the young are kept from their inheritance. Perhaps the answer is there: Rachilde would approve Beatrice's vengeful violence, but not her politics.

La Sanglante Ironie (1891) also takes a hero faced with a choice between Life, the Whore who deceives and cheats, and Death, the cold, consoling Mother. This novel, however, makes it clear that this set of symbols and choices is no more than the self-justifications of a particular narrator, constructed by a particular historical situation. The narrative has an analytical dimension that deconstructs the processes of male fantasy, and criticizes some of its definitions. At the same time, male authority is shown as more than fantasy. The narrator is a murderer, and his two female victims are dead before his text begins; their death, in fact, is the pretext of his writing.

The irony of the title lies partly in his discovery that death and prison are for him true freedom. It lies also in Rachilde's awareness that her exposure of the murderous violence on which male privilege rests is futile. As for Beatrice, death is the reward of opposition.

The narrator speaks from prison, and from experience, to explain that the desire to kill is a natural one. He has 'the cult of Death', an unknown, dreamy country, figured by a cool, elegant woman in a floating ash-coloured gown, with silky white hair, who offers no welcome, but a calm, neutral embrace.

Death is the aristocratic mother he never knew, and the place in aristocratic society that life has denied him. The son of a gentleman too proud to let him go to school with peasants and too poor to afford any but the cheapest of tutors, he is ridiculed and stoned by peasants' children whose freedom and vitality he envies. The woman he thought was his mother is his father's servant and mistress, dirty, stupid and unfaithful, whom he watches one night on the kitchen table with his tutor. Her liaison with his father shuts the family out of local aristocratic society. The boy inherits all the worst of the aristocratic tradition – arrogance, weakness, neurosis – and is cut off from the vigour of the peasantry. He knows them only as enemies, usurpers and thieves. When the Franco-Prussian War breaks out, he finds he would rather kill French peasants than Prussians.

Like Rachilde, he loves the father who has ruined his life. He adopts his aristocratic cult of blood and vengeance. When he murders a rival, or later his mistress, he is exercising in the private domain – the only one left to him – rights he has been told are traditionally his. The 'simple man's view' (p. 7) of national politics he gives from his cell are the clichés of post-1870 monarchism. War is a necessary 'periodic bleeding of nations' (p. 5). The lilies of feudal France, which flourished before the Americas were discovered and before Europe decayed, were pure because they 'grew from a crimson compost . . . In their day, the blessed day of noble massacres, our country was more picturesque, less neurotic, healthier. Blood freely shed is what makes bodies healthy, and to retain an excess of blood generates corruption' (p. 6). His health was too poor for him to join the army, to his father's disgust.

The symbol of his hopeless longing to 'return' to his aristocratic home is the still, lonely pool in the hills, surrounded by lilies, reeds and dragonflies, where he spent idyllic childhood hours, his only companions a wildcat and a snake. This Eden is forever unattainable, locked in the lost past, with his dead mother. All that is left for the present is the animal violence.

Denied his political and social heritage, he tries to carve an identity out of sexual relationships. He tries to marry Grangille, the illegitimate daughter of the local doctor, thinking she will make a submissive wife. Aware he has no future, Grangille makes use of him to get to Paris, but has no intention of saddling herself with his dead weight. In Paris, he finds Jeanne Simeon, his cousin's wife, an attractive blonde, dying of slow paralysis. Jeanne represents the sterile fascination of the aristocratic world – a dead past that resists all his necrophiliac desire to reclaim it. At her insistence, he enters her mother's tomb, and experiences a morbid thrill, as if he were violating his own dead mother.

Sexually and politically, he is caught between two extremes: peasant and princess, and life and death. Neither satisfies; he is determined to hold on to both; and in reality, neither is for him. Jeanne dies of shock and grief on hearing of her rival, and he himself stabs Grangille, as she turns to leave him for a grocer.

He waits now in the limbo of prison, the figure of the decadent condition, desiring death but clinging to life. The impotence that was originally the fault of circumstances is now his by choice. Compared to the women, imprisoned in the roles of paralysed wife or bastard daughter, his limitations were far fewer. He used his relative freedom to choose death for all three.

Rachilde's best work consists of the short stories that appeared in the early 1890s, first in the early issues of the *Mercure de France*, and then in the collection *Le Démon de l'Absurde* (1894). In these, she explored the role of tradition, highlighting the burden and the restrictions which the cultural inheritance places on the present. Traditional ways of seeing – in the form of images, symbols or values – can produce dangerous constructions of reality, of which both men and women are victims. Like Lorrain or de Gourmont, she shows desire caught, repressed, or glamorized in the distorting mirror of learned perceptions, turning into fantasies that terrorize and destroy their originator.

In these tales, her writing is more sensuous. Woman is the fertile force of Nature, not vampire but serpent, set against the crabbed and confining conventions of man's authority. But reviewers who saw her as 're-habilitating the flesh' (Camille Mauclair, *Mercure de France*, May 1893) were mistaken. In all her stories, the denying power of social and religious law still imbues pleasure, however intense, with a sense of guilt. 'Les Vendanges de Sodome' and 'La Panthère' (first published in March and October 1893) show how the voluptuous natural forms of sensuous and sensual life are constricted, crushed and perverted by the language of prejudice. These misperceptions are the result of a tragic blindness that pushes the destroyers into the pit along with their victims.

'Les Vendanges de Sodome' opens with images of rampant fecundity: the earth smoking under a red dawn sun, and a vine with 'leaves of blood and gold', heavy with giant fermenting grapes like huge black eyes, coiling convulsive tendrils over the ground, 'imploring arms stretching to the sun, in a delirium of suffering, all the guilty delight of Paradise'. Red, gold, black, green and silver, the brilliantly coloured symbol of all the ambiguous energy of female sexuality, the vine is the only living point in the Judaean landscape, except for a few sparse twisted figs and the distant bone-white stone town of Sodom. From the town comes a procession of young men to pick the grapes, led by a bony, twisted, old man, and trailed by a pretty youth. On the instructions of the old man, 'the sovereign image of eternal death', the pickers strip the vine, and 'angrily' trample the grapes into wine.

While they are asleep, a woman approaches, earth-spirit, fairy Melusine, faun and Virgin, clothed in her own awesome natural beauty:

> She was thin, pale-necked and covered from head to foot in red, downy
> hairs, which seemed like clothing of spotless linen embroidered with
> golden stars; her brow against the blue of the sky was smooth and
> polished as a dazzling swordblade; her hair swept the earth, gathering to
> itself the rustling yellowing leaves; her heels, round like peaches, hardly
> touched the ground, and her step had a gay animal spring; but the two
> nipples on her breasts were black, a burnt, frightening black.

Having eaten the leftover grapes from the boy's basket, she creeps
alongside him like a serpent and her 'impure fingers lay claim to his flesh'.
He wakes with a sigh of pleasure that turns into a scream as consciousness
returns and brings the men running. The woman is one of the wives and
daughters ('gulfs of lust') banished from Sodom to die in the desert or flee
to Gomorrah, so that the men's strength can be saved for the harvest. The
men denounce her as a thief, and a seductress. The child's accusation is
more complex, blaming her for the fascination and fear with which he
contemplates sexuality, in his enforced ignorance: 'I never knew you,
because I never wanted to!' Stoned, splattered with blood, she writhes into
the vine and crawls to hide in the grape-vat. They trample her underfoot
with the grapes, 'while from the miraculous black globules gleaming like
rolling eyes flickered a glance with the ultimate curse'. That evening,
drunk on 'the dreadful poisoned liquor of love', in a hellish moonlit
landscape, 'the men of Sodom for the first time committed the sin against
nature in the arms of their young brother Sineus, whose sweet shoulder
had the scent of honey'.

The story has a crude but vigorous message. The law of the Jewish
Father protects the interests of the impotent old men who impose it. It
destroys women, and it destroys its own male children. Repression poisons
the source of life.

The same theme reappears in 'Volupté', dedicated to Camille Mauclair.
Two adolescents sitting on the edge of a forest pool, on the threshold of
sexuality, are looking for a language from their own experience to describe
the paradoxical identity of intense pleasure and intense pain. They find
instead familiar images, expressing the traditional relationship of man and
woman. She recalls the scent of hyacinths, the sensation of drops of water
falling on the nape of the neck, and the image of the dying Christ. His
images are of violation and penetration, longing to scrape his nails along
smooth, glassy surfaces, or cutting his own finger with a razor.

She is afraid to let him touch her breasts, but allows him instead to drink the reflection of her face in the pool. Even fantasy is not safe. After he has drunk, leaning over the water, she sees at the bottom a real woman's dead face, with mouth wide-open. Unable to communicate the horror of what she sees, or draw back from the edge, she faints, and he carries her home.

There is no way out of the trap of tradition. In 'Le Piège à revenant', the enterprising son of a family who inherit a haunted mansion digs a trap to catch the spectre and then falls in it, spending the night wrapped in the terrors of the tradition he thought he could abolish.

The trick of these stories is to manufacture pleasure out of the knowledge that women are victims, by signalling their connivance with the executioners. In every case – wine-vat, pool, or pit – the source of death and fear, which is often also the source of nourishment and refreshment, is a female image. The guilt of being the transmitter of a poisoned tradition becomes part of the pleasure of the text.

'La Panthère' describes how the victim comes to cross to the side of the murderers. Hoisted from her underground cage into the centre of a circus to tear Christian captives to pieces, the young, elegant panther sits gravely licking her genitals. She ignores the men dying on the crosses, just as she ignored the spoiled, spiced meats served in her cage to excite her. She bites at last into the flesh of a dead elephant and sits eating it delicately. She has known freedom, and she intends 'to show her good breeding in the presence of appetites less natural than her own'. She 'whimsically declares herself for the weaker party', only to discover the price of virtue. She is attacked with dogs, spears and arrows; patricians and people fling stones, fruit, coins and jewels. Back in her cage, she is starved and tormented. The jailer burns out one of her eyes, and then leaves her to dream of her lost freedom. When the jailer's compassionate daughter comes into the cage with meat and fresh water the divine panther has turned into a demon. Suffering leaves no room for morality, or discrimination, only the blind desire for revenge:

> Then the panther lifted herself on to her haunches, which fortunately were still supple, shrank into herself, so as not to frighten the child, stared at her a moment with her twin luminous eyes, that suddenly turned into deep gulfs of shadow, and leapt straight at her throat and strangled her . . .

In their attribution of blame for the pain and suffering in her world, Rachilde's stories hit out wildly, in contradictory directions. This seems particularly true of those which first appeared in the enlarged collection of 1900. In 'La Mort d'Antinoüs', it is the patriarchy's web of blood and corruption that demands the sacrifice of the young. Decaying, dying authorities convince themselves of their potency by destroying a future they cannot share. The ageing Emperor Hadrian, in a fever of terror from the omens of death he has seen on the battlefield, still loves his favourite slave, the ephebe Antinoüs, whom he had once decreed a god; but jealous of his youth, and fearful of losing him, he turns on him with an unwitting curse.

Elsewhere, civilization is the destroyer. Florence is ravaged by plague, and only one man, a prince, left alive, with nothing to eat but the billowing roses sprung from the victims' dead bodies. The prince dies of a surfeit of poisoned roses ('Le Mortis'). In 'La Buveuse du sang', an incantatory prose-poem dedicated to Jean Lorrain, it is not civilization but Nature herself, in the form of the moon, who, like the Emperor Hadrian, decrees and thrives on death. Woman is the victim of her own sexuality. A young girl dreams of being kissed by the honey mouth of the red moon: 'the laughing moon, that drinks women's blood'. Under a pale moon wreathed in bridal mist the girl is raped and 'the moon sniggers on . . . a fiery flower that lives on women's blood'. Under a crescent moon, a thin spur signifying crime and death, the woman, beside herself with frenzy, strangles her new-born baby. The moon shines on victorious, pure as a wax taper.

'Le Tueur de grenouilles', far from being a 'rehabilitation of the flesh' blames female sexuality for men's perversion. Toniot was beaten by his naked mother, afraid he would betray her nightly visits to her lover in the forest. As he watched them making love in the dark, sexual pleasure for him became a complex blend of revenge, excitement, fear, jealousy and contempt:

> He won't forget what he sees, it's too funny! He sees a big white frog, yes, that's it, those wonderfully flexible thighs, open arms, precise, elastic, stretching limbs, so pale they look like silver! . . . He'll see that all his life, inside, in that very image, like a poisoned spring, with its sweet, painful reflections.

The frogs he catches and puts in a bag made from his mother's old nightdress wave their legs like 'girls being raped' and he skins and eats them with erotic precision, deflowering and devouring his treacherous mother:

> Kneeling before the heap of tiny corpses he undresses them, removes the double ring of their golden eyes, lifts off their pretty green satin dresses,

their sweet white velvet pants. It all slides off in a heap like dolls' clothes, and all that's left are the naked little thighs, very pale, nervously shivering, trembling . . .

And there is a strange flame in the man's staring eyes, a gleam of desire or hate . . .

But more often, for Rachilde, woman's 'crime' is not example but collusion, reflecting for man, uncritically, the image of his desire. 'L'Araignée de cristal', which was staged by Lugné-Poë at the Théâtre de l'Oeuvre, is a short dialogue between son and devoted mother, in a darkening house. The language is convoluted as both try to avoid admitting guilt; Rachilde is adept at exposing decadent evasions. The son demands, he knows, the impossible: that 'blind women might sometimes appreciate the frightening situation they create for men who can see, even if only in the darkness'. What the son sees in women are his own impossible desires or shameful secrets, and these ensnare him like the mirrors men use to catch skylarks:

Have you seen of a winter's morning the birds wheeling over the sparkling trap, thinking it a miraculous heap of silver oats or golden corn? Have you seen them falling one by one out of the sky . . . There's the mirror for skylarks and the mirror for catching men, that stands waiting at every dangerous corner in their dark existence, which will watch them die with their brows stuck to its icy enigmatic crystal . . .

He traces his hatred for mirrors back to the traumatic moment that marked his passage from child to adult – from infant dependency on the mother, to acknowledgement of the father's superior power, and the roles and responsibilities he must accept to function as an adult male in society. A ten-year-old schoolboy, writing his lessons in the shabby summerhouse, he found himself gazing absently into an old full-length mirror. In the stains in the glass he deciphered fluid, shifting images of waterlilies, and ghosts with streaming, slimy hair. He drifted into a reverie characterized as 'a muddy lake', 'dead water', 'this sleepy atmosphere'. The torpid, cloudy reflection in the glass of his own childish unselfconsciousness was broken into by a speck that became a spreading star-crack, a white spider, then a crab with a silver shell:

. . . its head starred with dazzling spikes, its claws stretching and stretching over my head, lost in thought, it overran my brow, split my temples, consumed my eyes, gradually erased my image, sliced off my head . . . sucked out my brain!

The glass shattered and he fainted, coming round to find the gardener with his drill who had been fixing a nail on the other side of the wall.

What the mirror fixed was the violation of his unself-conscious existence by the power of the father, pushing him roughly out of formless, maternal dream into a world shaped by patriarchal authority and intentions and forcing him to accept it as his own. The mirror also fixed his fainting, his sense of impotence before that alien father. In mirrors now he sees that self he first saw as victim and failure, and so he hates them. Women too mirror his double and contradictory desire to be both passive dreamer and active authority. They don't see the cracks in the image, but he does. All unknowing, their reflections confront him with his inadequacy.

His mother responds, in the only way she can, by mirroring his terrors, and demanding that he go out (as his father would have, she says) to fetch the lamps to drive away the gathering darkness. He too is frightened of the dark, but he obeys. In the hall, he falls on her long looking-glass, and cuts his throat.

The mirror scene in de Gourmont's *Sixtine* was a brave assertion of the hero's ability to force his own patterns of desire on the world outside. When that hero, and others, failed in their intentions, the fault was always in a world that fell short of their desire. What Rachilde is saying is that the fault is in men, or rather, in the present generation of men who lack their fathers' power. Until they change, there will be no change. There can certainly be no initiative from women, who are even more deeply marked with that formative dependency. The mother will see her son's throat cut before she will make a new beginning. And when his throat is cut, she is left sitting in the dark.

There is considerable distance between Rachilde's versions of the female challenge and those of the emergent feminist movement, which she became aware of in the 1890s when male journalist colleagues took up the 'Woman Question'.

The radicalism of the women's movement at this time was more feared than actual, but the fear was still considerable. It was given striking expression in Strindberg's *Miss Julie*, premiered at the Théâtre Libre in February 1893. Louis Dumur, theatre critic of the *Mercure de France*, wrote a lengthy review in the March edition, drawing on Strindberg's Preface to explain the social implications of the play.

There is little in Strindberg's polemic that is not already anticipated by

Rachilde's *Monsieur Vénus*. Dumur described a 'battle of castes' in which an aristocratic heiress, degenerate representative of a vanishing society, sells herself to a servant who 'aspires to rise, and carries in him the sap of future victories'. Julie acts in the name of a specious principle of female emancipation which in Strindberg's view is no more than egoism and fevered instinct. She is 'a half-woman, a man-hater', who learns the hard way that women are incurably weak by nature and training, and that outside the security of conventional duties and responsibilities offered by present society, there is nothing for them. If she joins forces with servants against masters, the servants will destroy her first.

On the first page of its January 1895 issue, the *Revue blanche* featured a translation of Strindberg's essay 'On the Inferiority of Woman'. Strindberg proposed arguments from evolutionary science to demonstrate woman's physical inferiority, which he equated with the negro's, or the child's. She had less grey matter than men, and her sense-perceptions were poorer. Natural incapacity, not lack of opportunity, was her problem. The tasks she was generally allowed to perform – drawing, music, or taking telegrams – were usually badly done. Her social inferiority was the result of her physical handicaps (menstruation and menopause), and of the division of labour in modern society, which was no more than the logical product of natural differences between the sexes. There was no reason to concede 'noisy' and 'raving' female demands for emancipation. Women could only merit it by working harder, which, Strindberg concluded with some satisfaction, was impossible given the present (natural) division of labour. As for the vote, there was no reason why inferiors of either sex should have it.

The *Revue blanche* was one of the few journals to run both sides of the feminist controversy. With a few exceptions, the voices countering Strindberg's authoritative pseudo-science were those of the occultists, using, more often than not, the language of their decadent origins. Paul Adam gave a positive account of the feminist congress of 1896, where most of the delegates, vociferously upholding family order, had demanded more jobs for women; only the radical Paule Mink, he thought, understood that the real task was to attack the values of patriarchy (Vol. X, p. 390). In 1895, in his *Chronique des moeurs* (Vol. IX, pp. 433–5), he had already included a lightly erotic, ironic piece on the dilemma of girls caught between changing notions of what women should be. A father who taunts his shy daughter for her unwillingness to say frankly how she reacts to the tale of *Sleeping Beauty* throws her out of the room in panic when she obeys: 'I thought of hot lips touching my own, hands clawing at my trembling breast, a whole body penetrating me with its odour, its vigour, its life . . . I thought of nakedness . . .' Jules Bois' lyrical account of the 'War of the Sexes' (Vol. XI, p. 363, 1896), rewriting his mentor, John Stuart Mill, found supporting evidence for feminist complaints in the history of 'man's constant, relentless oppression [of woman] through the centuries'. For Bois, both partners now take a perverse pleasure in woman's enslavement. She submits to the role of prostitute in exchange for a continuous supply of fresh golden chains. Men set the fruits of their labour at her feet, while she in return generates bloodshed, lies and rivalry. Man owns the world, but woman owns man, through his passions; both need liberation.

In contrast, Rachilde's contribution to the arguments of 1896 ('Questions brûlantes', Vol. XI, p. 193) is a retreat into platitude. She refuses to take seriously any of the issues contemporaries are wasting their time on. She pictures herself sitting in the literary 'fun train', just an 'old lady who likes reading', lost in her book, ignoring both the changing landscapes and the travelling companions she despises for their readiness to take sides on voguish questions.

The only *real* burning question of the day, she claims, is the eternal question: whether Love is finished. The fashionable 'emancipatress', 'the ludicrous lady swelling with pamphlets', clouds this fundamental point with her prattle of free love, hygiene, sex education, and sexual harassment in factories. (German and American feminists are intelligent, if dull. French feminists are merely persistent.)

She claims that any woman who likes can be free, and that freedom is not a question of votes or party politics. Her free woman is a wife who is proud to confess an adulterous affair to her husband. The freedom to love is what matters most, and her admiration goes to Lord Alfred Douglas for braving convention and declaring his love for Oscar Wilde (which she is convinced is platonic). Outside her flamboyant fictions, Rachilde's sentiments are robustly bourgeois, slipping away from major problems with maudlin sentimentality.

Forced to state her position in plain language, Rachilde is banal and conventional. The more conservative she becomes in reality, the more wildly perverted are her fictions. *Les Hors nature* (1897) is the drama of a repressed homosexual relationship between two brothers, Paul-Eric and Jacques Reutler de Ferzen, of whom the first, and younger, resembles his French mother and the second his Prussian father. The characterization is curious, implying on Rachilde's part a covert admiration for Prussian authoritarianism, which no patriot (however frustrated she might be by the democratic degeneracy of her country) could openly admit. Repressed homosexual desire becomes a symbol of the guilt-ridden, impossible longing of French weakness to be consumed by Prussian strength; decadent masochism finds its appropriate political form.

Paul-Eric is corrupt, effeminate, sadistic, self-indulgently sensual, and wholly dependent on his brother for survival. Reutler, the Prussian, is harsh but upright, and devoted to Paul, who despises him. His rigid brutality is the result of his determination to hide the extent of his feeling for Paul, afraid of playing Hadrian to his brother's Antinoüs. Self-control is his watchword. He intends to be 'master in his own house', to 'make nature no more than the setting of my will' (p. 384). The product of his repressed desire is a sadism that inevitably destroys them both: 'Death is the highest expression of my sensuality' (p. 232).

Woman plays two supporting parts. She is first the medium through which the two opponents express their differences, and second the bringer of welcome death. Marie is an incendiary, found hiding in the brambles after setting the village church on fire, and taken in as a servant. When Reutler beats Paul for cutting off her hair, he feels the same thrill of perverse possession as Marie watching the church blaze, frustrated by being denied possession of her God. Destruction, Reutler acknowledges, is the only way out of the impasse, and he admires Marie's courage: 'Sometimes, it would be so good to blow up the world or set fire to the heavens . . . Really, that servant has breeding!' (p. 252). By setting fire to the house, releasing all three of them from an untenable situation, Marie at last becomes part of the family. As the flames lick into the boudoir where Paul lies dead, strangled by Reutler to save him from the pain of slow suffocation, Marie can acknowledge Reutler as master of the house, and he can call her 'sister'.

The clearer the political commentary in Rachilde's work, the more marked is its pessimism. The house of tradition disappears in purifying flames, or stands decaying at the centre of eternal 'natural' cycles of desire and frustration. *La Tour d'Amour* (1899), the ancient Breton lighthouse Ar-men, is the monster of a tradition outwardly sound and powerful, inwardly full of decay, madness, cruelty and death, to which its victims cling; the alternative is to be swamped by the sea.

By tradition, maintaining the lighthouse is man's work. The narrative centre is the young keeper, held to his post by principle – a sense of moral and patriotic responsibility – and also by economic necessity. He needs a job; he has no alternative. The rafts of corpses who drift past the rock are all men. Women stay safe at home. But men are not too much to be pitied. The lighthouse is a refuge as well as a responsibility. With all its stresses, it is better than the unknown: 'When you've been a long time in the same place, you get to love the place where you're suffering. It's more natural than to go out looking for happiness' (pp. 234–5).

The rules of the system – systematic isolation – make it impossible to look for happiness elsewhere. The keeper thought he had found a fiancée on one brief visit ashore, but she moved away during his long spell of duty. He is left with unsatisfied desires which turn to violence. He knifes the whore who accosts him, as her image fuses, in a drunken mist, with those of the drowned women who in his fantasies drift past the lighthouse. There comes a point in this system when all its participants really want is death.

All his anger at the limitations of his world is turned into sexual resentment, directed against women. He identifies with his lighthouse, united with it by 'a necessary evil: the evil of living for yourself' (p. 186). He imagines it locked in sexual struggle with the moon and the sea. He watches in bitter envy one night as the moon, 'the great virgin', sailing high and seemingly free above the constraints of his own life, is embraced by the yearning arms of the lighthouse, 'the monster emerging from the darkness', and 'devours' it. The moon is an animal, shadowed and scarred every month, her face marked with the mouth that consumes men's mind and will. She floats on, and the lighthouse is quenched by dawn: 'human destiny is to burn out on one spot', to see eternally reiterated the evidence of its own futility (pp. 187–8).

The sea too is an image of woman and of life, cradling and consoling in her treacherous, murderous arms. She taunts the lighthouse like a mad whore:

> ... flaunting her nakedness to her very entrails. The whore swelled like a belly, then caved in, flattened out, parting her green thighs; and in the lantern-light you saw things that made you want to turn away. But she began again, her hair flowing wild, in disarray, in fits of love or madness. She knew the watchers belonged to her. It was all in the family . . . (pp. 198–9).

The sea also taunts the young man with an image of impossible freedom:

> The waves rose and fell, plump and opulent in a wealth of silk and jewels that insulted our poverty. Oh, the whore, the whores! All those little pussycat purrs, mad lioness screams, actresses dancing, and then in the end the torrents of blood and tears, streaming all round, and never tainting *them*. And their loveliness comes from all that freedom that men, prisoners of their own desire, can only admire from afar! (p. 235)

The young man's dreams of revenge are tame in comparison with those of his senior, who has kept the lighthouse for twenty years. The old man rows out to sea for the pleasure of putting two bullets into a drowned woman. He keeps the head of a rich young virgin, only two days drowned, locked away in the lighthouse in a bottle of spirits, its long hair streaming over the sides. The young man's initial horror and disgust develops into respect and finally collusion. When his mentor dies, he lives for weeks with the stinking corpse until the next supply ship arrives. When it comes, he accepts without demur the old man's job.

Men's power, the narrative suggests, may be limited, but within those limits it must be recognized as absolute. Since the world cannot be changed for the better, the lighthouse must be preserved. It must be accepted that in the lighthouse there is no room for living women. For the storm to be held off, women must let themselves be traduced to morbid fantasies.

After the Gothic self-denials of *La Tour d'Amour*, *La Jongleuse* (1900) is a welcome contrast, with its account of the satisfaction women can extract from their decadent roles. Yet even here, the illusion of women's all-sufficiency – Mother, Whore and Dream, Mary, Salome and Beatrice – is shown to be hollow at the centre.

The novel shows how women are defined by appearances, required to produce themselves through dress, decor and social rites and ritual as objects of pleasure for men. Women who are aware of this can juggle with men's fantasies as a means to power.

The text makes it plain these are sharp knives to play with, and they can cut; to challenge sadistic authority in its own language is a mistake. The ending shows the heroine, Eliante, forced to kill herself to preserve the fantasies, and with them the illusion that she, the Mother, is all-powerful. Rachilde writes her death as a perverse triumph that does indeed make Eliante the focus of all hearts and minds for eternity. But death is a poor kind of triumph, and the whole narrative, despite itself, throws up constant doubts and challenges. Who, it asks, does Eliante's play-acting really serve?

By choosing irony and parody rather than refusal, Eliante reinforces and internalizes the values she claims to reject. The centre of her house, her own bedroom, is furnished like a shrine with the erotic and exotic objects her husband brought back from his voyages to the East. Smoky light drifts through the topaz windows on to walls covered with skins and weapons set on cloth of gold, a red Turkish carpet, black furniture inlaid with iron, gold and mother-of-pearl, and – symbol of sexuality repressed and

perverted – a marble statue of a black Eros with emerald eyes, set at the
foot of the bed, his bow, hand and left arm cut off. These exotica, stolen
from colonies she claims to despise by a husband she claims to have hated,
represent all her identity and all her charm; she has nothing of her own.

Costume – masquerade – is the centre of the novel. Three distinct
moments enact the same female fantasy that power can be won by
pretending vulnerability. Men are to be fascinated with a display of
sexuality that concedes nothing, forcing them into the spectator's role.

Eliante makes her first appearance in a sheath of watered black silk that
gleams like metal, face blank white, hair flattened to blend with the lines of
her dress. At first sight, the gown emphasizes her weakness; she is 'draped
in thick shadow, apparently impenetrable mystery, rising high up her
neck, tight, almost choking round her throat'. But it is also a 'snakeskin';
her long gloves fall into snakelike folds, and her veins run like little blue
vipers under her white flesh. The dress is a snare. Her glance in the mirror
at the foot of the stairs is not for her own image but that of the mesmerized
Léon. She entangles him in his embarrassment as he treads accidentally on
her train, almost pulling off the 'chaste sheath', and closes the trap with
tantalizing fetishistic glimpses:

> . . . feet, lightly shod, edged with skin soft as her gloves, dark and naked
> in lacy stockings . . . eyes, dark and naked under a silky fringe of furry
> strands. The man halted, hypnotized, catching his breath (p. 28).

In this costume, she makes Léon watch her make love with the Greek
amphora in her bedroom, a kind of rape of an ideal phallus that she has
created, and which he could never match. It was already an exquisite work
of art when unearthed from its ancient site, but Eliante has improved it by
removing all traces of the handles that stuck out and spoiled its
harmonious lines, polished and scented it and set it on a carefully lit
pedestal, throwing her favourite ring inside as an offering – a parody of the
way men reshape and decorate women to suit their own idea of Beauty.
Rachilde's imagery for Eliante's masturbation is blatant, down to the
streaming 'starlight' from her eyes:

> Eliante, now poised over the neck of the white amphora, stretched up
> from nape to heels . . . Without a single indecent gesture, her arms
> chastely crossed over the slender form, neither girl nor youth, she
> clenched her fingers a little, in complete silence, and then the man saw
> her closed eyes part, her lips half open, and starlight pour from the white
> of her eyes and the bright enamel of her teeth; a slight tremor ran

through her body – a ripple creasing the mysterious waves of her silk dress – and she gave a little imperceptible groan of pleasure, the authentic breath of the orgasmic spasm.

Either this was the ultimate, splendid, manifestation of love, the true God descending to the temple, or the spectator had before him the most extraordinary actress, an artist who had transcended the limits of art's possibilities.

He was dazzled, charmed and indignant. 'It's shocking! To do that . . . in front of me . . . without me . . . No, it's abominable!' (pp. 50–1).

Eliante's performance flatters Léon with this privileged glimpse of her hidden self-sufficiency, and leaves him disposed to see the same threat to his masculinity in more common forms of female exhibitionism. When she appears in the juggler's costume at Missie's white ball, he recognizes the contempt beneath her apparent anxiety to please her audience. Her close-fitting leotard, powdered clown's wig topped with a diamond butterfly, and velvet mask leave nothing visible but her red mouth 'between brackets . . . on a black and white page!' With its blatant framing of the symbol of sexual availability, it pretends she is like all women, mere performers, offered on the open market. But Eliante has no intention of parting with the merchandise. The professional's trick that brings the act to a triumphant finale is to catch the last falling knife apparently in her breast – in reality, in a small concealed pocket. The costume has a life-preserver built in for the wearer with the skill to use it. Playing with others' desire feeds her own pleasure, and confirms her self-sufficiency:

[Léon] saw only too well that she wasn't juggling in his honour, or their honour, but for her own amusement. You could feel the vibration inside her of another blade, simultaneously treacherous and passive. She was innocently, absolutely amused by the original sensations of pleasure she procured for them, and at the same time she needed the sharp desire of those eyes aimed at her, the whole vibrating atmosphere charged with the electricity of passion.

Léon knew how that would end off-stage! . . . She would go on playing, vibrating with the pure metallic vibration of her knives, a steel blade tempered in the fires of passion, scornful of real flesh and blood, using only her own black sheath! (p. 143).

Her Spanish dancer costume is a parody of female self-denigration, an ironic 'confession' that all women are cheap, and that she, now that she is growing old, is herself one of the cheapest. She wears the whore's version of the costume, that pushes her breasts into prominence and splits open at the back to reveal her shoulders; she adds a red flower (a 'blood-coloured kiss') and crude make-up that underlines the savage contrast between ageing face and athletic body: 'The eyes blackened with kohl were too big, too dark, casting a shadow over the rest, and the mouth, slashed with red, invoked a feeling of pain, like the sight of a surgical wound' (p. 241). The dance is another masturbatory exercise, vibrating to her castanets, her own clicking heels and a demonic inner fever. It ends according to tradition, with the dancer 'dead' on the ground, covered in a black shawl. Eliante adds her own individual touch, reappearing from the 'wings' with a pot of red make-up thrown over her bodice, to kill the dancer off. Younger women are entering the picture, and Eliante is forced to compete through increasingly flamboyant disguises. Her downfall is grotesquely, tragically inevitable. The more the merchandise depreciates, the more risk there is of the buyer finally realizing that the market is, and always has been, his.

Eliante's fears of depreciation are linked to her knowledge of how completely she has made herself over into the image of man's dream. She tells Léon that she never loved her husband, 'and today is the first time I fear him, for your sake, because all he is now is what he's left behind in me. I am and shall always perhaps remain his humble servant, or yours . . . what can I give you that hasn't belonged to him?' (p. 116). All she can give is the sexual identity that her husband has formed. She has two secrets, both his gifts, which symbolize that sexuality: perverse, glamorous, cruel and corrupting.

The first is a case of double-sided Chinese figurines, ivory divinity on one side, wax mortal on the other, locked in an obscene embrace, and all carved with her face. The key ornament is the crown of pleasure, made of men and women entwined in the dragon chimera of passion:

> . . . the eternal dragon who represents all things . . . a mouth filled with flames, bloody eyes, golden claws and wings studded with rubies. His immense prehensile ringed tail fulfils all natural, supernatural and social functions. Men and Women are studded with his precious jewels. Temples are lit by his brightness and for him, lanterns hang humbly before shops! (p. 123).

Patriarchal power controls its subjects with the illusion that sexual desire, shaped in its own monstrous, glamorous image, is the centre of existence, snaring them in its shiny coils, and through its seductions dictating every aspect of their daily life. Eliante's face is now part of the chain, and she is no more than an instrument for handing on the patriarchal tradition.

Her second secret is the trunk of costumes that dictates in advance the parts she can play. Her most useful role is the maternal one. She shows her costumes off to Léon, or gives them away to Missie and her friends, again handing on the corrupt tradition. The Mother, like the goddesses on the figurines, has all the appearance of power as long as she concedes her essential subjection:

> I'm not cruel, wicked, or even arrogant in the modern style. I humiliate myself as and when it pleases people. At a sign from the children who come up to me (and all men who come up to me, curious or tyrants, are just children); I juggle to amuse them, and if they cry, I rock them to sleep with pretty stories. I must be forgiven for being . . . happy. No one will ever know I carry inside the great source of illuminating fire, the fire of saints, martyrs, and great courtesans, not those who are paid for, but those who pay for their right to be respected, by inspiring love! I want . . . to be happy all by myself, arms crossed firmly over my breasts, thighs tightly sealed, smiling like a virgin at Communion.
>
> Could you teach me anything better, dear little children, with your undignified shaking and trembling like puppets all hanging on the same string? It's my hand that holds the right end of the string! (pp. 166–7).

Eliante hands on the tradition that passion is all that matters, and passion means domination: '. . . to be truly passionate you must have a heart nearer the Devil than God, that is, be an arrogant man or woman . . . dreaming of infinity!' The text makes it clear that the dream of divine self-sufficiency can never be fulfilled; but implanting it in others is power in itself. Léon, and Eliante's niece Missie, both students, belong to a generation learning different ideas. Eliante intervenes to deride Missie's desire for independence:

> . . . born in middle-class suburbia, slightly bourgeoise, contentious, intoxicated by her new freedom, a raw beginner at everything, working haphazardly, piling up vulgarized information in the back of her mind so she can make her own vulgar deductions, to no great profit, so thirsty for pleasure, comfort and frills that she never remembers to wash her hands before she grabs; to be brief, always saying it takes very little to satisfy her – the little our grandmothers would have thought was a fortune (p. 159).

In Rachilde's book, Missie is certainly a contemptible creature, feminist because it is the fashion; smoker, cyclist, and would-be bluestocking. Ironically, it was Eliante's husband who decided Missie should be educated. Eliante is certain she might otherwise have made of her a good wife or a witty courtesan. As it is, she makes sure Missie will never change the form of men's dreams. The girl she finally pushes into bed and marriage with Léon is someone for whom no partner could feel anything but contempt; and Eliante's suicide secures her own place as the unattainable ideal of which Missie will always fall short.

Eliante's is something of a Pyrrhic victory. She may have marked Léon's life with her dream-image, but Missie has the reality. Ironically, her aristocratic delusion of her own freedom and power is the instrument that has set up and will sustain one more part of the middle-class world it so despises. Eliante herself is completely caught up in that world. She may have been the daughter of a marquise, but she was orphaned by the Franco-Prussian War. When she married, she accepted responsibility not for children of her own but for her husband's family. That marriage itself, made for money, turned her from heroine to commodity. The last, unexpected discovery of Rachilde's text is the corruption of her aristocratic ideal by the values of the market. The queens of decadent mythology earn their keep by glamorizing the union of the primary-school teacher and the doctor.

Le Meneur de louves (1905), another attempt to glamorize simultaneously heroic rebellion and submission to order, is set in the completely different context of France's first struggles from barbarism to national identity. In this romance, self-denial is a moral and patriotic duty. Princesses and common people, united in revolt, are both shown as victims of injustice, and repositories of energy that could tear the new, weak nation apart. Princess Basine was raped and beaten by her father's soldiers, on the orders of her stepmother, Queen Fredegund. Like the she-wolves of the title, driven by starvation to attack cities, her own survival is at stake. The young Church struggling to unite the warring Franks is already corrupt, and rules by deceit and superstition. In Basine's army is a nun walled up for twenty years in her convent, whose stinking, rotten flesh is a living indictment of ecclesiastical power. But the alternative to the rule of the Church is anarchy, which Rachilde no longer condones: in 1905, the threat of revolution is too great. The nun is pitiful, but also ugly, vicious, and too broken to be of use. The starving wolf has to be destroyed for the general good. Basine's thirst for justice is rewritten as a bloody obsession with revenge, which leads to the sack of the countryside and the deaths of children. Harog the wolftamer, who raised his rabble army to avenge her, bewitched by her beauty, finally forces her to submit to the Church and ask for forgiveness.

Le Meneur de louves is one of Rachilde's last attempts to play the rebellious young barbarian. In later works, as Rachilde feels herself increasingly part of an order not merely under threat but displaced, she aligns herself completely with the dying kings.

The First World War gave her fresh images for the conflicts inside Byzantium. A set of new moral and technological values challenged outdated hierarchy, at the same time as the war's bloody horror gave a new lease of life to the old monsters. What she draws is the impossibility of concessions to the new world: the old order is dead, but must be defended at all costs.

Le Grand Saigneur (1922), with its title pun on *seigneur/saigneur*, 'Lord' and 'Bloodletter', brings the Marquis de Pontcroix back from presumed death in the trenches to renew the vampire traditions of his family. He discovers Marie, the daughter of poor working-class parents, who is acquiring a reputation as a major young painter, and takes her to his gloomy Breton stronghold to marry her, murdering her brother, who opposes the match. The belated discovery that Marie is not a virgin means marriage with her – a union between equals – will not save the marquis. Instead, he demands the right to survive by drinking her blood, which Marie, in her guilt, concedes. She is saved at the last minute by discovering evidence that he is her brother's murderer, and so more guilty than she is. In this curious competition for the cleanest conscience, the marquis finally scoops the pool by shooting himself, having first provided apparent proofs of his inno- cence. He becomes a vampire on Marie's world for eternity, a tragic hero unjustly accused.

The novel writes a general exculpation of the aristocracy. Admittedly, they were vampires, liars and destroyers. But the fault lay with history, and with their opponents. If the people had been better, aristocracy could have ruled with them; if Marie had been a virgin, there would have been a marriage, and no need for blood.

Corrupting the generation that will inherit is again the theme of *Madame de Lydone, assassin* (1928). The white-haired old lady, dressed in her favourite costume of eighteenth-century marquise, charms her nephew Gaston, an airman back from the front, with the manners, morals and decor of the past. In contrast to the stark devastation he has seen from his plane, she offers a haven of peace. Together the ill-matched couple think they might build a new life. But when she takes him back to her home village in the forêt d'Argonne, the dream-world she had promised him, the war has wiped it out.

Even before then, Gaston's dreams are filled with warnings of the impossibility of their love, with nightmare images of his plane sucked from the air by a mysterious, devouring monster which turns into his mistress's crippled dwarf servant. The creature's twisted relationship with Madame de Lydone – pity and exploitation on one side, devotion and resentment on the other – figures the contradictory relationship between rulers and dependants that pre-empts all hope of collaboration. The dwarf attempts to murder his mistress out of jealousy, and she shoots him in self-defence. They die together, leaving Gaston with the debilitating memory of a passion he will always believe could have restored meaning to his life. Yet the truth is that the two generations and ways of life are irreconcilable. Madame de Lydone herself, looking at the ruins of her village, had called for revenge, not forgiveness; forgiveness only brings the same mistakes again.

Rachilde's last novels are contradictory. They recognize, more than many contemporaries, the destructive nature of the old patriarchal order, but their chief focus remains the tragedy of its passing and the belief that nothing better can take its place. François de Valerne, the last of his line (*Les Voluptés imprévues*, 1931), sternly puritanical, strong-minded, strong-willed, and growing old, has chosen an heir for his wealth and his way of life. Lucien Girard, the type of the post-war generation, is the child of failure. His father, a rich coalmerchant, came home from the war disillusioned and ruined. His employer is a communist deputy, whose eagerness for equality is for Rachilde the cult of mediocrity, and whose belief is that France was ruined by the egoistic, imperialist values Valerne represents.

In this novel, Rachilde's traditionalism has a clearly extreme edge. Lucien's world is café society, artificial, spineless, superficial and discordant, surrendering human dignity to the basest of animal instincts. To the delight of the café, Valerne rolls up his white gloves and rams them down the throat of a bawling negro singer, the symbol of the animality that dominates this world. Lucien, like his friends, is glad to be woken from the 'spell' of the music. But he is fundamentally unsympathetic to Valerne's values, however attractive the old man's fortune might be. Valerne's castle, at the end of a long damp drive, surrounded by ivy-wreathed oaks, is too antiquated to hold his frivolous attention, and he does not feel enough gratitude to his benefactor to endure his company for even a few days. Chafing at the old man's oppressiveness, he reveals that he is a homosexual, and Valerne collapses with a heart attack. Lucien inherits both castle and fortune, and all that the text can promise by way of justice is that great ancestral homes have been known to collapse on unworthy heirs.

Rachilde's work, for all its melodrama and its unevenness, is an important account of the possession and perversion of power in the years of the decadence, and the symbolic and instrumental role that women played. She is no feminist. From the beginning, she accepts dependency on men as the price of existence, and writes to extend dependency, glamorizing submission and painting the pleasures of self-delusion. She draws the political consequences of the unequal sexual relationships she prefers, and their interconnection. Hierarchy, authority and strong leadership are the principles by which she lives, dreamed into situations where their inappropriateness and ineffectiveness is increasingly obvious.

As a result, it is the death motif that predominates in her writing. The lighthouse that encloses the old man's rotting body and the young woman's head is the grotesque symbol of dying power: rigid order that kills the life it was built to sustain. Stifling the energy of the negro, handing over his wealth to Lucien's self-confessed weakness, Valerne deliberately chooses ruin.

In the end, all power drains into the decor. The old man's hoarded capital and ancestral mansion are left to wreak havoc in the weak hands of the future. In Rachilde's work, decadence makes the clearest confession of its own impotence. We do not live, or make history; our symbols do it for us.

5
Masking Murder:
Jean Lorrain 1855–1906

The decadent inheritance enshrined in *A rebours* passed directly from Huysmans to Jean Lorrain, to be transformed into the flamboyant vulgarities of the *fin-de-siècle* and transmitted wholesale to the twentieth century. Lorrain turned what had been the aristocratic pose of a would-be unique individual into a mode that a whole class could copy. The crude Romantic origins of decadent elitism stood revealed in his work and person. Colette describes him as she knew him towards the end of his life – ageing dandy, cynic and sentimentalist, flaunting with deliberate bad taste his cheap jewellery ('chalcedonies, chrysoprases, opals and olivines – huge rings of twisted gold'), tricolor-dyed hair, face powdered white over the broken veins, brows pencilled in over red eyelids and startlingly attractive brilliant blue eyes, offset by the blue iris in his buttonhole (*Mes apprentissages*, 1936, p. 183).

His closest counterpart in the European decadence is Oscar Wilde, whom he met in Paris in 1892–3 when the Irishman was in the first flush of his fame and whose pauper's death he mourned ('Pall-Mall Semaine', *Le Journal*, 6 December 1900) with harsh words for the hypocrisy of the English establishment that ruined him. Like Wilde, he combined extremes of cynical sophistication with ingenuous sentimentality and a redeemingly self-directed irony. Like Wilde, too, he found his eccentric individuality fully realized not in neurotic seclusion but on the centre stage of society, leading a troupe of like-minded performers in decadent carnival. He too was a journalist, with a style to propagate. His regular gossip columns and articles (*L'Evénement*, 1887–90; *L'Echo de Paris*, 1890–5; *Le Journal*, 1895–1905) kept his contemporaries aware of the latest fashions and poses; his sharp eyes and ears were alert to note the details of mask, costume, phrase, intonation, that could spell social acceptability or ruin, in a world where superficial individualism masked profound conformism.

In these pieces, art elbows reality into second place. *La Ville empoisonnée: Pall-Mall Paris* (Crès, 1936), a posthumous selection from Lorrain's gossip column in *Le Journal*, evokes the kaleidoscope of literary and artistic Paris, where society is procession and display. Streets are filled with student parade for the Bal des Quat'z-Arts, Pierrot and Pierrette, Harlequin, Scaramouche and Restoration marquises, jostling with Rome and Byzantium, the Orient, Ancient Greece and prehistoric Gaul (25 April 1899). Buildings are turned to galleries and museums for the paintings, sculpture, jewellery, furniture and bric-à-brac – on which all civilization is focused, in this age of Exhibitions. Passion is a literary affair. Lorrain charts faithfully changing fashions in feeling: the sadism of the English aesthetic school, channelled through the Goncourts and Maupassant ('Logis du poète', 25 August 1887); the sombre violence, disappointed idealism and frustrated eroticism of Octave Mirbeau's *L'Abbé Jules*, 'deceived in his dreams, betrayed by his senses' (23 May 1888); the obsessive, morbid sensuality of d'Annunzio, lavishly plagiarized from the French, including Lorrain himself (2 February 1896), and its counterpart in painting, Jan Toorop's 'Les Trois Fiancées', exhibited in photograph form at the Quai Voltaire, combining the realism of Holbein with the irrealism of the opium dream: 'fantasy and dream conveyed with amazing exactness . . . an almost monastic scene of devilry' (1 February 1896). On 5 May 1896, he notes the phenomenal success of Pierre Louÿs' pagan prostitute *Aphrodite*; 18 February 1900, it is the 'dangerous' convolutions of feminine sadism in Rachilde's *La Jongleuse*.

Lorrain knows, however, that another reality exists under the play of fictions. It may only appear as counterpoint, like the view of the rooftops of Paris in the turn of the stair to the fantasies at the Quai Voltaire. Or as fresh matter for artistic exploitation, like the urban poverty that brings a new note to the cafés-chantants of Montmartre, in the plaintive or violent laments of Louise France, Mévisto aîné, or Jehan Rictus (20 February 1896). But it presses with increasing urgency to the foreground, culminating in this volume in his sincere horror at the Boxer revolt (11 July 1900), fruit of the colonialism that funds Paris's pleasure:

It has been written that the colonization of Asia will remain as the great bloodstain on the nineteenth century. We must be careful that the damp, greasy stain doesn't spread over the whole of Europe.

The Boxer rising is humanity's reply to the cruel war declared on the Boers.

On 6 December, his sympathy is again for the Boers, victims of English and German duplicity and commercial enterprise. The decadent's pose takes on an edge of political criticism.

Lorrain simultaneously celebrates and criticizes decadence. He satirizes those who buy the contention that all is play and surface, and that modes count for more than moral values. *La Petite Classe* (1895), *Pelléastres* (1910), and most of all, the chronicles of *Madame Baringhel* (1899), are a vitriolic attack on the mindless followers of decadent fashion, who reduce books, paintings and politics to the same level of off-the-peg purchase.

Rampant snobbery leads Madame Baringhel into the worst excesses of japonoiserie, chinoiserie and diablerie. She scatters her salon with copies of Jules Boissière's *Fumeurs d'opium* and Edmond de Goncourt's *Hokousaï*. She buys every engraving described in her favourite novels. An ingenuous obsession with toads and frogs is her passport to degeneracy. She gloats over a battle of frogs: '. . . a seething, crawling, hopping assembly of flabby bellies, thin thighs and warty backs . . . all horribly streaked and spotted, a whole dying, rotting heap of bullfrogs and monster toads' (p. 8).

In Jeanne Jacquemin's studio, she delights in 'green goddesses in showers of pale blossoms, irises drowned in moonlit waters, faces of Christ hanging in naked branches' and everywhere frogs (p. 17). She owns all Rops' engravings – 'In art, there's nothing unhealthy' – and expounds to a red-faced marquise the meaning of the frogs in his 'Tentation de Saint-Antoine', with their throbbing throats and shameless bellies, one Herodias, she claims, and one the Queen of Sheba, and one in a corner, an 'equivocal touch', a pale bloodless frog with its front paws raised in ecstasy to the heavens, signifying Lesbos (p. 29).

This shallowness that so swiftly reduces strong sensations to the ridiculous reduces even the Dreyfus Affair to a question of fashion. In her salon, serious discussion, patriotic cliché, and mere gossip carry equal weight. Over the 'two terrible years' in which its implications slowly dawned on the Establishment, Madame Baringhel's contemporaries swivelled from the rabid anti-Semitism of Henri Rochefort and Edouard Drumont, to Zola, and back again; while Lorrain himself, traditionalist, nationalist and anti-Semitic, remained consistently opposed to Dreyfus, registering his delight, for example, in the municipal elections of 1900, at seeing the Dreyfusards 'floored' by the nationalist candidates

(P. L. Gauthier, *Jean Lorrain*, 1935, p. 207).

In his preface to Lorrain's *La Petite Classe*, Maurice Barrès challenged these caricatures of what in his view were mere imitators, poor pastiches of the genuine neurotics of the decadence (the heroes of Barrès' own books). Far better, he thought, were Lorrain's accounts of the tragic heroes of Individualism: 'He follows them through every shock, pity, pain and hallucination, mingled and exaggerated to the point of death . . . A magician in love with the dangerous side of nature.'

Barrès missed the originality and the truthfulness conveyed by Lorrain's more ambivalent vision, in which the modern decadent is primarily a playactor – not by choice, but out of a necessity forced on him by the decadent moment. In Sarah Bernhardt's Lorenzaccio, at the Théâtre de la Renaissance, Lorrain greeted an *alter ego*. Musset's would-be saviour of Renaissance Florence, bloodstained and debauched, dreams 'sumptuous dreams of art and liberty', 'dazzling yet pale, like a lily blooming in a boneyard'. He puts on a mask of decadence to charm the tyrant who is destroying the Republic, the better to plot his murder. Trapped and degraded by the mask, with no support from time-serving contemporaries, he is defeated both by his own pose, and by politics too complex and contradictory for one individualistic gesture ever to resolve. Bernhardt's frail black-suited youth finds his gesture of murder turns against himself. His identity vanishes under the mask in a self-consuming blaze of murderous hate and dream:

> In the cynical youth, this whole complex, contrived pose of cowardly insolence betrays the disgust of a world-weary soul, the suffering of the body smothered by the mask, while the shining blue-green eyes in the pallid cheeks, flickering with chilly steel, the wandering eyes that suddenly fix in a frightening stare or fill with distant dream, denounce the rage of insults swallowed in silence, hatred of the world, desire for ripe revenge and the determination to kill (3 December 1896, coll. in *La Ville empoisonnée*).

Criminal Passions

In its serious evocations of contemporary neurosis, Lorrain's writing combines reportage and creative imagination to re-create urban civilization in the shape of Baudelairean nightmare. This world, inhabited by monstrous, predatory egos, is a source of terrors to be turned into aesthetic pleasure. Sometimes confrontations are sudden and shocking; sometimes the slow accumulation of obsessive fears builds into morbid hysteria. Outlines are deliberately clouded by the smoke of cigarettes, the fumes of ether and opium, and the fogs of gaslit streets, tempting inhabitants to lose themselves in the landscape of their own fears. What is most real in this world are the obsessive symbols in which evil is focused.

Criminality has become the essence of society and of human personality: 'Every man, in his secret heart, is obsessed with robbing and cheating his neighbour. Modern life, in all its luxury or harshness, has given men and women the souls of bandits and slave-drivers' (*Sensations et souvenirs*, 1895, p. 165). Trawling among the *faits divers* of the daily newspapers, Lorrain finds the slums and back-street brothels supply tales as horrifying as any of de Sade's inventions. Under the title 'Crimes de Montmartre et d'ailleurs', the posthumous *Pelléastres* (1910) collects a sequence that first appeared in *L'Evénement* in 1888 and 1889. 'La Terreur à Londres' evokes Jack the Ripper's murders down among the fogs and gaslight of the East End docks. The mysterious Ripper, 'fantastic, invisible, a character out of Edgar Allan Poe', an English gentleman, Lorrain surmises, with that particular English brand of black humour ('the gloomily gay note of British FUN'), provokes fascinated and perversely sympathetic conjectures. 'What moral torments, what dreadful criminal, remorseful obsessions must rack him to bring him to such carniverous savagery, such atrocious thirst for blood!' as he piles up his score of prostitute victims:

> In dark backyards, alley corners, in the cellars of houses under construction, on the banks of the Thames, on deserted building sites, men find the disembowelled, quivering remains of their wretched pleasure-giving flesh, flesh sold cheap for sailors' lusts, now flesh for torture for a dilettante murderer.

In 'Le Métier de femme', Lorrain laments: 'These are dreadful days for women. For respectable and licentious alike, love comes down to a razor blade over the carotid artery, or two bullets in the head.'

The Ripper's female French counterpart is 'Mauricette', the lace-maker in the dock at the Bordeaux Assizes as an accomplice to murder. Amoral, vindictive, shamelessly self-interested, she hid her knowledge that her lover had murdered his previous mistress, and wore the dead woman's jewels without a qualm until he left her in turn for another woman, and she denounced him to the police.

At one moment, the criminal can be an object of pity. 'Fleurs de banlieue', recalling Huysmans' evocation in 'La Bièvre' of the poetry of the decaying suburbs, describes the sickly 'romance' of the whores who haunt them, driven by poverty to rob and kill. Against this, 'Verdicts littéraires' introduces a harsh, condemnatory note, shocked that so many 'crimes of passion' go unpunished. In 'Une morte', Lorrain changes tack again, and speaks up for the victims of the Darwinian ethos and against the cult of the powerful: 'In our busy, feverish era with its "struggle for life", it's the victims who are in the wrong. Never has the *vae victis* been howled with such victorious rage at deserted women, fallen governments and fallen reputations . . .'

Crime crosses social boundaries. At the top of society, however, it tends to be renamed perversity and judged as a work of art, or else it stays unpunished, as he points out in his dedication to *Le Crime des riches* (1905), evading publicity and the processes of justice, since it can pose no threat to social order.

Aristocratic crime is a dream of disorder that never encounters real consequences. When the aristocratic model for George Selwyn, de Goncourt's English sadist, visited Etretat, neighbours were terrified by the strange goings-on in his villa, renamed after de Sade's celebrated castle. Negroes were chased round the garden at night, gunshots echoed, little servant boys came and went with unusual rapidity, and after one night, filled with terrifying sobs and screams, a child's coffin left the house. The audience for this anecdote see in it one of Hoffmann's tales, or an English mystification ('Dolmancé', 25 August 1887) – though clearly they half wish the mystification were fact.

All the much-publicized sadistic excesses of the nineties, Lorrain would have us believe, were pure mystification, in France at least. In *Pelléastres*, under the subheading 'Le Poison de la littérature', Huysmans is blamed for the vogue for Black Masses. Everyone was desperate to attend one, but no one ever did, just as every woman claimed to be the original of the icy-fleshed Madame Chantelouve. The Adelsward affair (in the chapter 'Messes noires' *et passim*) was only an attempt by a literary snob to attract fashionable attention. (The Baron Jacques d'Adelsward Fersen, dabbler in royalist politics, Satanism and paganism, organized Neronic orgies in his flat in the avenue Friedland, beginning with processions of children in Greek costume, dramatizing Baudelaire's poetry, and ending in the 'regrettable excesses' that filled the newspapers in the second half of 1893.)

The real crimes of the aristocracy are acts of moral and intellectual cruelty, the last bitter gestures of a dying race that knows its traditional talents no longer qualify it for a place in history. One remaining skill still attracts poets and artists. Aristocrats are great actors and stage-managers of emotion. The novel *Très Russe* (1886) presents Madame Livitnof (Lady Sore), the archetype of 'the great cosmopolitan courtesans', and representative of the elegant world of the Second Empire which was dispersed by the disasters of 1870–1: 'Sedan, and the great humiliation of the Commune' (p. 113). In her mysterious past, 'there's a bit of everything: mud, gold and blood' (p. 33). For the poet Allain Mauriat, with his fatal penchant for perverse women, she represents an irresistible temptation. A self-proclaimed egoist, she demands from lovers the admiration and devotion her rank used to command. She gives herself only once, explaining with 'a cruel, painful Mona Lisa smile' that 'chastity is extreme desire' (p. 86). She envies Cleopatra and Marguerite of Burgundy, who murdered their lovers. No modern woman ever possesses a virgin lover, but if she can't be his first love, she can always be his last. She enjoys the power-play of jealousy, exciting rivals to intensify Allain's passion and refusing to give herself until the night before her husband comes home from his travels. For such women, love is all illusion and artifice: 'Between a woman like me and a poet, that is a sceptic, like you, there's nothing true or possible in love except the science of love itself' (p. 240).

The essence of love lies in imposing pain, to demonstrate power. Love is 'one sex dying in the embrace of the other' (*L'Ecole des vieilles femmes*, 1905, cit. P. L. Gauthier, p. 64). Most often, woman is the murderer. Nelly, the golden-haired Lorelei with mysterious blue-green eyes, exudes 'the philtre of Death, the fascination of Non-being' ('Les Yeux glauques', *Buveurs d'âmes*, 1893). She listens, entranced, to an old legend that the woman who looks into her lover's eyes as he dies will gain his soul, and with it, the gift of eternal youth. The couple go boating together, and he drowns in a mysterious accident. In 'Ophélius', a painter lies dying of an obsession with the smile and the eyes of Botticelli's 'perversely ideal' 'Primavera', who is 'Giaconda and Ophelia combined'. Lady Viane, his English wife, has the same enigmatic smile and starry eyes, promising an ideal that can never be possessed, as had the drowned sailor he saw three months before on the beach. As he dies, Viane tells the narrator, his friend, that she loves him, not her husband – and then immediately withdraws, leaving behind her another unfulfilled promise. The hint of Claudius' homosexuality is repressed, and the tale concludes with a denunciation of Eve:

> ... Flaubert's Ennoïa, the eternal enemy, the dancer drinking the blood of prophets, Salome, Herodias, the impure creature, the Beast. When she kills our bodies, we call her Debauch; when she murders our souls we call her Hate, or sometimes Love.

Women also kill women. Both artist and aristocrat, La Barnarina, the Wagnerian opera star, watches at her window for her stepdaughter,

Rosario, whose life she is sucking dry with her kisses, and from whose lips she takes the daily glass of blood prescribed by her doctor. A chill, cruel Russian blonde, she is surrounded by snow-coloured flowers, irises, narcissi, tulips:

> ... visionary, icy white ... a strange artificial bouquet, immaterial, but of a cruel, suggestive hardness, with the flowers' sharp, cutting edges, the irises like hauberk spikes, the jagged chalices of the tulips, and the starry narcissi, a mysterious blossoming of stars fallen from a wintry night sky.

'Le Buveur d' âmes' of the title story, however, is a man, an aristocrat enjoying an adulterous affair with an artist, fascinated by the pain in her eyes, and the obsessive anguish in her painting:

> ... a watery, distant gaze swallowed up by the intense blue of her eyes, while her wild, sensual mouth smiled like a mystic Bacchante ... I love those heart-breaking severed heads of women and martyrs she conjures up, inevitably sitting on an inverted dish or bathed like cut flowers in the bloody water of a glass shaped like a chalice; and I adore the cold, transparent blue of the eyes in those pathetic heads, those tired, forgiving eyes, where I see her own ...

On their first night together, he delightedly drank her tears: 'Cleopatra drank pearls. Why shouldn't he drink the blood of her soul?' (A longer version of this piece, condemned by the censor, contained the woman's whole past history, beginning with her rape by her guardian on the way home from her father's funeral, and including a pious condemnation of women who put their art before the role of mother or mistress. See 'Victime', in *Correspondance*, Editions Baudinière, 1929). In 'Un soir qu'il neigeait', a pimp prostitutes his wife to a rich man who likes to play de Retz. He runs a razor blade across her throat until she's mad with terror, then puts the blade away, takes her and goes. 'That's what turns those stinking rich on', says the pimp self-righteously, 'scaring workers' daughters and good proletarians' wives, victimizing poor people; so when our turn comes, the landlords had better watch out.'

The greatest refinement is to blend victim and executioner, source and object of pain and pleasure, in one single person and form. 'Sur un Dieu mort' contemplates a Descent from the Cross to reveal a pagan original under its Christian veil. The central figure is 'a Christ with the effeminate grace of Adonis', with a halo of peacocks' feathers, bracelets and rings on his arms and wrists, and two bleeding wing-stumps on his shoulders. This androgynous Cupid, slipped in to represent the death of Love, is said to be more arousing and obsessive in its ambivalence than the conventional images of suffering in the surrounding figures of Virgin, Magdalene and Baptist. Lorrain's writing lingers with horrified delight over its own perversity, in a tone of cautious sensuality, triply refined through the frame of the painting, the mythical nature of its content, and the abstract language:

> Through the purulent wounds of its torment, this bloody nakedness preserved a transparency of flesh, suppleness of contour and elusive grace which was not that of a man of thirty; this victim of the cross had the chubbiness and the slenderness of the ephebe, and even in his gentle, beardless Asiatic face, with its heavy dark eyelids and sinuous lips, and their contemptuous, cruel lines, this Jesus had a kind of ambiguous charm and perverse attraction that intrigued me . . .

'L'Homme aux têtes de cire' models a wax head which might be either a woman or a youth, a work of 'visionary art' in which the only certainty is the anguish in its eyes: 'You were seized by pity, spiced with an indefinable unhealthy curiosity, before these child's eyes which had become woman's eyes as they gazed on some dreadful nightmare.' The model was an Italian boy who died of poverty shortly afterwards. The narrator buys the head, both for its formal genius and for the real pain it represents.

If there is an underlying pattern to the criminal acts that are the substance of Lorrain's world, it is that figured here in childhood corrupted, innocence thrust into guilty knowledge by treacherous elders, or in the parallel image of the couple, where Eve, mother turned temptress, lures an innocent lover to destruction. The dominant partner is condemned, for preying on weakness. But the victim is also guilty. The erotic nature of these criminal relationships stresses the victims' active desire for complicity.

Behind all this, the larger crime at issue is that of a dying generation's desire to revive its own decaying world, seducing the young to its service. Ultimately, the victims are not the sufferers of sexual but of political relationships: it is the Italian pauper who provides the substance of both the sculptor's and Lorrain's artistic invention.

One last striking feature of Lorrain's account of contemporary crime is the way in which blame for its worst excesses is shifted to foreigners, refugees from European revolution (the Russians) or predators from rival nations (the English). These become centres of corruption within a national aristocracy which by contrast, and in a contrived haze of self-righteousness, acquires a new innocence.

It is the smoky fantasies of the opium den which, in *Coins de Byzance* (1902), generate scabrous anecdotes about the dubious international set that gravitates to the melting-pot of the Riviera. Their narrator, Count Germont, enthusiastically adds the latest atrocity to his collection: 'I cultivate the orchid of the exquisite corpse . . . I'm the Robert de Montesquiou of carrion flesh.' Russian officers, princesses, secret policemen fleeing the Tsar's purges, have turned the Riviera into 'a corrupt suburb of Byzantium'. Count Sternoskef, former rake, now neurotic mysogynist, pays his male secretaries to attend him everywhere, constant, silent and chaste companions – a 'vampire' on their young lives. Baroness Nydorf is another kind of predator, out of a child's storybook, with 'those heavy, dark eyelids, that triangular smile over her ogress's teeth, that greedy mouth and those devouring, damp, enamel eyes, set off by her grey complexion . . . and her supple, gliding gait like a hunting cat' (p. 103). Worse still are the English, exporting their gin-sodden indifference and the fumes of ether and opium out of their little island to corrupt an entire continent. The stews of Naples are their proper home: 'Wherever he goes, the true Englishman inhabits the brothel; he carries it with him over the whole world, with his antiseptic toilet waters, his Sheffield razors and his boredom' (p. 58). The old English lord, who really prefers little girls, terrorizes Continental prostitutes, and the smouldering passions of bespectacled English misses put stalwart gondoliers to flight.

This, though, is trivial malice compared with Lorrain's onslaught on the Jews. *L'Aryenne*, the novel published posthumously in 1907, blames Jewish influence for the economic, moral and cultural decadence of France. Two Aryans in love, Breton aristocrats, are captives of a Jewish 'Barbarian'. The Prince de Ragan d'Helyeuse married Rebecca to exchange his status for her money. The Countess Marthe Ilhatieff is a poor parasite, who pays for her bed and board by introducing Rebecca into society. Both Ragan and Marthe feel that Rebecca has the better bargain. Common resentment drives them to a flirtation, which she discovers. Her punishment is to 'forgive' them. Stopped from committing suicide, Marthe sinks into a limbo of morphine, to blunt her humiliation and despair. Rebecca now has both money and position – the enemy within the gates.

The symbol of her victims' painful dependency is the Lalique ring Rebecca gave her husband, which he gave to Marthe, and which Rebecca insisted she go on wearing, as a sign of servitude. Of semi-precious stones, rock-crystal and enamel, the ring figures a tragic mask supported by laurels and myrtles, coiled through with an enamel serpent, all in evil greenish-blue. When Marthe first slipped it on to admire it, she found it stuck to her finger, and could not be removed:

> My puffy, bruised finger swelled over both edges of the ring, and Lalique's clear enamels were incrusted in my flesh; my whole hand is burning and painful, and I spent a feverish night. I was tormented by a terrible nightmare: the enamel serpent squeezed me until I screamed, the purple crystal mask sniggered and bit me till I bled, its savage teeth cutting down to the bone, and the mask looked more and more like Rebecca, Rebecca transformed into a vengeful Fury, knowing our fault.

The three are bound together in a fatal dependency. Racist resentments combine with the admission that the Jews are needed, and that the Aryans are not only helpless without them but equally evil. The horror of the situation is that they come to love their subjection. Marthe sinks into masochistic resignation tinged with innuendoes of lesbian attraction towards Rebecca, who throughout is the image of the cruel Goddess: Moreau's Salome, posing in her salon in jewel-studded silk, or, in her blue-green silk tunic, a slender jade icon.

Lorrain's two great novels, *Monsieur de Phocas. Astarté* (1901) and *Le Vice errant* (1902) are both images of a society made of and moved by violence and transgression. In both books, the hero's viciousness is a symptom of his displacement. Despite appearances, he is not the centre of his text. Phocas' self-obsessed quest for his heart's desire, and Noronsoff's despotic attempt to transform the Riviera into his own private theatre, are games played on the margins of history. Each in turn is subject to someone greater: the English lord, be it Férédith or Ethal, in whom the real wealth and power is concentrated. Consuming, using and killing are not choices that mark out individuals for distinction. They are acts of submission and co-option to a system which, like Phocas' Astarte, is both repugnant and desirable.

Both novels present Woman as the temptress, Eve responsible for the heroes' fall. But rapidly the text establishes that the true images of desire are male. The hero wants to submit to an image of his own masculine power. Modern society is founded on collusion between men to preserve the power of the Father. Yet even in the homosexual obsessions in the texts, ambivalence remains. The guilt that Lorrain associates with homosexual desire conveys his simultaneous rejection and acceptance of the structures by which he lives.

Monsieur de Phocas is by reputation an evil and debauched man. The framing narrator reports this, and the reader's first sight of him confirms it. But ambivalence is introduced with the manuscript autobiography he gives to the narrator, which is both self-disclosure and confession of error. The repentant libertine quotes Musset, and Swinburne's 'Laus Veneris':

> Sin, is it sin when men's souls are thrust
> Into the pit? Yet had I a good trust
>
> To save my soul before it slipped therein,
> Trod under by the fire-shod feet of lust.
> . . . sad hell where all sweet love hath end,
> All but the pain that never finisheth.

The repentance is itself double-edged, for in presenting the narrator with his seductive account, Phocas is effectively extending the chain of corruption.

The many different hands in which the text is written disclose a personality in disarray, seeking unity through the byways of the hidden and the forbidden. Phocas will have peace when he unravels the fascination of the '*yeux glauques*', the ambivalent blue-green gaze that has obsessed him since childhood. He has found it in jewels, especially emeralds, and in women's eyes – Salome's, those of his mistress, the actress Willie Stephenson, and those of Astarte, Demon of Lust and Demon of the Sea. The contradictory image of the sea is that of Phocas' desire: for an eternal, unchanging reality with a superficially changing face.

The source of his obsession is discovered in two dramatic entries for 28 and 29 March 1899, tracing the slowly emerging recollection of an idyllic childhood moment. He was riding home on the haywagon, eleven years old, with a young farmhand, Jean Destreux, who delighted all the children with his games, and tales of military service in Africa. The hayload collapsed, and Destreux fell under the cart. The bright blue stare of his dead eyes fixed for Phocas the image of total satisfaction, combining the maternal security of the warm, enfolding, swaying hayride with paternal promises of excitement and challenge. When Phocas goes back to his country home to try and recapture the memory, the bliss is gone. There is a paradox: the corrupt adult can understand, but not experience, the bliss that the innocent child experienced without knowing it. For Phocas, the paradox is both pleasure and pain – the wound at the centre of his being, that he cherishes. His dream is not of a new future, but an irrevocably dead past which, were it not dead, would not be desirable. Homosexual love is a

dream Phocas would not dare contemplate in reality.
He devotes his life to re-creating another such moment of intense
pleasure. Too late, he discovered that such moments are always
gratuitous. His experiments with whores were futile:

> Whores for me have never been anything but flesh for experiment, not
> even for enjoyment. Greedy for sensations and analyses, I used them for
> documentation, like anatomical objects, and none of them gave me the
> thrill I expected; because I was on the lookout for such a thrill, lurking in
> ambush in the undergrowth of my neuroses, and there is no self-
> conscious pleasure, only unconscious, healthy joy, and I lavishly wasted
> my life contriving it, instead of living it; and because all refinement and
> quest for rarity leads fatally to decomposition and the Void (p. 288).

The self-conscious seeker finds only his own reflection in the world.
Phocas' quest is echoed in the narcissistic poetry of Charles Vellay,
desiring: 'To be mirrored in others' eyes, drown in eyes like Narcissus at
the fountain' (p. 37). But the mirror, says Phocas, only reflects the eyes
that look into it: 'There is nothing in eyes, and that's their terrifying,
painful enigma, their hallucinatory, abominable charm. There is nothing
but what we put there ourselves' (p. 39). What Phocas sees is humiliating –
nothing but animal instinct and disappointed desire.

Phocas searches among objects that are bought, collected and consumed
– emeralds, 'with their translucent aquamarine poison' (p. 10), sex, drugs
and works of art. In his sensual life, the morbid blue-green gaze of Astarte
inspires dreams of artifice and perversion. His first preference is for the
androgyne; a statue of Antinoüs is for him the epitome of art. In history, it
is the corrupt young Caligula, Otto, Messalina and Poppaea, who charm
him with their expression of lascivious weariness. Exhaustion, morbidity,
viciousness enhance beauty. It is 'the charm of the hospital' (p. 27) that
marks the fashionable beauty of the twentieth century, the venal
androgyne with cavernous eyes and emaciated face. These women awaken
in him a 'spring of cruelty' (p. 36) which takes him by terrifying surprise.
Art reinforces the corruption of his instincts. He copies the lovebite
sequence from Swinburne's 'Laus Veneris' at the head of an entry
describing the bruise on the neck of the sleeping woman beside him, and
the longing it stirs in him to suck out her life and soul. The scent of death
lingers on her breath: 'The sickly smell all human creatures exhale in their
sleep' (p. 24). When the impulse recurs, he remembers how, at eight, he
squeezed the life out of two doves, and wonders: 'Twice now I've caught
myself thinking of murder in the depths of passion. Am I two people?'

(p. 25). Willie Stephenson's slender neck, like Anne Boleyn's, stirs dreams of execution and rape. Ize Kranile, dancing naked under her black veil, smiling like a sardonic vampire, recalls Salome, 'the eternal, impure animal, the malicious little girl, unconsciously perverse, who . . . makes old kings hoarse with desire' (p. 50). Both women turn from dreams into whores. Just once in a young sailor's eyes Phocas saw the green gaze of his dreams and 'I felt the pull of the abyss' (p. 64). But the glance flickered past him.

Masks might conceal the eyes of his dream. But masks too are only delusions. In an ether-induced nightmare, he dreams of a darkened Marseilles, peopled with silent prostitutes, all identical, and all dead under their masks, except for their glassy eyes. Awake or asleep, he sees nothing but masks, covering dead faces, a painfully lucid vision of modern life and its 'envy, despair, hatred, and egoism, and avarice' (p. 79).

He is easy prey now for the English painter Claudius Ethal, whose fluent, satirical tongue brings nightmare into the salon, whispering of scandals that transform Phocas' fellow guests into devils. With his collection of Japanese masks he initiates Phocas into the exquisite, artistic forms of vice. He liberates the evil double in Phocas' personality: 'This mysterious raconteur tells me my own tale, gives flesh to my dreams, *he speaks me out loud and I awake* in him as though in another self more subtle and precise' (p. 104).

Ethal – a more vicious version of the Lord Henry who destroyed Dorian Gray – exploits Phocas' sexual insecurity. He sends him paintings. From Jan Toorop's 'Les Trois Fiancées', the eyes of the Bride of Hell stare threateningly; Goya's 'Dream of Reason' fills his sleep with nightmares; he is haunted by Ensor's mask of Lust. Phocas struggles against Ethal's definition: 'Am I a lover of death?' (p. 151). He shrinks from Ethal's own sculptures (the head of a dying child, a wax Infanta with decomposing flesh, modelled on a dying marquise) and from his preference for art over reality: 'artistic emotions . . . which are the most intense, and the richest in complex sensations'. He struggles against Ethal's suggestion that he too could find pleasure in murder and crime, watching the poor and the prostitute suffer in 'the rotten civilization of a big city, Paris, or London . . . what you're looking for is the gaze of torment' (p. 153).

With Ethal's friends, grotesque, ageing decadents, Phocas for the first time tastes opium. He experiences the pleasure of absolute degradation, and the double pleasure of being both observer and observed, dominant subject and passive object. As the opium takes effect, the naked Javanese dancers at the orgy vanish in a swirling cloud, to be replaced by a dark lamplit street where two thieves carefully saw at a woman's throat with a delicate knifeblade. From this cruel vision, Phocas soars into dizzy flight from which, suddenly, he plunges to destruction, into oozing depths where clinging vampires suck his blood, until he almost swoons into spasm. Suddenly, 'something hairy, limp, cold entering my mouth' turns out to be the antidote (p. 205). The mysterious, vicious, double is on the threshold of existence; Phocas sees himself as Gilles de Retz in the forest of Tiffauges, haunted by obscene desires.

Welcôme, a former protégé of Ethal's, plans to leave the murderous world of Europe and take refuge in the East. Ethal sends Phocas a new icon, an image of Astarte as the destroyer, Kali, with a Death's Head and crudely displayed genitals. Phocas must choose between two selves and two ways of life: desperate, evasive idealism or the murderous pleasures of instinct.

In the end, his decision is not his own, but is imposed on him by the force of art. The genius of Gustave Moreau has pre-empted every solution to the decadent dilemma. Both Ethal and Welcôme press him to see the 'Triumph of Alexander', the apotheosis of the new life of Benares. Ethal wants him to look into the eyes of Moreau's portraits.

Phocas has his own preconceptions of Moreau's work. It is perverse religion revived, a mysticism of cruelty and sexual excess conceived for the bankers and shareholders of modern times, depicting the force that moves the modern world, which is murder. For Phocas, his name evokes the enmity of body and spirit and the malaise of nostalgia for dead days: 'the dangerous love of dead women and their long, staring, empty eyes, the hallucinatory dead women of long ago, whom he brings back to life in the mirror of time' (p. 350). His white coral 'Sirènes', with their living branches, restate the paradox of death-in-life, and life-in-death, which confronts the decadent generation.

On the second storey, Phocas finds the 'Triumph of Alexander', where the solitary leader sits on a throne like an altar, washed by enthusiastic crowds. His is a sensuous response to the colour, structure, symbols and textures of the painting, produced in Lorrain's prose-poem reconstruction in language that implicitly urges the reader to see the political invitations of the canvas. This is a demagogic fantasy, in which the crowd joyfully submits to the young representative of the old elite who seizes power, declaring himself the solution to all the old contradictions, marrying Greece and Asia, old order and new, Reason and Violence – the old elite and the challenging mob. In the background is a terrifying but thrilling cliff, from which the temples and pagodas of the city are carved. The relationship of crowd and leader is in the foreground. A careful admixture of fantasy turns tired old tyranny into something new and strange.

Elephants mix with the crowd, massive strength domesticated; dragons, sphinxes and lotus flowers jostle on the throne in carved profusion, figuring the complex mystery of leadership. The whole scene is bathed in an atmosphere of liquid gold and iris petals – phallic power in softer, more seductive form. Phocas is moved by excitement, and also nostalgia – an appropriate response to a picture that offers not the new life of the East, but a more seductive disguise for the old values of the West.

The rest of the gallery is haunted by empty eyes and the smell of blood, wrapped in that atmosphere of beauty and terror which, Ethal had said, always envelops the killer, and which rekindles Phocas' fears of seeing his murderous double emerge. Turning to leave, Phocas suddenly finds his own answer in the painting of 'Les Prétendants', one of Ethal's recommendations. Ulysses, returned from his wanderings, is an obscure figure in the background, aiming his arrows through the hall. At the centre is the flaming image of Athene, guiding his aim. Death is inevitable. The suitors are caught at the height of an orgy of flowers, jewels and naked flesh. Moreau has consciously heightened the effect, Phocas notes, by making all his male figures adolescents, giving his picture a cruel, Neronic sensuality. The foreground displays the different ways in which these heroes of decadence meet their inevitable end. A group in the centre sits stoically drinking, oblivious to the carnage. On the far right, a would-be martyr bares his breast to the arrows; on the far left, one proud individual takes poison before the arrows can reach him. Phocas is fascinated by the eyes of these last two, filled with the pain and resolution of death, a gaze more compelling than any look of love. They are men 'become decisive, supernatural and, finally, themselves in the anguish of their last moment of life' (p. 358).

He suddenly realizes that the way to create the gaze he has longed for all his life is to kill – but not as Ethal had intended. Like Ulysses, he performs 'an act of justice' (p. 401), of which Ethal himself is the victim. If Europe is rotten with murder, it should be the wicked, not the innocent, who die. Phocas turns Ethal's own artistic poison against him, forcing him to swallow the poison hidden in his own emerald ring. He wonders at his own calm: 'the coolness of the sleepwalker with which I accomplished the act' (p. 396). The police swallow, without difficulty, the explanation he concocts.

With this murder, Phocas enters into possession of himself. He feels a sense of liberation. It is he now who is the artist, in control of his own life, beyond all definitions of good and evil. He still dreams of a city in ruins, but filled with the calm of night, the air quivering with plumes and soft whispers, which are the rustling jewels that clothe the sweet-faced Salomes of Moreau's watercolours. Those blue-green jewels, pale in the dark, are still the eyes of Astarte, but now at peace: 'I never had such a sweet dream' (p. 404). Cool contempt replaces his raging hatred for his Parisian contemporaries. He is able to leave Europe and join Welcôme to make a new beginning in the East.

The conscious irony of Lorrain's text is that Phocas' end is not triumph, but a total capitulation to the image Ethal created of him. The repose he feels is the temporary calm of passion spent, the idol momentarily sated by a sacrifice which will have to be renewed. Dorian Gray stabbed his own portrait. Phocas turned his violence outward, and freed the vampire double from his tomb. What flees to Benares is a reincarnation of Ethal, intending to draw fresh energy from a whole fresh race of victims, to write again its own futile dream of life without change, longing 'to travel, to live fervently a life of passion and adventures, to annihilate myself in the unknown, in infinity, in the energy of young peoples, in the beauty of unchanging races, in the sublimity of the instincts' (p. 405).

The novel concludes on a vision of Astarte in an emerald diadem and a gauzy cloak that hides her genitals, the image of life's mystery which is not necessarily, claims Phocas, a mystery of death. At least, he has decided, there will be no death for him. Her eyes are closed; to remake the deathly gaze he craves, he sets off for Egypt, and more murders.

In Phocas, Ethal has succeeded in embodying the madness of decadence. The pathological symptoms are faithfully recorded: exacerbated sensual responses, sexual confusion and guilt, obsessions, alternating lethargy and violence, unmotivated fears, and the sense of alienation and 'possession'. But ironically, what Phocas becomes is a personality finally at home in society, whose word carries weight with the police, and who commands the narrator's respect. In transferring his dangerous energies to the colonies, he is performing a socially acceptable action. The twist in Lorrain's tale is that this madness, in society's terms, is in fact sanity.

Noronsoff's madness is of a different kind. The Count has neither the wish nor the ability to disguise his criminal instincts. The last remaining aristocrat, he has no alternative but to repeat the old role in front of the new Barbarian tyrants. The English, and the mob, are the beneficiaries of the humiliating spectacle of his degeneration and his futile revolt – a contemptible audience, before which the most vile and vicious gestures become perversely heroic. Lorrain's ogre is a grotesque Samson, pulling down the pillars of the Philistine temple:

He called down flames and destruction on the town that had held him up to ridicule, destruction and flames, fire from heaven and the fire of the Barbarians on the old Europe of his corruption; in his frenzied death agony there was a last magnificence . . . And in one final spasm he at last spat out the old soul of Byzantium that for too long had lingered with him (p. 363).

Once again the narrative frame shifts the story into the recent past. Spoken in the now abandoned garden of Noronsoff's villa in Nice, the story conjures up the ghosts of monsters whose power to harm is gone, rewriting them in the forgiving perspective of Nature and nostalgia as part of history's cycles, a moment of poisonous decay that has generated the beauty of the present. The horror now lies hidden in the landscape:

Mountains and seas vanished in the distance, in a powdery heat haze, but here all was chiaroscuro and shadow, the shadow of a sacred wood: nameless flowers, daughters of solitude, bloomed in the topmost branches, with huge petals like great butterflies. There were African, American, and Indian corners. In the camellia grove, the withered calyxes had dropped in a snow of pink and white decay, and their slow decomposition lent an additional charm to the torpid silence . . . The park seethed with a living world of maggots and poisons. Over it brooded the heavy heat of the graveyard, and I thought of d'Annunzio's books, with their descriptions of the gardens of Sicily and farthest Italy, melancholy under the sun's brilliance, with their obsessive, oppressive charm . . . A superb frame, don't you think, this enchanted park, for the death agony of a race? (pp. 117–18).

Like the flowers in the branches, literary form masks the ugliness of corruption. D'Annunzio is only the latest in a line of chroniclers of aristocratic decline, of a story that 'starts like a fairytale and ends like a chapter in Suetonius, with notes by Saint-Simon inserted in the margins' (p. 119).

Noronsoff draws together in his own person all the corruption of old Europe, East and West, the naïve, superstitious and extravagant temper of his Russian fathers joined to the Florentine inheritance of his mother. He carries in his blood the curse laid on his family in the fifteenth century by the gipsy whose betrothed an ancestor had stolen. All Noronsoff wives become faithless, whoring furies. Noronsoff is unmarried, but he has a Polish countess for a mistress.

Like des Esseintes, he is the victim of 'a neurasthenia acquired by every possible nervous expenditure and all the excess of a life already deplorably famous . . . worn out by sensation and ruined by debauch . . . [and] the misuse of anaesthetics' (p. 135). He holds audiences of his parasites dressed in jewelled robes, sitting on his commode. The symbolism is deliberate: the show of wealth and the exercise of power delights in the foulness on which it is founded.

Noronsoff is a physical and moral ruin, held together by artifice. Physically, he is preserved by the skills of his doctor, the narrator, who disapproves of his excesses, but in return for a fat fee is willing to put his talents at the service of the monster's will to live. That will is sustained by a different kind of skill – the storytelling gifts of the young sailor, Marius, he picked up at the harbour along with his friend, bringing both back to the villa to charm his black moods like a male Scheherezade, with 'invitations to voyages', stories like Lorrain's own, alternating heroic, romantic dream with cheap perversion, 'all the words and the specialities from the gutters of the rue Ventomagy and the rue de la Rose down to the sailors' dives in the old harbour'.

His life is a series of staged performances, suppers, receptions, fetes and masques. He seeks to co-opt the rest of society as actors in his fantasies, from dependants, such as his mistress, or Marius and the mob from the old city and the harbour, to the new arbiters of the fashionable world, Lord Férédith, the English owner of the yacht that ties up in the harbour below his villa, carrying Algernon Filde, the Wildean poet-satirist on board, whose ridicule undercuts the Count's pretensions.

In exchange for their co-operation, the mob demands that the Count acts out its own dreams of opulence, and that he pays. The mob rules Byzantium, and its so-called tyrants only live in exchange for bread and circuses. The relationship of actor and audience is fragile, and easily broken by the ascendant star, Lord Férédith.

His instrument is Noronsoff's mistress, Polish and Jewish, seeking revenge for years of humiliation. To impress the English lord and his poet, she sets Noronsoff on to give the performance of his life. The garden is remodelled for a festival of Adonis, with all the inhabitants of the town for extras, an orgy of roses and torchlight whose centrepiece is Bacchus in triumph, played by one of the Countess's beautiful adolescent sons. The tableau displays Noronsoff's power to transform his world into the image of his desire. His wealth wraps the future – the child – in the morbid forms of the past, and induces the crowd to acclaim his fantasy as its God. The procession builds into an intensely sensuous moment of perfume, light, shouts and music, all caught and focused in the costume of the child, a web of Noronsoff's jewels that completely masks the human flesh:

. . . a mad [costume], defying description, like that of Salammbô in Gustave Flaubert, or Heliogabalus in Jean Lombard's *L'Agonie*; Gustave Moreau does the same thing. He is dressed in a kind of ash, ash shivering with the reflections of watery gems. The material of his robe is woven of nothing but moonstones, opals and sards; a pectoral of amethysts clasps his torso, and he wears a massive wreath of huge purple poppies – shadowy poppies with ruby pistils, monstrous, crazed and adorable, an emperor's dream, a poet's invention, the apotheosis of a god!

The spectacle collapses because Lord Férédith refuses to watch. He sails away with the Countess, leaving a mocking note of excuse, a vulgar vaudeville and Noronsoff in collapse. As he lies near death in his room, the crowd, bored and unpaid, surges round the villa, throwing stones through the glass, threatening to swamp it. The well-drilled procession turns into a half-naked mob, shrieking in near-unintelligible patois, the torchlight flickering on tragic faces under antique diadems and naked torsos wrapped in stained togas. There is a sickening atmosphere of rut, carnival and riot, roses streaming in tangles of hair, 'bleeding, streaming, brilliant, stagnating, like rivers of wine'.

In its orgiastic climax, the focus turns from the hero to the mob. It is not the egoist, but the mob that is the danger, that needs to be held on a tight rein, and at arm's length, and which despises the show of a common humanity in its leaders. To hold back the mob, the flamboyant, honest viciousness of the old aristocratic tradition can no longer be indulged. A grotesque death reluctantly severs the Noronsoff connection. The Count, his passion finally become total madness, roaming the harbour in search of a partner for his homosexual cravings, is slapped in the face with a sole by a fishwife whose lover he accosts; he dies of apoplexy. The solution for political survival, as Phocas learnt, belongs to the English: to indulge in oneself the criminal, animal instincts of the crowd, but never confess a common identity; to hide vice below decks on a private yacht, and under the cold, indifferent mask and the plain black suit of the dandy.

Childish Fantasies

Lorrain may recoil in horror from the murderous fantasies of his contemporaries conveyed in his nightmare satire. His own escape routes are equally morbid and obsessive. Through masks, drugs, art and fairytale, he enters the lost childhood world of pretend mysteries, factitious terrors, which struggle to screen realities even more terrifying.

For the mask is truth deformed:

> . . . mystery in laughing mood, a lying face twisted out of truth, the deliberate ugliness of reality exaggerated to hide the unknown.
> Masks have always impressed me, driven me to hallucinations; the fascination they exert generates unease. For me, the mask rises and forms in things and people with pathological ease; and the kind of delightful terror with which it grips me makes me a fervent devotee of the streets of Paris at carnival time . . . But however terrifying the mask may be, there are human faces still more frightening, and if Fate wills it, a chance conjunction of ugliness can reach such grotesque, unforeseen intensity that reason loses its grip and the reality of life itself is transposed into nightmare ('Trio de masques', *Histoires de masques*, 1900, pp. 94–5).

Histoires de masques acknowledges its debt to E.T.A. Hoffmann, 'the machinator par excellence of fantasy and surprise . . . in my view, the finest of the artists of distortion'. In 'Lanterne magique', the narrator complains to the physicist that science: '. . . has killed the Fantastic, and with it, Poetry, which is also Fantasy! . . . You're destroying Madness, Madness, the last citadel where an intellectual, at the end of his patience, could still retreat!' But thanks to Hoffmann and Poe, the fantastic still survives as psychological and moral mystery: 'we walk in a world of witchcraft, surrounded by the Fantastic; it's invasive, pervasive, obsessive, only the blind and prejudiced could refuse to see it' and 'every day, we rub shoulders with ghouls and vampires'.

Hallucination is conjured from the moral ambiguity of the mask. 'L'Un d'eux' speculates with a thrill of delight on the sicknesses the masked are trying to hide; what is disguised must be evil. The sexual ambiguity of the mask stirs a special malaise, rousing men to 'vicious dreams' of the double transgression of homosexuality ('outside nature, outside the law'). This is 'lust spiced with fear, the piercing, delightful hazard of the challenge to the curiosity of the senses'. Alternatively: 'Why should there not be a void, nothingness, under those vast Pierrot smocks draped like shrouds over sharp-angled legbones and armbones?' Des Esseintes' pastoral fancy of Pierrots turning somersaults in the moonlight takes a macabre turn on the *fin-de-siècle* Paris streets, as the Romantic pantomime sours. In an article in *L'Evénement*, 20 May 1888, Lorrain spoke of Pierrot's scepticism turned to pessimism by the influence of Schopenhauer, and his clowning become demonic and macabre. Under the powder is a murderous death's head: 'Willette's Pierrot from Montmartre, stained bright red with the stabbing

knives of the outer boulevards, Willette's Pierrot, with Greedy Mag for
Columbine, replacing the white puppet from the Opera ballets . . . And . . .
Paul Margueritte, the obsessed and obsessive *Columbine Forgiven* and
Pierrot Murders his Wife, . . . ousting with his gravedigger's panto-
mime the delightful, dreamy fantasies of the old actor Paul Legrand'
(cit. P. L. Gauthier, p. 243).

A new kind of dream setting heightens the terror. Modern life may have
done with Gothic tombs, but a lonely mask strayed from the carnival
crowd can be just as disturbing in the shivering dawn of the townscape:
'puppets of the night, born, maybe, in the pale light of gaslamps and
electric light, vanishing at the break of day'. 'L'Un d'eux' wears an
Arabian burnous embroidered with frogs, topped by a green velvet
monk's hood and a silver helmet with holes for his eyes, and on his legs
black silk tights, one with a blue-green silk stocking and a watered-silk
garter, and another with a man's evening shoe:

> . . . he reeked of dungeon, marsh, graveyard; and he stirred the senses
> with his firm, supple nakedness emphasized by the black tunic . . . the
> spectre of eternal Lust, the Lust of the Orient and the cloisters, Lust with
> its face eaten away by cancers, Lust with its heart limp and cold as a
> reptile's body, androgyne Lust, neither male nor female, impotent Lust
> – as a finishing touch, the masker held in his hand a huge waterlily
> flower.

The epicene monster takes the same train as the narrator, hands over his
ticket and goes out into the cold, dark countryside – a harmless terror.

In these tales, the decadent craving for novelty and surprise confesses its
childishness. As a bored child, looking through the rainy window on to his
dull province, Lorrain found the same thrill of mystery in the sudden
emergence of faces in the street as he later found in masks ('Trio de
Masques'). Chance absurdity provokes innocent delight. In 'Heures de
villes d'eaux', he speaks of the 'supernatural' effect of finding oneself
ranging the town on a rainy day in a mackintosh, carrying a dead swan for
stuffing. Or, in 'Trio de Masques', he enters a room while a travelling fair is
in town to encounter: 'a bearded woman in a low-necked ballgown,
smiling as she waltzed with a man dressed as a woman, to the sound of a
guitar strummed by a Japanese dwarf, in an empty hall blazing with light!'
It is nurse's admonitions that create that greedy child's version of the cruel
mistress, the nightmare delight of 'La Reine Maritorne', a glassy-eyed
jumble of kitchen pots and pans, a soup tureen round her waist, a necklace
of black puddings, two great eels hanging from her waist like household

keys, and a bunch of leeks, onions and carrots in her hand.

Not all masks are play menaces. The society that invented carnival for the temporary release of repressed passions is also responsible for the antagonisms which make repression necessary. 'La Dame aux portraits' is an ugly old Jezebel whose neck is ringed with a wide collar of pearls set on a broad silver ribbon. The pearls may only mask ageing flesh. But speculation has it that they hide an old scar – that the rich woman's throat was sawn by miners in a colonial revolt, or thieves in a London slum. 'La Pompe-funèbre' is a new version, after Huysmans, of Rops' lesbian absinthe drinker, the silent spectator at circuses and bullfights, waiting for the death of the tightrope walkers and the matadors, to arouse 'her bored, cerebral sensuality'. 'La Marchande d'oublies' is a pleasant old lady who haunts the city parks, offering poisoned sweets to soldiers and small children. At any moment, Anarchy, pervasive and deathly as ether, can step forward to reclaim its inheritance ('L'Impossible Alibi').

Like the Ensor whose masks obsessed Phocas, Lorrain identifies the mask with real evil. The theatre audience of 'Lanterne magique' recalls Ensor's deformed creatures: the chalk faces, kohl-blackened eyes, red lips 'like an open wound' of the 'ghouls', with their 'smiles, all wet with blood', who drag young men to ruin, the china cheeks, silken hair and pearly teeth of the '*jeune fille comme il faut*', like Dr Coppelius' doll, the flaring nostrils, linen-like pallor and huge eyes of the drugged aristocrat, and the fresh rose-pink of the honest citizeness who never misses a public execution. In 'Le Masque', one hideous face stands out from the cardboard carnival grotesques, with its pink, lashless eyes, thick wads of bloody flesh in place of lips, bright pink cheeks and no nose. Reaching out his hand to thrust away its obsessive ugliness, the drunken reveller touches real flesh, 'a poor wretch just out of hospital'.

The hallucinatory effect of the mask is enhanced by ether. Without warning, the ether-addict's tale, 'Les Trous du masque' slips into an ether trance, the narrator surrounded by cloaked and masked figures with no face or body under their disguises. To his horror, one member of the threatening circle is himself. In 'Un crime inconnu', a recently cured addict watches hypnotized through a hole in the wall of his cheap hotel room the drunken male couple next door. Innuendos of guilty homosexuality compound his unwilling complicity in murder. The murderer, slipping on a green silk domino and a mask, becomes the spectral, undulating embodiment of ether. Under the mask, 'two eyes, terrifyingly alert', catch their victim in 'an unspeakable look of complicity'. The watcher through the wall and the reader are swept into the web of guilt as they succumb to the sadistic pleasures of Lorrain's text. Humiliated, crazed, the victim of disguise collapses into a final sub-human scream, as the murderer slips away, untouched:

> . . . oh, the pallor of those outstretched, tortured hands, trailing ecstatically in the tumbling folds of the spectre's gown . . . and while he croaked his last agony, in a long strangled shriek from the black hole of his wide open mouth, the form evaded his grasp, slipped back, dragging after it the hypnotized wretch sprawling at its feet.

In the 'Contes d'un buveur d'éther', collected in 1895 in *Sensations et souvenirs*, ether gives an epic dimension to the banal crimes of everyday life and transforms intimations of just retribution into sensuous pleasure. Serge Allitof ('Un mauvais gîte'), engaged on a study of necromancy, suffers from ill-health, and his flat smells of ether. The tale manufactures panic. Footsteps are heard passing inside the walls, and strange knocks and rattles shake the doors. Serge flees to a hotel, where he's pursued by the smell of corpses. The fantasy becomes ambiguous when the tenant who succeeds him in his flat, pursued by the same strange noises, commits suicide. Serge's private fears are part of a collective madness.

'Réclamation posthume', on the other hand, dedicated to Oscar Wilde, is an unashamed descent into fantasy and private delusion. The narrator, in a fit of black humour, had painted a wax head of Donatello's 'Unknown Woman' with dark blood clots, bright pink lips and green eyes. His crime is against form, and his guilt is absolute. Alone in the house, surrounded by silently falling snow and a mysterious scent of ether, he feels a sense of strange presence, and sees an exquisite female foot under the green silk hanging behind his door. A few weeks later, two moving feet and a female shape appear under the silk. Finally, the apparition is complete. A halo of light slowly grows around the maltreated wax, and its eyes dart to the door to watch the materialization of its headless body. They dart back, and the narrator is transfixed by their threatening gaze.

For all the self-punishing humour that deprecates his transformation of pure Muse into garish whore, in art it is bright colour, intense sensation, and crude contrast which are Lorrain's springboard into dream. Like Huysmans, his texts on contemporary art are overlaid with his own obsessions. He too prefers the makers of icons, pedlars of would-be profound philosophies, cherishing their aristocratic anguish. And he too looks for an elegance spiced by gamey contrast. In 'Bâle' (*Sensations et souvenirs*), he finds a new Salome to set against Moreau's ritual splendours. Manuel Deutsch's version, Herod's daughter and worthy

Bavarian citizeness, stands aloof and smiling in a jangling pantomime of grotesque masks – a plumed comic-opera soldier-executioner, a tight-mouthed, wax-faced harridan of a Herodias.

Under the section headed 'Les Artistes mystérieux', *Sensations et souvenirs* evokes the alternative decadent world on display at the Champ de Mars in 1893. (Most of the pieces, he grimly notes, are owned by Jewish bankers and businessmen.) Decadent dream is a skilful combination of old forms and modern feeling. Aman Jean's private dream, or prayer, envelops his 'Venezia bella regina maris', who owes her stiff grace and conscious naïveté to the Italian Primitives, and the cut of her cloak and her vitrified blues to the German Renaissance.

Gustave Moreau's witchcraft works through the 'pale and silent heroines of his watercolours', whose loveliness recalls Baudelaire's sonnet to silent, motionless Beauty. These dream princesses, naked flesh armoured in jewels, distant, almost ghostly, languid and lethargic, offer themselves without hesitation. Simultaneously, they arouse the senses and tame the will, creating a self-enclosed and self-consuming circle of morbid pleasure. Poet and scholar, Moreau's charms work because his ancient legends embody insights into modern neuroses, stressing, like Flaubert, the cruel and sinister side of myth. Flaubert's Carthaginian priestess, surveying from Hamilcar's terrace the young warriors' corpses, is sister to Moreau's Helen, standing on the pile of bodies at Troy, or to Salome: '. . . slender, pensive Salammbô, her flesh steeped in cosmetics, grown to womanhood amid prayer, fasting, ecstasy and perfumes, rustling with jewels in her robes woven with sardonyxes, more numerous than the rustling scales of her serpent'.

'La Dame en vert' looks at three female portraits by Antoine de la Gandara, whose grey, fluid shadows create an atmosphere reminiscent of Reynolds, Burne-Jones and Whistler. An old woman, a child, and the Lady in Green are straight from one of Poe's fantasies. The wide-eyed, hopeless, melancholy blue gaze of the Lady, the aristocrat confronting death, recall the novelist's Ligeia, Morella, Berenice. The same eyes look from the face of the precocious, frightened child. Lorrain links all these creations of the artistic imagination with a true anecdote. Set in the Normandy village where he lived as a child, 'Sonyeuse' evokes the tragic death of the local marquis' distant and lovely fair-haired English wife, whose daughter was mysteriously kidnapped and never returned.

Three pastels by Jeanne Jacquemin, described in 'Trois têtes', evoke the same passive, pallid, strangely menacing female victim. A pale, emaciated face with open mouth and starry eyes fixed on dangerous infinity stimulates satanic dreams – this woman is destined to be the naked victim at some Black Mass: 'the whiteness of that victim flesh, that long, bloodless neck and the thin oval face framed by hair like plaited vipers all seemed to me stamped with the irreparable Kiss'. A Botticelli fairy princess with flowers in her hair, pearls and lace in her blonde ringlets, sad, sensual mouth, distant blue-green gaze, wearing a purple gown and ropes of pearls, is an exiled Melusine. Last of all is an autumn princess, with long shining eyes and a calm smile, behind her a palace and a strongly coloured sky, and two morbid, monstrous dahlias, faded white, pinned in the place of her heart. Behind her, against a stormy sky, stands the palace of forgetfulness of which she is the figure.

In the same book, a piece on the Odilon Redon retrospective at the Durand-Ruel gallery, 'Unétrange jongleur' (first published in *L'Echo de Paris*, 10 April 1894), surveys the surprising and contradictory variety of Redon's work. The artist is the creator who fills an empty universe with a myriad of flashing, changing worlds of pure, dazzling Spirit. The centre of that universe is his own eye and brain, grotesquely, painfully deformed by the force of his vision of the ideal. Lorrain notes the 'ghouls, spectres and monsters' already evoked by Huysmans in *L'Art moderne*. But Redon's style now has a new dimension. Beyond the nightmares are 'serene, haughty visions', the Classical harmonies of Baudelaire's still Beauty revived in the golden aura of Byzantine princesses, or the bloodless pallor of Egyptian mummies, petrified yet imbued with erotic, vital fascination, 'living the magnificent life of ideas and idols', enveloped in a halo of light reminiscent of the art of George Frederic Watts. Or again, Redon paints the nostalgic landscapes of Celtic Gaul, of Arthurian or Wagnerian legend, settings for Merlin, Parsifal, and the flower-maidens.

For Lorrain, the most interesting painting of this exhibition belongs in this category; the 'Chevalier mystique' on which he closes his study. The dialogue of the Knight with the Goddess Chimera challenges the philosophy of the 'Etrange jongleur' in which the quest for the ideal was an ascetic renunciation of the flesh. Quoting Jules Bois' poem, 'La Chimère', which makes intelligible this, the 'finest' of Redon's visions, Lorrain marks a major shift in modern sensibility. The knight confesses his disillusionment with the sterile quest to which he has sacrificed the mistress whose head he carries in his hand. For Bois, occultist and humanist, 'the intoxications of death', 'blood spilling from gaping wounds', are terrifying errors. What is required are inner sacrifices, coupled with tolerance for the sins of the flesh. The sense of guilt remains, but is coupled now with a demand for absolution. Halfway between Huysmans and de Gourmont, Lorrain's peculiar blend of confession, repression and self-indulgence finds its own image in the art of Redon.

The best of all Lorrain's flights of fantasy is to fairytale. In a kingdom all his own, he blends myth, legend and folktale in an attempt to recuperate not the innocence, but the vigour, colour, mystery and terror of childhood. All the fears and desires of the child's unconscious, repressed in the formation of the 'responsible' adult, find expression in a world which is not a dream of something different, but a recapitulation of an old self. Like Phocas in Benares, he invents an alien landscape for the irresponsible indulgence of familiar desires.

This is a world of rich colour and intricate detail, whose characters, like Moreau's heroines, are weighed down with ornate symbolism. Artifice is paramount. In 'Les Contes', (coll. *Sensations et Souvenirs*), Lorrain argued that landscapes, like feeling and experience, only had meaning and beauty when transfigured by art:

> . . . the soul of a landscape lies entirely in the memory of the traveller journeying through it, more or less rich in recollections, and there are no mountains, forests, dawns rising over glaciers, nor twilight falling on pools, for the man who does not both long and fear to see Oriane rising from the edge of the wood, Thiphaine in among the golden broom, and Melusine at the fountain's edge.

Nature for Lorrain is only the dream of an ideal, utopian or nostalgic, by which the present can be judged, but never transformed. In 'La Princesse des chemins' (first published as 'Le Roi Cophétua', *L'Echo de Paris*, 22 August 1892), the young king marries a beggar-girl to possess the vision of a purer, simpler world he sees in her eyes. The beggar queen sits silent on her throne, gazing through the windows for her world, which is elsewhere; she has nothing but dream to give a sophisticated world. Eden is gone for ever; and perhaps just as well, Lorrain seemed to suggest in 'Les Contes'. Tales of unsophisticates are dull and untrue. If sometimes he dreams of the pleasure of being a child again, curled up with nurse by the warm fire, he knows also that her stories are no match for his. Her version of the Snow Queen tale that shaped his childhood is the simple picture of popular tradition: the queen of the snow bees, all made of ice, with two frozen moonrays for wings and a long cloak of ice edged with a fur of snowy mist. The adult Lorrain watches his listening childhood self transform that figure, from lessons nurse is less aware of giving, into the image of the fatal mistress who nurtures and punishes. His Snow Queen is lethargic and frozen like the bees in winter (with, by implication, all their latent power to give sweetness or pain). Her attendants are the old packwolves of the Arctic, howling for the kill, and hungry black crows –

the consuming force of passions repressed by maternal teaching. He lived in fearful anticipation of his initiation into passion, waiting for her dead, distant eyes to look in at his window.

In place of the drama of salvation which is Andersen's tale, Lorrain puts the single obsessive image of his Snow Queen, the cruel mother and mistress in whose icy form all energies are frozen. Lorrain's fairytales repeat this image of menacing inertia, which is the decadent's world, and dramatize the destructive effects of energies and passions released.

The section heads of Lorrain's tales (coll. in *Princesses d'ivoire et d'ivresse*, 1902, and first published in *L'Echo de Paris* and *Le Journal*, 1892–9) are themselves images of the hard, pure beauty of powers held in suspense: 'Princesses d'ivoire et d'ivresse', 'Princes de nacre et de caresses', 'Princesses d'ambre et d'Italie', 'Masques dans la tapisserie', 'Contes de givre et de sommeil'. In these stories, set mostly in the Orient, recurring images of a reflected double (in mirrors, pools, polished jewels) enforce the idea that self is a simple reflection of reality, voluntarily confined in a narrow, carefully constructed frame. The attempt to look beyond the given frame is an act of rebellion, which courts and deserves disaster.

Lorrain's virgin princesses are images of a perfection that does well not to look too closely into its origins, and to accept its privileges without seeking further favours. Virginity – ignorance – is a precious gift, only appreciated when it's gone. Knowledge is always of unpleasant realities, and delusions of possessing power are better than the certainty of being a victim.

Ilsée, 'La Princesse au sabbat' (*Le Journal*, 22 October 1895), is in love with her own reflection in the 'dead water' of her palace mirrors, which for her is 'natural' truth. The illusion is enhanced by her costumes, green dresses embroidered with river flowers, reeds, irises and anemones, symbols of the sexual desire from which her beauty takes its power, so long as that desire remains unfulfilled. Her palace is filled with ugly frog statues, grotesque intimations of the degrading reality of female sexuality.

Ilsée's mistake is to step from still mirror to moving river, tempted by the desire to know what it is that makes her desirable. She is swept by the current to a witch's island, and carried off to the Sabbat. There, the only mirror is Nature's, 'a rainy sky lit by a green moon' displaying the flesh's commitment to decay and death. As the Sabbat builds to its climax, she becomes the helpless focus of the onslaught of carnal instinct in all its humiliating ugliness:

Young and old, fat and skinny, ugly and pretty, naked forms buck and leap, swirl down screaming, dishevelled, swoop on to the forest;

creatures flutter down through the air . . . Princess Ilsée is dying: a swarm of turkeys covers her, puffing out their plumage, a rat's tail caresses her, a fox sniffs her, a viper with cock's wings whips her; nipped by claws, embraced, bitten, licked, ridden by a thousand invisible beasts, the princess Ilsée wakes with a great shriek.

Her painful wakening shatters the mirrors and breaks her frog statues to pieces.

Illys, 'La Princesse aux miroirs' (*Le Journal*, 25 January 1899), almost suffers the same fate. This time her fault is not curiosity, but her arrogant demands that her beauty, and her power, should last for ever. The witches sweep her off on a frenzied journey through a desert that becomes first a swamp and then the 'frightening, shifting softness' of a pack of satanic beasts. She reaches out instinctively to a green jasper sphinx at her side, which carries her, swooning, away. Culture, with its riddles and mysteries, means safety; Nature tells truths that only the demons of the mob can survive.

The prince 'Narkiss' (*Le Journal*, 18 June 1898) dies of his deluding image. Reared in the temple by the priests of Isis, in the image of the goddess, he is not the androgyne Narcissus of Ovid's *Metamorphoses* but a silky-fleshed, obscenely exquisite embodiment of the carnal dream. He is the instrument through which the priests rule the people: the 'feminine', passive and unself-conscious force of erotic power. He does not know his own beauty and power, because the priests have taken away all the mirrors, and told him nothing of the blood sacrifices demanded of the people, in his name, which sustain their power. Narkiss is the passive instrument and victim who unwittingly reinforces and reproduces his own servitude.

All Narkiss is allowed to know is the life of the senses, in forms chosen by the priests. In his introductory pages, Lorrain describes the power of art to transform Nature's monstrous force into instruments of fascination. In his incantatory prose, the irises, lilies and peonies on his writing table, 'monstrous gaping throats', become 'not flowers but works of art, living works of art with a strange occult power'. These are the mirrors in which Narkiss is allowed to see himself: 'Narkiss loved the scent of flowers, the smell of cosmetics and perfumes, the brilliance of sparkling gems and the damp coldness of the fleshy lotus. Narkiss knew nothing of the look in his own eyes and the colour of blood.'

This limited vision which makes him a god is also a fatal snare. When he accidentally strays into the temple, the scent of flowers masks the smell of blood. As he walks down the steps to the river, in the dark, the corpses polluting the water are hidden by banks of flowers. When he leans over the water and sees his own seductive eyes, he does not recognize them as his. He drowns in his own delusion.

Like Narkiss, the 'Princesse aux lys rouges' (*L'Echo de Paris*, 11 June 1894), is an instrument of patriarchal authority, a dream whose function is to destroy her father's enemies. Another Snow Queen, 'always pale and cold in her gown of white wool embroidered with golden clover-leaves . . . always silent . . . white and frail', she stands in her flower-garden while her father fights on the battlefield, magically assisting the slaughter. Every lily she tears up from the ground is a dead enemy; every foxglove she kisses opens an enemy wound. As long as her garden remains inviolate, and she remains obedient, 'her father's daughter', Audovère shares his power. When she relinquishes the role of simple reflection, with the intrusion of carnal reality into her symbolic world, she is destroyed. Battlefields 'flatter a virgin's pride', but mothers turn from bloodshed in 'anguished horror'. When a wounded fugitive takes refuge in the castle crypt, Audovère disregards his claim to sanctuary and goes down to her garden that night to kill him. There she is finally forced to face Love, in a vision of the sorrowing Christ whose authority she has challenged. The magical symbolism of the flowers is transformed into deadly reality:

. . . a gust of sighs and death-rattles, a rain of lamentations. The flowers in her fingers pressed and yielded like flesh; something warm fell on her hands, that she thought was tears, and the lilies had a sickening smell, strangely different, heavy and sickly, their cups full of a noxious incense.

In the morning, the princess is found dead among the red lilies.

The same image of murderous virgin appears in the sequence of prose-poems based on Eugène Grasset's art nouveau calendar, 'Les Douze Mois', which the Catholic writer Léon Bloy wrote between 1896 and 1900 and published in the *Mercure de France* in November 1903 ('Les Douze Filles d'Eugène Grasset'). The virgin whose castrating scissors, reflected in her cold eyes, deny the supplicant entrance to her garden, is threatened with a similar, if less sensual, end: 'I'm afraid the pointed branch she's about to cut will spring back into her face, put out her eye, and pierce back to her brain, her tiny brain that never had room for heaven's humble pleas.' Bloy's attack on the resistant virgin, like that of Lorrain, and, indeed, of Péladan, is prompted by more than sexual frustration. A new generation feels itself passed over not simply by the Woman who apparently holds the key to satisfaction, but also by the Patriarch who stands behind that woman, and on whose law her own power depends.

Unlike Bloy and Péladan, whose Catholicism provided a language to mystify resentment into submission, Lorrain's writing is forthright in exposing the Father's culpability, and his own desire to be free of the attraction of his brooding power. The child-prince 'Hylas', ('Conte d'Orient', *Le Journal*, 6 February 1896), runs away from the dark mystery of the king, for whose unspoken purposes he has been reared. The insinuation of a projected homosexual violation conveys the child's desire and fear of recruitment. Hylas has been schooled as a woman, washed and scented, taught to sing to the lyre and to dance holding the hem of his robe like a courtesan.

Lorrain approves his flight. But the difficulty is that outside the king's palace there are no known worlds. The story falls silent as he crosses the threshold. Similarly, nothing more is known of the princesses who escape from their father's locked towers when Love beckons ('Légende des trois princesses', *L'Echo de Paris*, 23 February 1894), or those who listen to the 'Conte du bohémian' (ibid., 27 March 1894), 'gipsy Love, who sings in the woods for the poor and the disinherited, is silent in palaces, is mirrored by Death, and loves only himself, Love free and untamed as solitude'. Life, with or without the Father, is death.

The decadent solution to the dilemma is to displace the guilt and fear it creates on to women, or men rewritten in the female image. In the end, it is women who pay for the Fathers' misuse of power. When the mob sacks Byzantium ('La Fin d'un jour') and the little black kitchen slave at last inherits the palace treasures and the empty throne rearing over a heap of corpses, what he sees borne off into the distance by the mob, 'a strange flower', is not a king's body, but the head of an empress, dripping blood.

In the collection 'Masques dans la tapisserie', Lorrain invokes the Arthurian legends, relearned from Tennyson, to which he also gave poetic and dramatic form (the poems of *La Forêt bleue*, 1883, for example, or the play *Brocéliande*, staged at the Théâtre de l'Oeuvre, December 1898). Here too the fairy world offers no escape. Lorrain's Celtic dreamworld is lovely because it has been superseded. His tales evoke the moment of its fall from innocent, unreflective harmony with Nature to painful self-knowlege. Like de Gourmont, he blames Christianity for the fall. The princely heroes of these tales, like the hero of Redon's painting, suffer from the realization that the Christian quest for perfection is futile, and the loss of the irresponsible, pagan self irreparable. Chivalrous adventure is replaced by lament.

The hero of 'L'inutile vertu' (*Le Journal*, 1 November 1895) wastes a life that should have been lived for joy and pleasure, in a dutiful quest for revenge imposed on him by his mother. Burdened by this grey, pointless progress inherited from the past, he turns aside from life's most tantalizing mysteries – the three noble maidens beckoning at the forest's edge, a pale corpse in the marshland, a phantom boat, the lady on the unicorn. In 'Mélusine enchantée' (*L'Echo de Paris*, 18 November 1892), misty voices prophesy the coming of the warrior Lusignan to release the fairy Mélusine from her enchanted form, embracing the virgin, drinking her venom and dissolving the enchantment. The fulfilment of the prophecy is drawn in the language of utopian dream.

Promises of happiness are all delusion. 'Le Prince dans la forêt', meeting the forest's guardian, is offered by her a choice between Dream and Reality – death or suffering. Dreams always destroy. 'Oriane vaincue' (*L'Echo de Paris*, 20 January 1893) tells how the fairy Oriane over the centuries ensnared dreaming warriors in her enchanted cave. Oriane in her turn was held captive by their desire. While the warriors dreamed, their horses roamed wild in the night forests. The vigour of that image of free animal instinct is set against the horror of the living death of enslavement to the dream of sensuality, and against the guilt that underlies that dream (and distinguishes it from, for example, Burne-Jones' 'Briar Rose' sequence). The knight Amadis, the disciple of the monks, brings the message of the Cross into the cavern ('Christ, the enemy of joy, pleasure, love'), and the warriors wake to their own corruption. In a powerful sequence of metamorphoses, the sleeping, but living, heroes become skeletons, carrion, and liquefying flesh, and the fairy collapses into dust.

The advent of Christianity represents awareness of accountability and responsibility, of time and change, and of divisions and difference. Decadence wants the abolition of all these. The decadent ideal is imaged in the 'Conte des faucheurs' (*L'Echo de Paris*, 14 June 1895), Raymondin's vision of the identity of Love and Death, which is a plea for the abolition of history, for enjoyment of the pure present. Death and Love share the planting and the harvesting. Death who ploughs and reaps is hand-in-hand with Love, who gleans as well as sows.

As Love sang, Raymondin realized there was no more need for tears, for love is death and rebirth; that he need not fear to know life, but should look it in the face and live each day as he found it; that each of life's moments belonged to Death's scythe, as each pleasure that passed belonged to Love's sickle, and that their instruments of murder are, after all, only their wings.

Lorrain's own seductive song pretends that the eternal circling is a moment of growth and development. It pretends that all historical moments are the same, and that ends are just as good as beginnings. But it undercuts its own pretensions, declaring itself only song, an incantation which is as good as truth. As Lorrain makes his final evasions, writing dreams of death he would have us believe are as exquisite as life, he has to confess that the instrument of his escape is also the instrument of murder: the wings of his song are the strokes of Death's scythe.

6
Crossroads in Byzantium:
Pierre Louÿs and Octave Mirbeau

Ultimately, the decadent generation confronts two choices. The hero-artist can walk deeper into the labyrinth, the forest, the high-walled garden, or the temple, losing all sense of time and self and locking himself into the guilty pleasures of repression. Or he can set fire to the palaces and pull down the temples, like Lombard's Adel, turning the weaknesses of the rulers to their destruction and opening the gates to his own dream of a 'natural', 'barbarian' unknown. The first of these paths is taken by Pierre Louÿs; the second, by Octave Mirbeau.

The Temple Prostitute: Pierre Louÿs 1870–1925

The heart of Pierre Louÿs' work is the Temple of Cottyto, the centre of the high-walled gardens of *Aphrodite* (1896). Within the temple is the emblem that sustains the ideology of the world in which he lives: the ritual, voluntary death, in a frenzy of poisoned pleasure, of the female slave who sells herself to underwrite others' desires and dreams. In the temple, life and death are purely matters of price:

> . . . thirty-six courtesans lived there, so sought after by rich lovers that they never gave themselves for less than two *minae*: they were the Baptes of Alexandria. Once a month, at full moon, they came together in the compound by the temple, crazed with aphrodisiac draughts and wearing

ritual phalluses. The oldest of the thirty-six had to take a deadly dose of
a fearsome love philtre. The certainty of a speedy death enabled her to
experiment fearlessly with all the dangerous pleasures living women
would shy from. Her foam-covered body became the centre and the
pattern of the whirling orgy; amid wailing shrieks, cries, tears and
dances the other naked women would embrace her, trail their hair in her
sweat, rub themselves against her burning skin and draw fresh ardour
from the uninterrupted spasms of her raging agony. For three years
these women lived in this way and after the thirty-sixth month this was
their ecstatic end (Bk.II, ch.1).

The contradictions of decadence are at their most extreme in Louÿs'
world. Within the modern imagination, formed by the logic and the guilts
of Christianity, he tries to re-create a pagan ideal of unself-conscious
sensuality. The result is a detailed, dynamic, brilliant vision of life that
draws all its colour from the fear of death and loss which stands beside it.
Victor Hugo's Romantic deformation of Christian mysticism, with its
intense death-cult, and Ignatius Loyola's *Spiritual Exercises*, are among
the major influences on a mind that crystallized into self-awareness
between the death of his father and fear of his own dying. On the first
anniversary of his father's death, he recorded in his *Journal intime* his
decision to draw a firm dividing-line between spiritual ideal and carnal
reality which would enable him to enjoy both, secure in the timelessness of
his own imagination. Art produces a world that lives alongside and knows
of the degrading, decaying world of the flesh, but remains untouched by it:

I shall love no one with my soul. I am the hermaphrodite Sphinx,
creating outside himself a Chimera for himself alone. My sole aspiration
is to the Ideal, and the Ideal rises up from my own thoughts . . . I
recognize no other desires but those whose end is aesthetic pleasure . . . I
shall spend my life contemplating the Ideal I myself have created, like
Zeus, forever virgin, confronting Athene . . . What does it matter what
the body does, if the soul does not give its consent (14 April 1890).

That diary of a personality in formation closes definitively on 1 March
1891, with the note that he believes he has tuberculosis, and is filled with
panic at the thought of 'dying without having done anything'. Both belief
and panic were unjustified; but from that point he clung firmly, and
exclusively, to the divided world he had inherited, with all its privileges
and all its limitations, never moving out of the circle of dream and willed
impotence.

Of all decadent fictions, his is the most blatant claim for self-indulgence. Morality and Beauty, he argues, are eternal opposites; reading more closely, he is suggesting that immorality and Beauty go hand in hand. He borrows the tongues of Pericles, Socrates, Sappho and the Areopagite to declare: 'that not only did Beauty justify vice, but Beauty was vice's sole excuse!' (*Journal intime*, 28 August 1890). Like Péladan, he emphasizes that his is doctrine for an elite: 'It is no longer the crowd that generates progress. It is only individual minds that pass on the torch, *quasi cursores*, and Beauty is the purer for being desired by the elite' (2 September 1890). Three years earlier, under the influence of his adored stepbrother George (possibly his real father), he had expressed fear of socialist revolution, but this had been coupled with the assertion that socialism (in moderate form) was just, and inequality wrong (25 December 1887). Now, like Lorrain's Lord Férédith, he hides his claim for sensual and aesthetic freedom below decks, and makes it plain that he will not share it with the populace.

His fantasy world has a double foundation: art, and the image of woman. Art holds off the barbarian unknown of the outside, and also the barbarian threat within himself. It has a social dimension, creating icons, emblems and divinities which inspire the crowd to worship the principles they embody, at the same time as it holds the worshippers at a respectful distance. It enables Louÿs himself to enjoy the seductions of carnal reality without personal confrontation with its taints and threats, enabling his texts to play dangerous games with their own repressions.

Woman is both the embodiment of the real world and the bulwark against it. In his work, she belongs to the single type of the prostitute. She knows her place and her purpose, always ready to be used, blamed, or made to suffer in the service of her employer's dreams. The property of no single class, time, or place, she is the ideal mother-mistress who presents no resistance or refusal. Her place as the presiding deity of Louÿs' fiction, declaring the importance of the body in defiance of conventional moral taboos, gives at first sight some credence to that fiction's claim to be liberated and liberating, the expression of the desire noted in his diary, 28 September 1890, to challenge the hypocrisies and obscene repressions of his age. But like the real-world prostitute, the female figure in these texts is only part of the machinery that constructs a strictly limited fantasy of freedom. The only freedom is in Louÿs' own imagination.

Aphrodite (1896), Louÿs' first and most famous novel, keeps a discreet distance from the pornographic literature of prostitution – though as he composed it, Louÿs sketched a parallel version, with more specific accounts of the perversions practised in the Garden, lists of the obscene caresses in which the Temple prostitutes were trained, and headings for a blason of the intimate parts of the female body, their flavours and their function (*Notes sur* Aphrodite, 1928). In the published version, obscenity is discreetly veiled by style, but the repression is deliberately incomplete. Coppée's review in *Le Journal*, 16 April 1896, was precisely the response Louÿs had written to evoke: 'I recommend *Aphrodite* to all artists, but only to artists . . . a beautiful book, but singularly impure; and I think it my duty to play here the part of the curator who doesn't allow everyone to enter the "secret museum", or the librarian who doesn't make available to all-comers a volume catalogued among the forbidden books.'

In this novel, the exploitative relationship of artist and woman is at its most explicit. The real centre of the book is not Aphrodite herself, ruling deity of Alexandria, despite the title. Nor is it Chrysis, the courtesan with whom the first chapter opens, whose demand for tribute (her rival's silver mirror, the ivory comb belonging to the high priest's wife, and Aphrodite's pearl necklace) provokes the crimes that are the substance of the plot, and whose burial closes the narrative. Both are raw material for the sculptor Démétrios' dream. It is by his grace that Aphrodite rules the people, through the statue in the Temple made in the image of his own ideal:

> Divine Sister . . . I saw you, summoned you and caught you . . . I revealed you to the earth. It is not your image but yourself to whom I have given your mirror, and whom I have covered with pearls, as on the day you sprang from the bloody sky and the foamy smile of the waters, dawn dripping with dew, acclaimed to the very shores of Cyprus by a procession of blue tritons (Bk.I, ch.3).

Chrysis, like Aphrodite, is just another inspiration. Standing deep in boredom on the jetty at Alexandria, he finds a new, piquant challenge in her beauty, spiced with arrogance, indifference and cruelty, which invites him to risk crime and death. Answering the challenge enriches the artist, transforms him, and produces the new statue which is the end of Chrysis' story. The climax of the book is Démétrios' sudden awareness of how much he has been changed by this new experience. His new vision immediately transforms the obedient landscape of Alexandria, just as it transforms the body of Chrysis. Both woman and Nature are shown to be subordinate to the artist, who invents his own virility at the price of their death. Chrysis' suffering opens up for Démétrios a new world of light and colour:

He stopped abruptly on the threshold, stunned by the vast brilliance of the African noon.

The street and the houses must still be white, but the flames of the sun directly overhead washed the dazzling surfaces with such a rage of reflections that the whitewashed walls and flagstones vibrated simultaneously with marvellous, glowing shadowy blues, red and green, violent ochre and hyacinth. Great quivering bands of colour seemed to move through the air and lie transparent on the wavering, burning façades. Lines changed shape behind the dazzling brightness . . . A dog lying by a milestone was turned crimson.

Struck by amazed enthusiasm, Démétrios saw in the spectacle a symbol of his new existence. For some time now he had lived in lonely darkness, silence and peace. For some time, he had taken the moon's rays for his light, and for his ideal the careless line of over-refined movement. His work had lacked virility. An icy chill lay on the skin of his statues.

In the tragic adventure that had just overwhelmed his understanding, he had felt for the first time his breast swell with the great breath of life (Bk.V, ch.3).

Woman not only gives the artist the means of realizing a new self. She also enables him to impress that self on the crowd. Despite his declared aloofness, Démétrios needs the people's adulation. They must admire him: the women of Alexandria long to make love with the artist, and men and women alike press to touch the hem of his robe. They must accept his creations as the image of their own dreams, and the object of their aspirations, like the stream of supplicants who hang their offerings on his statue of Aphrodite.

Even those he destroys should worship him, for, after all, his dream of them is lovelier than their reality. The women who give themselves to Démétrios' fantasies are in return made goddesses. Queen Bérénice models for his Aphrodite. The statue he makes of the dead Chrysis is a work so marvellous that we never see it, and far lovelier than the dead, decaying corpse the little flutegirls bury. Even before she dies, merely holding the ornaments he has stolen for her, she is transformed into a figure of inhuman beauty. As she climbs the high lighthouse at Alexandria in the setting sun:

Her veil shivered like a flame. The burning twilight reddened the pearl necklace into a river of rubies. She climbed upwards, and in all that glory, her dazzling flesh displayed all the magnificence of flesh, blood,

fire, bluish crimson, velvet red, bright pink, and turning with the great
stone walls she ascended into heaven (Bk.IV, ch.6).

For all the women in this book, the artist's dream of passion means
death. The mystery of the temple of Cottyto is prefigured in the song the
fluteplayers sing in the second chapter, on the jetty at Alexandria, of Eros,
god of love and death, 'Desire, both sweet and painful', and the cruelty of
satyrs to nymphs, Cybele to Attys, Pan to Syrinx. The high priest's wife
welcomes death at Démétrios' hands, in a landscape transformed by
Louÿs' lyricism to suggest a natural link between death and femininity.
Around the sleeping woman, images of swelling sea and moon are coupled
with ambivalent figures of blood:

The eternal sea shivered from the wide blue terrace up to the sparkling vastness of night. Like another breast of another priestess, it swelled
up to the stars, lifted by the ancient dream with which it still quivers
under our late-come eyes, and whose mystery the last human creatures
will still be seeking before they disappear at time's last end. Above her,
the moon poured out its wide cup of blood. Above the purest air that
ever joined heaven and earth, a thin red trail scattered with dark veins
trembled at sea level beneath the rising moon, like the tingle of a caress
lingers in the night on the soft flesh of a breast, long after it has gone . . .
(Bk.II, ch.3).

The slave Aphrodisia, unjustly accused of stealing her mistress' mirror,
dies on a cross, tormented by her spiteful mistress – in bliss, with a former
lover's kiss on her lips.

The text writes its own apology, arguing that it is women, not men, who
bring death into the world. Cleopatra, the queen's twelve-year-old sister,
destined to destroy Egypt, Antony and herself, keeps a lover locked in
prison, and visits him to torment him. It was Chrysis who first taught
Démétrios the pleasures of sending a lover to death, in her eagerness to
make him her slave. He accuses her:

You all have just one dream . . . to break man's strength with your
weakness and govern his intelligence with your vanity . . . you don't
want to love or be loved, but to bind a man at your feet, demean him,
bend his head and set your sandals on it (Bk.V, ch.4).

For her Hindu slave Djala, in the opening chapter, Chrysis is 'the face of
Medusa', as she contemplates her bejewelled image in the mirror after her

lengthy toilette, singing the blason of her own body, until she comes to the heart of her mystery:

> It is like a crimson flower, full of perfumes and honey. Like a sea anemone, soft, living, that opens at night. It is the moist cave, the warm resting-place, the Refuge where man halts on his long march to death.

But in the end, it is only Chrysis herself who is turned to stone by the image in the mirror. Nothing touches Démétrios. In prison for her blasphemy against Aphrodite, she is the one who confronts the raw reality of death:

> Taking her head in her hands, to still her thoughts, she suddenly, unexpectedly felt the shape of her dead skull through the living flesh: the empty temples, the huge eye-sockets, the short nose under the cartilage and the jutting jaw (Bk.V, ch.1).

She drinks the poison he refuses to share. He disowns his promise to spend a last night with her, which was the wager for which she put on the goddess' stolen pearls. Démétrios' new virility is paid for with Chrysis' final humiliation, the knowledge of herself as an object, with no more use.

The violence and cruelty of Louÿs' eroticism is contained in a series of frames. Chrysis is framed in the mirror in which she becomes Medusa, and in her own hair, whose coiling, fearsome vitality envelops her as she steps from the bath, as she lies in bed with the two fluteplayers, and finally on her deathbed, where Démétrios drapes it for his statue. The Temple of Aphrodite is enclosed by a series of stone walls, made of the houses of the sacred prostitutes, and by a river. The novice prostitutes are surrounded by frescos and friezes from which they learn to re-enact the artist's dreams of love. Démétrios dreams of possessing Chrysis on an island, in a room embedded within other rooms.

Unexpectedly, at the end of the novel the frame motif is turned back on itself, an ironic revelation of the deadly power of style. These images of erotic vitality intensified by art are all reversed in the last tableau of the decaying corpse of Chrysis, art's victim, carried into her dusty tomb. The sensual colour of the text is enclosed by a corroding awareness of the price of self-indulgence. The preface makes it clear why the price must be paid. The intimidation and the ugliness that Louÿs experiences in the real world completely justify, for him, the sensual dream:

> The modern world is drowning under a flood of ugliness. Civilizations

are returning to the North, back to the mist, cold and mud. Such darkness! a whole people dressed in black walks the foul streets. What does it think of? We don't know; but our twenty-five years shiver at the thought of our exile among these old men.

Still, the shiver runs through *Aphrodite*, and the death of Chrysis fails to exorcize it. At the end, the text is left not with Démétrios' dream work, but with her dead body.

Like *Aphrodite*, Louÿs' other fictions are attempted evasions into other worlds. Sometimes the world is Utopia (*Les Aventures du Roi Pausole*, 1901). At others, it is a romanticized Spain, as in the masochistic fantasy *La Femme et le pantin*, 1898, which re-creates Goya's painting: two women, on a lawn, tossing a man-sized puppet in a shawl. Fifteen-year-old Conchita, discovered in a tobacco factory in Seville, teases and torments her middle-aged would-be lover, with promises she never keeps and real and fantasized infidelities. Her pleasure is in giving and receiving pain. He finds her dancing naked in black stockings for two Englishmen in a brothel, or in bed with her friend's brother, or making love to Morenito on the ground in front of him. Goaded to fury, he locks her in her room and beats her for fifteen minutes: 'I never heard such dreadful shrieks . . . she was weeping like a little girl . . . I can still see the incessant movement of her bruised shoulder and her hands pulling the pins from her hair . . .' (pp. 224–5).

Most often, and most effectively, the scene of escape is Ancient Greece. Dreams of dead women, clothed in scholarly respectability, weave softly pornographic fancies that the sternest critics found 'charming'. *Les Chansons de Bilitis* (1895) declared itself 'the first translation from the Greek' of texts discovered in the tomb of Bilitis, a woman born at the beginning of the sixth century BC. Until the hoax was discovered, the reader enjoyed the additional pleasure of seeing all the sensualist's dream-versions of woman apparently confirmed as historical truth.

Bilitis' poems were found in her tomb, along with her perfume and eye-pencil, a statue of Astarte and her golden jewellery, decorating bones that fell into dust when the lid was opened. The four cycles begin with the Bucolics of her childhood, flirting with the nymphs and Aphrodite. Her Elegies at Mytilene, capital of Lesbos, where she knew Sappho, are discreetly sadistic:

The only marks, Mnasadika, that I want to see on your body, are the stain of a protracted kiss, the scratch of an over-sharp nail, or the crimson bar of my embrace (No. 47).

Her Epigrams on Cyprus are an orgy of Maenadic possession, evoking Aphrodite's secret rites, and the courtesan's pride in her profession and her possessions – beauty, perfumes, money and slaves. Water washes away all her sins, until age exacts retribution. The courtesan discovers too late she has lived her life as a mirror for others. She steps of her own will into the tomb, accepting that woman's destiny is man's pleasure: 'If I was a courtesan, why should I be blamed? It was my duty as a woman' (No. 99).

Keats supplies the epigraph – 'Beauty is truth, truth beauty' – but even with this encouragement, Bilitis makes no claims. A woman's immortality lies not in her verses, but in her memories of pleasure: 'And now I wander, an intangible shade, over the pale fields of asphodel, and the memory of my life on earth is the delight of my life in the world below' (No. 100). Her delight in the body earns her death and dissolution. If there is rescue, it is by the art of her 'translator'.

Louÿs' dreams of nymphs, published in the miniature 'Lotus Alba' collection and collected in the single volume *Le Crépuscule des nymphes* a few months before his death, are also dreams of women made into Beauty by pain and death. Byblis (1898), the incestuous lover searching the world for her lost twin brother, is transformed into a fountain of tears, her pale skin turned to marble, an eternal, inhuman emblem of anguish. Lêda (1898), with her blue eyes and skin and dark blue hair, unfathomable Night, is woman in all her ignorance, who is there to be used by man to re-create his ideal, or to perpetuate the race. Penetrated by the swan's 'bloody beak', she produces Helen; raped by the rough satyr, the warrior twins Castor and Pollux. Ariadne, deserted by Theseus and torn apart by the Bacchantes on the shore at Naxos, is restored by the immortal Dionysus, who then destroys her in his turn.

The dead women of Greece walk the streets of modern Paris in the short story 'Une volupté nouvelle' (1898, rpt. *Sanguines*, 1903). Smoke from the narrator's cigarette summons Callisto, daughter of Lamia, buried in her tomb by Antioch for almost two centuries, and now resting in the Louvre. She is a pleasure to watch – young, sensual, with black eyes, red mouth and dyed blonde hair, wearing a green silk dress that reveals her nipples, a gold serpent with enamel eyes twined round each arm and two rows of pearls about her neck. He listens with delight to her stories of the erotic pleasures invented by the women of her time. But nothing she offers equals the pleasure of his cigarette smoke, the image of the dream of art that summoned up all her beauty. Louÿs' nymphs, however exquisite, are only there to represent the power of dream, and the dreamer.

The stylistic opposites of the sophisticated courtesans of Ancient Greece, Callisto or Chrysis, are the vigorous modern enthusiasts of Louÿs' pornographic classic, *Trois Filles de leur mère*, published in 1926, after the writer's death. The contrasts between this book and, for example, *Aphrodite*, are immediately clear. Sexual acts and sexual parts, left in the earlier work to periphrasis and discreet innuendo, are here described in precise and explicit detail. An informal, impromptu tone replaces the slow, sober ritual of the Temple that legitimized obscenity: the narrator's adventure is a passing fancy which begins as an interlude on a staircase. With the repressions of language and ritual removed, the morbid, vindictive and obsessive element of the earlier work disappears. There is a different kind of intensity – a frenzy of physical activity that rivals the orgies in the Temple – but the poison, literally, is gone. The child-prostitutes of the Temple reappear as Teresa's three daughters, but not, this time, forced by poverty to sell themselves. Like the heroines of the *Histoire du roi Gonzalve et les douze princesses* (1927), they offer themselves to the hero freely, and confidingly, out of pure affection. Coercion and brutality are consciously ruled out as sources of sexual pleasure, at least in the episodes in which the narrator himself takes part.

There is still the same careful use of form to enclose the fantasy, both to intensify its effects and to preserve the writer from the dangers of his subject-matter. The whole tale is theatre. Teresa is an ex-actress, from a circus family, whose sense of drama has been passed on to her daughters. Each stages her own little confrontation with the hero, one at a time, or with her mother, while Teresa stage-manages the whole drama up to the climax, which is an impromptu play to celebrate the imminent loss of Mauricette's virginity.

The story is also a bundle of fictions. Charlotte and Teresa spin their life-stories into the string of dramatic tableaux, and even fourteen-year-old Mauricette has a past to narrate, in which her mother whipped her, beat her, stuck her with hot needles – a useful device for introducing the cruelty of which this hero prefers to be absolved ('I'd a hundred times rather listen to you than beat you'). Louÿs himself plays games with his readers, constantly reminding them that this is only writing. Faced with Mauricette in erotic frenzy, he breaks off to tell the reader how much in control he is – concluding, however, with a neat double-take:

> The calmness of the commentaries I've been absent-mindedly reeling off (this story doesn't turn me on at all, I may tell you, and I'm writing these pages as coolly as if I were telling you how I learned Greek grammar) . . . I'm so absent-minded I've started a sentence I can't finish, which has

never happened before. Since it's there, I won't cross it out (p. 189).

The female characters' masochism also remains the same and, for all his shocked, censorious comment on its extremism, the passive hero shares it. Mauricette's preference for physical pain is put in the shadow by Charlotte's delight in humiliation. Her life-story is a mechanism to provoke insults from the hero, long lists of the degrading things she's been forced to do with men, women and animals, which work her up to a pitch of madness where she masturbates grotesquely in front of her partner, mouthing pathetic obscenities as frightening, to him, as the obscene songs of mad Ophelia.

Pornography, in a sense, is the ultimate form of decadent literature, with so much energy locked away and deliberately withheld. Self-denigrating, like Charlotte, the text turns on itself, using its own language to underline the futility of its fantasy, even as it clings to it. Prostitutes, she says, prefer to masturbate – when you're in the trade, it's all the pleasure you have. The fantasy is sustained by deliberate refusal of commitment. Mauricette, in the last few pages, decidès she would prefer after all to keep the saleable commodity of her virginity, which was only promised as the pretext for the play. At its end, the play turns momentarily serious, collapsing in a crisis of hysterical screams and tears from Charlotte which alarms even her mother. But the crisis passes, as they all do, and the adventure concludes in an atmosphere of sentimentality and light cynicism. The only dark note is the threat of the police in the background, but their attentions are reserved for the prostitutes. Young men, the whores' innocent victims, dream on safely in their rooms.

Unlocking the Garden: Octave Mirbeau 1848–1917

For Edmond de Goncourt, the contradiction between Octave Mirbeau's anarchist politics and his comfortable middle-class lifestyle was deeply offensive:

> Those partisans of anarchy and the egalitarian regime it intends to install, Mirbeau and Scholl, are gentlemen who can't live without women and drink and expensive dinners, gentlemen who spend 60,000 francs a year: I can just see them subjected to the cheap pleasures of an anarchist regime (*Journal*, 6 May 1892).

Mirbeau himself turned that contradiction into the subject of his work.

He drew himself, and his heroes, as men corrupted by the times. Educated by the Jesuits 1859–63, 'brought up in perfect, total idiocy and in the most pathetic, crudest superstition' ('Pétrisseurs d'âmes', *Le Journal*, 10 February 1901), sampling the delights of university and opium in Paris in the late 1860s, fighting in the Franco-Prussian War, and then in the 1870s back to Paris and journalism, politics and, briefly, the Stock Exchange, he had every opportunity to observe and absorb the workings of an unlovely, undesirable, yet apparently irresistible system. He recognized and succumbed to its seductions, and he loathed their effects.

In the early eighties, Catholic and monarchist, he blamed republicans, democrats, Jewish financiers and the corrupting culture of the European decadence for France's decline. In *Les Grimaces*, the weekly satirical review he founded and edited, he made himself spokesman for a public demanding, he said, an end to all the stench and decay: 'Wherever there is a wound to cauterize, rogues to unmask, decadence to lash, or virtue to praise, we shall be ready' (11 August 1883, cit. M. Schwarz, *Octave Mirbeau*, 1966, p. 33).

When he switched to the Left, it was to attack the same vices, but from a better understanding of causes and effects, and of the mechanisms by which a society makes over into its own image the individuals that compose it, disguising from them the extent of their incorporation.

His three autobiographical novels, *Le Calvaire* (1887), *L'Abbé Jules* (1888) and *Sébastien Roch* (1890) trace this process of demystification. Mirbeau learned to reconstitute those categories which decadent ideology so carefully distinguished – 'nature' and artifice, individual and society, instinct and education. He recognized the function of the scapegoat, be it Jew, democrat, or woman. He understood that the solutions he had previously found for his discontents – escape into religious ideology, and reliance on strong leadership – were not in fact solutions, but a major part of the problem.

As he himself acknowledged through the confusions of his heroes, caught helplessly in a transitional moment of society, his vision was never able to clarify completely. It was too much shaped by the old world. In an article of 1896, 'Questions sociales' (coll. *Les Ecrivains*, 2e série, 1926), listing with delight those forces waking in the depths of society as yet unrecognized by the politicians, 'anarchism, socialism, feminism, anti-Semitism, all the harbingers of inevitable revolution', he made no distinction between progressive and regressive currents. What he appreciated in all of them was their capacity to produce violence, and thereby change. As he had written in his famous preface to Jules Grave's *La Société mourante et l'anarchie* (1891), terrorist violence was the storm that brought rain to thirsty land. If the lightning blasted oaks which had grown too tall, that was a regrettable but inevitable side-effect: 'We shouldn't get too emotional over the death of greedy oaks . . .'

In his view, he had established the real enemy. The Dreyfus Affair confirmed his position. In his novel *Le Journal d'une femme de chambre* (1900), the Dreyfus case is a binding force for the complex economic and psychological relationships that hold together servants and masters, keeping the servants, and the system, safely in place. Joseph is a rapist, a murderer and a thief, who despises his masters. He respects, however, the mystique of power centred on the Army and the Church, disseminated by Drumont, whose *La Libre Parole* is read avidly by the servant classes. Respect for the prestige of power is bred into the bones of Joseph's people. Célestine, the chambermaid, is drawn despite herself to the ugly, brutal old man:

> He has the fascination of the mysterious and the unknown, and he exercises it over me besides the harsh, domineering, powerful magic of strength. And that magic – for it is magic – works more and more powerfully on my nerves, conquering my passive, submissive flesh (p. 319).

Once Joseph is married, and established in his own café on the proceeds of his robbery, that same murderous violence becomes the backbone of solid conservatism:

> What I admire in him is his moral tranquillity . . . You can tell that his life has a solid foundation. He supports more violently than ever family, property, religion, the Navy, the Army, the Motherland . . . I think he's wonderful! (p. 442).

In the tales swapped by the inhabitants of the sanatorium in the Pyrenees, where the narrator of *Les Vingt-et-un Jours d'un neurasthénique* (1901) goes for his rest cure, the rich count up their crimes while the poor are starved and beaten. The best are caught in impotent nightmares. Apathy and ignorance are the enemy; and Mirbeau, through the mouth of the starving worker, declares the parallel roles of the literary and political anarchist. If the rich refuse to see, he will smear their crimes, and his own, in their faces:

> I want to be a social threat . . .
> I shall go to Rome and tell the Pope that the people of Paris and my

friends the peasants want no more of his Church, his priests and his
prayers . . . I shall go and tell the Kings, the Emperors, the Republics,
we've had enough of their armies and their massacres . . . all that blood
and tears they cover the world with, for no reason . . .
     And I shall wipe my knife and my red hands over all those faces and
bellies.
     That's how I shall be a social threat . . . (pp. 331–2).

Mirbeau's three autobiographical novels are an exploration of the
neurotic condition of alternating lethargy and frenzy which is the fate of
the best of his contemporaries. They look at their morbid eroticism and
the violence with which it is usually associated, and the two images on
which it focuses: Woman and the crucified Christ. Painstakingly, they
disengage the images from the reality that produces them, and which they
reinforce. The origins of good and evil are not in God or Woman, but in
systems.
     The process of dissociation is a slow one. The firm grip which the old
authorities have on power is directly connected with their success in
inducing individuals to accept what Mirbeau elsewhere calls the heroic lie:
the illusion that private life, personal sensibility and personal relations,
and not political and economic systems, are the stuff of which life is made.
What Mirbeau sets out in his fictions are the distractions of the decadent
dream.
     Le Calvaire (1887) is a denunciation of the eternal feminine. Lirat, the
painter, denounces the mothers who bear sons for a 'sick', 'exhausted'
race, and bring them up to be easy prey for mistresses who degrade and
debilitate. For the hero, Jean Mintié, Lirat's views are close enough to his
own experience to have the ring of truth. Jean's childhood centred on his
unhappily married mother. Since discovering, as a child, her own mother
hanging from a candelabra, she had suffered morbid hallucinations. Her
fear of passing on her neuroses to Jean, the only person who could rouse
her to life, drove her to alternate between neglecting the child and
smothering him in passionate embraces. His most vivid memories are the
sight of her suffering, and her frightening, animal-like '*rages de tendresse*';
she was more of a mistress than a mother. He was shattered by her early
death, and resentful at being abandoned to a cold father.
     With Juliette Leroux, the mistress who takes his money and cheats him,
but also genuinely cares for him, he re-creates the emotions aroused by his
mother. Her entry into his life is marked by his dream of a consoling Virgin
Mother who suddenly strips herself naked and lasciviously offers herself.
(This is the dream of de Gourmont's Guido della Preda in his Tower.) He

looks for ways of perverting their pleasure with suffering. On their first night together, he torments himself with fears of her dying, and with jealous fantasies of her previous lovers. When their relationship ends, his masochistic pleasure in being rejected is coupled with sadistic dreams of Juliette humiliated, whipped and prostituted to men and animals. He is filled with frenzied desires to rape and murder; finding Juliette absent from her flat, he tears her dog to pieces.

Both narrator and text hold Juliette responsible for feelings which should properly be attributed to the mother's influence, and through her, to the complex institution of the family. Before he met his mistress, he was subject to bouts of torpor, like his mother's; he was 'a corpse who knew he was dead'. Living with Juliette, when that same lethargy prevents him writing, he experiences its cloying darkness as something intensely physical, erotic and evil, the woman's fault: 'I felt its darkness sticking to my hair, clinging to my fingers, rolling its viscous coils round my body . . .' (p. 184).

Lirat's painting is devoted to a vision of woman that confirms Jean's prejudices. Like Rops, he draws not love but lust, passion in the mask of death and corruption: 'Love smeared with blood, intoxicated with filth and slime, Love in onanistic frenzies, accursed Love that sticks its sucker-like maw on a man and dries out his veins, sucks his marrow, strips the flesh from his bones' (p. 105).

He is a past master of the corrupting half-truth. He plans an engraving of a woman rising from a dark pit on the back of a beast with a gross, living death's head and greedy lips; old men will be bending over her, with lustful faces. Such images of a hated father stir in Jean unresolved envy and resentment which are immediately diverted to the female at the centre. Lirat takes advantage of Jean's confusion to suggest he leave Paris and forget Juliette. In Jean's absence, Juliette's affections are easily transferred to the painter.

The enemy is not woman but man, and his readiness to exploit other men, women, animals, in short, the whole of his world. In the Franco-Prussian War, the enemy is not the Prussians, who are met in open conflict, but those who claim to be on the same side but are ready to use the slightest shred of advantage against those who are weaker. In a chapter that caused a scandal when published, Mirbeau describes ordinary French soldiers sacking French peasants' houses for firewood and stealing their food, or pulling carts from refugee columns to build their barricades. Officers take peasants' sons for cannon fodder. On the battlefield, the Establishment's political language – 'justice', 'love', 'fatherland' – appears as the confidence trick it is.

The only glimpse of goodness is Jean's sighting of the Prussian scout, innocently savouring the beauty of dawn. The proper response here would be for Jean to hold out a hand to the enemy, across the lines of conflict which others have drawn, for their own interests. He realizes this, but too obscurely to be of use. His 'instinctive' reaction is to kill. Reproducing the childhood model of his father shooting a cat in the garden, as it sat mesmerized by the beauty of a butterfly, Jean shoots the Prussian. There is one difference; too late, overcome with remorse, he kisses the enemy's dead face.

A similar revelation awaits Mintié in the city. Watching a workman admiring the carriages passing in the Bois de Boulogne, he is swept by the urge to seize the man, shake him and tell him the women inside should be guillotined. They're 'ferocious animals' stealing his bread and his place in the sun; his labour is the price of their luxury; the society that grinds him down is there for their protection. He gloats in anticipation: 'How well the good corn would grow, tall and nourishing, in the earth where their bodies lay rotting!' (p. 312). At the same moment, he sees Lirat with Juliette. As with the Prussian, he is suddenly and devastatingly aware of how his hatred has been deflected from its proper targets.

Having seen through the delusions of the decadent world, the only answer for Jean is to abandon it. His only alternative is a utopian vision: down a luminous road, 'nature' beckons, promising an end to suffering and evil. Putting on workmen's clothes, he strikes off for the unknown, leaving the city peopled with the lovers of death:

> In the street, men seemed to me like mad spectres, ancient skeletons falling to bits, their bones held together with pieces of string, dropping on to the pavement, stirring strange echoes . . . And all those shreds of human bodies, stripped by death of their flesh, were hurling themselves at one another, for ever swept by murderous fever, whipped on by lust, fighting for ever over foul corpses . . . (p. 319).

In *Sébastien Roch*, the sins of the fathers are again the source of the children's corruption. The adult Sébastien must rid himself of a double nightmare, in which his father hands him over to the priests and their followers to be torn to pieces, and the priests feed their creatures on the crushed souls of children:

> There was a kind of tub, filled to the top with quivering, bright, vivid butterflies. They were the souls of little children. The Father Rector . . . plunged his hands into the tub and pulled out handfuls of pretty souls,

that quivered and uttered tiny, plaintive cries. Then he put them in a mortar, pounded and crushed them, and made a thick, red paste that he spread on lumps of bread and threw to the dogs, great greedy dogs, standing all round him up on their hind legs, wearing birettas (pp. 308–9).

The novel is set in Catholic, Royalist Brittany in 1862. To satisfy the vanity of his father, a well-to-do ironmonger, Sébastien is sent to a prestigious Jesuit school for young gentlemen. The Jesuits' choice of Brittany for their establishment, Mirbeau points out, was deliberate. The heroic legends of the Counter-Revolution and the mystical legends of the Middle Ages which still flourished there were the perfect context and vehicle for the conservative ideology with which the Fathers sought to impress their students.

Mirbeau explains that the function of these colleges, microcosms of the world outside, is to teach children to respect social hierarchy. Sébastien rapidly learns that he is to be one of life's losers, while Guy de Kerdaniel, the local marquis' spoiled and arrogant son, a pale weakling, 'stamped with the stigmata of an exhausted race' (p. 120), is an unquestioned leader.

Sébastien is easy prey for the corrupting forces of the adult world, which are aimed directly at his awakening adolescent sexuality. A prurient confessor gives his imagination mysterious new desires to feed on. Romantic literature ensnares him in sensual dream. As he listens:

Sébastien felt himself sway in strange hammocks, his brow cooled by the perfumed breath of fans, while behind him to infinity stretched misty, pearly dream landscapes, crimson forests haunted by female figures, seductive shadows, plaintive souls, tender flowers, sad, wandering desires . . . Father de Kern had a tendency to tender melancholies, ecstatic repentance, intangible embraces, hopeless mysticisms, where the idea of love and the idea of death are always hand-in-hand – everything that was both carnal and immaterial, everything that corresponded with all that was vague, noble and headstrong in Sébastien's soul, a young soul too fragile and delicate to bear unharmed the lightning shocks from those clouds, and the corrupting fumes of those poisons (p. 190).

Christianity, with its love of humiliation and morbid attachment to pain, has a sensuality all its own in the image of the crucified Christ: 'Ah, to let one's repentant lips wander over the adorable body, to fix one's mouth on the bleeding wounds of those suffering sides, to embrace those broken limbs, to feel that heavenly flesh burn against one's mortal flesh! . . . Where are delights that can compare?' (p. 203). The priest makes Nature an accomplice to his seductions – 'sun, mists, sea, languid evenings, starry nights, all Nature obedient, like an old procuress, to the monstrous desires of one man' (p. 203). With no defences, the child is easily raped by his master.

This is the misuse that plunges him into nightmare. To his imagination, obsessed with evil, all his friends seem fallen into the same trap; his prayers and poetry are stained with corruption; when he thinks of Marguerite, his playmate at home, he pictures her offering him 'her prostitute body, covered with foul filth' (p. 231).

Falsely accused by Father de Kern of homosexual practices with the doctor's son, Borobec, his only friend, he is sent home in disgrace. At home, he sinks into torpor. He can understand how the corrupting forces of education and social institutions have worked against him. He knows the priest for what he is and despises him. But he is powerless to revolt, unmanned by guilt: 'I cannot formulate a moral concept of the universe, however confused, that is free of all hypocrisy and all religious, political, legal and social barbarities, without at once being seized by the social and religious terrors instilled in me at college.'

The people in his own town will never rebel: 'There is there a force of inertia, strengthened by centuries of religious and authoritarian tradition, that cannot be overcome. Man . . . is weakened and emasculated by the lie of heroic sentiment; he is kept in his moral abjection and slave-like submission by the lie of charity' (p. 304).

He feels the futility of things too keenly to go to the barricades or the scaffold for the sake of an idea (p. 305). He has one hope left: 'A younger generation who, faced with the morality established by the priest and the laws set up by the policeman, the priest's right hand, will say with resolution: "I shall be immoral, and I shall rebel" ' (p. 298).

Woman is the scapegoat for all these fears and resentments. Obsessed by learned images of the evil of the flesh, he is tempted to kill Marguerite, whose complexion seems to invite murder, 'moon-pale, pale with the pallor of death' (p. 343). Instead, they exchange the perverted dreams which are all they have. He makes her describe in obscene detail how she was stirred by watching the servants make love; he, as he listens, remembers his old hallucinations and the rape that broke his will, leaving him 'between an abyss of blood and an abyss of mud'. His desire to murder is transformed into the desire for sexual possession. The act of penetration, made brutal by the need to overcome taught repugnance and inhibition, restores them both to animal innocence.

Theirs, however, is an historical tragedy that cannot be resolved in private life alone. The authority of the fathers still rules in the wider world, and war is declared. The same war that drafts Sébastien to death on the battlefield gives his father a new lease of life, with committees to organize and orders to be given.

On the battlefield, the old playground enemies are still in command, plunging their soldiers into deadly combat with their careless gunshots. But also present is Bolorec, who for years has silently waited and prepared for 'the great event', which will bring 'Justice'. Bolorec shoots his captain in the back, too late, unfortunately, to save Sébastien, who dies caught in the cross-fire.

In this novel, war is the purifying flame prefigured in the closing pages of *L'Abbé Jules*. The transformation of sexual practices is a step on the road to recovery; but without purification by violence, destroying the authoritative figures of the old world, the end of decadence will not be complete.

For the hero of *L'Abbé Jules*, contemporary decadence is less a question of excessive self-indulgence than of unjustifiable repressions.

The priest is an enigma to himself, his Church and parishioners, and to his family, including his young nephew (the narrator) over whose childhood he exerts a formative influence. With a strange, hallucinatory realism, echoing the nightmare state of alienation in which its hero lives, the novel unravels the mystery. By the time he dies, he has at least salvaged an honest understanding of his wasted life, and bequeaths to his nephew his knowledge of the sources of decadence and the cure. Its grotesque fascinations must be openly confronted; there is no purification possible without violence and destruction.

Jules is the neurotic, who oscillates between demonic desires to cause pain to others as a mark of his revolt, and equally inexplicable fits of sick remorse. He enjoys evil. His decision to become a priest, at the end of a libertine adolescence, scandalizes his mother: 'I want to be a priest, by God! . . . A priest, by bloody God!' (p. 62). He enjoys the power over others that the priesthood gives him. He torments his colleagues by threatening to reveal their thefts and debauch; every one has guilty secrets to hide. He steals from his bishop to buy books. But his greatest sins are those of the flesh. He humiliates and assaults a peasant girl, pressing her to confess incest and bestiality, urging her to blasphemy:

> . . . he grabbed her neck and with his free hand he seized her breasts, raked and pinched them, crushed them furiously in a cruel, wild embrace. He felt under his fingers a scapulary, a cross, holy medals that

the poor wretch wore next to her skin, hanging on a little gold chain, and experienced a hideous, sacrilegious pleasure in twisting them, breaking them, thrusting them into the woman's flesh, making them part of his profane, brutal caresses. And he belched out foul words, horrifying, incoherent blasphemies, panting sobs (p. 88).

The robust peasant contemptuously knocks him away, and leaves him bewildered, frightened and sick with remorse, 'crushed', 'annihilated', in 'a feverish dream', experiencing 'a kind of drugged pleasure as he drifted into emptiness, oblivion, Nothingness'. In his feverish hallucinations, he sees obscene images written across the clouds, piling up 'like some terrifying construction, some black Sodom built in honour of etèrnal, triumphant Debauch' (p. 90).

The same obscene visions obsess him in the church:

Kneeling at the foot of the crucifix, he would watch, as in the famous picture, the body of Christ sway on the bloody nails, leave the Cross, leaning, falling into emptiness, and in the place of the vanished God, there was Woman, in triumph, naked, the eternal prostitute offering her mouth, her genitals, holding out her body to foul embraces (p. 137).

Jules' remorseful confessions are for him another perverted source of pleasure. But his display of corruption serves a double function. To speak evil rather than veil it is to oppose decay, not reinforce it. The sermon Jules preaches at his first Mass, listing his youthful blasphemies and criminal debauches, is a pleasurable exercise in self-humiliation: 'like those men of old, looking for martyrdom, flagellating and rending his own flesh, parting the streaming wounds with his fingers, scattering under fearsome voluntary blows shreds of his own flesh and drops of his own blood . . .' (p. 67). But it is also a painful shock to the complacency of the congregation, forcing tears that release their repressed humanity, and turning them to face Nature, who will, Jules claims, restore them.

Gradually the sources of Jules' lack of willpower and his contradictions are revealed. They are not inscribed in nature, but rather the results of nurture: 'I've wasted my life . . . I wasted it because I could never tame my filthy passions, the repressed passions that came from my mother's mysticism and my father's addiction to alcohol' (p. 236). After the family, the Church too betrayed its purpose and profession, giving an example of evil and of weakness. The old bishop who boldly forged a will to make his own fortune was too timid to perform his duty to his flock, and attack the corruption of society at its political roots. Jules urges him:

On all sides, society is cracking, religion collapsing, everything falling apart. At the top, on the throne, lolls shameless orgy, orgy made law . . . below, the starving beast howls, greedy for blood . . . You have charge of souls . . . and souls need to be upheld in their faith, encouraged in the struggle, reassured in danger . . . (p. 128).

The Church spends its efforts on the empty shows and shadows of its own declining power. Like Jules' mother, it is never there to console. His bishop was too sleepy to hear him confess to trying to rape the peasant girl.

Catholicism has corrupted both life and death. Death, which should be a deliverance, is haunted by religious terrors. Life's pleasures are perverted by false idealism, that imputes guilt and sin to innocent Nature. The insinuations of George Sand's *Indiana* are (as Baudelaire noted) far more obscene than the simple facts of life. Jules burns the book, explaining to his nephew:

Instead of keeping love as it should be in Nature, a normal, calm, noble act . . . simply, an organic function . . . we introduced dream . . . dream brought us dissatisfaction . . . and dissatisfaction, debauch . . . Religions – especially Catholicism – have become the chief pimps for love . . . they have developed its perverse, unhealthy side, invoking the sensuality of music and perfumes, the mysticism of prayers, and the moral onanism of worship . . . they knew that was the best and surest way to turn man into an animal, and keep him in chains . . . Love has dominion over life, like the whip has dominion over the back of the slave it tears to pieces, or the murderer's knife has dominion over the breast where it digs! . . . And God! . . . God is only one more form of debauched love! . . . He is the last inexorable delight, to which we yearn with all our exacerbated longing, and which we never reach . . . (p. 221).

The child is not uncritical. Jules is hard to understand, and often gratuitously cruel. Much of his advice is wrong. The boy describes one of his speeches as 'these tirades of vague, sentimental anarchism' (p. 205). But they are a vital alternative to 'the future baccalaureate that was my parents' ambition for me'. He watches Jules' corruption; he shares in it, as he reads *Indiana* or listens to the obscene song his uncle sings on his deathbed. He sings it himself, with tears in his eyes, while the rest of the family scrabble for the priest's inheritance. But he remains untouched by his uncle's decadence. Jules, with his honesty, puts an end to the debilitating hypocrisy and conformity of his generation. When his will is read, his entire fortune is promised to the first priest in the parish to renounce the Church.

His final legacy is the mysterious trunk he orders to be burned after his funeral. It collapses in the flames to liberate a magnificent collection of pornography:

> . . . spilling a flood of papers, strange engravings, monstrous drawings, and we saw twisting in the flames huge female rumps, phallic images, naked wonders, breasts, bellies, waving legs, entwined thighs, a whole swarm of tangled bodies, satanic ruts, extravagant perversions, all in fantastic movement as they shrivelled in the flames (p. 255).

Though the boy's father hurries him away, he goes on watching at a distance. His old life must start again, without Jules' protection; but from now on, in the background to his parents' worst atrocities, he hears his uncle's snigger.

Mirbeau's attacks in *L'Abbé Jules* and *Sébastien Roch* on the deformations of woman, love and Nature by Romantic artists are eclipsed by his denunciations of the morbid perversions of full-blown decadence which they prefigure. Pre-Raphaelites, aesthetes, decadents and Symbolists play with an absurd symbolism that colours what is at best, he says, an acknowledged absence of values, at worst the smug self-regard of the philistine middle classes. It is not so much the lily that inspires the Pre-Raphaelites as the English umbrella: 'See how it exudes femininity, dream, mystery, melancholy, Hamletism, pessimism and the absence of love' ('Portrait', *Gil Blas*, 27 July 1886).

This mode of painting, disclosing 'a singularly morbid frame of mind', has poisoned a generation. The failed painter confesses:

> I can't draw, and I don't know what *values* are! . . . that's all it is, their ideal, that's poisoned a whole generation! It's ugliness exacerbated and the hidden side of Nothing at all! Oh, those princesses with bodies like beanpoles and faces like poisonous flowers . . . Oh, those long emaciated mistresses like fishing gaffs, who can walk without legs, see without eyes, speak without mouths, and make love in the absence of organs, who stand in leafy bowers cut out by machine, lifting their hands, bent back flat at the wrist, in the same boring gesture! And those heroes stinking of neurosis, sodomy and syphilis! ('Des lys! Des lys!', *Le Journal*, 7 April 1895).

Burne-Jones is the major source of mystification, England at her most ridiculous. Ignorant of design, colour and composition, he is idolized by Liverpudlian merchants, for whom his work is a rich source of obscenities.

England's parks are filled with gliding Souls, red-haired, long-gowned, clutching arum liles, poor imitations of Burne-Jones' equally poor pictures of prisoners, virgins and hermaphrodite chevaliers. Brilliant red sensual mouths and black-ringed eyes send confusing signals of lust and chastity. 'Nothing exalts lust like a nun's disguise; a hairshirt, properly worn, is a marvellous prop for accursed passions' ('Toujours des lys!', *Le Journal*, 28 April 1895). The bruised eyes express it all, in their willed ambiguity: 'When people explained Burne-Jones to me, they would say: "Just look at the quality of the bruises round the eyes: it's unique. You can't tell whether it's from masturbation, lesbianism, natural love or tuberculosis. It's all there!" ' ('Les Artistes de l'âme', *Le Journal*, 23 February 1896).

In another satire, Botticelli himself is summoned to complain that his style has been usurped by mystics and pseudo-intellectuals, and that he loathes being 'followed everywhere . . . by a devilish procession of lesbians and homosexuals'. He knows what moves his self-styled heirs: they're equally incompetent as artists and human beings: 'Theories are the death of art, because they're a confession of artistic impotence. When you can't create according to Nature's laws and the normal course of life, you have to find some semblance of an excuse, and go looking for pretexts' ('Botticelli proteste!', *Le Journal*, 4–11 October 1896).

In the novel which engages most directly with the forms and values of the decadence, *Le Jardin des supplices* (1899), these same charges reappear. Pretentious self-presentation veils real incompetence and impotence; Nature and truth are deformed to satisfy an egoistic ideal. But what in the art criticism gave rise to comic gibes is here taken with deadly seriousness. Mirbeau draws together all the emblems of decadent style – flowers, peacocks, the green eyes and blonde hair of the mother-mistress, blood, pain and death – in a quintessence no less heady than *A rebours*, whose purpose is to settle accounts with the decadent poison. Oscar Wilde wrote to Frank Harris in May 1899:

If you want to read a terrible little book, order Octave Mirbeau's *Le Jardin des supplices*: it is quite awful: a *Sadique* joy in pain pulses in it: it is very revolting to me, but, for all that, wonderful. His soul seems to have wandered in fearsome places. But you, to whom fear is unknown will face the book with courage: to me it is a sort of grey adder.

Arguably the most seductive account of sadism produced in the decadent era, the novel is also the most precise analysis of how power works in society. It discloses the patterns of cruelty and dominance on which relationships between individuals and between individuals and State are founded, and shows how individual imagination and instinct are drafted into the service of collective oppression.

In this novel, moments of most intense feeling are moments at which characters react most automatically, repeating learned responses. Their emotions and their objects of desire are not their own. Cruelty, which they label instinct, would seem rather to be a practice, a habit taught by a society based on competition. Where cruelty is rewritten to appear as intense, exquisite pleasure, everyone will aspire to be an executioner, and no one realize the extent to which all are victims. With reason clouded by the sensuous excitement of the decadent theatre, all become willing accomplices in the action, equally deluding and deluded. Mirbeau's book is frightening, as Lorrain's *Monsieur de Phocas* is frightening: it shows the madness of decadent egoism become the way of life, plausible and seductive, with, to all appearances, no cracks in its surface.

The book is dedicated to the members of the institutions that shape modern society and modern sensibility: Church, Army, Judiciary, Faculties and Government. In the frontispiece, an after-dinner conversation, it is the academic members of the club who speak, giving their apparently objective and authoritative account of the instincts as unchanging acts of life, products of Nature rather than environment, fearsome forces that can only be repressed, never modified or redirected – another heroic lie, that turns instinct into an object of respect as well as fear.

What academics say is not necessarily true. The English academic whom the narrator meets later on his travels, the admirer of Darwin and Haeckel, is a laughable idiot. Anyone can claim academic credentials for his own purposes: the narrator passes himself off as a naturalist to get funds for his trip to Asia. And none of the academics challenges his assertion: 'Do things need proving? They only need to be felt' (p. 27). Academics express their preferred truths, with well-trained articulacy.

For a 'Darwinian scholar' who takes the floor, Hobbes and Darwin are sources of a language that reinforces his own social position. At the same time, it expresses the fears and repressed desires which that position represents. For him, the basis of civilization is murder; not simple 'killing', but a value-loaded action that presumes the existence of guilt and punishment. Murder justifies the existence of Government. Without it, there would be anarchy. By this he means there would be no elites, castes, or positions in a hierarchy. In his view, industry, colonial trade, war, hunting and anti-Semitism are safety-valves for the instinctive desire to kill. (Another guest speculates briefly that these might be causes rather than products of the thirst to kill, but this idea is unhelpful, and he drops it.) A philosopher adds that in modern civilized society the pure instinct cannot be exercised freely, but there are other outlets. At one extreme are the fairground shooting booths with their increasingly realistic targets; at another, there is Dreyfus. With a frisson, the academic confesses that he himself has felt overwhelming impulses to murder. He is upstaged by a young man who on the same impulses very nearly did murder a fat, repulsive bourgeois citizen asleep opposite him in his first-class carriage. The victim woke up to see the youth reaching out for his throat, and died of fright. Mirbeau's irony is neat. A bourgeoisie which tells its children that instinct is both admirable and irrepressible will find its sins come home to roost. The young man adds to his unconscious indictment of decadent ideology by confessing that he enjoys the 'mystery' of impulse and instinct, and has no intention of spoiling his pleasure by an analysis that might see it as a social and human question.

A diversion is provided by a stranger, a prematurely aged man with ravaged face, who declares that woman – aristocrat or whore – is the source of all cruelty and crime, and the symbol of the identity of the sexual instinct and the instinct to kill. He has met Eve, free of all civilization's restraints, displayed 'in her truth, her original nakedness, among gardens and torment, blood and flowers'. He had asked her for salvation, and she had dragged him into 'crimes I never knew existed, darkness where I'd never before descended'. He refuses to blame her. She is irresponsible, one of the forces of Nature, in whom love and death are two faces of the same coin: 'Being the matrix of life, she must therefore be the matrix of death . . . since it is from death that all life is perpetually reborn . . . and ending death would mean killing the sole source of life's fertility' (p. 27).

His tale makes clear that he *cannot* blame her. If she could be blamed, she might also be changed into something else; and he can imagine nothing else. Before he met her, he had a career of failure to look back on. When he tried to leave her, his only option was to join an English mission into the fever-ridden jungle. The woman was beautiful, she flattered him, and gave him an illusion of living. For all its untruth, the illusion was better than any alternatives he could invent. And if he can now repeat it, in a way that catches his audience in its contagion, it becomes the guarantee of his continued existence. This tale will be his admission ticket to the clubroom, where others like him sit wrapped in the drugged fumes of cigarettes and alcohol, perpetuating the lies.

What is at issue is social corruption. Clara is not Eve. She is heir to a man who made his fortune exploiting the colonies, selling opium in Canton, and she has been formed by the Europe she so despises. She spends summer in England, for business reasons, goes to Germany for her health, and France for pleasure, like any other member of the wealthy English upper classes. The narrator is equally a creature of French public life. Narrowly escaping prison for a business fraud, failing in his attempt to enter the Assembly on a corrupt ticket, he is packed off East on misappropriated monies until the scandals at home die down. He is the parasite of a Minister who is himself one of the parasites of the Opportunist faction, devoted to making large promises to the electorate in order to rob it blind. Both Minister and narrator come from a petty bourgeois background, and had the whole of society to climb. The narrator learned his morality from his father, a corrupt merchant who had a lucrative contract with the army. Theft and fraud, punished when committed by the poor, are a 'natural' part of trade and commerce. Justice, which is arbitrary, is the arm of established power. This is precisely the situation which the narrator will rediscover in the East.

These are the ugly truths for which the bloodstained flowers of the Chinese garden provide a welcome mask. The narrator learns to present himself as a Romantic victim, the centre of a heroic and fatal drama. Without the mask, he is no different from the grotesque Europeans on the ship, whom he and Clara affect to despise, but whose murderous obsessions are at least their own invention. (A Normandy gentleman, obsessed with hunting, baits for peacocks with tiger's droppings. A cannibal explorer, a connoisseur of human flesh, explains frankly that he is paid by Governments and business enterprises to civilize the blacks: 'that is, take their stocks of ivory and rubber' and kill them. An English officer, who is on the look-out for more efficient ways of killing, has invented a bullet that can cut through twelve Hindus in its flight.)

Trapped on the boat, the narrator turns to Clara as his only resource. He is drawn by her heavy red hair and green eyes flecked with gold, like a wild beast's, and by the purity he invents in her gaze ('the heavenly regard of this lustral creature'). He confesses to her all the squalor of his past; she will be mistress and mother confessor. For her sake, he abandons his mission to Ceylon. He leaves the ship for the unknown of China with a goddess who carries with her all the guilts of Europe.

Though all his actions are his own choice, his story is so constructed that Clara is turned into its driving force. In the two principal acts of their drama, it is Clara who rushes him into the abyss. The race out of her boudoir, through her garden and the docks, in the intense heat and filth, is to satisfy her haste to be on time to feed the convicts. Their second, even more horrifying course through the Imperial gardens, with all their mud, flies, blood, heat and poisonous flowers, is to satisfy her desire to reach the site of the bell torture before the criminal dies. It is Clara who gives him the words to justify the passion for death. These are the commonplaces of sadism, but in her mouth, he claims, they sound suddenly new and convincing. Western eroticism for her is 'a poor, stupid, chilling thing', spoiled by the guilty fear of natural instinct which Christianity has instilled (p. 140). Lust, not love, is the source of greatness. 'In lust . . . all man's intellectual faculties are revealed and sharpened.' It inspires crime, which is the supreme exercise of the ego, the desire 'to lift your individuality above all social prejudice, all laws, everything' (p. 141).

There is a stark contrast between seductive theory and actual practice. It is embodied first in the poet Clara feeds in the prison, incarcerated for his satires on Imperial corruption and his hatred of the English. Clara recites to him one of his own love poems, hymning the morbid beauty of decay:

And her I love for something more mysteriously attractive than Beauty
                itself: corruption.
Corruption, the dwelling place of the eternal warmth of life
Where metamorphoses are forever made and made again! (p.157).

The poet can no longer hear his poem; gangrenous, bloody-eyed, inhuman, the victim of real corruption, he is wholly absorbed in the fight for the rotting shreds of meat Clara has brought. Clara is not moved by the beauty of his poetry but the thrill of her own power as she watches him kill for what she distributes. As the prisoners, chained hand and foot, reach like Tantalus for the near-inaccessible meat, her phrases on the pleasure of unsatisfied desire are patent untruths: 'It passes the time for the poor devils . . . It gives them a little illusion . . .' (p. 152).

At first sight, the real beauty of the Imperial garden seems indisputable. But it comes from the 'natural' humus of the bodies of thirty thousand coolies who died of fever during the twenty-two years of its construction, enriched by the blood and excrement of the prisoners it was built to enclose. The narrator notes that it is this institution built on blood which preserves the exotic flowers and near-extinct species of fish that grace the decadent poetry of Robert de Montesquiou.

As the narrator looks more closely at the flowers, the truth about the garden pierces through. Colours, scents and lines are grouped in what seems a natural and inevitable harmony. Peach, apple and almond blossom, cataracts of vines, stephanotis and viburnum, are carefully placed to make 'an inflexible harmony, an artistic whole' (p. 175). Like all established societies, the life of the garden seems spontaneously generated and self-sustaining, but it is in fact a careful construct, to which hierarchy is the key.

As the couple advance, the flowers become more exotic. There are grotesques, that play games with the strict categories that 'nature' has ordained for the lesser breeds. Some plants look like animals. There are dwarf cedars like human heads of hair, ribbon-like leaves resembling snakes' skins, obscene orchids and flowers that look like insects. There is one that smells 'like when I make love to you'; Clara smears her face with it. There are shrubs with leaves of leather and mica. These perverted hybrids, fresh from a des Esseintes' nightmare, lead straight into the arms of the executioner.

This man is an artist. His 'Torture of the Rat' is the perfect synthesis of humiliation and pain. In language which parodies that of his Western equivalents, this pillar of the Establishment explains that he is in the 'classical tradition' of Chinese culture; that it is so little appreciated is a sign of the nation's 'decay' (p. 193). He gives a cruder version of Clara's apology for the identity of love and death, denying that the flowers in his garden are perverse: 'our flowers are violent, cruel, terrible and splendid . . . like love!' (p. 194). Their function is to make love and die, which is the way of life he urges on Clara, charming her with his account of the twenty male stamens that stand ready to serve one female pistil. Like the poet, the executioner is skilled in devising exquisite masks for the evil system he perpetuates.

Like the poet, too, he is a victim of the system. He was passed over for promotion, he complains, but he still works loyally at his job. Much of the garden's fascination is in its complete irrationality. It endures not only through violence but also by the promises of personal advantage with which it tantalizes its servants. The mystery is that broken promises create no revolt. Even more mysterious is that the people of the garden go on working to maintain a system that destroys them. The bell that rings in the centre of the garden, to madden and shatter the victim beneath with its vibrations, is pulled by two prisoners with blistered hands and strained muscles, one of whom dies with the condemned man.

In the last section of the garden stands an avenue of dead trees, each enclosing the tortured body of a living criminal, innocent of the charges manufactured by the authorities, who has refused to play the game of confession and guilt. These too die in agony, but not, at least, subscribing to the myth of the garden's beauty, harmony and propriety.

Religion helps forge the myth. The bell that tears the prisoner's body to pieces is the same bell that calls to prayer, preaching that crucial, murderous message of the beauty of inaccessible desire and the pleasure of pain. In the English countryside, it 'makes amorous virgins as they pass weep with ecstasy and divine melancholy' (p. 218). Heard in the distance, 'it gives you the impression of mystical Easters . . . joyful masses . . . baptisms . . . marriages . . . And it's the most terrifying death of all!' Clara herself speaks a fierce indictment of Christian sexual repression, and of the rapacity and venality of Anglican clergyman and Catholic priest alike in their 'civilizing' missions outside Europe. But all religions are evil, because all ultimately serve authority. When he first enters the garden, the narrator is moved by the calm, merciful face of Buddha, who, long before Christ, preached purity, self-denial and love. In the depths of the garden, the face changes. After Clara's attack on Christianity, 'The Buddha himself seemed to be twisting his features into the executioner's sniggering face' (p. 173), while the young girl praying has a yellow dress that brings to mind images of Narcissus. Religion is no more than the egoist's mirror. And religion consumes the hopes of the future. A little later, another image of Buddha appears, 'whose convulsed face, devoured by time, writhed in the sun. A woman was offering him branches of sidonia, whose blossoms looked like tiny children's hearts . . .' By the end, the divinity is completely exposed as demon, a head with horns and bat's ears, perched on a crumbling pillar whose decay is hidden by coiling honeysuckle, jasmine and hibiscus, and guarded by a foul-mouthed, money-grabbing priest.

In *A rebours*, Huysmans drew the disappointment of decadent aspirations. Des Esseintes gave up the attempt to impose his own cruel dreams on life, and returned, defeated, to a healthier 'real' world. In Mirbeau's novel, there is no alternative reality. After the exposure of all the tricks by which a mountebank society holds its victims fascinated, as the narrator stands chilled and horrified by the obscene truth finally spoken in the avenue of dead trees, the *tour de force* is to draw him back into the illusion, so that he becomes a consenting victim, taking pleasure in the deceits that destroy him. In the familiar pattern of decadent art, all the resentment, frustration, and excitement which have been generated turn back in on themselves not to destroy the system but to refuel it. Mirbeau's novel concludes with three images of chaotic, deadly violence, fixed in unbreakable, enclosing circles.

The couple's last moment in the garden is focused on the flower-strewn pool that contains a whole universe in its margins. In its stillness, the only signs of life are the darting red goldfish, like 'red thoughts in a woman's brain' (p. 226). They dip out of sight into the depths as a flock of cranes descends, to stand motionless, like bronze statues, alongside the phallic irises, 'devilish flowers . . . fatal signs'. All that moves are the waterlilies, like floating heads, swaying in the wake of the vanished carp. The narrator reads these images with the eyes of his own experience and self-interest. For him, the pool is an image of the garden, which in its turn is the image of a world of human cruelty and its 'monstrous flowers' – passion, self-interest, social institutions, justice, heroism, religion – all the instruments of 'eternal human suffering' (p. 232). In Europe and Asia alike, experience has taught him, all Nature 'driven by the cosmic force of love rushes to murder, thinking to find outside life a way of slaking the raging desire for life that consumes it and springs from it in jets of filthy foam!' (p. 233). His vision confuses Nature with artifice, cause with effect, and executioner with victim. Clara's red dreams, the goldfish which to his mind animate the pool, are not the source of cruelty but one more of its objects. The presiding deities are the cranes, the phallic predators masked by the irises.

Briefly, a different truth pierces through, but only to be twisted back to reinforce his chosen version. As Clara, like the pool, falls into unresponsive silence, he wonders whether he has misunderstood her.

> Does she really exist? . . . Does she not spring from my own debauch and fever? . . . Is she not one of those impossible images nightmare brings? . . . One of those criminal temptations that lust foments in the imaginations of sick murderers and madmen? . . . Is she perhaps none other than my own soul, projected outside me, involuntarily, incarnate in the form of sin? (p. 230).

This is too unpalatable a truth. It is easy to evade; the two are locked close together by the erotic intimacy of the garden, and her immediate presence is too 'real' to be understood for what it really is – that is, the mirror-image of his, the product of social relationships and social institutions. Because she stands before him as a physical reality, he attributes to her autonomy and responsibility, just as he chooses to define the garden as it stands as autonomous, spontaneously generated Nature. The choice is made, however blindly, and there is no way out.

As day declines, the flowers vanish from sight and the instruments of torture are clearly revealed. The garden is dominated by the dizzying silhouettes of five impaled prisoners, each turning in another closed circle. The phallic authority that rules the garden is also its own victim: 'On top of a mound, against the dying crimson of the evening, I see turning, turning, turning on stakes, slowly turning, turning in the void, swaying, like huge flowers with their stalks showing through the darkness, turning, turning, the black silhouettes of five condemned men' (p. 231).

Under the presiding authority of the stakes, the garden draws back into harmony, just like the pool. But where the female 'red thoughts' in the pool were repressed, the narrator's black mood is lifted upwards in a purging thrust of religious idealism. The evening mists lift the smell of blood and dead flesh to the heavens. Geckoes call at regular intervals, like bells, and darkness hides the ugliness of the flowers, leaving only their caressing touch. Tension is released as the terrors of the day are muted into new harmonies.

In the third circle, in the flowerboat brothel, it is made plain that Clara, far from being his executioner, is the victim who pays for his pleasures in her own body. The women in the novel are engaged in a bizarre conspiracy, glossed as erotic pleasure, that perpetuates their own pain, humiliation and submission. Ki-Pai takes Clara and her lover back to the flowerboat in her punt, as she has always done. The whores welcome Clara back as an old friend and set about restoring her, as always, with perfumes and caresses.

To the narrator, the air seems filled with the power of the Great Goddess. Clara's whispered name fills the boat. He grows dizzy at the sight of so many fetishes – naked female bodies, 'mouths, hands, breasts', jewels, perfumes. At the same time, apparently without understanding, he notes that the women waiting, in obscene poses, have 'lustful faces sadder than the faces of the tormented'. Equally without understanding, he registers the evidence of the male authority by which the boat is ruled. Two 'robust' men carry Clara in on a stretcher. A young man lies on a bed with wide eyes, in the anguished ecstasy of an opium trance, dreaming it all – just like the men in the frame, lingering over their liqueurs, dreaming the narrator's adventures all over again through their cigar smoke. The idol at the centre of the women's dance is the phallic Idol of the Seven Rods, a three-headed horned demon. The hellish frenzy that focuses on him is almost – but not quite – beyond the narrator's power to convey:

> Shouting, shrieking, seven women hurled themselves on the seven bronze rods. The Idol, embraced, ridden, violated by all this delirious flesh, vibrated under the repeated shock of these rapes and kisses that echoed like the blows of a battering ram on the gates of a beleaguered city. And around the Idol rose a mad clamour, a wild, mad lust, a mêlée of bodies welded together in a frantic embrace that took on the wild face of a massacre, reminiscent of the slaughter of the condemned men in their cages fighting over Clara's scrap of rotten meat! . . . (p. 248).

The narrator blames the 'slaughter' on Clara. But the passions that he censures are generated in his name, in forms chosen by men, those who control the prison, the garden and the brothel. Clara, waking up from her fits and fevers, is full of remorse and promises not to sin again, just like those made by the narrator as he left Europe. Ki-Pai leaves her to sleep off her weariness, convinced she can do nothing but sin again, with different partners, throughout eternity. Ki-Pai is right; and the fault lies with the narrator. Lovingly watching over her sleep, he says he wishes she would never wake up. But at the edge of his vision, he is aware of a bronze monkey with a ferocious snigger holding out to her a monstrous phallus. Clara's remorse is irrelevant. What she is, is dictated by man's desire, and his refusal to understand what he desires. Nature – Woman – is the malleable material, not the sculptor; the decadent is the artist, who will not be responsible for what he has made.

Bibliography

This Bibliography gives the first editions of works referred to in the text, together with a select number of important background works. Most page references in the text are to first editions. Where another edition has been used, this is given in brackets.

Primary Sources

Aldington, R., *Rémy de Gourmont: Selections*, Chatto & Windus, London, 1932.
Balzac, H. de, *La Fille aux yeux d'or*, *Scènes de la vie parisienne*, Vols 3–4, Madame Charles-Béchet, Paris, 1834–5.
Barbey d'Aurevilly, J., *Les Diaboliques*, E. Dentu, Paris, 1874.
Barney, N.C., *Souvenirs indiscrets*, Flammarion, Paris, 1960.
Baudelaire, C., *Les Fleurs du mal*, Poulet-Malassis et de Broise, Paris, 1857.
  (*Oeuvres complètes*, Bibliothèque de la Pléiade, Editions Gallimard, 1961.)
Bloy, L., *Un brelan d'excommuniés*, A. Savine, Paris, 1889; Blaizot, Paris, 1906.
Bois, J., *Le Satanisme et la magie* (with pref. by J.-K. Huysmans), L. Chailley, Paris, 1895.
Bourges, E., *Le Crépuscule des dieux*, Giraud et Cie [1884].
Bourget, P., *Essais de psychologie contemporaine*, A. Lemerre, Paris, 1883.
  The Century Guild. Hobby Horse.
Colette, *Mes apprentissages*, Ferenczi et fils, Paris, 1936.
  Le Décadent.
Ellis, H. Havelock, *The New Spirit*, George Bell and Sons, London, 1890.
  Affirmations, W. Scott, London, 1898.
  Studies in the Psychology of Sex, Vol.V, F.A. Davis Co., Philadelphia, 1905.
Flaubert, G., *Salammbô*, Michel Lévy frères, Paris, 1862.
  La Tentation de Saint Antoine, Charpentier et Cie, Paris, 1874.

Trois Contes, G. Charpentier, Paris, 1877.
   (*Oeuvres I*, Bibliothèque de la Pléïade, Editions Gallimard, 1966.)
Goncourt, E. and J. de, *Journal. Mémoires de la vie littéraire*, Charpentier, Paris,
   1889–96 (Fasquelle, Flammarion, 4 vols, 1956).
Gourmont, Rémy de, *Merlette*, Plon-Nourrit et Cie, Paris, 1886.
   Sixtine, roman de la vie cérébrale, Albert Savine, Paris, 1890.
   Le Latin mystique (Pref. by J.-K. Huysmans), Mercure de France, Paris 1892.
   Lilith, Des Presses des Essais d'art libre, Paris [1892].
   Litanies de la rose, Mercure de France, Paris, 1892.
   Le Fantôme, Mercure de France, Paris, 1893.
   Histoires magiques, Mercure de France, Paris, 1894.
   Le Livre des masques, 2 vols, Mercure de France, Paris, 1896–8.
   Les Chevaux de Diomède, Mercure de France, Paris, 1897.
   D'un pays lointain, Mercure de France, Paris, 1898.
   Le Songe d'une femme, Mercure de France, Paris, 1899.
   La Culture des idées, Mercure de France, Paris, 1900.
   Le Chemin de velours: Nouvelles Dissociations d'idées, Mercure de France, Paris,
      1902.
   Physique de l'amour: Essai sur l'instinct sexuel, Mercure de France, Paris, 1903.
   Une nuit au Luxembourg, Mercure de France, Paris, 1906.
   Promenades littéraires, 3ème série, Mercure de France, Paris, 1909.
   Lettres d'un satyre, G. Crès et Cie, Paris, 1913.
   Lettres à l'Amazone, Crès et Cie, 1914.
   Journal intime (1874–80), Typographie François Bernouard, Paris [1923].
   (*Oeuvres complètes*, Mercure de France, 1925–32.)
Huret, J., *Enquête sur la littérature contemporaine*, Bibliothèque Charpentier,
   Paris, 1891.
Huysmans, J.-K., *Le Drageoir à épices*, E. Dentu, Paris, 1874.
   Croquis parisiens, Henri Vaton, Paris, 1880.
   A vau-l'eau, Henry Kistemaeckers, Brussels, 1882.
   L'Art moderne, Charpentier, Paris, 1883.
   A rebours, G. Charpentier et Cie, Paris, 1884.
   En rade, Tresse et Stock, Paris, 1887.
   Certains, Tresse et Stock, Paris, 1889.
   Là-bas, Tresse et Stock, Paris, 1891.
   En route, Tresse et Stock, Paris, 1895.
   (with O. Mirbeau, J. Péladan, and others), *Félicien Rops et son oeuvre*, Edmond
      Deman, Brussels, 1897.
   La Cathédrale, P.-V. Stock, Paris, 1898.
   (*Oeuvres complètes*, Lucien Descaves ed., 1928–34, rpt. Slatkine Reprints,
      Geneva, 1972.)
James, H., *The Princess Casamassima*, Macmillan & Co., London and New York,
   1886.
Lévi, E., *The History of Magic*, tr. A.E. Waite, 4th ed., Rider & Co., London, 1948.
Lombard, J., *Adel. La Révolte future*, L. Vanier, Paris, 1888.
   L'Agonie, A. Savine, Paris, 1888; P. Ollendorff, Paris, 1901 (with pref. by
      O. Mirbeau).
   Byzance, A. Savine, Paris, 1890; P. Ollendorff, Paris, 1901 (with pref. by
      P. Margueritte).

Lorrain, J., *La Forêt bleue*, Alphonse Lemerre, Paris [1883].
Très Russe, Librairie Giraud et Cie, Paris, 1886 (P.-V. Stock, 1914).
Buveurs d'âmes, G. Charpentier et E. Fasquelle, Paris, 1893.
Sensations et souvenirs, G. Charpentier et E. Fasquelle, Paris, 1895.
Le Petite Classe, Paul Ollendorff, Paris, 1895.
Une femme par jour: Femmes d'été, Librairie Borel, Paris [1896].
Madame Baringhel, Fayard frères, Paris [1899].
Histoires de masques, Librairie Paul Ollendorff, Paris, 1900.
Monsieur de Phocas. Astarté, Librairie Paul Ollendorff, 1901.
Princesses d'ivoire et d'ivresse, Librairié Paul Ollendorff, 1902. (Collection Les Maîtres de l'Etrange et de la Peur, choix, préface, bibliographie de F. Lacassin, Union Générale d'Editions, 1980.)
Coins de Byzance. Le Vice errant, Librairie Paul Ollendorff, Paris, 1902.
Poussières de Paris, Librairie Paul Ollendorff, Paris, 1902.
Le Crime des riches, Pierre Douville, Paris, 1905.
Théâtre, Paul Ollendorff, Paris, 1906.
L'Aryenne, Paul Ollendorff, Paris, 1907.
Pelléastres, Albert Méricourt, Paris, 1910.
Correspondance I. Lettres . . . suivies des articles condamnées, Editions Baudinière, Paris, 1929.
La Ville empoisonnée. Pall-Mall Paris, Editions Jean Crès, 1936.
Louÿs, P., *Lêda ou la louange des bienheureuses ténèbres*, Librairie de 'l'Art indépendant', Paris, 1893.
Les Poésies de Méléagre, Librairie de 'l'Art indépendant', Paris, 1893.
Ariane ou le chemin de la paix éternelle, Librairie de 'l'Art indépendant', Paris, 1894.
Scènes de la vie des courtisanes, Librairie de 'l'Art indépendant', Paris, 1894.
Les Chansons de Bilitis, Librairie de 'l'Art indépendant', Paris, 1895.
Aphrodite. Moeurs antiques, Mercure de France, Paris, 1896.
Byblis changée en fontaine, Libraire Borel, Paris, 1898.
La Femme et le pantin. Roman espagnol, Mercure de France, Paris, 1898.
Les Aventures du roi Pausole, Bibliothèque Charpentier, Eugène Fasquelle Editeur, Paris, 1901.
Sanguines, Bibliothèque Charpentier, Eugène Fasquelle Editeur, Paris, 1903.
Le Crépuscule des nymphes, Editions Montaigne, Paris, 1925.
Trois Filles de leur mère, Aux dépens d'un amateur et pour ses amis [Paris, 1926].
Histoire du roi Gonzalve et des douze princesses, Aux dépens d'un bibliophile, Madrid [Paris, 1927].
Notes sur 'Aphrodite', Bagration Davidoff, Tiflis, 1928.
Journal intime (1882–91), Editions Montaigne, Paris, 1929.
Maupassant, G. de, *Oeuvres complètes: Chroniques littéraires et chroniques parisiennes*, Albin Michel, Paris, n.d.
Mendès, C., *Les 73 Journées de la Commune*, E. Lachaud, Paris, 1871.
Richard Wagner, G. Charpentier et Cie, Paris, 1886.
La Première Maîtresse, G. Charpentier et Cie, Paris, 1887.
La Maison de la vieille, Bibliothèque Charpentier, G. Charpentier et E. Fasquelle éds., Paris, 1894.
Mercure de France.

Mirbeau, O., *Le Calvaire*, Paul Ollendorff, 1887.
  L'Abbé Jules, Paul Ollendorff, Paris, 1888. (10:18, Union générale d'éditions, 1977.)
  Sébastien Roch, Charpentier, Paris, 1890, (10:18, Union générale d'éditions, 1977.)
  Le Jardin des supplices, Bibliothèque Charpentier, Eugène Fasquelle Editeur, 1899. (Fasquelle Editeur, 1957.)
  Le Journal d'une femme de chambre, Bibliothèque Charpentier, Eugène Fasquelle, Editeur, 1900. (Editions Fasquelle, 1937, rpt. Le Livre de poche, n.d.).
  Les Vingt-et-un Jours d'un neurasthénique, Bibliothèque Charpentier, Eugène Fasquelle Editeur, 1901.
  Pref. to J. Grave, *La Société mourante et l'anarchie*, Tresse et Stock, Paris, 1893.
  Des artistes: Première série (1885–96), Ernest Flammarion, Paris, 1922.
  Les Ecrivains: Première série (1884–1894), Ernest Flammarion, Paris, 1926.
Moore, G., *Mike Fletcher*, Ward & Downey, London, 1889.
  Confessions of a Young Man, Sonnenschein, Lowrey & Co., London, 1888; rev. ed. T. Werner Laurie, London, 1904.
  The New Freewoman; afterwards *The Egoist*.
Nietzsche, F., *Der Fall Wagner*, C.G. Naumann, Leipzig, 1888 (tr. W. Kaufmann, Vintage Books, New York, 1967).
Nordau, M.S., *Entartung*, Berlin, 1892. (*Degeneration*, W. Heinemann, London, 1895.)
Papus (Encausse, G.), *L'Occultisme contemporain*, Carré, Paris, 1887.
Péladan, J., *L'Art ochlocratique: Salons de 1882 et de 1883*, C. Dalou, Paris, 1888.
  Le Vice suprême, Librairie des Auteurs Modernes, Paris, 1884.
  Femmes honnêtes (pseud. le Marquis de Valognes), Ed. Monnier et Cie, Paris, 1885.
  Curieuse!, A. Laurens, Paris, 1886.
  L'Initiation sentimentale, Edinger, 1887.
  A coeur perdu, Edinger, Paris, 1888.
  Istar, Edinger, 1888.
  Femmes honnêtes, C. Dalou, Paris, 1888.
  La Victoire du mari, E. Dentu, Paris, 1889.
  Coeur en peine, E. Dentu, Paris, 1890.
  L'Androgyne, E. Dentu, 1891.
  La Gynandre, E. Dentu, Paris, 1891.
  Comment on devient mage: Ethique, Chamuel, Paris, 1892.
  Comment on devient fée: Erotique, Chamuel, Paris, 1893.
  Diathèse de décadence. Psychiatrie. Le Septénaire des Fées. Mélusine, Ollendorff, Paris, 1895.
  Le Théâtre complet de Wagner, Chamuel, Paris, 1895.
  Le Dernier Bourbon, Chamuel, Paris, 1895.
  Finis Latinorum, E. Flammarion, Paris, 1899.
  La Vertu suprême, Flammarion, Paris, 1900.
  La Science de l'amour, Albert Messein, Paris, 1911.
  La Guerre des idées, E. Flammarion, Paris, 1917.

(*La Décadence latine*, 21 vols, rpt. Slatkine Reprints, 1979).

La Plume.

Pound, Ezra, tr. and annot., R. de Gourmont, *The Natural Philosophy of Love*, Casanova Society, London, 1926.

Literary Essays of Ezra Pound, ed. T.S. Eliot, Faber and Faber, London, 1960.

The Selected Letters of Ezra Pound (1907–41), ed. D.D. Paige, Faber Paperbacks, London, 1982.

Rachilde (Marguerite Eymery), *Monsieur Vénus*, Auguste Brancart, Bruxelles, 1884; F. Brossier, Paris, 1889 (with pref. by M. Barrès).

Nono, roman de moeurs contemporains, E. Monnier, 1885.

La Marquise de Sade, Ed. Monnier et Cie, Paris, 1887.

La Sanglante Ironie, Léon Genonceaux, Paris, 1891.

Théâtre, Albert Savine, Paris, 1891.

Le Démon de l'absurde, Mercure de France, Paris, 1894.

Les Hors nature Mercure de France, Paris, 1897.

La Tour d'amour, Mercure de France, Paris, 1899.

La Jongleuse, Mercure de France, 1900. (Editions des Femmes, Paris, 1982.)

Contes et nouvelles, suivis du Théâtre, Mercure de France, Paris, 1900.

Le Meneur de louves, Mercure de France, Paris, 1905.

Le Grand Saigneur, E. Flammarion, Paris, 1922.

Madame de Lydone, assassin, J. Ferenczi et fils, Paris, 1928.

Pourquoi je ne suis pas féministe, Editions de France, Paris, 1928.

Les Voluptés imprévues, J. Ferenczi et fils, Paris, 1931.

(et Vallette, A.), *Le Roman d'un homme sérieux*, 5th ed., Mercure de France, Paris, 1944.

Quand j'étais jeune, Mercure de France, Paris, 1947.

Raffalovich, M.A., *Uranisme et unisexualité*, Storck, Lyon-Masson, Paris, 1896.

Redon, O., *A soi-même: Journal (1867–1915)*, Librairie José Corti, Paris, 1961.

The Graphic Works of Odilon Redon, Dover Publications Inc., New York, 1969.

Odilon Redon, Gustave Moreau, Rodolphe Bresdin, Exhibition Catalogue, Museum of Modern Art, New York, 1961.

La Revue blanche.

La Revue indépendante.

La Revue wagnérienne.

Sade, D.A.F., le Marquis de, *La Philosophie dans le boudoir*, London [Paris], 1795. (*Oeuvres complètes*, ed. G. Lély, Au cercle du livre précieux, Paris, Vol. III, 1962.)

Swinburne, A.C., *Poems and Ballads*, E. Moxon & Co., London, 1866.

Symons, A., 'J.-K. Huysmans', *The Fortnightly Review*, March 1892.

'The Decadent Movement in Literature', *Harper's New Monthly Magazine*, November 1893.

Silhouettes, 2nd ed., 1896.

London Nights, 2nd ed., 1897.

Studies in Two Literatures, L. Smithers, London, 1897.

The Symbolist Movement in Literature, Heinemann, London, 1899.

(*Collected Works*, 9 vols, Martin Secker, London, 1924.)

Villiers de l'Isle-Adam, A., comte de, *Isis*, Dentu, Paris, 1862.

Akëdysséril, M. de Brunhoff, Paris, 1886.

L'Amour suprême, M. de Brunhoff, Paris, 1886.

L'Eve future, M. de Brunhoff, Paris, 1886.

Axël, Quantin, Paris, 1890.

(*Oeuvres complètes*, Mercure de France, Paris, 11 vols, 1914–31.)

Wilde, O., *Complete Works of Oscar Wilde*, Collins, London and Glasgow, 1966.

The Letters of Oscar Wilde, ed. R. Hart-Davis, Rupert Hart-Davis Ltd, London, 1962.

Yeats, W.B., *The Secret Rose*, Lawrence and Bullen, London, 1897.

Autobiographies, Macmillan & Co., London, 1955.

Secondary Sources

Arwas, V., *Félicien Rops*, Academy Editions, London, 1972.

Baldick, R., *The Life of J.-K. Huysmans*, Clarendon Press, Oxford, 1955.

Bellot, E., *Jean Lombard: sa vie, ses oeuvres*, nouv. éd., Librairie Léon Vanier, Paris, 1904.

Cardinne-Petit, R., *Pierre Louÿs inconnu*, Editions de l'Elan, Paris, 1948.

Carr, R., *Anarchism in France: the case of Octave Mirbeau*, Manchester University Press, Manchester, 1977.

▪ Carter, A.E., *The Idea of Decadence in French Literature (1830–1900)*, University of Toronto Press, Toronto, 1958.

Clive, H.P., *Pierre Louÿs (1870–1925): A Biography*, Clarendon Press, Oxford, 1978.

Coeuroy, A., *Wagner et l'esprit romantique*, Collection Idées, Gallimard, Paris, 1965.

Colloque de Nantes: L'Esprit de Décadence, Minard, Paris, 1980.

Cooke, D., *I Saw the World End: A Study of Wagner's Ring*, Oxford University Press, London, 1979.

Crespelle, J.P., *Les Maîtres de la Belle Epoque*, Librairie Hachette, Paris, 1966.

Curzon, Henri de, *L'Oeuvre de Richard Wagner à Paris et ses interprètes (1850–1914)*, Maurice Senart et Cie, Paris [1920].

David, A., *Rachilde, homme de lettres*, Editions de la Nouvelle Revue Critique, Paris, 1924.

Deleuze, G., *Sacher-Masoch: An Interpretation*, tr. J. McNeil, Faber and Faber, London, 1971.

Delevoy, R.L., *Symbolists and Symbolism*, Skira M., Macmillan, London, 1982.

Doyon, R.-L., *La Douloureuse Aventure de Joséphin Péladan*, La Connaissance, Paris, 1946.

Durant, A., *Ezra Pound: Identity in Crisis*, The Harvester Press, London, 1981.

Evans, R.J., *The Feminists: Women's Emancipation Movements in Europe, America and Australasia (1840–1920)*, rev. ed., Croom Helm, London, 1979.

Exstéens, M., *L'Oeuvre gravé et lithographié de Félicien Rops*, Pellet, Paris, 1928.

Fletcher, I., ed., *Romantic Mythologies*, Routledge and Kegan Paul, London, 1967.

▪ ed., *Decadence and the 1890s*, Stratford-upon-Avon Studies (17), Edward Arnold, London, 1979.

Furness, R., *Wagner and Literature*, Manchester University Press, Manchester, 1983.

Gauthier, P.L., *Jean Lorrain*, André Lesot, Editeur, Paris, 1939.

Gibbons, T., *Rooms in the Darwin Hotel*, University of Western Australia Press, Nedlands, Western Australia, 1973.

Griffiths, R.M., *The Reactionary Revolution: the Catholic Revival in French Literature, 1870–1914*, Constable & Co., London, 1966.

Guichard, L., *La Musique et les lettres au temps du wagnérisme*, Université de Grenoble, Paris, 1963.

Hause, S.C., and Kenney, A.R., *Women's Suffrage and Social Politics in the French Third Republic*, Princeton University Press, Princeton, New Jersey, 1984.

Hone, J., *The Life of George Moore*, Victor Gollancz, London, 1936.

Hough, G., *The Last Romantics*, Methuen University Paperbacks, London, 1961.

Jackson, H., *The Eighteen Nineties*, Grant Richards, London, 1913, rpt. Harvester Press, London, 1976.

Jeffares, A.N., *Anglo-Irish Literature*, Macmillan, London, 1982.

Jullian, P., *Oscar Wilde*, tr. V. Wyndham, Constable, London, 1969.

Esthètes et magiciens, Librairie académique Perrin, Paris, 1969.

The Symbolists, Phaidon, London, 1973.

Jean Lorrain ou le Satyricon 1900, Fayard, Paris, 1974.

Kahane, M. and Wild, N., *Wagner et la France*, Bibliothèque Nationale et Théâtre Nationale de l'Opéra, Paris, Editions Herscher, Paris, 1983.

Laugaa-Traut, F., *Lectures de Sade*, Armand Colin, Paris, 1973.

Lhombreaud, R., *Arthur Symons: A Critical Biography*, The Unicorn Press, London, 1963.

Lidsky, P., *Les Ecrivains contre la Commune*, François Maspero, Paris, 1982.

Lucie-Smith, E., *Symbolist Art*, Thames and Hudson Ltd, London, 1972.

Magraw, R., *France 1815–1914: The Bourgeois Century*, Fontana Paperbacks, London, 1983.

Mann, T., 'Sufferings and Greatness of Richard Wagner', in *Essays of Three Decades*, tr. H.T. Lowe-Porter, Alfred A. Knopf, New York, 1947.

Mascha, O., *Félicien Rops und sein Werk*, Albert Langen, Munich, 1910.

Mendel, G., *La Révolte contre le père*, Paris, Payot, 1968.

Millan, G., *Pierre Louÿs ou le culte de l'amitié*, Pandora Editions, Aix-en-Provence, 1979.

Milner, M., ed., *Entretiens sur l'homme et le diable*, Mouton et Cie, Paris-La Haye, 1965.

Moers, E., *The Dandy. Brummell to Beerbohm*, Secker and Warburg, London, 1960.

Montgomery Hyde, H., *Oscar Wilde*, Eyre Methuen Ltd, London, 1976.

Nouvelle Revue du Midi, No. 10, December 1924 (no. spécial sur Joséphin Péladan).

Pierrot, J., *L'Imaginaire décadent, 1880–1900*, Presses Universitaires de France, Paris, 1977. (*The Decadent Imagination, 1880–1900*, tr. D. Coltman, University of Chicago Press, Chicago and London, 1981.)

Praz, M., *La carne, la morte e il diavolo nella litteratura romantica*, 'La Cultura', Milan-Rome, 1930 (tr. A. Davidson, 2nd ed. reissued, Oxford University Press, London, 1970).

Raitt, A.W., *Villiers de l'Isle-Adam et le mouvement symboliste*, Librairie José Corti, Paris, 1965.

Reade, B.E., *Sexual Heretics: Male Homosexuality in English Literature from*

1850–1900, Routledge and Kegan Paul, 1970.

Romantisme: Revue du dix-neuvième siècle, 'Décadence', No.42, 1983.

Sandstroem, S., *Le Monde imaginaire d'Odilon Redon*, tr. D. Naert, Berlingska Boktryckeriet, Lund, 1955.

Schwarz, M., *Octave Mirbeau: Vie et oeuvre*, Mouton & Co., The Hague-Paris, 1966.

Seznec, J., 'Odilon Redon and Literature', in *French Nineteenth-Century Painting and Literature*, U. Finke ed., Manchester U.P., Manchester, 1972.

Sieburth, R., *Instigations: Ezra Pound and Rémy de Gourmont*, Harvard U.P., Cambridge, Mass., 1978.

Sonstroem, D., *Rossetti and the Fair Lady*, Wesleyan University Press, Connecticut, 1970.

Souffrin, E., 'Swinburne et sa légende en France', *Revue de littérature comparée*, XXV, 1951.

Thomas, D., *Swinburne: The Poet in his World*, Weidenfeld and Nicolson, London, 1979.

Thornton, R.K.R., *The Decadent Dilemma*, Edward Arnold, London, 1983.

Uitti, K.D., *La Passion littéraire de Rémy de Gourmont*, Princeton University-Presses Universitaires de France, 1962.

Wirth, O., *Stanislas de Guaita*, Aux Editions du Symbolisme, Paris, 1935.

Zayed, F., *Huysmans, peintre de son époque*, Nizet, Paris, 1973.

Zeldin, Th., *France 1848–1945: Ambition and Love*, Oxford University Press, Oxford, 1979.

Index